TRUST
NO ONE

ALSO BY JAMES ROLLINS

Arkangel
Tides of Fire
Kingdom of Bones
Unrestricted Access
The Last Odyssey
Crucible
The Demon Crown
The Seventh Plague
The Bone Labyrinth
The 6th Extinction
The Eye of God
Bloodline
The Devil Colony
Altar of Eden
The Doomsday Key
The Last Oracle
The Judas Strain
Black Order
Map of Bones
Sandstorm
Ice Hunt
Amazonia
Deep Fathom
Excavation
Subterranean

BY JAMES ROLLINS AND REBECCA CANTRELL

The Blood Gospel
Innocent Blood
Blood Infernal

BY JAMES ROLLINS AND GRANT BLACKWOOD

The Kill Switch
War Hawk

TRUST NO ONE

A THRILLER

JAMES ROLLINS

wm

WILLIAM MORROW

An Imprint of HarperCollins*Publishers*

Pages 405–407 constitute an extension of this copyright page.

HarperCollins books may be purchased for educational, business, or sales promotional use. For information, please email the Special Markets Department at SPsales@harpercollins.com.

hc.com

FIRST EDITION

Library of Congress Cataloging-in-Publication Data has been applied for.

ISBN 978-0-06-341323-8
ISBN 978-0-06-348230-2 (international edition)

Printed in the United States of America

25 26 27 28 29 LBC 5 4 3 2 1

To Dr. Mimi Sato-Re,
Thank you for your dedication, friendship, and compassion

دوب اناد هکره دوب اناوت
دوب انرب ریپ لد شناد ز
[Mighty is the one who has knowledge.
By knowledge, the old hearts grow young again.]

—a Persian couplet from Ferdowsi's epic poem *Shahnameh* (*The Book of Kings*) from the tenth century AD

*   *   *

A little knowledge is a dangerous thing. So is a lot.

—often misattributed to Albert Einstein, which ironically proves this very point

TRUST
NO ONE

Historical Fact:

The tapestry of history is woven as much by charlatans as it is by those true of heart. Sometimes to distinguish between the two proves impossible. This is the story of one such historical figure: an eighteenth-century alchemist named the Count of Saint-Germain (*Comte de Saint-Germain*).

Engraving of Saint-Germain by Nicolas Thomas, 1783, secured at the Louvre

This mysterious man spoke a dozen languages and was an accomplished painter, violinist, and scientist. He quickly gained the respect of nobles across Europe. Encounters with the man are mentioned in the writings of Voltaire, Mozart, and Casanova, and across dozens of memoirs. Music composed by him can even be found in the British Museum. Yet, all that barely touches upon the true mystery and wonder surrounding this historical figure. It is said he could remove flaws from diamonds and commune with spirits, and sightings of the man continued long after his supposed death. The claims, suppositions, and tales found within this book—as wild as they may seem—are based on recorded accounts.

To quote Voltaire concerning Saint-Germain: "He is a man who does not die, and who knows everything."

* * *

Modern Fact:

In the seventeenth century, the last executions of witches in England took place in the city of Exeter. Today is a different story. As of September 2024, the University of Exeter now offers a postgraduate degree in magic and occult science. Coursework does not involve waving wands or casting spells. Instead, it is a rigorous academic study of the history, practices, and beliefs that separate our world from the hidden realms beyond.

Still, many deem this to be a perilous line of study. And not just for religious reasons. For some, certain knowledge is too reckless to explore—especially for the unwary.

[The following is a diary entry taken from *Souvenirs sur Marie-Antoinette* (*Memories of Marie-Antoinette*) by Countess Gabrielle Pauline d'Adhémar.][1]

* * *

February 12, Year of our Lord 1820
Château d'Évecquemont, outside Meulan-en-Yvelines

I had just finished my evening's toilette in preparation for bed when a loud knocking, frantic in nature, echoed through my country estate. My aged heart did quicken in trepidation. An intrusion at this late hour could only bode ill—especially considering who had arrived.

"He awaits you in the family chapel," my maid insisted with a deep bow of apology.

"*Merci,* my dear. Tell Monsieur Saint-Germain I will join him shortly."

Once the maid left to deliver this message, I stepped to my desk in my private salon and drew forth my diary, a journal written back in 1780. I had no trouble finding the correct entry, as four decades later the moment recorded there still haunted me. It marked my failure to Marie-Antoinette, a duty I was bound as the Queen's *dame du palais,* her lady-in-waiting.

I read again what I had written:

"*Who is this strange man, the Comte de Saint-Germain? All I know is he appeared at the Court of France in 1743, a time well before my joining the Queen's service. From the diamonds and rubies that*

1 Published in 1836, under the full title *Souvenirs sur Marie-Antoinette, archiduchesse d'Autriche, reine de France, et sur la cour de Versailles, par Madame la Csse d'Adhémar, dame du palais.* Countess d'Adhémar kept a daily diary from 1760 to 1821, from which was drawn upon to form her *Souvenirs* (*Memories*), which was published after her death.

adorned his fingers and were sewn into his clothing, all believed he had come from great wealth. Yet, from whence did he hail? No one could truly say."

To this day, his origins remain a mystery.

Though, after Saint-Germain's arrival in Versailles, the Count quickly grew to be a favorite of the court—and a plague upon my well-being. I feared this visit would be much the same. It all started four decades ago, when he had arrived at my Paris apartment on a Sunday morning with a warning of ruin and death.

To return to that moment, I only had to reread what I had written in my diary back in 1780.

As I did now, memories flooded through me.

I had been in a rush that Sunday morning, late for Mass and irritated at the intrusion. My dearest waiting woman at the time—now deceased—had announced the visitor, much to my amazement, to be the Comte de Saint-Germain. The man had been absent from the court for four years. By then, many had believed him to be dead. Yet, there he had stood at my door, unbidden and unwelcome and traveling under a false name, such was the secret he carried.

He arrived with a warning for the King and Queen, one he wanted delivered by my hand rather than his own. As Marie-Antoinette's lady-in-waiting, I had the Queen's ear, and thus in turn, the King himself.

I had recorded his warning in my diary from that time:

"The King of France must act!" he told me with firm conviction. "A conspiracy builds to overthrow the government. Ill intent sweeps toward the royal family, along with the clergy and nobility. While time remains to thwart this plot, it will not be long before this will prove impossible."

I had asked how he could possibly know of such a foul design, especially having been gone for these past four years. His words were equally cryptic: *"Much I heard with my own ears, but other details came through a revelation that I must keep secret."*

He would elaborate no further and pressed me to deliver this warning. When I asked why he did not bring this message himself, he explained with words that I knew to be true. The Count had fallen afoul of the King's minister of state, the Marquise de Maurepas, who had grown jealous of the King's affection for Saint-Germain. The Marquise would certainly discount any warning from the Count.

Instead, Saint-Germain had pressed me:

"You must speak of me to the Queen on my behalf, press upon her the services I have rendered most honorably to the government. If her Majesty agrees to take audience with me, I will reveal what I know. If she judges my warning to be sound, she can intercede to bring me to the King—but without the intervention of the Marquise de Maurepas. That I must insist."

And while I had agreed and did just that, it came to no avail. Saint-Germain took audience with the Queen, laying out the plot with exacting detail. Marie-Antoinette heeded this warning, but the conniving Marquise de Maurepas intercepted her. Within a day, an order was sent out to hunt down Saint-Germain, to have him imprisoned in the Bastille, but the Count—guided by whatever preternatural foresight fueled him—vanished. Still, Saint-Germain persisted in trying to warn the Queen through secret missives over the next years, warning of the Revolution to come, presaging the deaths that would follow—which all proved true!

To my great guilt, I should have supported the Count with greater alacrity and fervency, but I did not. In the end, the Terror rose as he predicted, with bloodshed and murder, casting down the government and taking the head of my dear Antoinette.

I only survived because of another visit from the Count shortly before the end. He met me in secret at the Récollets church. His words haunt me even now: *"Alas, I have been a Cassandra; my warnings have fallen on deaf ears. Heed me now, though, my dear friend. Take yourself into retirement. Be prudent, and you will survive the storm to come."*

I did as he asked, but not before pressing him about his own future and whether I would see him again.

He offered one promise—or perhaps a curse:

"Five times more we will meet. But never a sixth."

This also proved to be true. He has indeed visited me over the decades—four times so far—and always to my unspeakable surprise. The last encounter happened seven years ago. I had thought him surely dead by then.

Now he comes once again, when I am eighty-five years old. In the mirror above my desk, I see the folds that mark my age, the thin gray of my hair. My heart is but a failing quail in a cage. I have no doubt this will be my fifth and last encounter with the mysterious Count, as he stated with such portent.

"But what does he want of me now?" I asked the ancient reflection in the mirror.

Knowing the only answer lay in the family chapel, I drew an evening wrap over my shoulders and collected my cane. I headed down the steps, past oils that had darkened by age. I crossed the marble floor and down the hallway to the small chapel that had served my family for three generations.

A small fire burned in the hearth. The light and warmth drew me. My maid waited at the threshold to announce me, but I dismissed her with a wave of a hand. The tapping of my cane on tile was announcement enough.

Still, I noted a pale look on the maid's face as I passed. The reason behind it became clear. The night's visitor had not arrived unscathed. The Count stood by the hearth, silhouetted against the flames, which cast him in an infernal light. As I approached him, he turned and revealed a bloodied and bruised face. His right arm hung in a sling; the shoulder secured by a bloody bandage. He crossed in some haste toward me.

I allowed him to take my hand, to bring it to his lips with much graciousness. Taken aback by his appearance, I did not object. Yet, his injuries did not offend me. Rather, the state of his physique shocked me. He looked little changed from when I last saw him seven years ago, which again was much like he had appeared when I first crossed with him decades past. Even now, he still appeared a man of forty-five or fifty, with the same unlined countenance, unblemished black hair. Even wounded, he kept a pliant ease to his movements. He smiled, showing the same dimpled chin and the most perfect teeth. But it was the blue of his eyes that were the most disconcerting, both soft and penetrating, as if able to pierce to one's bones.

"Madame, I apologize for the late intrusion, but my need is most urgent."

I finally found the breath to speak. "Am I dreaming or awake?"

"It is no dream, I fear, but more of a nightmare that I bring to your threshold."

"A nightmare, you say? Does it explain the bloodied state of your being, good sir?"

"Ah, it does. Dogs are set upon me once again, those who still do the bidding of the Marquise, a man long dead but who had formed a foul covenant that still seeks what I hide. It is why I have come to you with an earnest request. One last time, my dearest friend, I must ask for your help."

"In what manner?"

"A simple one, but not without grave import."

I sighed. "The hour is late, Monsieur. Please speak plainly of your need."

From under his riding cloak, he removed a leatherbound book, well worn, with a gilt symbol engraved on the cover. He held it toward me.

"I remember your advocacy for the written word," he said. "Your renown as a memoirist is well remarked upon. So, I would ask you to take my own account, a diary of my own, and secure it in your library."

"But why?"

He touched his wounded shoulder. "Shortly, I must travel abroad, and where I go, I fear I cannot keep this volume safe or the secrets inscribed within."

I must say curiosity made me take his journal in hand. I studied the symbol gilded into the leather. It depicted eight radiating arrows pointing to strange, indecipherable symbols.

I had never seen its like before, but I knew Saint-Germain belonged to many secretive organizations, including the Rosicrucians and Freemasons. Yet, I had never seen a sigil as inscribed here.

The Count noted my attention. "A work of my own design. Consider it the author's signature." He tried to diminish his statement with a grin, but it faded with his next whispered words. "Or perhaps a ward against those who seek it with dark resolve. For this book holds the key to riches and dangers beyond all imagining."

I cast him a furrowed brow. I recalled the quandary as to the Count's origin and the mystery of his apparent wealth. But he waved away any further inquiry.

Still, the symbol was not the only oddity to this volume. Two bands of copper bound the book full around, locking its pages tight. The release appeared to one side, a squarish tin the size of a snuff box, but without a discernible keyhole. Instead, a small crystalline sphere lay embedded into it, which rotated under my thumb. Inscriptions were engraved upon it, but my eyes, clouded by age, could not make them out.

"Take care," Saint-Germain warned. "The diary's pages are suffused with a combustible elixir, an alchemy learned from my travels in Arabia. Misuse or abuse of its lock or straps will ignite the book."

I removed my thumb from the incendiary lock. "Should I fear keeping such a tome in my library, where my books could become dry tinder if this should ignite?"

His smile returned in its more natural manner. "There is no danger if the book is left unmolested. This I promise you."

Still, I balked, and the Count read my hesitation.

"Dearest lady," he said, "we have seen much ruin and did our best to avert it, but here again is a chance to avoid a disaster of far greater import—not only here in France, but across Europe and beyond."

"By keeping this volume safe?"

He remained silent, but those penetrating eyes answered my question.

"I will do as you ask," I finally answered. "But I have one last query."

His gaze turned down, as if he already knew what I would inquire.

"This is your *fifth* visit upon me," I pressed him. "You claimed before that there would not be a *sixth*. Yet, you leave your diary in my care. So then, who will collect it if I never see you again?"

I had thought to stymie him, to make him deny his prior declaration. Instead, he raised his eyes, which shone with a grief that struck my heart. "I must vanish, and so must this book. When both next appear, a time of great tribulation will be upon the world. I cannot say what will happen, only that the book must not fall into the wrong hands even then."

It all sounded like such folly, but so had his assertions of destruction and chaos years before the Revolution. So, I agreed to take on this burden. Besides, as he had asserted, it did indeed seem a simple matter.

With promises made, we set again to part ways, surely for the last time. I stepped out to speak to my maid to arrange for his departure, but when I returned to the chapel, I found it empty. Inquiries across my staff revealed no one had seen the Count depart. He had simply vanished as if he were never there. The only evidence of his presence was the book in my hand and three drops of blood that had seeped from his bandage.

In the end, I stood before the chapel hearth until the last chimes of the day echoed through the château. I debated throwing the copper-clad book into the flames to be done with it, but I had failed the Count once before—and my beloved Queen had died.

Knowing this, I clutched the book to my bosom and turned my back to the fire. Still, I found myself staring at the three crimson droplets on the marble tile. I sensed more blood would be spilled before this tale truly ended.

Yet, I would not see it happen.

As was foretold, I never saw Saint-Germain again.[2]

---

2 Countess Gabrielle Pauline d'Adhémar died on March 19, 1822—two years after these events. Her *Souvenirs* that relate this story would not be published for another fourteen years. The fate of her library—and what was hidden there—still remains a mystery.

FIRST

I

October 28, 10:33 a.m. GMT

Exeter, County of Devon, England

Sharyn Karr was no witch—despite what local townsfolk might believe of her and her classmates. Even her mother back in Tulsa, who was devoutly Catholic, all but disowned her after learning Sharyn had fled across the Atlantic to pursue a postgraduate degree in witchcraft at the University of Exeter.

She'll eventually get over it, Sharyn repeated to herself for the umpteenth time.

Her mother certainly would not approve of this morning's sojourn across the city. Even Sharyn saw little reason for this pilgrimage. She had a paper to start and had just completed a two-mile run when her two roommates had insisted she accompany them on this journey. The day was sunny, a rarity this past month, and clearly her roommates wanted to escape the three-bedroom flat they shared. They cajoled and browbeat and pressed upon her the morning trip's academic interest, while also stressing the respect that was owed the past.

Ultimately, Sharyn was persuaded by a promise of the city's best coffee and doughnuts—the latter being a particular weakness of hers.

And what the hell, I did finish a two-mile run.

After a bus ride and short walk through the crisp autumn air, their goal appeared ahead: the crumbling gatehouse of Rougemont Castle. Its archway, constructed of rough-hewn red stones quarried from local hills, was all that remained of the old Norman stronghold built by William the Conqueror in the eleventh century. She gaped at its towering height, which looked ready to crumble upon her. Down lower, modern black iron gates stood open, allowing traffic into the courtyard beyond, where a music festival was being set up.

She and her friends had not come to participate in such festivities. Though, one of the pair looked enviously upon the trio of stages being set up by bustling crews of roadies.

"I attended a Coldplay concert here several years ago," Naomi said. "Back in my wild youth. I snuck out of the house with a group of friends. On the eve of my A-level exams. Supposed to be studying, but I had a crush on the group's bass player. So, I could not be dissuaded."

"Seemed to have done you no harm," Tag noted, leaning heavily on his cane as he kept up with them. "You still did crackin' well on those tests, didn't ya? Got accepted to Oxford with a full ride. Graduated with a dual masters. Archaeology and anthropology."

Naomi shrugged. "Took me until I was twenty-one. If I had reined in that rebellious streak, I could've completed the coursework a year or two earlier."

Sharyn detected no conceit behind the woman's words, only a matter-of-fact resignation. Naomi Wren, who had grown up in Wales, was not only the youngest in their study group at Exeter, but also the youngest accepted into the university program. Only months into their first semester, Naomi had already proven to have a nearly eidetic memory and an uncanny ability to wend together disparate disciplines. Her mind was as slippery as it was sharp.

Though, from the bright crimson dye of her hair and buxom shape, few suspected the brilliance shining behind Naomi's forest-green eyes. Even more daunting, the woman's legs seemed to stretch forever, presently accentuated by skin-tight jeans, which were topped by a vintage denim jacket embroidered with the Welsh battle standard: an emerald-and-white flag emblazoned with a crimson dragon balanced on one foot.

Sharyn could not help but feel inadequate in Naomi's shadow, not that her roommate ever sought to diminish her. Still, Sharyn's bachelor's degree from the University of Oklahoma in library sciences, with a minor in art history, seemed a paltry accomplishment in comparison. Like Naomi, Sharyn had earned herself an undergraduate scholarship—though in her case, it was not for academics, but for track-and-field. Still, her Sooners' team had become national champions, for which she took great pride.

Despite continuing to keep fit, Sharyn looked the part of a librarian. She kept her blonde hair in a trim ponytail, wore dark-rimmed glasses when her contacts bothered her after too much eyestrain (which was often), and her figure, while slim and athletic, had none of Naomi's dangerous curves.

"There it is!" Tag announced, pointing his cane down the street while hobbling a step.

Sharyn steadied the young man with a hand on his elbow, but he brusquely shrugged her off.

"I can manage," he groused, clearly not wishing to be coddled. He swiped aside a drape of fiery red hair, which matched his trimmed beard. His pale cheeks reddened as he lowered his cane and stepped away.

Sharyn mumbled an apology. Her actions had been instinctual, reflexive, a part of her nature to help, something ingrained in her from her years under the unpredictable bearing of an alcoholic father—or so she had come to understand from Al-Anon meetings, where she had learned codependency came in many forms.

In Tag McKnight's case, she recognized her coping mechanism could be misconstrued as condescension. Her roommate, who was gay, had grown up on the outskirts of Edinburgh and had been diagnosed with cerebral palsy at the age of four, but he had set out to show the world that he would not be constrained by his body's limits. He had already earned a master's in biochemistry and had joined the Exeter program to study medieval pharmacology, specifically with an interest in ancient herbal medicines and psychedelics.

Tag continued forward, aiming for a wall to the left of the gatehouse. He pointed ahead, wheezing a bit from the exertion. "We made it."

Sharyn followed him into the shadow of the gatehouse's arch, where a plaque had been secured to the rough red stone. The title at the top read *The Devon Witches.*

Naomi stepped closer. "Let me get ready."

They gave her room as she extended her phone's selfie stick. Beyond paying homage to the persecuted women, Naomi had come to immortalize this visit on TikTok, specifically on a subsection of the site known as WitchTok, a niche community with billions of views that centered on all aspects of witchcraft and magic: from herbal recipes to tarot reading, and the daily lives of Wiccans and their practices. Naomi had gained a large following as she shared her interest in the subject matter, though from a more erudite and educational standard, sharing her experiences and reasons for coming to Exeter along with documenting her ongoing coursework and campus life.

Once ready, Naomi flipped her hair and turned to Tag, trusting his judgment more than Sharyn's—and for good reason. "How do I look?"

"Posh Spice has nothing on you."

She touched his arm, thanking him. "Such a dated reference, but I'll take it."

She cleared her throat and began to record. As she stood before the placard, she ran a finger across the engraved names of the women.

"Here is a marker commemorating the last four women hanged in the UK for witchcraft: Temperance Lloyd, Susannah Edwards, Mary Trembles, and Alice Molland. The women were tried and found guilty here and hanged at the Heavitree Gallows. Afterward, their bones were buried in unconsecrated ground. Where, you might ask?" She dramatically pointed straight down. "Supposedly right here at the Exeter, beneath the car park at St. Luke's campus. I hope to confirm this in the year ahead. So join me. Hit the follow button and let's dig into this together!"

She cut off the recording and sighed. "That should do. I'll add some captions and music once we're back at the flat."

Sharyn frowned at the plaque. "Was that all true? About these women—"

"You mean *witches*," Tag reminded her, tapping his cane on the sign.

Sharyn frowned at him. "Who were no doubt innocent of those accusations."

"Ah, but all four women *confessed* to be witches."

"I'm sure they did. Under duress. A forced admission."

Tag shrugged. "Records suggest otherwise. Temperance Lloyd was accused of casting a hex that sickened a local shopkeeper. Others came forward with similar incriminations, along with wild talk of communing with the devil. Eventually, Lloyd confessed. Even the day she was hanged, she continued to assert that the devil forced her hand. The other women were similarly accused and were tied to Lloyd's actions."

Sharyn turned to Naomi. "And their bodies are buried on our campus? Were you making that part up?"

"That's what's believed and what I hope to confirm. This winter, I'll bring in ground-penetrating radar and search for any evidence of a mass grave. Once verified, I hope to set up a dig site in the spring. I'll make it part of my doctoral thesis on urban archaeology."

"Above and beyond that," Tag said, "if their bones are discovered, those women deserve a proper burial. I've also read they were interred with their journals, which reportedly contained recipes for herbal brews and potions. If the books were preserved in an adequate manner, it might offer great insight into early folklore and medicine?"

Sharyn stared between her two roommates, grasping the reason behind this pilgrimage. The trip here was plainly tied to their own particular interests.

But not mine.

She studied her roommates, whose eyes glowed with a matching avidness. She had no interest in digging up bones or divining the medicinal mysteries buried in moldering journals of disparaged women.

Instead, she simply loved libraries. The smell of dusty shelves, the lingering hint of resin from leatherbound texts. But mostly, it was the secrets buried in faded ink that captivated her. Her primary interest in traveling to England had been to gain access to the university's growing archive of ancient texts, some dating back to the Dark Ages. Many of them were said to be richly illuminated with stunning art that had not seen the light of day in centuries.

The latter was the center of her own academic interest. With her minor in art history, she wanted to work on a thesis pertaining to medieval illuminated manuscripts. Yet, the exact direction of her pursuit still escaped her.

I just need to find the proper approach.

She hoped to discover that path during her time here. A year ago, she had read how Exeter's new program had garnered donations of rare texts pertaining to magic and the occult, everything from alchemical treatises to monastic doctrines, even encrypted works that had yet to be deciphered.

She knew that somewhere in those stacks had to be the answer that had troubled her since she had graduated.

Where do I go next in my career . . . and my life?

Naomi offered a more immediate answer to this question. She nudged Tag. "We should head back, but first we promised to show our new American friend where to find the best coffee in Exeter."

"And doughnuts," Sharyn reminded them pointedly.

"Come!" Tag turned and thrust his cane forward like a call to arms. "Off to the Toadstool!"

Sharyn shook her head at the nickname for the establishment, which was actually called the Toad on a Stool. But considering its proximity to this marker and the program they were enrolled in, the name seemed apropos.

Naomi hooked an arm around her waist. "Let's get you properly caffeinated and carbo-loaded before we return to campus."

Having paid homage to the witches, the trio set off. Shortly thereafter, the weather proved to be as fickle as her father's moods, going from sunny and pleasant to dark and windswept. A low layer of clouds rolled in from the nearby river, propelled by a drizzling rain. By now, they had entered a warren of narrow streets, lined with cobbles. It was as if the trio had turned a corner and ended up falling into the medieval past.

"The café is not far," Tag promised, ducking from the wind and wet. "And besides the excellent espresso, the barista is a sight to behold. While sadly he does not bend in my direction, a man can certainly look on with appreciation."

"Tag is not wrong," Naomi said. "I find myself tipping far too generously when he's working."

Despite such appeals, Sharyn considered skipping the detour. The weather made her ill at ease. As did the story of the four persecuted women. Instead, she longed to return to the university library, to ensconce herself among its stacks. After her difficult childhood—where danger was only an empty bottle away—the quiet of a library offered a steadfast measure of security and contentedness.

Books had always been her refuge.

As an adult, she recognized this was yet another coping mechanism. But it was one that had never failed her. Even now, she took solace in the stillness of a library, in the quiet turn of a page, in words that transported. It was a balm against the panic attacks that still plagued her.

While she knew such escapes were an emotional crutch, she had come to recognize her faith was not misplaced.

For truth be told, what harm could come from a book?

2

October 29, 11:04 a.m. CET
Larvik, Norway

Jakob Haugen fought the restraints that bound him to the steel chair. His efforts were less about freeing himself as escaping the body of his wife. She had been forced to her knees before him. Still, she had not begged for her life. Instead, she had stared resolutely at him, remaining silent as her throat was slit. Her blood had washed across his lap.

Afterward, his captors had thrown her body at his feet and continued ransacking his home, leaving him to keep vigil over the price of his silence.

Oh, Elli . . .

From the runnels that flowed from his shattered nose, he tasted iron on his tongue. His only solace was the angry crashing from the library around him, where two levels of books were being tossed and searched.

You bastards are too late, he silently cast out to the marauders, allowing himself this small amount of satisfaction.

Unable to bear the sight of the ruin at his feet, he cast his gaze out the library's tall row of windows. They narrowed to gothic points at their tops, as if this space were a cathedral, one dedicated to preserving knowledge. Only this library's true purpose was far simpler: to hide a single volume among the many. He was the Twelfth Keeper, dedicated to protecting the book from those who hunted it.

He knew he would not survive the day, not that he had many days left to him. The diagnosis had come a month ago. Pancreatic cancer, a highly aggressive adenosquamous carcinoma. At stage four, he would be lucky to make it to Christmas; certainly he'd never ring in the New Year.

Still, it would not be cancer that killed him.

He tugged again at his restraints as he stared past the windows to the beechwood forest outside. The snows had yet to come. The forest floor remained a crimson swath of fallen leaves. He and Elli had spent endless days exploring the parklands, lazing along Farris Lake, hiking the Passion Path trail.

But no more . . .

Knowing the end was near, they had reached a measure of peace, finding solace in quiet moments, grieving and laughing, all in a long, slow goodbye—never suspecting the end would come so swiftly and brutally.

Still, the two had taken the necessary steps, not just legal and financial, but also in safeguarding the treasure that had been entrusted to them.

He returned his gaze to the sprawl of his wife, to the spreading pool of blood on the stone tile. The shock had dulled, replaced with a fury that sharpened his breath and spurred a heavier flow from his broken nose.

How had the bastards known? Who had betrayed us?

Jakob had believed he had attended to all the precautions in transferring the book to the Thirteenth Keeper, a number that now struck him as ominous. Last week, he had shipped and hidden the volume in crates holding hundreds of texts. The bill of lading and provenance declared it to be the bequeathment of a dying historian, which was the truth. Once the shipment reached the United Kingdom, the Thirteenth Keeper would secure the crates. The man had already found another library in which to ensconce the book, to again bury the treasured text amongst many others.

Over the centuries, such a transfer—from one Keeper to the next—had always been a risk, a rare moment of potential exposure.

Which proved the case now.

Jakob knew what this must mean.

Someone betrayed us, possibly within our own organization.

Still, if their enemy was searching this estate, the traitor clearly remained unaware of the transfer, of its destination in England. He hung his hope upon this thinnest of threads.

They must never know where I sent it.

It must vanish into history again.

A commotion drew his attention to the mahogany doors leading into his study. A tall figure strode into the room, flanked by two others, all three enrobed and hooded in crimson, their faces hidden behind folds of black cloth.

Jakob scowled at the trio, at their artifice and pompous garb. He focused on the man in the center, clearly their leader, whose eyes were as black as his scarf. His complexion, what little that could be seen of it, was a pallid shade.

"You will never find the alchemist's book," Jakob assured the man, spitting a gobbet of bloody mucus at his toes. "It is already beyond your reach."

"Nothing is beyond the reach of the *Confrérie*," the man said.

The leader waved to the two men who flanked him. The pair dragged Elli's body off. Watching her limp form be manhandled so callously, her arm scribing a bloody trail, inflamed Jakob's fury. Anger tightened his chest and strangled his breath.

Once the way was clear, the tall man sidestepped around the pool of blood to approach the chair.

"Professor Haugen, I apologize. This savagery should never have happened. If I had reached your estate sooner, I would have prevented it. Our methods need not be so crude."

Jakob had a hard time reading this one's sincerity. The other's eyes remained cold, his voice matter-of-fact. Jakob heard a slight French accent, but he could not even be certain of that.

The leader nodded to one of his companions, who carried a steel briefcase. The man crossed to a neighboring lamp table and snapped open the case. Jakob had expected to see a splay of sharp instruments of torture. Instead, a set of three syringes rested in velvet, along with a row of vials.

"Truth serums have been notoriously unreliable," the leader intoned as his two companions prepped the drugs. "At least in the past. Today's intelligence agencies have refined their methods, which are kept tightly guarded. Yes, analogs of thiopental and scopolamine continue to be useful, but the concurrent addition of oxytocin and MDMA encourages complete cooperation."

Once the syringes were filled, the two companions closed upon Jakob. He fought and writhed, but strong hands pinned an arm. Needles stabbed: one, then another, but he never felt the third. By then, the room had darkened, and his chin fell to his chest.

Words trailed him into oblivion. "In twilight, no secrets can be kept."

By the time Jakob woke again—which felt like no more than a long breath—he found himself alone. The forest outside had gone dark, but the room inside blazed with flames. Shelves and books burned all around. Smoke choked high. The heat seared with each breath. Panic cleared the haze from his head. He fought his restraints, but it was not the fire that set his heart to pounding. Death had already been coming for him.

Instead, it was the unknown that horrified him.

What did I tell them?

He had no memory of any interrogation.

He craned at the spreading flames and feared this manner of death was the leader's cruel way of letting Jakob know that the truth *had* been stolen from him.

Weeks ago, Jacob had been amused upon learning of the book's next hiding place, a location that he had deemed sardonically appropriate, particularly considering the book's contents. He had even shared an adage with Elli from a revered writer: *Any sufficiently advanced technology is indistinguishable from magic.*

As the fire and smoke closed upon him, he knew these flames were meant as a final message to him—especially knowing where he had sent the alchemist's diary.

For in the past, they burned witches.

3

October 31, 4:15 p.m. GMT

Exeter, County of Devon, England

Sharyn sensed the press of time, but she refused to rush her efforts. Due to the holiday, the library would be closing early, in less than an hour.

I must finish this . . .

Alone and ensconced in the reading room of the university's Old Library building, she carefully centered the illustrated book under her digital camera, which balanced on a tripod. The volume was a hand-painted Elizabethan atlas, mapping the counties of Wales and England, drawn by the famed British cartographer Christopher Saxton, in 1579. She had it propped open to a double-page spread. Through her camera, she stared at the emerald hills, the buttery yellow county lines, the crimson townships. She tried to imagine the hands that had so meticulously illustrated this chart.

A voice spoke at her shoulder. "You're wasting your time."

Startled, she accidentally snapped a photo, but the heel of her hand nudged the camera and blurred the image.

With a pained exhalation, she turned to the student who had slipped into the reading room behind her. She recognized the young man, Duncan Maxwell, a fellow postgrad student. He was enrolled in her same program, but he was part of another study group, one composed of four friends who had graduated from Oxford. All were men, all from rich families, all full of themselves. She had heard Duncan was sixteenth in line to the British throne.

At present, he looked as if he had just arrived from a foxhunt, dressed in a tweed coat over a canary yellow vest with tan breeches and polished black boots. The only mark of casualness about him was the shaggy, rakish cut to his black hair and the persistent stubble that always darkened his face, which only accentuated the confidence that shone from his ice-blue eyes.

He stared at her with one brow raised—maybe in curiosity, maybe in disdain.

She had to turn away.

How long had he been standing there?

She returned her attention to the book. It rested on a pillow to protect its spine. Soft weights gently held open the pages. She had spent a half hour prepping the text, and this was after a five-day wait to obtain permission to take a photo of the rare book.

"It's *not* a waste of time," she stated crisply, wishing her cheeks had not flushed so hotly. "And yes, the library staff did inform me that copies of the atlas had already been digitized by the Humanities Lab."

"Then, Ms. Karr, why photograph them yourself?" Duncan's hard accent struck each consonant with a haughty condescension. Even addressing her by her surname felt as if he were a schoolmaster disciplining a student.

"Not all of us take the easy path in the pursuit of scholarship." She scowled back at him. "Why are you even here? The library's about to close."

Duncan held up a gray package, tied with archival tape. "I came to retrieve an order from the special collections desk. Something sent to me from the British Library. Then I saw you working in here . . ."

"So, you barged in."

"Only to try to help." He sighed and the hard edges to his voice softened. "I saw you were taking a photo of a volume that had already been digitized. I had hoped I could save you some needless labor."

She swallowed and let her guard down—slightly. "I'm working on Dr. Plinth's assignment, on the essay about the intersection of medieval science and magic."

"Same here. In fact, it seems we've both targeted the same person of interest: the astronomer and alchemist, John Dee."

She eyed Duncan. "How did you know I picked him for—"

He held up a hand. "People talk. Especially after too many pints at the Ram."

She gave a sad shake of her head. The Ram was a student hangout, a bar operated by the university. Both Naomi and Tag had tried to lure her out there a few times, but the reek of spilled ale, the raucous laughter, and drunken barks were all too triggering for her.

The only time she had visited the Ram was for a quiz night with her study group. Unfortunately, they were bested by Duncan's team, who lorded it over the pub that night. Later, clearly inebriated, he had tried to make up for it by buying a round of drinks for all the competitors. Tag had commented upon this largesse after his first sip: *Oy, Guinness has never tasted so bitter.*

Sharyn squinted at Duncan. "So, you're also working on a paper concerning John Dee?"

She had already been fascinated by the sixteenth-century scholar and polymath. Not only did Dee serve as an advisor to Queen Elizabeth I, he was also the court astronomer and a skilled mathematician. But in addition, the man had a keen interest in alchemy, divination, and astrology. When it came to merging science and magic, there were few who matched his devotion.

She studied Duncan. "So what's *your* angle for the assignment?"

He stepped closer. "I'm looking into the science of encryption and how codes were used both to mask and enhance the mysticism of occult knowledge. It's said Dee possessed a copy of the Voynich

Manuscript with its bizarre drawings and indecipherable language. While this fact remains in dispute, it is known that he *did* possess and was fixated on a copy of the *Book of Soyga*, a sixteenth-century Latin text on magic, of which large sections remain deeply encrypted. The British Library holds one of only two extant copies of that mystical book in its collection."

Sharyn stared at the package in Duncan's hands. "They loaned it to you?"

"To me? Never. But I was able to get photographs of a few significant pages and have them sent to me. Cryptography has always been an interest of mine. My undergrad degree at Oxford was in Cybersecurity and Information Assurance. My focus was on AI and digital encryption."

She frowned in confusion. "With such a degree, why enroll in this program?"

He snorted, which came out with an edge of bitterness. "My father—who's in banking—questioned the same. He certainly favored the practicality of my Oxford studies." He shrugged heavily. "But after learning of my postgrad application, he threatened to disown me. And may still."

Sharyn could relate, remembering the castigation from her mother. "Yet, you came here. Why?"

He glanced at a clock on the wall. "A long story. Too long for now. Like you said, the library is about to close."

She grimaced, recognizing she had at best another fifteen minutes. She returned her attention to her camera and the open book. She made a final adjustment of the pages with her freshly scrubbed fingers. Unlike many institutions, the Old Library forbade gloves, which interfered with tactile dexterity and caused more damage than they prevented.

Oddly, Duncan did not leave her side and leaned in closer. "I'm puzzled," he said softly. "How does Saxton's atlas relate to your essay on John Dee?"

She glanced back, finding him standing far too close. At six foot two, he towered over her a bit. She swallowed before answering. "Later in life, Dee became the warden of Christ's Church in Manchester. During his tenure, he commissioned Saxton to survey the city's parish boundaries. No copies of that work exist, but this hand-painted atlas of Saxton's includes the Manchester region." She pointed to the splay of pages. "It's why I wanted to photograph them myself, to use this as a stand-in for the lost work commissioned by Dee."

"Ah. But still, how does this pertain to your thesis?"

She talked it out as she took her photos. "While Dee dabbled in the occult—even believing he could communicate with angels—he was devoutly Catholic. All of his esoteric work, some of which could be deemed demonic, always had a Catholic slant to it. My treatise is to look at the merging of art, astronomy, and religiosity in Dee's work."

"To what end?"

"To prove how the lines between the occult, religion, and science are blurrier than ever. Both in the past and now."

"With the truth lying somewhere in the cracks . . ."

She hid a smile at his words.

Exactly.

Duncan pointed to the tabletop, where a chained loop held a tarnished pendant. Sharyn had taken it off, along with a couple rings, before handling the book.

"I see you have a Saint Christopher's medal. You're Roman Catholic yourself?"

"Actually, it was my father's. He was a police officer. Died in the line of duty—a crash during a high-speed pursuit."

"I'm sorry," Duncan whispered.

"That was four years ago," she muttered, as if time could excuse the pain.

Sharyn covered the medal with her palm and scooped it into

the pocket of her jeans. She was not sure why she had divulged any of this. Still, she had left off one significant detail, maybe out of shame. Her father's body was found to have a blood-alcohol level of 0.06 percent. While it was within legal limits, it was enough for the carjacker to sue the city and her family. Even with the union's support and life insurance, the judgment had left the family desolate. Afterward, her mother had taken a reactionary hard turn into a faith that had long since lapsed.

Sharyn, too embittered and angry, could not follow the same path.

Even now, she remained conflicted about his death, about him. Her father's alcoholism had been a slow progression. From doting parent to a monster who haunted her life. Even in those hard depths, when shouts woke her, when an angry bull roughed through the house, there remained moments of tenderness and concern. When she was a teenager, he would often take her to the gun range. His instructions were firm but softened by humor and compliments. He also enrolled her in self-defense and martial arts classes, where she earned a brown belt in jiujitsu. Unfortunately, she hadn't had time to gain her black belt before her father passed, and afterward the classes had been too expensive.

While Sharyn had enjoyed the challenge, down deep she suspected the reason behind her father's encouragement. It wasn't just to gird his daughter against the harshness of the world, but possibly also to protect her from himself. Often when she dropped an opponent to the mat, he would smile and nod, but there remained a troubled look to his eyes.

While she had suffered verbal abuse during his drunken rages, it had never turned physical. That was the burden of her mother. Black eyes, bruises, broken fingers. Still, she suspected her father feared his anger might one day fall upon his daughter and maybe—consciously or not—sought to give her the means to protect herself.

With his death, Sharyn would never know the truth. Was her father the alcoholic who haunted their house like some dread beast . . . or the man who cheered her at track meets and who so clearly loved her?

She remembered Duncan's words from a moment ago and knew they applied here, too: *The truth lies somewhere in the cracks.*

She took a final few snapshots of the atlas, then straightened. "That should do it."

Which proved timely, as the door to the reading room swung open. The librarian who staffed the research desk popped her head inside. She was an older woman who wore her gray hair in a tight bun and reading glasses hanging from a chain. "We'll be closing in five minutes. All material must be returned to their strongrooms."

"I'm finished," Sharyn said. "I'll get everything tidied up and re-box the atlas."

The woman nodded and ducked back out.

"I can help you," Duncan offered.

"No need. I can manage."

"Very good." He stepped toward the door, then turned back. "Are you going to the Halloween party at the Lemmy?"

"I'm afraid not." The Lemmy—the nickname for the Lemon Grove nightclub—had a bash planned for the night. "Those tickets are rather steep."

"I do have a couple extra, if you'd like."

She shook her head. "My friends and I already made plans to go to the Forum."

Where there will be no cover charge.

She was on a tight budget, not that she particularly wanted to go either way. The party at the university commons was open to the public and notoriously rowdy. Unfortunately, she had been unable to discourage her flatmates from browbeating her into attending.

"Well . . ." Duncan patted his pockets, then pulled out a set of black tickets stamped in crimson with the logo of the Lemon

Grove. He tossed them on the table. “For you and your friends . . . if you change your mind.”

She made no move toward the tickets.

“I hope to see you there,” he added as he headed out.

She lifted a hand and made a noncommittal noise. She had no intention of going. In fact, if possible, she planned on making it an early night.

That’s if Tag and Naomi will let me.

And that was certainly a big *if.*

4

5:02 p.m.

With Duncan gone, Sharyn carefully lifted the Saxton Atlas from its pillow and returned the large tome to its acid-free storage box. She then collected her things, shouldered her backpack, and drew the heavy box under both arms. Holding it aloft like a tea tray, she headed out of the reading room.

The research librarian noted Sharyn struggling with the door and came to help. As Sharyn exited, the older woman touched her arm. "I'm the last one here. Could I trouble you to carry the box to the strongroom for me? I can lead you there."

Sharyn understood the reason behind this request. The Saxton's atlas, large and unwieldy, weighed close to twenty pounds. The thin-limbed woman, while prim and tidy, would certainly struggle with the load.

Sharyn noted her nametag: Margaret Peele.

"Of course, Ms. Peele. Put me to use."

"Thank you, my dear."

Actually, Sharyn needed little goading. She had always wanted to peek into one of the library's many strongrooms. In those temperature-controlled chambers, the most valuable and rare collections were preserved and protected. Sharyn had already spent weeks searching through the library's catalogs, retrieving material that she would never have access to back in the States.

She had spent days reviewing the library's Syon Abbey Collection, which consisted of rare books and manuscripts gathered from a monastic order founded in the fifteenth century. Many richly illuminated books included gilded illustrations of the Virgin Mary. It surprised her to discover several pages showing examples of mirror writing, with the script written backward across a page. Such writing was both a crude means of encryption and a way to force a reader into a deeper introspection into what was written so challengingly.

She remembered Duncan's treatise on coded texts.

Maybe I should let him know what I found . . .

Then again, maybe not.

She still recalled him thumping his chest in triumph when his team won the pub's quiz match.

Putting such thoughts aside, she followed Ms. Peele, who paused to lock the front doors before continuing deeper into the library. Sharyn glanced to the exit. This deep into autumn, the sun had already set. Outside, lampposts glowed across a twilit park. A few figures rushed by on foot or bicycle, likely hurrying off to enjoy the start of the campus festivities.

Even inside the library, only a few lights illuminated the maze-like spread of rooms. The staff had squandered little time in shutting the place down. Sharyn glanced across the shadowy rows of shelves and spotted no other movement.

A shiver of misgiving shook through her. The night had always held a particular fear for her. A dread not born of superstition, but from real danger: the crash of a door in the dark, the stumble of heavy feet, the slurred burst of accusation, the sharper cry of the assaulted.

She pulled her box closer.

It didn't help matters that they passed a cabinet displaying an Agatha Christie exhibit. Many items came from the library's heritage collection, including letters and early drafts of the mystery writer's work—where murder was only a page away.

As they continued deeper into the library, Sharyn studied Ms. Peele, taking a cue from the other's calmness. The woman showed no twinge of discomfort as she headed off the main hall.

"The Rare Books strongroom lies this way."

Sharyn kept close on her heels. "Who guards this place after hours? Is there a nightwatchman?"

Ms. Peele turned and peered over the top of her glasses. "This isn't the British Museum, young lady. The building is alarmed, of course, and monitored by CCTV cameras. Plus, campus security regularly sweeps by and checks doors." She squinted at Sharyn with an amused smile. "Aren't planning on robbing us, are ya, miss?"

"Not on Halloween. Wouldn't want to disturb any ghosts."

"Wise. Especially as Exeter is the most haunted city in all the UK."

Sharyn glanced over. "Is that true?"

"That's what they say. And if they're right, you definitely don't want to get on the bad side of this place."

"I'll try my best."

They finally reached a door stenciled with the words *Rare Books* on it. Ms. Peele slipped out a keycard and tapped the glowing lock. A brief chime sounded, followed by a whisper of sliding bolts.

Before the door could be opened, a muffled crash rose from inside. Sharyn stepped back, ready for a fast retreat, but Ms. Peele yanked the door open.

A flare of light momentarily blinded Sharyn, but the older woman barged across the threshold. "Why didn't someone tell me you were back here?" Ms. Peele blurted out.

Sharyn got drawn in the librarian's wake. Still, adrenaline spiked through her, tightening her chest. Raised in an alcoholic household, her body had honed a quickfire fight-or-flight response when it came to a threat.

"You're supposed to log in and out," Ms. Peele scolded whomever was inside. "You should know better. Just because you were once the director of the libraries does not give you the right to flaunt our rules."

"I apologize." The voice rose from behind a stack of wooden crates, well over a dozen. One box had toppled over and lay broken—likely the source of the noise a moment ago. A crowbar rested on the floor next to it. "I had thought I'd only be here a few minutes."

A tall gray-haired man with a matching goatee straightened from a crouch beside the cracked crate. He swiped a fall of hair from his sweaty brow. He was dressed in a crisp white shirt with the sleeves rolled to the elbows. A suit jacket hung on a nearby dolly. He dusted off his hands and stepped over to greet them.

Ms. Peele admonished the man. "I could've accidentally locked you inside." She waved to Sharyn. "If not for a student who checked out the Saxton Atlas, I would've never known anyone was still in here."

The man offered a slight bow of his head in apology. "Fear not, I still have my own keys to the building. I could've freed myself if need be."

"Still, I should've been informed."

"Of course. It was an inexcusable lapse."

He stepped over and hugged Ms. Peele, which warmed the woman's scowl into a soft smile. Clearly, they knew each other well.

Once free of the man's arms, she wagged a finger at him. "Don't do it again."

"Never, my dearest Ms. Peele."

The man's eyes fell upon Sharyn with a slight raise of his brows. "Ms. Karr, is it not?"

Sharyn struggled to respond, shocked that the former director of the libraries knew her name.

He stepped closer and relieved her of the boxed atlas, which he placed on a nearby cart. "I remember your application to our MA program in Magic and Occult Sciences. We've not formally met. I'm Professor Julian Wright."

He held out his hand, which she took reflexively, and finally freed her tongue. "You're the head of the Exeter program."

"Indeed. Next spring, I'll be teaching coursework on paleography."

She nodded, anxious to delve into this very subject. Paleography, the study of ancient writing systems, covered everything from deciphering languages to dating texts. It also explored the history of illuminated drawings, a particular interest of hers.

Ms. Peele interrupted with her hands on her hips, staring at the crates, especially the broken one. "I heard there was a delivery this morning, a donation of books."

"A bequeathment," Wright corrected and turned to the stacks, his eyes taking on a haunted cast. "From a friend and colleague of mine. To expedite cataloging, I had the crates delivered and secured in the Rare Books Collection. I came to retrieve the lading slip and take it to my office for review. I thought I'd be in and out."

Sharyn eyed the crowbar on the floor.

"You've been doing more than that," Ms. Peele scolded.

"True. A quick glance down the list revealed several extremely rare books that I thought should be set aside before we bring in archivists to catalog the collection."

Sharyn noted most of the boxes had their lids pried off, revealing cloth-wrapped books packed inside and cushioned by dry hay. Many of the volumes had been unbound to reveal dusty texts with faded titles. She found herself frowning, recognizing the work had been done hastily. Several books looked as if they had been haphazardly tossed to the side.

"Did you find what you were looking for?" Ms. Peele asked.

"Not everything."

Ms. Peele scowled. "If you're so determined in this pursuit, I can stay until you're finished." She waved an arm. "All these heavy boxes. And with your heart condition. You shouldn't be doing this alone."

"I'm fine. I can't ask this of you, my dear. It's All Hallow's Eve. It was foolish of me to even begin this task so late. You go home. As I said, I have my own keys. Once done, I can secure the building."

"Very well, but don't forget to set the alarm."

Ms. Peele motioned for Sharyn to accompany her out, but Sharyn nodded to the broken box. "Professor Wright, Ms. Peele is right. This isn't a task you should be doing by yourself. I'm happy to stay. In fact, I'd love to be the first to see these new books."

And that wasn't her only reason.

It'll be the perfect excuse to skip the night's party.

"In truth, I could use an extra hand," Wright admitted. "But perhaps—"

A cell phone rang in his pocket, cutting him off. He pulled it out, checked the number, then stepped aside. "Excuse me. I must take this."

Ms. Peele drew Sharyn aside. "Your offer is very generous. And you should know you have nothing to fear in being alone with him. He is a most honorable man. Plus, his inclination leans not toward women, if you understand."

Sharyn smiled at this attempt by the older woman—clearly from another generation—to be discreet. "Thank you for letting me know."

The woman nodded sagely. "Then I'll leave you to it." She touched Sharyn's arm. "But don't let him keep you all night. You're too young and pretty to spend Halloween cooped up in here."

"If that happens, I'll have those Exeter ghosts to keep me company."

Ms. Peele patted her arm. "Ghosts don't keep you warm at night, my dear."

True . . .

This was something Sharyn knew all too well. She'd not had a proper date in more than a year, and it had been even longer since someone shared her bed.

Sharyn walked Ms. Peele to the strongroom's exit and said her goodbyes.

As Sharyn closed the door, Professor Wright's voice rose behind her, sounding both alarmed and angry. He was speaking German or some other Nordic language. All those hard consonants only accentuated his growing agitation.

Sharyn used this time to collect the boxed atlas and cross to the rows of white steel shelves, all hung on sliders, which could be wheeled apart by black winches on their sides. She checked the box's catalog number and returned the atlas to its proper spot. Luckily, the location had already been left open after the book had been retrieved and delivered to the reading room.

Once done, she stepped out and found Professor Wright's call had ended. He stood with his back stiff, his cell phone clutched at his side. His gaze stared a thousand yards off.

"Is everything okay?" Sharyn asked.

"No," Wright mumbled. "Not at all."

Sharyn inwardly winced. Maybe volunteering here had been a mistake. But she had committed herself.

"Is there anything I can do to help?"

The professor shook his head, then his eyes focused on her, pinching somewhat. "Maybe . . ."

He turned and crossed to the broken crate. He retrieved the crowbar and pried off the damaged lid with three strong cranks. "It must be in this last box . . ."

She came over to assist him, but he held her off with a raised palm. He hurriedly yanked out books, parted cloth wrappings, while grimacing in frustration. Then finally he freed one book and ripped away its covering. His shoulders sagged with relief, but his hands shook.

"It's here."

He stared at the old volume for a long breath, then rewrapped it with some haste. Sharyn only caught sight of its dark cover and a glint of metal.

Wright stood and stepped over. With his eyes pinched, he stared at her, too long, enough to make her uncomfortable.

Then he finally spoke. "Ms. Karr, as program director, I reviewed your application and transcripts. Read your essay explaining your interest in Exeter's program. What impressed me most was your dedication to the written word. As a librarian—like myself—you recognize the importance of preserving that which is threatened, to protect knowledge that should never be lost."

She nodded, her mouth gone dry.

"To that end, I must ask for your help. It may be a needless safeguard, but I would rather err on the side of caution."

"I . . . I don't understand. What do you want me to do?"

He shoved the wrapped book toward her, his expression pained, as if passing over his firstborn. "You must take this."

She backed a step, her heart in her throat. "What? Why?"

"I fear it's not safe here." He closed on her again, still holding aloft the wrapped volume. "You must hide it. Tell no one where you put it. Not even me until I deem it safe."

His urgency drew Sharyn's hands up, forced her to take the book. "Why is this so important?"

"I wish I had more time to explain." He guided her to the strongroom door, then out into the library. "But perhaps the less you know, the better."

Sharyn hurried alongside him, struggling with this responsibility, wondering if she should refuse it. But she remembered Ms. Peele's judgment of the professor: *He is a most honorable man.*

Clutching the book harder, she made her decision. "What am I to do with it?"

"Don't attempt to open it. Just keep it safe."

They reached the exit, and Wright unlocked the door. Before Sharyn could step outside, the professor grabbed her arm.

"If something happens to . . . if you don't hear from me by the morning, call this number." He shoved a business card into her hand and clutched it there. "I'm sorry to place this burden on you."

He freed her hand, pushed her outside, and locked the door. She stared back through the glass, his figure now a dark specter. She suddenly sensed there was more to this matter than he had been willing to admit—which became clearer when Wright pressed his palm against the door.

Muffled words reached her.

"Trust no one."

Then he was gone.

5

11:00 p.m.

"The witching hour draws near," Naomi warned with a spooky waggle of her fingers.

Her friend had to lean near Sharyn's ear to be heard. The thumping music threatened to deafen the crowd packed into the Forum. Their small group had arrived an hour ago and had taken up roost on a second-floor balcony, where they could gaze down at the mass of bodies below.

The raucous bash filled the spacious hall—called "The Street"—which connected the various facilities of the university's central hub: the student center, an alumni auditorium, and the main campus library. Still, the cavernous space failed to adequately hold in all the revelry. Partiers spilled out through the north and south exits to the open plazas beyond.

"If it's the witching hour," Sharyn shouted, "we're certainly dressed for it."

She smoothed the black dress that hugged her figure much too tightly. The rented outfit, courtesy of Naomi, came with a matching cowled cape, which Sharyn kept demurely draped.

"Aren't we a tad on the nose with these costumes?" Sharyn tipped up the silver pentagram that hung on a chain between her breasts.

Naomi shrugged. "If the student body is convinced that we came to Exeter to cast spells and perform dark rituals, then we might as well look the part."

"As witches?"

"As *sexy* witches," Naomi corrected.

Tag leaned on his cane. "I prefer *sexy* necromancer."

The young man wore a black suit with a blood-red vest over a frilly collared white shirt. He had powdered his face to a paler-than-usual complexion, while hollowing out his eyes with dark makeup. He had also swapped out his usual cane for a more elaborate one with a silver owl gracing its top.

"We're sexy indeed," Naomi concurred, circling an arm around Tag's waist. "So we might as well flaunt it."

Sharyn stood at the balcony rail. Below, revelers danced to pop music, while others gathered in groups, laughing and carousing. It was supposed to be an alcohol-free event, but she spotted flasks being surreptitiously passed around. The more brazen drank openly.

She shook her head, intent on getting out of here as soon as possible.

And for good reason.

Directly across from her was the entrance to the university's new main library. It stood as a stark reminder of the responsibility thrust upon her. In the rush of the evening, she'd had no time to adequately digest what had happened.

Professor Wright's final warning echoed in her head.

Trust no one . . .

Earlier, on the walk back to her flat, Sharyn had hurried between lamplit pools, searching for anyone following her. Eventually, the cool night and the lack of any obvious threat calmed her pounding heart. Still, once home, she had tried to back out of the party, but Naomi had already rented their costumes. Plus, if her friends left, she did not want to be alone in their flat.

"What's wrong?" Tag asked, as he stepped next to her. His brows were knitted in concern, proving his empathetic nature. "You've been unusually quiet."

Another remained oblivious.

Behind them, Naomi swayed by herself to the beat of the music, while holding out her phone on its selfie stick, commemorating this night on her WitchTok site.

Tag waved below. "Is it this pissed lot? Everyone's already pretty scuttered. I know you don't like being around—"

"It's not that." Sharyn stared up at the spread of the roof, which was divided into large triangles of glass and slatted wood.

"Then what is it?"

She shook her head. She hadn't told her friends what had transpired. Her silence had less to do with the professor's warning—*trust no one*—and more to do with her own struggle to come to terms with this sudden responsibility.

Keep it safe.

Back at her flat, she had hidden the book in her room. She remained nervous about leaving it behind. Their corner of town—what she could afford even with two roommates—was in a sketchy area. Last week, there had been a break-in down the block. And with the boisterous nature of Halloween night, she questioned the wisdom of letting the book out of her sight.

Still, she had no other choice. Her tight dress, even with the cape, offered no place to hide anything, especially something as cumbersome as the book.

"Do you want to get some fresh air?" Tag offered. "It's getting stifling in here."

Sharyn nodded, unable to hide her relief. "Dear god, yes, let's get out of here."

Naomi glided over. "Sounds good. I'm gonna try to bum a fag."

Tag frowned. "Smoking? Really?"

With his cerebral palsy, Tag found it distasteful for anyone to take needless health risks.

"I don't do it much. Only on special occasions." Naomi smiled as she headed off. "And it is a holiday."

They crossed down the stairs and worked through the crowd—which amped Sharyn's tension. She shoved hurriedly through the exit. Outside, the crisp autumn air was tinged with the smell of weed and cigarettes, but it was wonderfully cool and less crowded on the open plaza. Most of the students here, many in amorous embraces, lounged across a set of wide, terraced steps to her right.

She drew her friends to the left, where a series of eco-ponds had been installed to store rainwater runoff. To enhance the look of a natural wetlands, the dark waters were fringed by reeds and dotted by lily pads.

Nearby, excited chatter rose from clusters of students at the plaza's edge. Only now did Sharyn hear the blare of sirens past the loud music. Faces stared to the south, toward the rising noise.

Naomi headed toward the gathering crowd. "Something's up."

Sharyn swallowed and followed. The sirens jangled her already fraught nerves. When they reached the edge of the plaza, which overlooked the campus to the south, a fire engine blazed down Prince of Wales Road, followed by a blaring ambulance.

"Looks like they're coming this way," Naomi noted, which proved true as the emergency vehicles made a sharp turn onto the entry road, which led to the Forum.

Only, the fire engine braked a short distance up the side road, its lights strobing, its siren still screaming.

Tag pointed his cane. "Is that smoke?"

Lit by the emergency vehicles, a thick black column rose from a neighboring building. A ruddy glow shone from several of its windows. One of them shattered and cast out a gout of flames that licked across the brick façade.

"The Old Library," Naomi said.

Tag lowered his cane and leaned toward Sharyn. "Weren't you over there this afternoon?"

Sharyn backed up a step, as if trying to deny what was happening. She remembered Professor Wright's warning: *It's not safe here.*

Tag stared at her with those darkly painted eyes.

"We . . . we must get home," she gasped out. "Now."

6

11:27 p.m.

Sharyn stopped her friends at the edge of a dark park. Across the street, a line of brick rowhouses formed a continual barricade. "Hold here."

Naomi crowded next to her. "When are you going to tell us what's going on?"

Sharyn simply shook her head. Back at the Forum, their group had retreated inside the hall and exited out its north side, away from the smoke, flames, and sirens. There, they had ordered an Uber. Sharyn had the driver drop them off on the far side of the park. Her father had instilled in her a healthy (or perhaps unhealthy) level of paranoia.

She studied the houses. Their apartment was a third-floor walk-up at the top of the rowhouse across the street. She spotted nothing untoward or suspicious. Their flat's lights remained dark.

"Okay," she said and headed quickly across the street.

The other two kept at her heels, clearly responding to the tension exuding from her. Still, they trusted her enough to not press her further.

At least, for now.

She climbed the steps and tapped in the code for the lock, but a shadow swept into view on the far side of the entry door. Sharyn stumbled back. But it was only Mrs. Kenworthy, the middle-aged caretaker who kept a small flat on the ground floor. She opened the door and waved them inside. A chair sat outside her door with a tub next to it, shaped like a cauldron and half full of candy. Her apartment door had been propped open, and a television droned inside.

"You're all home early, aren't you?" she said. "I was about to lock the place up."

"Thank you," Sharyn said. "But we may be headed out again."

Tag cast Sharyn a quizzical look.

Mrs. Kenworthy only smiled with a knowing wink. "Of course. How foolish of me. Something tells me you're just getting started."

Sharyn prayed that wasn't true. She wanted all of this to end.

Their group climbed the three flights to their floor, which they shared with four other flats. Once inside their own, Sharyn took a breath, while leaning on the door.

Naomi pointed a finger at Sharyn's chest. "You need to tell us what's going on. Why are you in such a fright?"

Sharyn swallowed, pushed off the door, and came to a decision. "I'll show you."

While Professor Wright's warning still burned inside her—*tell no one*—she could not stomach keeping this secret any longer. She trusted her friends and wanted their counsel. The fire at the Old Library could not be a mere coincidence.

Something had gone wrong.

But *how* wrong remained to be seen.

Until then, she needed help and led the pair into her bedroom. She crossed and dropped beside an old blanket chest. She pulled it open, sifted through her folded sweaters, past an old Army jacket, and retrieved the book. It still remained protected in its cloth wrap. She had not dared uncover it, fearful of being drawn further into this mystery, sensing the danger it represented.

But there was no shirking from that responsibility now.

She knelt back and parted the folds of cloth. "Back at the Old Library, Professor Wright gave this to me."

"Wait . . . Professor Julian Wright?" Tag pressed her. "The head of our program?"

She nodded and did her best to explain all that had happened, stressing the urgency in the man's attitude. "He believed the book wasn't safe at the library, not even in his own possession. But I don't know why."

Anger spiked though her for being thrust into all of this against her will. Though, she knew that wasn't entirely true. She had accepted the responsibility. While it would be easy to say she did it to curry favor with the director of the postgraduate program, she knew the blame lay deeper. She had difficulty saying no. It went back to having to always be the good daughter, to stave off triggering her father's outbursts—as if she had control over him. Now she knew better, but such self-awareness didn't stop those deeply ingrained reflexes.

What have I gotten myself into?

Both her roommates dropped and crowded next to her, eyeing the strange text on her knee. The leather bindings were clearly old, centuries at least. She fingered two bands of copper that held the text clamped shut. The release appeared to be a small metal tin, embedded with an eyeball-size crystal orb. As she wiped dust from it, the sphere rotated under the thumb.

She warily drew her fingers away. "I don't know what the hell this is or why it's so important."

Naomi leaned in, her eyes bright with curiosity. "Do you see any title? Or the name of the author?"

Sharyn flipped the volume back and forth. "Nothing."

Naomi wiggled to free her phone. "I should record this."

Sharyn pushed her friend's arm down. "No, not until we know more."

Tag pointed to the cover's center. "Look at that embossed emblem. Like the spokes of a wheel, all pointing to various symbols."

"Very cryptic," Naomi noted.

"Whatever it is, the book must be valuable," Sharyn added. "Enough for Professor Wright to send it off with me. Just prior to that, he had taken a call. He had sounded shocked, even angry."

"Maybe the call spooked him," Tag offered, then used his cane to push back to his feet. "Still, why give it to you? If he was concerned for its safety, why not take it himself?"

Sharyn recalled the professor's urgency. "He warned me to keep it hidden. To not even tell *him* where I hid it until he deemed it safe." She stared over at the other two. "I think he feared whoever was after the book might know *he* had it."

"So he sent you scurrying off with the prize." Naomi sat heavier on her heels. "Away from him."

Sharyn clutched the book harder, aching to know why this was so important, but she remembered Wright's other warning. "He also told me not to attempt to open it."

"Like we could," Tag scoffed. "It's clearly locked with some code tied to that crystal. I can see symbols engraved into it. Am I right?"

Sharyn held the book at an angle toward the room's lamp. "You are, but it looks like the symbols are *inside* the crystal, like flaws in a diamond."

"Truly?" Tag reached over to see for himself.

Sharyn pulled the book away with a twinge of possessiveness. "We can leave this mystery for later. Right now, we must change and get out of here."

Tag frowned. "You mentioned that to Mrs. Kenworthy. Why?"

Naomi stood up. "Sharyn is right."

Tag looked between the two women with confusion.

Sharyn explained, "Someone clearly attacked the Old Library, setting fire to it. Professor Wright could've been caught there."

Naomi continued, "And if Wright was there, he might have been forced to reveal where the book was—and *who* he gave it to."

"If they got my name, it wouldn't take them long to find out where I live." Sharyn frowned. "Again, I could be wrong about all of this, but I'd prefer not to take any chances."

"Then shouldn't we go to the police?" Tag asked. "Tell them what you told us."

She remained silent, unsure. Wright's last warning blazed in her mind's eye: *Trust no one*. Instead, she reached into a pocket and removed the business card given to her by the professor. She had already studied it earlier. It was blank, except for a single phone number engraved on it.

"The professor told me to call this number if there was any trouble." She fished out her cell phone. "Let's try this first."

Naomi and Tag shifted closer.

Sharyn dialed the number, noting the international code for France. As the connection was made, the phone rang and rang.

"Anything?" Naomi pressed.

"No one's answering. It's not even going to voicemail."

"It is almost midnight," Tag noted. "Maybe no one's there at this hour."

Sharyn waited another half-minute, then hung up.

"What do we do?" Naomi asked.

She stared at the other two. "For now, let's get moving. Retreat somewhere and lay low."

After growing up in a volatile household, she had learned to live by this credo. Her father had reinforced it during her training: *When there's danger, keep your head down. Heroes only get themselves killed*. While it wasn't the most noble of sentiments, it was a practical one.

Sharyn stood. "After we're clear of here, we can reach out to the police."

"Sounds good," Tag said.

The three separated and quickly shed their costumes and climbed into streetwear. Sharyn pulled on jeans, a warm turtleneck, and thick-treaded boots. She packed the strange tome into a crossbody bag and slung it over her shoulder. She then draped an oversize Army jacket over everything and tugged on a ball cap.

"I'm ready!" Naomi called from her room.

"I need another minute," Tag answered.

Sharyn used the time to cross to her nightstand. She collected a few extra precautions. She snapped a small Kevlar sheath to the strap of her crossbody bag. It held a combat knife—a folded stainless-steel karambit. Her father had drilled her on the weapon's use, assuring her in tight situations that it would serve her better than a gun. Not that she could have attained the latter in the United Kingdom. Even the knife only had a three-inch curved blade, the maximum allowable here.

She also grabbed a flat leather pouch from the drawer—another gift from her father—and shoved it into her jacket pocket. She flashed to standing before her father with her wrists bound in plastic zip-ties in front of her. He had her bite the loose end of the binding and tighten it until the ties dug into her skin. He then instructed her: *Raise your arms above your head, elbows wide, then thrust your arms down as hard as you can.* As she did, the tie miraculously broke, snapping apart at the lock, and fell away. She stared down in amazement.

Nothing can trap you if you keep your head, her father had warned her.

She prayed that still held true.

She joined the others in the small common room with its tiny kitchen. Tag had donned a fashionable ankle-length duster over a black hoodie. Naomi wore her denim jacket with the Welsh symbol embroidered on it, pulling it over a puffy pink vest. She had also changed into jeans and a scuffed pair of Doc Martens.

"All set?" Sharyn asked.

Tag frowned and stared past Sharyn's shoulder. "Looks like we may be talking to the police sooner than we expected."

She turned. The window behind her flashed with a strobe of

blue lights, rising from the street below. But she had heard no siren—which only set her heart to pounding harder.

"Move quietly," she warned and headed to the door.

One after the other, they crept out onto the third-floor landing. Sharyn held them back, then crossed and peeked down the center of the stairwell. Harsh voices echoed from below. She heard her own name.

Then Mrs. Kenworthy blustered angrily. "At this bloody hour? I don't see why you must—"

A pair of sharp pops cut her off.

Sharyn covered her mouth. From her time spent at the gun range, she recognized the muffled spats of a silencer

A heavy shadow fell into view.

Mrs. Kenworthy . . .

Her body was quickly dragged off. A breath later, a door slammed, likely from the caretaker's flat as the murder was hidden away.

Then a trampling of boots pounded toward them.

7

11:44 p.m.

Sharyn turned to the others. "Up," she mouthed, barely making a sound and pointing.

Her friends remained silent, their eyes huge, but they heeded her instruction. The three of them quickly ascended a half-flight to a sealed door that led to the roof. Tag reached to the push bar, which would automatically unlock in case of emergency.

Which this definitely counts.

Still, Sharyn grabbed Tag's arm. "Stop," she hissed softly.

She shifted him aside and freed her knife from its sheath. She flipped the blade to unfold its short length and reached for the door. Two months ago, she had already inspected it.

Always have an exit strategy.

It was the caveat to *nothing can trap you if you keep your head.*

She used the knife's tip to slice the alarm wire. She held her breath, fearful that severing the power might trigger the alarm, but thankfully it did not. Huffing out her relief, she pushed the door wider, waved the others across the threshold, then followed.

Behind her, the pounding of boots had nearly reached the third floor.

Wincing, she carefully closed the exit door as quietly as possible.

"What now?" Naomi whispered, her face pale in the moonlight.

"This way."

Sharyn rushed to a waist-high brick parapet that separated their rowhouse from its neighbor. With the line of buildings tightly packed, there was no gap between them. She hopped over, then helped Tag.

For once, the man did not object to her assistance.

"Keep moving," Sharyn urged and led them across the roof's gravel and tarpaper surface, sidestepping satellite dishes, boxy air-handling units, and rusty old flues.

She cast a glance behind her. It would not take long for the attackers to discover the apartment was empty and recognize their targets could only have fled in one direction.

Moving swiftly, she crossed two more rooftops. She wished these old buildings had been retrofitted with fire escapes. Instead, if flames drove someone to the roof, the only means of escape was to flee across the adjoining rooftops, to buy time before a rescue could be mounted.

Time we don't have.

At the fourth rowhouse, she headed to its rooftop door, dropped to a knee, and removed the flat leather pouch. She thumbed its flap open and shook out two lockpicks. It was another defensive skill taught to her by her father. As a cop in Tulsa—which was ranked among the most violent cities in the States—he had witnessed too many bodies, many of them women who had been victims of kidnappings or abductions.

No wonder he took to the bottle . . .

With her heart pounding, she fumbled the steel hooks into the keyhole and fished for the tumblers. Panic dulled her dexterity.

"You're proving to be a woman of many hidden talents," Tag noted.

"Let's hope you're right," she said. "Still, be ready. I can't cut the alarm wire from this side. It'll go off once I open the door. After that, we must move fast."

"You'd better hurry *now,*" Naomi warned, ducking and pulling Tag down beside her.

A door crashed open in the distance, accompanied by a muffle of angry voices. With their flat's rowhouse sitting in the middle of the block, the assailants would not know which direction their quarry had fled, which might make them hesitate.

But not for long.

With her teeth clenched, Sharyn forced herself to concentrate. She heard her father whispering in her ear: *Take deep breaths. Panic is your worst enemy.*

She heeded this advice, while still struggling with the darkness her father represented. She inhaled deeply, then let it out slowly through her nose.

Finally, the lock clicked under her efforts. She did not wait. She grabbed the handle and yanked the door wide. As she feared, an alarm blared inside. Worse, light from the stairwell blazed out like a spotlight, bathing them brightly.

"Go!" She waved the two ahead of her, while she huddled behind the swing of the open door. "Head down. Don't slow for anything."

As she followed, a flurry of rounds peppered the far side of the door's reinforced steel. Gasping at the enemy's swift response, she slammed the door behind her and rushed after the others, who had reached the landing below.

"Keep moving!" Sharyn called out.

The three fled headlong down the steps. In the lead, Tag struggled with his cane. The stress had clearly worsened his palsy.

Rather than scold him, Naomi offered encouragement. "We've got this."

They rounded landing after landing. Doors popped open in their wake, roused by the blaring alarm. Questions and curses trailed them as they ran. Finally, they reached the main floor. Sharyn sped past Naomi and Tag and shoved the door open.

"Make for the park. Keep low."

They burst out the door, fled down a short flight of steps, and raced across the street, aiming for the dark shadows of the park. Only a few lampposts glowed out here. Several others had been broken long ago, likely by those who had sought to hide their illicit activities.

Sharyn suddenly appreciated the due diligence of drug dealers.

As she raced for the tree line, she glanced down the road. A black sedan sat at the curb, with a flashing blue light sitting on its dash. Across the street, another larger vehicle idled, half bathed in one of the few remaining lamps. She did a double take, noting the hood ornament's spread of silver wings.

A Rolls-Royce . . .

Such a vehicle looked as out of place here as a diamond ring on a panhandler's finger. She squinted at the oddity for half a breath—then from inside the cab, the red flare of a cigarette spurred her onward. She ducked past a hedgerow and into the park, hoping she had not been spotted.

Once they had gained enough distance, Sharyn used her cellphone to light the way. She muffled its glare with her hand. She only took this risk once she heard the growl of engines erupt behind her, then fade off in another direction. Still, she kept their group moving, fearing the assailants could have sent someone on foot.

They only slowed once they exited the park and lost themselves in a maze of side streets and alleys. By now, Tag wheezed heavily, but he made no complaint. Still, Sharyn drew them to a stop.

"I can keep going," Tag coughed out.

Sharyn had read up on cerebral palsy, wanting to know more about Tag's condition without overtly prying. People with CP were prone to respiratory compromise due to reduced lung capacity and an impaired elasticity to the muscles of the chest wall. Guilt ached through her for putting her friend in danger.

Tag lifted an albuterol inhaler and took a hit from it. He held his breath, then let it out with a long sigh. "That's the good stuff," he mumbled and forced a smile. "Truly. I *can* keep going."

"But to where?" Naomi asked. "Do we just keep running the streets all night?"

Sharyn weighed their options. "No. If those gunmen were truly cops, they could access the city's CCTV cameras to find us. To avoid that, we must get out of sight as soon as possible."

"How?" Tag asked. "Where do we go?"

"Somewhere public. With many people. A crowd to get lost in."

Naomi frowned. "What are you thinking?"

Sharyn reached into her pocket and pulled out a set of black tickets emblazoned with a crimson logo. "Luckily, someone already invited us to a party."

SECOND

8

November 1, 12:20 a.m. GMT

Duncan stood at the urinal, eliminating a portion of the night's beer. With his eyes closed, he tilted his head back. He was unfortunately far more inebriated than he had planned on being by this time. While it was after midnight, he had hoped to extend his evening.

"Why do you want to go to the Forum?" Archie asked from the neighboring stall. "Why go slumming with the commoners when there are plenty of fit birds right here at the Lemmy?"

Duncan tapped off and zipped up. "I'm already tired of this place," he lied. "It's getting too crowded and lairy in here. I could use some air. And it's only a ten-minute walk to the Forum."

Archie finished and followed him out of the restroom. "I'm game enough. As they say, horses for courses. But I'm not sure about Seb or Dom. Both of 'em are still chatting up those two girls. No doubt it's a wasted effort on their part, but those two will not cut bait this early."

Duncan shrugged. "Just as well. I'm fine going by myself."

In fact, he would prefer it. He'd have better chances of "chatting up" someone at the Forum if he didn't drag along an entourage of drunken hooligans.

Unfortunately, Archie failed to take the hint. "And leave you wandering the campus alone? In that get-up?" He sized Duncan up and down. "Someone might think you went AWOL."

Duncan scowled. He had decked himself in a wool Army jersey with reinforced epaulets at the shoulders. He had paired it with regulation trousers in desert camo and a matching cap. The gear was no rented costume, showing ragged repairs and significant fraying. He had collected the military fatigues from his grandfather's wardrobe after the man had passed at the age of ninety-five.

By donning the uniform, Duncan had wanted to honor his grandad, but at the same time, it felt like stolen valor. Still, when Duncan was a teenager, the old man had once caught him sizing up the former uniform and encouraged him to wear it: *Our history shouldn't be resigned to dusty bins. . . . I'd be chuffed to see my old kit out in the world again.*

Archie nudged Duncan in his shoulder. "I'll let Seb and Dom know we're headed off."

Duncan sighed, accepting that he could not shake loose his friend. Archibald Bailey had been his roommate going back to his first term at Oxford. The two had also been teammates on the same university rugby team, the Men's Greyhounds. Though that name was a poor fit for Archie. *Pitbull* was the more apt description. Archie had been the team's tighthead prop, one of the roughest positions, requiring a bullish strength in shoulders and legs. While a head shorter than Duncan, Archie outbulked him by a third.

"If we're heading outside, I better grab my warmers," Archie said. "It's getting to be brass monkeys outside."

The stocky man shoved through the packed crowd, as if fighting a tough scrum.

For Halloween, Archie had simply donned his old rugby kit. Once inside the nightclub, he had stripped to his jersey, shorts, and ankle-cut boots, abandoning a woolen track suit at their booth.

Duncan considered using this distraction to sneak out of the club, but he knew such an Irish goodbye would wound his friend.

As much as Archie looked like a tough-skinned pugilist—with a crick to his nose and his hair shaved to a stubble—he had a big heart that could be easily bruised. Archie took great stock in their friendship, far more than Sebastian and Dominic. Duncan suspected Archie had only enrolled in Exeter to dog along with him. Archie's father had served with the diplomatic core and changed embassies every three years, which made it difficult for Archie to find a circle of friends.

And now that he had, Duncan refused to break it.

While waiting, he took in the chaos of the Lemon Grove. Partiers, most of them in costume, packed the small dance floor. The music pounded his ears and thumped his ribcage with each bass beat. A pair of fog machines wafted misty clouds throughout the club, reflecting the swirling lights, while masking groping hands and grinding hips.

Archie finally fought his way back, tugging on his jersey jacket. He carried his track pants over a shoulder. His eyes shone with his usual excitement.

"Like I thought, Seb and Dom aren't budging. They're dug in deep. But I come with news about the Forum."

"What news?"

"People are saying the Old Library caught fire. Bunch of sirens, flashing lights. They've cordoned off the road and cleared the party at the Forum."

Duncan turned to the club's doors, doing his best to hide his disappointment.

I waited too long. Should've left earlier.

Still, guilt twinged through him for such a selfish misgiving.

"Anyone hurt?" Duncan asked.

Archie shrugged. "Don't know. But I wouldn't mind legging over there and taking a looksie."

Duncan had the same thought and headed toward the exit. "Let's go."

He pictured his visits to the library over the past weeks and hoped its treasure trove of old books and manuscripts had been spared the flames.

"Weren't you just there today?" Archie asked.

"Not just me . . ."

As if summoned by his words, the club's front doors opened and a trio of figures rushed across the threshold, stopping short of the velvet rope that cordoned off the club. The one in the lead flagged a set of tickets toward the bouncer.

Sharyn Karr looked flushed and breathless. She wore a loose Army jacket, but it was no costume, just casual streetwear. Her long blonde hair had been tied in a ponytail and tucked through the back of a ball cap, the brim of which was pulled low over her eyes.

What's she doing here?

He guessed the fire must have driven her and her friends over to the Lemmy. Still, Sharyn did not strike him as someone who would blithely go club-hopping after such a tragedy. He noted the furtive glances she cast back to the door. Her two friends did the same.

Something's up.

Duncan remembered his earlier regret about waiting too long. Clearly the opposite was true.

I waited just long enough.

9

12:44 a.m.

Sharyn crossed past the velvet rope as it was lifted away—then balked at entering the packed club. The Lemon Grove had a capacity of eight hundred. The Halloween party looked to have surpassed that limit, or maybe the artificial fog only made it seem so.

Her two friends stuck close to her shoulders.

"We're the only ones without costumes," Naomi noted.

"Not that anyone can tell through this mist." Tag waved a hand before his face and covered a cough with his fist.

Despite several hits off his inhaler, he still wheezed heavily. Recognizing Tag needed to catch his breath, Sharyn led them onward and searched for a place to retreat and regroup. As they crossed deeper into the club, the music thundered, rising from a DJ booth on the far side, where a helmeted figure waved an arm to the beat. It all made Sharyn dizzy, especially the spinning dazzle of lights.

A hand suddenly snatched her elbow, while someone shouted at her.

She seized the offender's thumb and bent it backward, breaking the grip and raising a yowl. She shoved off the attacker—a figure in a uniform.

Naomi shouldered protectively in front of Sharyn. "Maxwell, what the hell do you think you're doing? Never grab a woman like that."

The tall figure stepped back, bumping into someone outfitted in rugby gear. "I was only trying to get your attention."

Sharyn refocused on her assailant and recognized Duncan Maxwell. From boots to cap, he looked authentically like someone from the British army.

"Sorry," Duncan apologized, rubbing his injured thumb. "Still, I'm chuffed to see you were able to use my tickets."

Tag cast Sharyn a scathing look. "You got the tickets from this pompous ass?"

Clearly Tag still held a grudge from quiz night.

The rugby player shoved forward. "Who you calling *pompous*, mate?" The man clapped Duncan on the shoulder. "Though, you did get the *ass* part right. I'll give you that much."

Sharyn saw it was Archibald Bailey, another student. She took a deep breath and fought down her pounding heart. The night's tension—the fire, the bloodshed—strained her nerves.

Before she could break away, Duncan stepped closer. "I heard there was a fire at the Old Library. Is that true? Did you see it?"

He clearly only meant to engage her in conversation, but something must have registered on her face—something wounded, maybe guilty.

Duncan moved closer. "Do you know what happened? How it started?" His voice lowered. Yet, it remained deep enough to be heard past the music. "You must've been one of the last ones in the building when it closed."

"I . . . I don't know what happened," she stammered. "And Professor Wright was still inside when I left."

Naomi touched her elbow in warning.

Sharyn swallowed. "That's all I know."

Duncan's eyes narrowed on her, then he nodded. "Let's hope the professor wasn't there when the fire broke out."

She prayed for the same, but she held out little hope. She pictured Mrs. Kenworthy's body slumping to the entryway floor. She shuddered, still struggling to come to terms with all that had happened, still furious at Professor Wright for putting them all in such danger.

The weight of the crossbody bag hung heavy on her shoulder.

What is so important about this book?

Tag searched around. "Is there somewhere less deafening in this place? Where a guy can talk without straining his vocal cords?"

Duncan pointed to the left. "We have a corner booth. With table service."

Archie shook his head. "Sorry. Won't do. That spot is currently overflowing with hormones and Paco Rabanne cologne." He turned. "But follow me."

As he swung to the right, Sharyn cast Duncan a questioning glance, but he only shrugged.

Archie led them to a side door marked EMPLOYEES ONLY. He shoved through, then held the way open for everyone else. "There's a breakroom ahead."

"Are we allowed back here?" Naomi asked as she crossed the threshold.

The same question must have been on a server's mind. A lanky woman in a Lemon Grove polo headed down the hall toward them. She carried an empty drink tray tucked under an arm and scowled as she sidled past them. Then her eyes spotted Archie, and the hard set to her lips softened.

"Hey, Arch, coming to see the boss?" She nodded down the hall. "As usual, Haran's holed up in his office."

"Nah, I'm sure he's too busy. Friends and I just wanted to rest our ears a bit."

"All right then." She called back as she exited into the club, "But stay out of trouble."

Sharyn knew it was far too late to heed such advice.

Archie led them down the corridor. As they crossed an open door, a shout called from inside. "*Masa' alkhayr, sadiqi!*"

Archie stopped, shoved his head through the doorway, and answered back in Arabic. The exchange was brief, but clearly warm.

Duncan leaned toward Sharyn. "Archie's father was with the British diplomatic core. Did a stint in Riyadh. Don't let Archie's exterior fool you. He can speak nine languages. Some better than English."

Archie rejoined them and waved onward with a grin. "The manager offered to send a few free pints our way. I thought it impolite to decline."

Sharyn had no interest in partaking, but Tag and Naomi looked relieved.

As they passed the office, Duncan nodded back to it. "A few years ago, Archie's father helped smooth the visa process for the manager's family. A favor that proved uncannily fortunate, considering where Archie ended up being enrolled. Though, truth be told, his father has connections everywhere. In fact, it's how I got so many free passes to the club."

"And now free beer," Sharyn noted.

Duncan shrugged. "All further proof of the effectiveness of British diplomacy."

As they reached the breakroom off the hall, Sharyn hung back and searched farther down the corridor. She spotted a glowing Exit sign at the end. The sight of another way out eased the tension in her chest—but only slightly.

Still, it was enough to push her into the breakroom, where concert posters plastered the walls, as if someone had decoupaged the interior. The skunky notes of weed hung in the air, likely pickled into the bones of the place long ago.

Sharyn did not complain. She crossed to the long table that split the room and sagged gratefully into a hard plastic seat. Duncan stepped over to a small fridge and retrieved two bottles of water. He passed her one and took the chair next to hers.

"Thanks," she said, but she left her bottle unopened. Her stomach was too knotted to take anything in.

She also felt Duncan's gaze on her, probably weighing whether or not to challenge her on the night's activities. To deflect any questions, she spoke first. "Sorry about your thumb. From earlier. I thought you were with the military police or something."

His brows rose higher. "And your first go-to is to attack a British officer?"

"You startled me. That's all."

"I suppose I can understand your mistake." He brushed a palm down his woolen jersey. "These are real fatigues. Belonged to my grandfather."

"Your grandfather?"

"He was with the British SAS during World War II. Lost a leg while serving in North Africa."

"How horrible. I'm sorry to hear that."

"I'm not. If not for his injury, I wouldn't be sitting here."

She frowned at him until he explained.

"Once back home, my grandad wanted to continue to serve and was assigned to guard a codebreaking team. It's where he met my grandmother, who was a mathematician with the group. From their stories, it was not love at first sight. They butted heads at every turn."

Despite the night's terrors, Sharyn found herself smiling. "But clearly they worked out their differences."

"Eventually." Duncan matched her grin. "Before they passed, the two used to regale me with tales from their time during the war."

Sharyn noted the wistful glimmer in his eye. She imagined it must have been those stories that had whetted Duncan's interest in cyphers and codes. She wished her legacy was so blessed. She remembered the counsel from her Al-Anon sponsor: *For better or worse, our past forges who we are. It's the steel that strengthens us or chains us down.*

Still, this line of thought—about codes—reminded her. She reached for a yellow legal pad left on the table, where someone had doodled crude figures in graphically obscene poses. She grabbed a loose pen, flipped to a fresh page, and quickly jotted down a series of letters and numbers, fearing she might forget them.

Naomi frowned at her effort. "What are you doing?"

"Back at the house, I spotted a Rolls parked at the curb."

Tag nodded. "That's right. I saw it, too."

"It might be nothing, but it seemed out of place, so I memorized the plate number." Her father had schooled her to be ever vigilant, especially in suspicious situations. She shifted the pad over and tapped at what she wrote. "*This* number."

SCV 91345

Duncan's brow furrowed as he studied the page. "What's this about?"

Naomi opened her mouth, but Sharyn shook her head.

No need to get others involved in this mess.

Archie grunted. He had been standing on the table's far side, tugging into his track pants, which proved difficult due to his rubber-cleated rugby boots. He abandoned his effort and rapped his knuckles on the pad.

"SCV," he said, reading off the first three letters. "You know what that means."

Sharyn did not. And from the confused looks, neither did anyone else.

Archie tapped each letter. "*Status . . . Civitatis . . . Vaticanae.*"

As this clarified nothing, Archie continued. "The license plates of official vehicles registered with Vatican City start with those three letters."

"You know that?" Duncan frowned. "How? From your embassy days?"

"Nah," Archie scoffed. "From *Who Wants to Be a Millionaire?*"

Sharyn didn't know if he was being serious or sarcastic, but it didn't matter.

Duncan turned to their group and asked a question they all shared: "Why would someone from the Vatican be on your street?"

10

1:09 a.m.

Duncan read the tension across the faces of Sharyn and her two roommates. The three had retreated to a corner of the breakroom and argued in low tones. He caught snatches of the conversation as it grew heated, but it made no sense.

What the hell is going on?

"Just tell them," Naomi urged.

"And draw them into this mess?" Sharyn said.

"They could be useful," Tag offered. "Archie knew about those Vatican plates."

Duncan turned back to the table, wondering what other knowledge his friend might have. "Arch, where would such a car possibly come from?"

Archie had returned his attention to the yellow legal pad, but he was no longer studying the plate number. Instead, he meticulously added anatomical flourishes to the crude sketches on the front page.

As he continued his work, he answered, "Probably an embassy vehicle. The Vatican has an Apostolic nunciature in London. Their equivalent of a diplomatic mission. Most embassies haul in their own cars. All about national pride. The Germans bring in Beemers and Benzes. The French drive Peugeots. The Finns love their Saabs. They shuttle the vehicles by rail to the UK through the Chunnel."

"But what would a car from the Vatican nunciature be doing in Exeter?"

"Can't say. The university does have a Department of Theology and Religion. Maybe they brought in a speaker. London's only three hours away."

"In a Rolls?"

Archie tilted an eye up at him. "The Holy See has never been known for their humble trappings." He returned to his artwork. "And where your new friends live—as dodgy as it is—sits only a handful of blocks from Exeter Cathedral. Whoever was in the car could've come to minister to the poor . . . or maybe they were looking to score some coke or meth."

"I don't know," Duncan muttered. "Still seems odd."

Archie shrugged. "My pops probably knows both the nuncio in London and our ambassador to the Vatican. I can give him a call in the morning. Check and see if he can shed any light on this."

By now, their conversation had drawn back the attention of Sharyn and the others. Tag pointed a hand toward Archie, silently indicating that here was another example of their usefulness.

Naomi agreed. "We do need help."

Sharyn refused to budge. "For now, we need only *one* thing from them."

Duncan shifted toward them. "What's that?"

Sharyn ignored him and turned to Archie. "What time does the club close?"

Archie leaned back in his chair, stretching a kink from his shoulders. "Sometimes it's open twenty-four hours. But tonight, it'll be shutting down around two, so the staff can do a deep cleaning after the party. Especially due to the—"

"That's in less than an hour," Naomi blurted out. "I thought we'd have more time."

Sharyn turned to Duncan with a wince and offered the barest explanation. "We can't go back to our place."

Duncan opened his mouth to ask why, but Sharyn lifted a palm.

"We need somewhere to hole up for the night," she said. "Nothing more. Until we can figure out what to do next."

Duncan wanted to press the matter. He considered leveraging this request with a demand for answers. But Sharyn swallowed hard, looking both resolute and scared. While he had only known these three for a few weeks, he sensed no illicit intent—just trepidation. He knew any further explanation would have to wait.

Still, he needed one matter clarified. "So, you want to go to *our* place? Not a hotel or something?"

"Just for one night," Sharyn stressed.

Duncan took a deep breath, then sighed it out. "All right then. A slumber party it is."

Before they could move, a thunderous eruption rose from the nightclub. Even muffled, the ruckus shook the walls.

"What's going on?" Naomi asked.

Archie swore and cast a longing look in the direction of the commotion. His entire body looked crestfallen as he shoved to his feet. He glowered at the rest of them. "Look what you're making me miss . . . it had better be worth it."

Duncan herded everyone toward the door. Once out in the corridor, he pointed to the glowing Exit sign at the other end. "Let's go out the back."

Archie led the group in that direction, while casting a wounded look over his shoulder toward the nightclub. Because of that, he missed the rear door swinging open ahead of him. A single lamp in the alley revealed a pair of shadowy figures in body armor and helmets. Behind them and to the right, flashing blue lights bathed the two in flickering glows.

Sharyn grabbed Duncan's arm and tugged him back.

"They found us . . ."

11

1:18 a.m.

Sharyn retreated backward down the hall, dragging Duncan with her, while herding Tag and Naomi behind her. Archie came along, looking confused. For the moment, Archie and Duncan blocked the view of Sharyn's huddled group.

"Into the club," she urged everyone.

But would it do any good?

Through the open doors, sirens could be heard blaring outside, rising from the front of the building.

They must have the place surrounded.

Still, she kept everyone moving, backpedaling, never taking her eyes off the two gunmen. Before they made it halfway down the corridor, someone called from the direction of the club.

"Where are you all going?"

Sharyn glanced over her shoulder and spotted the server from earlier. Atop a raised palm, the woman balanced a tray, laden with foaming pints.

The promised free order.

The group closed on the server, then tried to get past her. In the shuffling confusion, Sharyn ended up exposed, in full view of the armed men.

The two remained at the back door, guarding the rear exit. One stood with his head tilted to his shoulder, likely radioing in. Then the other one snapped straighter. The glint of black steel reflected as he lifted a handgun toward her.

"Run!" she yelled, shoving into Tag and Naomi.

Down the corridor, the two gunmen rushed with pistols raised.

Sharyn grabbed for the only deterrent at hand. She snatched the server's tray, sending mugs tumbling and shattering, then flung the platter like a Frisbee down the hall. As the cork and metal rebounded and ricocheted off the walls, she hoped the confusion would throw off the gunmen's aim for a few seconds.

Twisting around, she got her friends racing toward the far door. She had to abandon the server, who had fallen to a knee, knowing the woman was not the target.

Archie tried to help her up, but Duncan bowled into him and carried him along. "Move!"

Sharyn appreciated that Duncan had not abandoned her, but it was a foolish act. He was putting himself and his friend in needless danger. He and Archie were also not the targets this night.

Then gunfire broke out behind them. Muffled by silencers, the noise was barely discernible above the club's roaring crowd. A glance back showed the server collapsing to the floor, shot in the head.

No . . .

Then Archie lurched forward with a cry and grabbed his shoulder, but Duncan kept him on his feet. They were almost to the door, but they would never make it.

Duncan must have recognized this, too, and crowded behind her, trying to shield her.

But another victim heedlessly interceded.

Behind them, the manager stepped angrily into the hall—right into the line of fire. He must have noted the commotion but failed to hear the muffled shots.

His body jolted under the barrage.

Still, his sacrifice bought Sharyn and the others enough time to reach the far door and crash headlong through it. The sights beyond nearly drew her to a stop. The ear-shattering crescendo of house music battered her senses, adding to her confusion. The club had become another world. The fog had solidified into a dense, churning mass, where screaming figures writhed under technicolor lights.

Sharyn struggled to understand.

Naomi gasped out the answer, "Foam party . . ."

Her friend dove into the shoulder-high froth, dragging Tag with her.

Duncan pushed Sharyn into the thick of it, but she squirmed to the side and waved him onward. "Go!"

Archie hung on his arm, the shoulder of his track suit bright with blood.

Sharyn rushed back to the door. There was no way to block it, but earlier, ever paranoid, she had spotted something that might add to the confusion.

She lunged to a fire alarm on the wall and yanked hard. The music immediately cut off, likely a failsafe measure during an emergency. The ratcheting scream of a klaxon took its place, intercut with a loud robotic voice repeating the same warning again and again: *Fire, Fire, Fire, Fire . . .*

The door next to her swung open, but she was already moving. She shoved off the wall and spun into the foam. She dropped low, burying herself. Before diving in, she caught a glimpse of Duncan wading through with Archie, their heads barely above the froth. She blindly aimed in their direction, trusting Duncan to stay on Tag and Naomi's trail.

She gasped and choked on the suds, but she dared not come up for air. As bodies battered into her, she kept her head down and fled toward where she had last spotted Duncan. Still, the spinning house lights and shadowy shapes challenged her sense of direction.

Around her, the tumult of bodies slowly formed a tide flowing in one direction—toward the front doors—as confusion turned into a panicked rout to escape. She let herself be carried with the surge, trusting the others would do the same.

Sharyn shivered as the bubbling dampness soaked through her clothes. She gagged against the soapy taste. As the crowd neared the exit, the foam's depth lessened. She risked lifting her face, her head crowned by lather. She searched across the mass of people, all packed tightly, bottlenecked at the lone pair of exit doors.

Where are the others?

Then a hand grabbed the collar of her jacket and tugged her backward. She jabbed an elbow, earning a hard *oof* from her assailant.

"It's me," Duncan coughed in her ear. "This way."

He drew her to the left, fighting through the tide. In an eddy off to the side, Naomi stood with an arm around Archie. Tag crossed to meet Sharyn, hobbling badly, having lost his cane at some point.

"Police are outside," Tag wheezed heavily. "Or at least someone pretending to be them."

Sharyn turned to look. The Lemmy's front doors faced a small park. The only roads were a crisscrossing of narrow paths meant for bikes or service carts. Two black sedans with flashing lights flanked the exit, parked crookedly on the grass.

A trio of helmeted figures in body armor stood posted beside the bumpers of each vehicle. Flashlights swept the foamy faces of those fleeing the club. Still, it was clear the searchers were being overrun. The enemy had failed to account for a panicked surge of hundreds rushing past them.

Naomi looked on. "We can make a run for it. Hope they miss us in the crush."

It was risky, but Sharyn knew they couldn't stay here. Turning, she searched for any helmeted shapes forging through the foam, but she spotted no one. Most likely, the pair had been ordered to continue guarding the employee exit, to keep their suspects from circling back and escaping that way.

Archie offered his own warning. "If we wait much longer, I may bleed to death."

Tag scowled at this concern. "I checked. You'll live. Nothing more than a graze. In the meantime, what do we all do?"

"We stay put," Sharyn said, coming to a decision.

Duncan frowned at this plan.

She pointed past the two parked sedans. Off in the distance, blue lights spun angrily, heading this way, sitting atop far larger vehicles.

"Fire engines," she said.

After the inferno at the Old Library, the local brigades already had manpower and resources nearby, a portion of which were now speeding toward the club, responding to the alarm.

Fortunately, others also noted the approaching emergency forces.

The six men outside did a sweep of the faces closest at hand, then clambered into their vehicles. Moments later, the two sedans reversed rapidly, scattering everyone aside.

Sharyn had counted on this retreat. Whether fake cops—or a group on the take—they wouldn't want to be caught by the arriving emergency forces.

Especially with people shot in the club's hallway.

Guilt at those deaths warred with a rising fury—at herself, at the professor, at whoever hunted them. Once the sedans fled fully out of view, Sharyn waved to the others, her voice bitter but determined.

"Let's go."

She got everyone into the tidal mass of people fleeing the club. Still, she took additional precautions. Someone had clearly tapped or hacked into the city's CCTV to track them to the club.

Still daubed in remnants of foam, she tugged the brim of her ball cap lower. She had Tag draw his pullover's hood over his head.

Naomi wrapped a scarf across her features. To further confound any spying eyes, their group kept to the remnants of the departing crowd as hundreds dispersed through the park.

As they headed across the green, keeping under trees, the changeable British weather proved fortuitous for once. The clouds burst and a heavy rain fell. Duncan paid a handsome sum to buy three umbrellas from a drunken bunch of revelers.

By the time their group exited the park, they were all huddled under the additional cover. Sharyn found herself sharing a refuge with Duncan. He hooked an arm around her waist and drew her farther under the umbrella's bonnet.

As cold and wet as she was, she did not object.

He leaned his face closer, as if about to kiss her, but there was no amorous intent. Instead, he fixed her with a hard look, his voice equally flinty.

"When we get back to my flat, I need answers."

She swallowed, nodded, and stared ahead.

So do we all.

12

2:55 a.m.

Inside Duncan and Archie's apartment, Sharyn stood with her back to a glass dining table. The others remained seated there, studying the strange book. She could barely stomach looking at it, knowing how much blood had been spilled just to carry it across the city.

With her arms hugged around her, she stared out a set of panoramic windows. The view overlooked the storm-swept snake of the River Exe. Lightning chased across the bottom of the low, dark sky. Morning seemed an impossibility.

Duncan's flat consumed a corner of the fourteenth floor of a new tower in St. Leonards, one of Exeter's toniest neighborhoods. The room's furnishings fit the polished building. Everything looked Scandinavian modern, with sleek lines, cool leathers, all softened with faux-fur throws. An electric fireplace glowed along one wall with a huge TV screen above it.

While tasteful, it was not her style.

Still, Sharyn appreciated the building's other amenities, especially its security features. In the foyer below, a reception desk was manned 24/7. On Duncan's phone, he had pulled up a feed from the lobby camera. Normally it allowed residents to approve any guests. Now he kept watch for anything suspicious.

Additionally, Sharyn had taken her own safeguards: memorizing the location and number of elevator bays, the routes to the north and south stairwells. Still, she felt exposed, waiting for the next damned shoe to drop.

She lifted a hand and rubbed the back of her neck. She had considered tossing the book down the building's incinerator chute, to be done with this once and for all. Yet, she could not. It wasn't out of respect for a rare text that was centuries old. Nor was it from any sense of duty or obligation. Instead, she knew the copper-bound book remained their group's only leverage.

But how best to use it?

Before reaching his flat, Duncan asked her group to turn off their phones, even removing the SIM cards. His explanation spiked her fears: *Maybe it wasn't the CCTV cameras that led them to the Lemmy. Maybe they traced your cells.*

Duncan kept his own phone powered for a couple of reasons. First, it was unlikely the enemy would connect her group to these two men. At least not quickly. So the risk was low. Sharyn also asked Duncan to dial that mysterious number on the business card, but still there was no answer—which meant only one thing.

We're on our own.

Naomi spoke up behind her. "Come look at this!"

The shock in her voice drew Sharyn's attention away from the windows. Suppressing a groan, she returned to the others. Earlier, she had explained to Duncan and Archie all that had transpired, starting with how she had come to be burdened by the book. Afterward, she had expected Duncan to toss her out. Instead, he had merely gone darkly quiet, clearly needing time to digest this all.

With book in hand, Naomi sat between Tag and Duncan. On the other side of the table, Archie slumped in his seat, his chin resting on his chest, half-asleep. Tag had treated his bullet graze. Apparently, Tag's own health challenges had gifted him with some basic medical knowledge. The wound—mostly a bloody burn—had been pasted with an antibiotic salve and wrapped. A handful of ibuprofen helped dull the pain, but Archie assured them he had suffered far worse on the rugby pitch.

Still, the long night had taken its toll on him.

On all of us.

Sharyn crossed to stand over Naomi's shoulder. "What did you find?"

Her roommate held Duncan's phone over the book's leather cover. She fixed its camera light on the crystal eye, setting it aglow, and studied it closer using the phone's magnifying feature.

"You were right," Naomi said. "The symbols aren't engraved *into* the surface but lay *within* the crystalline structure itself."

Sharyn had already suspected as much. "What about it?"

Naomi, her eyes as bright as the crystal, glanced to Sharyn. "Come see."

Sharyn leaned down, drawing Tag and Duncan closer. Naomi slightly rotated the orb, while attempting to hold the phone steady. The image on the screen jittered, then settled enough to make out one of the symbols.

Tag gasped.

Duncan swore.

Embedded shallowly into the crystal, a stylized gold centaur shone in astounding luminous detail. In its hands, it held aloft a stretched bow with a notched arrow.

Sharyn gaped at the sight. The image had to be no larger than a matchhead. Yet, the artistry—the exquisite detail—stole her breath. She remembered visiting a museum in New York that held an exhibit of carvings made from single grains of rice: birds, roses, busts of famous people, even a rearing stallion like shown here.

"I've never seen anything like this," Naomi murmured.

Tag squinted at the crystal. "The skill and know-how to do this seems impossible for a book of this age."

"And it's not just this *one* symbol." Naomi rotated the orb.

With each halting stop, she revealed more tiny golden figures: a ram with curled horns, a crab with menacing pincers, a charging bull with its head held low, a scorpion threatening with a raised poisonous tail.

They all knew what these shapes represented, but Duncan was the first to voice it.

"Zodiac signs." He pointed to the centaur, which Naomi had returned to again. "That's supposed to be Sagittarius. Look at those silver lines that cut across the gold. They link together brighter blebs . . . stars . . . forming the constellation for the symbol."

"Tiny celestial maps," Sharyn whispered. "The entire crystal orb is a chart of the heavens."

"But what does it mean?" Tag asked.

No one had an answer, but one thing was clear.

"The crystal sphere," Sharyn noted, "the rare artistry on display, it alone must be worth a small fortune."

Tag stared at the book. "If something this amazing sits *atop* the book, imagine what might be *inside*."

"Whatever it is," Naomi noted, "someone locked it up tight for a reason."

"But who and why?" Duncan asked.

Archie interrupted with a gruff snore, loud enough to stir himself fully awake. He lifted his face and gazed blearily around the room. "What's going on?"

Duncan sighed, shook his head, and stood up. "Enough of this. At this point, we're just faffing about. We're all shattered and need sleep. In a few hours, it'll be morning. We can figure out a plan then. Maybe we risk going to the police. Maybe we reach out to Archie's dad, who has a lot of pull. Right now, we're too tired to think straight."

Sharyn tried to raise an objection but all that came out was a jaw-straining yawn. She recognized he was right. Adrenaline could only carry one so far.

Duncan pointed across the common area to a short hall. "Sharyn, you and Naomi take my room. Tag can bunk with Archie."

"What about you?" she asked.

"I'll take first watch." He lifted his cell, which still displayed a view of the lobby. "Someone needs to keep an eye out for the bastards."

"Then wake me in an hour. I'll take the second shift."

"If I can last that long."

Guilt stabbed at her, but Duncan waved her off with a tired smile. "Fear not. I'll not dishonor my grandad's uniform by falling asleep at my post."

Sharyn still hesitated, until Naomi grabbed her arm and drew her across the common area. As they headed away, Sharyn wondered if the apartment had come outfitted this way or if Archie and Duncan's parents had hired a designer for this chic bachelor pad. The answer came when she entered Duncan's bedroom.

It was like stepping into another century.

A tall Edwardian wardrobe commanded one wall. Bookshelves covered another, packed with a disorderly muddle that spoke of its well use. There was even an old Victorian washstand with a marble bowl. Its scarred walnut surface held toiletries and grooming gear, including what appeared to be an old badger-hair shaving brush.

She wondered if the furnishings, like Duncan's fatigues, had been passed down from his grandfather. If so, she struggled to balance this sentimental side of Duncan with his otherwise cavalier attitude.

"That bed . . ." Naomi said, gliding past everything else. "I could sink into it forever."

The four-poster looked as much of an antique as the rest—and as well-used and worn. The mattress rose just shy of her waist. Layers of mussed blankets and quilts, all in tartan patterns, formed a masculine nest.

Naomi shed clothing with every step.

Sharyn followed, but she only removed her Army jacket, ball cap, and boots. Anxiety kept her otherwise dressed—ready in case they should need to run. Naomi had no such restraint. She stripped to panties and a loose-tailed shirt, then buried herself into the pile, nearly vanishing away.

As Sharyn climbed onto the other side, a soft drone of voices rose from down the hall. Duncan had turned on the television, likely to keep himself awake. She half-listened to what sounded like a soccer match as she cocooned herself into the blankets. The bed proved to be as comfortable as it looked. The sheets were silken, the duvet as soft as velvet. It all tempted her to remove more clothing, down to the skin.

Still, she refrained.

As she settled in, she noted the coverings and pillows smelled like Duncan, a muskiness that further lulled her, reassured her that someone had her back. She closed her eyes, but she knew any sleep would be fitful at best, especially as the night's terrors replayed in her head.

I may never sleep again.

She was proven wrong when time slipped, and a hand suddenly shook her hard. She shattered out of a dreamless void into a room lit by blinding rays passing through folds in the drapery.

Morning already . . .

She shifted up to an elbow, still bleary-eyed, to find Naomi leaning over her, somehow fully dressed again. Her friend's eyes were huge, her features flushed.

Sharyn coughed to clear the hoarseness from her throat. "Why didn't someone—"

"You must see this." Naomi tugged her up. "Right now."

13

8:38 a.m.

Duncan paced before the warm fireplace, but he remained chilled. His heart thudded hard as he struggled to find his center.

Naomi returned with Sharyn. Tag had already fetched Archie. The two men sat on the leather sofa, both looking equally ashen.

Sharyn entered with a complaint for her flat mate. "You should've woken me earlier. I could've taken a shift."

Naomi spoke rapidly. "Tag offered to take your place last night. He couldn't sleep with Archie's snoring. Then Tag made Archie pull the next shift—both as punishment and to banish him out of the bedroom. So, the boys had us both covered. For once, chauvinism proved to have its benefits."

Sharyn turned to Duncan. Her gaze flicked to the side, to the muted television, which was paused on a BBC morning newscast. "What's going on?"

Tag answered. "Rewind and show her."

Duncan picked up the remote. "It's not good," he warned lamely, but there was no way to lessen the blow.

He turned up the volume, while reversing through the newscast. He stopped at a red banner emblazoned with *Breaking News*, then let it run. The two anchors wore matching grim expressions, while reporting on the latest from the campus fire. They were intercut with nighttime footage of shining engines and arcing sprays of water. The Old Library lay engulfed in flames.

Duncan glanced over to Sharyn. She stood with a fist clenched to her chest, clearly girding herself.

She knows what's coming.

A reporter in the field appeared on the screen, backdropped against the smoking remains of the library at dawn. "We've just heard from the head of Fire and Rescue. They report one casualty, a body found inside badly burned. An investigation is pending."

The feed switched to a man in a suit standing before a cluster of microphones. "We are treating this as malicious arson. It appears the fire-suppression system may have been sabotaged or disabled. But more importantly, the body inside shows clear evidence of foul play."

In the background, someone asked for the identity of the victim.

"Until we can confirm, we aren't—" The man was interrupted by an aid, who whispered in his ear, and the interview abruptly ended.

The feed switched back to the anchor desk. The newscaster cupped a palm over one ear, likely listening to the control room, then lowered his hand and addressed the camera. "We've just received CCTV footage from a camera in the park that might offer insight into the night's tragic events. Be warned. What we're about to show is graphic and disturbing."

Next appeared grainy footage. The darkness reduced everything to muted shades of gray. The view showed the front doors to the Old Library. A cluster of figures appeared, all concealed in robes and hoods. They dragged a man in a dark suit up to the doors. The victim's face was bloodied and swollen, his arm cradled crookedly to his chest. One of the assailants unlocked the library, and the group vanished inside.

Sharyn moaned, lowering her fist as if in defeat, "No . . ."

The anchor desk reappeared. "After consulting with the university, we believe we can confirm the identity of the victim."

On the screen, a frozen snapshot of the bloodied face appeared beside a formal school headshot. It was clearly the same man.

The anchor continued, "Julian Wright was a humanities professor at the university. Latest word from campus security is that the police have cordoned off his office, which was said to have been ransacked . . ."

The broadcast ran on, but Duncan muted it and turned to Sharyn. "Someone clearly came for the book. First at Wright's office, then the library. The professor may have lied about it being there. Maybe to buy you more time."

"But eventually they tortured your name out of him," Tag said dourly.

"Then killed him," Naomi finished.

Sharyn backed away, as if trying to deny it all.

Still on the sofa, Archie rested his face in his palms. "What the bloody hell do we do now? We have to go to the police, right? They can't *all* be bad. Not like at the Lemmy."

Sharyn waved to the television. "What about the deaths at the nightclub? Have there been any reports?"

"Briefly. Deemed a robbery gone bad, timed to the height of the Halloween bash. The area remains locked down as the police correctly suspect the arson attack and nightclub murders are all tied to the same crime spree. But the authorities are remaining cagey."

A heavy silence followed, weighing them all down.

Archie was the first to move, stirring to his feet, still in a robe and boxers. "Don't know about you all, but I'm going to make us some brekkie. If we're gonna be chased or arrested, it'll be on a full stomach."

Before he could take more than a few steps, Naomi swore, drawing back Archie's attention and everyone else's. She pointed to the television. "Unmute it!"

Duncan turned and spotted the same anchors on the screen. Only between them was posted a graphic of a pentagram. With the remote still in hand, he turned the sound back on.

"—Satanic ritual, according to our source in the field. The body in the library is said to have been found sprawled inside a painted pentagram. With a dagger still lodged in his heart." The anchor turned to his partner. "Mind you, these reports are tentative, and we await confirmation."

The other newscaster nodded. "What we do know is that the victim—Julian Wright—was not only a humanities professor at Exeter, but also the director of a new postgraduate program on Magic and Occult Science. According to a police source, this angle is already being investigated, with a person of interest targeted."

"I wager they'll be looking to pin his murder on someone in our class," Tag said. "A Satanic death on Halloween night. The victim, a man who taught witches."

Naomi looked sick. "Not just *anyone* in our class. If the professor's death was purposely staged to incriminate a student, they would've targeted someone specifically." She stared over at Sharyn. "They forced your name out of Wright. They were at our flat."

Sharyn's features went pale as she clearly understood. "They could've easily planted evidence. And I was the last seen with the professor." She closed her eyes, moaning a name. "And Ms. Peele . . ."

Duncan shifted closer. "The head librarian? What about her?"

"When I was returning the Saxton Atlas back to the strongroom . . ." She opened her eyes, looking pained and scared. "I asked her about the library's security, what safeguards were in place, as if I might be scouting the place."

Archie sighed heavily, clearly having given up on breakfast. "If so, then we know *who* the police's person of interest must be."

Naomi grimaced. "And not just Sharyn."

"What do you mean?" Tag asked.

Naomi explained. "In a search of our flat, they'll undoubtedly discover the body of our caretaker, Mrs. Kenworthy. I wager the murder weapon will be found at our place. The same type of handgun used to kill the two at the Lemmy."

Duncan nodded. "If the enemy traced you three to the club via CCTV, the police will eventually do so, too." He swept his gaze across the trio. "You're the common thread to all those deaths."

Tag swallowed. "Then what do we do? If we go to the police, they'll never believe all those murders are tied to some old text."

"Even if we brought up the book," Sharyn said, "they'd only suspect we stole it. When I was in the strongroom, Ms. Peele was present when Professor Wright warned us that the new cache of books held several priceless volumes."

"Then we're doomed." Naomi ticked off on her fingertips. "Motive, opportunity, and means. The perfect trifecta."

Sharyn swallowed hard. "They're making it impossible for us to go to the authorities. Forcing us to remain at large. Where it will be easier for them to hunt us down."

Duncan suddenly wondered if this slumber party was such a good idea. He and Archie would surely be implicated, too. If not for the murders, then for failing to report a crime, for leaving the scene, for harboring fugitives.

As he struggled with all of this, a vibration thrummed against his thigh. He reached into his pocket and retrieved his cell phone. He checked the incoming number and bit back a groan.

"Who is it?" Archie asked.

Duncan held the phone toward Sharyn. "It's for you."

14

9:19 a.m.

Sharyn took the phone and noted the number on the screen. It matched the one written on Wright's business card. She feared answering it, but she knew she had no choice.

Someone must have finally noted the missed calls.

"Put it on speaker," Duncan urged.

She nodded as she answered, holding the phone toward the group. "Hello?" she said hoarsely, then tried again more firmly. "Who is this?"

A stern male voice replied, the accent French. "I have the same question, *mademoiselle*. How did you get this number?"

Sharyn glanced to the others and got a smattering of shrugs and nods. She decided to stick with the truth.

"From a professor at the University of Exeter," she said. "Julian Wright. He told me to call this number."

The speaker remained silent before snapping harshly. "*Merde* . . ." Then he could be heard faintly speaking to someone else in French.

Sharyn turned to Archie, remembering what Duncan had told her about his friend's fluency in many languages. She mouthed quietly to him, "Can you make out what they're saying?"

Archie shook his head. "Too muffled. But the guy is pissed."

The speaker returned, his voice low and urgent. "Do you have the book? Saint-Germain's journal?"

She glanced to the dining table, where the text still sat. She recalled Professor Wright mentioning how the strange volume was an account by some alchemist.

Could it be this Saint-Germain?

"I have *a* book," she admitted. "Bound in copper with an embedded crystal. But I don't know what it is. Only that it was given to me by Professor Wright yesterday. He asked me to hide it. He thought it wasn't safe at the library."

Another long pause, followed by a statement that almost made her drop the phone. "Then you must be Ms. Karr?"

She gasped at hearing her name from this stranger. "How did you—"

"Our group has been monitoring events in Exeter all night. Through resources across multiple authorities and agencies. While it's not been made public, we've already learned the police have named you as a primary suspect in his murder. If you have the book, it's no wonder you've been targeted by the *Confrérie.*"

She didn't understand the last word, but Archie whispered a translation. "The Brotherhood . . ."

Sharyn gripped the phone. "Who are you talking about? Who is after the book?"

"That requires a very long answer, the knowledge of which is as dangerous as the text given to you. But know this. You must leave. Now. Make for London. I will give you an address."

"If I run, I'll look even more culpable."

"If you stay, you'll be killed. Even if arrested, they will get to you. The *Confrérie* is older than our group, going back centuries. They are powerful, with unlimited resources and deeply rooted connections. You are not safe."

Or anyone around me.

Sharyn pictured the burning library, the bodies left in her wake.

The speaker continued, "Your only hope is to keep moving. To get to the safehouse in London."

Duncan interjected, "What's so damned important about this book?"

The Frenchman scoffed, then swore, plainly irritated, likely only now realizing he was being eavesdropped upon. "How many are with you, Ms. Karr?"

Sharyn cast a look around the group. No one voiced an objection. "Five of us."

"Five? *Merde.* And they all know about the book?"

"They do."

"Do you trust them?"

After everything, despite her normally guarded nature, she had to admit the truth. "I do."

"Then you must all make for London."

Sharyn clutched the phone, but Duncan took her hand, again challenging the Frenchman with the same query. "First, the book? Why's it so bloody important?"

"There's no time—"

"Tell us . . . or we'll take our chances with the police."

A chuff of exasperation burst from the cell. "*D'accord!* Fine. Then first know this. What you are protecting is not a *book*. It's a *map*."

Sharyn glanced again to the copper-bound tome. "A map? To what?"

"To a treasure beyond all imagining. One that could change the fate of humankind. For centuries, we have been its Keepers, its guardians, carrying this torch against the darkness to come."

Tag shifted closer. "If so, then why haven't you secured this treasure already? Why bother with this book, or map, or whatever?"

Silence stretched to a strained edge. "Because we've not yet learned to fully read this map. But we are close. Until then, it must not fall into the wrong hands."

Naomi rolled her eyes. "Then it could be total bullshit. Just a bunch of fanatics fighting over nothing."

"*Non!* Back in 1939, we deciphered the book's First Adage. This revelation led to the discovery of a huge cache of ancient gold coins found in North Africa. They were said to come from the mines of King Solomon. Many of us believe, encrypted in that glittering horde, was the location to the mine itself, possibly even other Solomonic treasures. But it came to naught."

"Why is that?"

"During the height of World War II, with the help of the *Confrérie,* the Nazis stole this golden treasure, after which it vanished into history—along with all its potential. Such is the irreparable harm done by our enemy. And why they must never secure the book."

"Then there are more of these Adages in the text?" Sharyn asked.

"*Oui*. Three in total. The *Seconde* has been partially decrypted and seems to point to a location in the Alps. Where exactly and what it holds remain a mystery. But according to Saint-Germain, the *Troisième*—the third and final Adage—holds his greatest *secrète.* Again, we can't know with precision what that might be, but some suspect it may be the key to immortality itself."

"Why do you think that?" Sharyn asked.

"For a very simple reason. From the words that open Saint-Germain's journal: '*C'est là que réside le secret de mon immortalité. Viens me trouver si tu l'oses.*'"

"Which means what?"

"'Herein lies the secret to my immortality. Come find me, if you dare.'"

A stunned silence spread across the room.

"Now, please, you must go. Toss this phone. Buy a burner and call me again from it. I'll give you an address in London where I'll meet you and explain more, but—"

The Frenchman cut off, speaking again to someone else.

"I have a car," Duncan whispered to Sharyn, while they waited. "In the building's garage."

The speaker returned to the line, his voice sharp and abrupt. "Ms. Karr, are you currently in the St. Leonards neighborhood of Exeter?"

Sharyn glanced out the row of windows that overlooked the River Exe. "We . . . we are."

"Then run. You've been found. A police task force is already en-route to your area. Go!"

The line disconnected.

Before anyone could move, a fierce pounding shook the front door.

15

9:44 a.m.

Duncan flinched at the hard knocking and grabbed the phone from Sharyn. He pulled up the lobby's security feed as he crossed toward the door. During the call with the Frenchman, he had assigned Archie to monitor for any suspicious activity below.

"Did you see anything?" he hissed back to his friend. "Were you watching the lobby?"

"Bollocks . . ." Archie snatched up his own phone, which rested on the sofa next to him, clearly abandoned during the tense conversation.

With the feed now filling Duncan's phone, he searched the screen for any sign of an armed task force, but the lobby looked as calm and quiet as usual. Once he reached the front door, he tapped the security screen next to it, bringing up a view of the hall outside.

Two men filled the frame. The larger pounded a fist on the door.

Duncan sagged with relief, momentarily resting his forehead against the door. "False alarm," he called to the room. "It's only Seb and Dom."

Archie fell back heavily into his seat. "Those barmy bastards' timing couldn't be worse."

Duncan unlocked the door and yanked it open. His two friends had the flat directly under this one. He confronted the pair, blocking the way inside. "Seb. Dom. We were just headed out. To . . . to get some breakfast."

Need to get these two clear of here as quickly as possible.

Sebastian Kroner stepped forward, shouldering past Duncan to barge inside. The man—the son of an MP with the House of Commons—had no respect for boundaries. His twin brother, Dominic, followed with a more apologetic look. They were not identical, but fraternal. Seb was all wiry muscle and had his father's hawkish nose and jet-black hair. Dom had a wider gut and softer features.

"We'll go with you," Seb said. "Coffee and a ciggie sound perfect."

"We've been up all night," Dom explained.

That was obvious, as both were still in their costumes. Under an ankle-length peacoat, Seb wore a pirate's outfit with an eyepatch pushed to his forehead. Dom had a matching coat, but under it, a tight bodysuit bore the outline of a skeleton on it.

"Lost you after that ruckus with the fire alarm." Seb nudged his brother. "But lucky for us, we found some damsels that needed rescuing."

Duncan had no interest in the details and grabbed Seb's arm to try to get him and his brother out the door.

Seb shook free, only now noting that Duncan was not alone. "Ah, I see you found some company yourselves. No wonder you vanished."

Dom winced. "Bruv, maybe we're intruding."

Duncan opened his mouth to agree, but Seb cut him off.

"Nonsense. The more, the merrier."

Archie intervened, flashing open his robe to show his boxers. "We're not ready to go yet. As cold as it is outside, we debated staying home. But the Tower Cafe doesn't deliver. Pick up only. But since you're both dressed, maybe you could dash over there for us . . . and we can all extend this little party of ours."

Archie gave Duncan a weighted look, the intent clear.

Get them the hell out of here.

As Archie headed to his room to change, Duncan took advantage of the opening. "We'll call an order in. My treat." He reached into a pocket for another way to put these two to use. He tossed a set of car keys to Seb, who had no choice but to catch it. "Take my Aston. It's been sitting idle for weeks and can use some warming up."

Duncan knew Seb lusted for a chance to drive his new DBX707, a graduation gift from his father.

Seb smiled and retreated for the door, plainly fearing such an opportunity might be taken away. He dragged Dom with him. "Can't promise we might not be a little late in getting back."

"Take your time," Duncan said and closed the door on his two friends.

Naomi strode over, her eyes pinched. "You gave them your car? Does Archie have another?"

"Not here."

"Then why did you—"

Sharyn answered, clearly understanding his intent. "With the authorities headed this way, they must know of Duncan and Archie's involvement. If the police haven't already, they'll put a trace on any registered vehicles."

Duncan nodded. "With luck, Seb and Dom will draw away the task force, buying us a bit more time. The restaurant lies in the opposite direction from St. Davids Station. Where trains head to London twice an hour."

"Won't the authorities get an alert when we buy tickets?" Sharyn asked.

"No. On British railways, as long as you're not leaving the commonwealth, anyone can buy tickets for someone else. We can pay cash at the kiosks, even make up a name. If an inspector should check—which is rare on those commuters—it won't matter as long as we have paid tickets in hand."

Tag hobbled up, using one of the umbrellas Duncan had bought last night as a cane. "We'll still need to be mindful of CCTV cameras."

"I've got plenty of extra mufflers and hats," Duncan assured them. "No one should question us being all bundled up. It's a bitter morning out there."

In more ways than one.

Archie returned, dressed in sweats and tugging into a black puffer jacket. "Let's get cracking."

Duncan got everyone properly outfitted, checked the lobby feed, saw it was clear, and led the way out. Once at the curb, he hailed a cab. The boxy carriage pulled to a stop, and they all clambered inside.

"Where to?" the cabbie asked.

"St. Davids." Duncan handed forward a fold of bills. "We're late for our train."

"No worries. I'll put my boot into it."

The cabbie took off, wending quickly through the morning traffic.

Behind them, a distant wail rose.

Sirens.

Duncan shared a worried look with Sharyn. Neither of them was under any illusion that they had made a clean escape—especially considering the murderous bastards who pursued them. The question remained:

Who the hell are they?

16

11:47 a.m.

Damn it all . . .

Keir Marchand grimaced as he watched the *Confrérie*'s efforts continue to be thwarted. As the founder of NeuVentis Pharma—a French biotech company—he was unaccustomed to having his ambitions stifled.

He leaned over a laptop at the end of a long reference table. He and the others had commandeered the library housed in the west wing of the Bishop's Palace, which lay in the shadow of Exeter's monumental Cathedral Church of Saint Peter. The arrangements were facilitated by Cardinal Tissot, who stood posted at the door, a phone at his ear, updating others in the group. For now, information was on a need-to-know basis, limited to only a few of the organization's cells.

On the laptop screen, a live feed showed the arrest of two students, who were being pulled from a sleek SUV. An armed cadre of MO19 officers surrounded them and cordoned off the street. The team—part of the Specialist Firearms Command—had been pulled from London by the woman at Keir's left side.

Saanvi Burman stood barely to his shoulders. Her diminutive size belied her power and ambition as a senior liaison officer with MI5. She worked under the deputy director and maintained a no-nonsense attitude. Of Indian descent, her dark hair had been cut efficiently to the shoulders of her crisp navy-blue suit. An earpiece was wired to a radio clipped to her lapel.

"We've confirmed the two young men are not our targets," Burman reported aloud. "They claim to have been sent to fetch a breakfast order."

"A purposeful misdirection," Keir scoffed.

"No doubt."

On another window on the laptop, a second feed showed a high-end flat being overturned by an investigative team, looking for some clue to a question that plagued them all.

Keir voiced it, allowing his frustration to show. "Then *where* have the American and her allies gone?"

Burman straightened. "Maybe to ground locally. We're continuing to monitor CCTV cameras. But I suspect they're trying to make it out of the city."

"And go where?"

The woman glanced over to the cardinal. "Hopefully, Tissot can shed some light on this. His contact within the *Gardiens du Livre* may offer some insight."

"We can't lose this opportunity. Not after so long. It's taken us decades to secure a mole in their organization. After this, we may never get another chance. This fumble of the book's transfer may never happen again."

"Understood, but no one suspected these students would prove so resourceful. In hindsight, we should've moved faster. We lost valuable time while framing the professor's death so it could be pinned on his students. Still, by doing so, we've boxed our targets in and won't underestimate them again."

"That's if we can find them."

"Only twelve hours have passed, so it's still early days." Burman tapped at a row of folders on the laptop screen. "I had our specialists work up dossiers on all five. We'll put pressure on any and all contacts. Surveilling the same. If our targets reach out, we'll know."

Keir paced away from the table, trying to dispel his anger. The failure here lay further back than this past night.

We've been too cautious.

Days ago, Keir's group had learned the name of the Twelfth Keeper from a mole within the *Gardiens,* along with the possible identity of the Thirteenth, but they could not be certain of the latter. Notoriously paranoid, the *Gardiens* could have set a false trail. Fearing that—and hoping to secure the book before it got shipped off—he and members of his echelon had accosted Professor Haugen at his estate in Norway. While the journal had already been dispatched, they had been able to corroborate the name of the Thirteenth Keeper.

After that, it became a waiting game. Once in Exeter, Keir's group had to sit tight until the shipment arrived. Unfortunately, once delivery was confirmed, they had to move faster than anticipated. Last night, their mole had sent frantic word that the *Gardiens* had altered their plans. Worried the Twelfth Keeper might have revealed where the book was sent, the *Gardiens* had arranged to move it again.

This warning forced Keir's group to accelerate their plans. But unknown to them, upon learning this, Julian Wright had already taken matters into his own hands, perhaps fearing *who* might reach him first.

In doing so, the bastard ruined everything.

Still, a wariness iced through Keir.

Has this misadventure been a matter of poor timing—or had it been plotted that way?

He returned to Burman's side and raised this concern. "I find it suspicious that we only received word about the *Gardiens'* plan to move the book *after* Wright had already sent off the book. Could the warning to us have been purposefully delayed?"

Burman glanced over to him. "You're wondering if another cell within our organization might have attempted to make a play for the book? To steal it away from us? To usurp our authority over the matter?"

"It wouldn't be the first time."

Keir looked across at Tissot. Unlike the two of them, the cardinal was not a part of the *Confrérie*'s inner circle. Instead, Tissot belonged to an outlier cell, one of the oldest. It traced back directly to the Marquise de Maurepas, the minister of state to King Louis XVI and the founder of the *Confrérie des Illuminés.* His cell continued to believe the book was demonic in nature, possibly the source code to Satanic magic—a fear once shared by the Marquise himself.

Yet, over the centuries, the organization evolved and refined its ambitions. Even the name—*Confrérie des Illuminés*—was no longer in vogue. It conflated too much with another secret society, the *Illuminati.* Though, truth be told, their two organizations had overlapped in membership in the past. The same was true for many other groups across history: the Rosicrucians, the Freemasons, the Italian Carbonari, and its French offshoot, the Charbonnerie. Even today, the *Confrérie* remained deeply involved with the Bilderberg Group, where political leaders and captains of industry met privately and discussed world concerns without fear of exposure or reprisal.

Over time, the *Confrérie* systematically wove its web throughout the world's secret organizations—both in the past and now. All to seek the betterment of humankind. That was their ultimate goal. In the past, their efforts had centered on seeking lost knowledge—like what could be found in Saint-Germain's journal. But now the *Confrérie* had merged forces with a new growing movement, called *longtermism,* which advocated that it was the moral duty of those living today to improve humankind's future, to look past short-term problems for long-term solutions—no matter the cost, if it ultimately improved the chances of humanity's survival.

It was how Keir had been recruited, along with many other wealthy members, mostly in the tech industry. The *Confrérie* sought to build a secret army of like-minded individuals, to make the hard choices that politics and shortsightedness would not allow.

Yet, that didn't mean the Brotherhood was of one mind. Over the centuries, exposed to so many different ideologies, it had splintered into disparate factions, each with its own agenda, some in conflict with the others.

Like perhaps now.

Burman looked skeptically at Keir. "Remember, Cardinal Tissot brought the mole to us."

"A mole whose identity he keeps to himself," Keir reminded Burman.

"Would you do any different? By keeping his contact under wraps, Tissot makes him and his cell an essential part of this operation. And even if you're right, with the book loose out there, both sides are equally handicapped, so it doesn't much matter."

"Maybe . . ."

Keir stared over at the cardinal. Tissot was in his early seventies, the same age as him, but the cardinal, with his white hair and frail form, looked decades older. Whereas Keir maintained a well-muscled frame, which filled out a suit tailored to accentuate his physique. Similarly, his dark hair, while speckled with salt, remained thick.

Such youthful vigor was not solely due to genetics. One of the latest ventures of NeuVentis Pharma was in the field of biogerontology, the study of anti-aging, which had proved to be a veritable gold mine. And Keir had taken full advantage of the field's many treatments and innovations. His regimen involved weekly testosterone injections, a fistful of daily supplements, regular hyperbaric oxygen sessions, along with IV therapy and blood transfusions.

"Before you cast aspersions," Burman warned, "there are many who still admire Cardinal Tissot. His modalities and beliefs may be outdated, but it was his father who worked with Rommel during

World War II to secure the cache of gold coins found in North Africa, a treasure whose location was encrypted in Saint-Germain's journal. Though we only obtained a quarter of the haul, it was still worth tens of millions in today's dollars."

Keir scowled. "And the Nazis took the rest—shattering apart the greater mystery hidden within all that gold. There's no telling what wonders were lost to the world when the Nazi gold train vanished in Poland."

"Yet, the *Confrérie* still learned a valuable lesson."

"Which was what?"

"That Saint-Germain buries his secrets in ever-unfolding layers. We will know better next time. To look beyond the glitter and wealth for the greater truth hidden behind it."

Keir nodded, finding some measure of solace.

For the longest time, Saint-Germain's journal—the foundation stone to the *Confrérie*'s existence—had been nearly forgotten. Even after the scuffle during World War II, where the book had proved its value while hinting at greater mysteries, it had faded again, relegated to an outdated relic that had little bearing on the world's mounting troubles.

But now . . .

He stared at the laptop, at the frantic search on the screen. "Do you remember reading Countess d'Adhémar's *Souvenirs,* her account of Saint-Germain's vanished journal?"

"What of it?"

"According to her diary, Saint-Germain claimed his book would return to the world during a 'time of great tribulation.' And look at the state we're in now. The threats we face. Nuclear war. Engineered pandemics. Collapsing ecosystems. The emergence of AI. More than any time in the past, humankind teeters on the brink of extinction. Don't you find it strangely opportune—possibly even providential—that the lost journal has come into play during this time in history, a *time of great tribulation.*"

"Providential?" Burman raised a brow. "Now you're sounding like Cardinal Tissot."

"Am I? The last time the book rose into prominence was during World War II. Another pivotal moment in human history. And here it rises again out of the dark vault of the *Gardiens* and back into the light of day."

Burman frowned. "There is nothing mystical about this. You're placing divine power onto coincidence. The simple reality is the journal contains secrets to astounding riches and potentially arcane sciences. For those reasons alone, we must possess it, to use its wealth and knowledge to move humanity forward. The *Gardiens* have kept this book buried for too long, spitefully keeping its wonders from humanity."

"Wonders like the key to immortality." Keir touched his hairline, a robust growth accentuated by transplanted plugs. "One consistent story about the Count is that he never seemed to age."

"Such tales are suspect."

Keir wasn't so sure. Over the centuries, whispers seeped out of the *Gardiens* concerning this very possibility. Keir had taken special interest in such rumors. Beyond the financial and political advantages of the *Confrérie* network, this prospect had been a driving force behind his involvement with the *Confrérie*. If he could discover the truth—whatever that might be—it could potentially transform NeuVentis Pharma into one of the most powerful corporations in the world.

Not to mention, extend my own life.

Despite a vigorous fight against aging, the unflinching march of time still wore at his body, slowly eroding it—which both frustrated and terrified him. NeuVentis had more than eight hundred laboratories across sixty countries. His net worth at the end of the last fiscal year was more than twenty billion. Yet, all his wealth and resources could not extend his life in any significant degree.

He stared at the two feeds on the laptop.

But what if that could change?

Burman pointed to the same videos. "The book remains too important to let it vanish again. We must find where our targets fled. We'll dog their trail until they're run to ground. It's only a matter of time."

"No need," a voice scolded from behind.

Both of them turned as Tissot crossed closer. The cardinal had shed his formal red vestments and wore a crisp black suit with a white roman collar. The only marks of his station were the pectoral cross and ring.

"I know where our targets are going," Tissot announced. "It took some finessing, but my contact within the *Gardiens* came through once again."

"Where?" Burman pressed him.

"London."

"How?" Keir snapped, still irritated that Tissot remained so guarded about his mole. "By car? By train?"

"That I cannot say. But it doesn't matter."

"Why?"

"I have the address where they're headed." Before they could respond, Tissot raised a palm, as if blessing them. "And with the help of my contact, I've already baited a trap—one they will not escape."

THIRD

17

November 1, 3:30 p.m. GMT
London, England

Sharyn shivered with trepidation as she passed the wooden expanse of the Traitor's Gate. She tightened her grip on the cross-body bag, all too aware of the weight and responsibility she carried.

This place can't be right . . .

On the train ride from Exeter, a set of coordinates had been texted to their burner phone, marking the location of the safehouse in London. They had all expressed various levels of incredulity upon realizing *where* those coordinates led. The location lay within the grounds of one of the most fortified and historic locations in the city.

Sharyn gaped at the spread of ramparts and fortresses that made up the infamous Tower of London. According to a plaque near the entrance, the main castle—the White Tower—had been built by William the Conqueror in the eleventh century as a key defense to the city, commanding a hill overlooking the Thames. Circling the central keep, massive curtain walls bristled with towers and barracks, all enclosing more than a dozen acres of parks and gardens. It had now become a tourist attraction, where one could visit the vaults that held the Crown Jewels or be entertained by colorfully dressed Yeoman Warders—known as Beefeaters—who shared stories of the Tower.

Sharyn had no interest in such tales. She had her own pressing question that she wanted answered.

Why were we sent here of all places?

Sharyn turned her back on the Traitor's Gate, where prisoners were hauled in chains to be interred in cold cells within the ground's many towers. She kept her shoulders bowed, her head down, expecting to be nabbed for trespassing—though, their group *had* bought entry tickets and traveled with the crowded press of tourists.

Duncan must have been worried about the same. "If the police catch us here," he commented, "we'll be joining a long list of the Tower's famous prisoners: Anne Boleyn, Lady Jane Grey, Guy Fawkes."

"If it comes to that," Tag said, "I'll accept incarceration." Still using his umbrella for a cane, he hobbled along the cobbled path, which passed under an archway, guarded over by the spikes of a black-iron portcullis. Ahead, a groin-vaulted tunnel burrowed through the base of a hulking fortification. He waved his free hand overhead at it. "Let's hope we don't suffer the same fate as those interred in the Bloody Tower above us."

Sharyn looked to him for elaboration, but Naomi explained.

"Two boys—Edward V and his younger brother Richard—were imprisoned at the order of their uncle Richard III. Most believe he had them murdered inside the tower to clear his path to the throne."

"Or it could've been Henry VII, as the boys blocked his kingship, too," Duncan added. "Either way, the tower is said to be haunted by their ghosts."

"Enough with the spook stories," Archie groused. He clearly had enough of this nervous banter and hurried them out of the tunnel. He also cradled his arm. His wounded shoulder must be paining him worse than he let on. "This place closes in less than an hour. We need to get ourselves tucked away before that."

They exited into the ground's main courtyard. The afternoon

had turned gloomy with low skies. Misty scraps of fog drifted like ghosts all around. A road led the way forward, flanked by two walls: one newer and firmly bricked, the other a crumbling ruin of an inner castle wall. A large black raven perched atop there, eyeing them with clear disdain.

Sharyn had read about the winged guardians, the ever-present residents of the Tower of London. Legend held that if the ravens ever abandoned these grounds, the British kingdom would fall.

She met the creature's dark gaze and prayed such protections extended to her group.

"We need to get to the park above us." Tag pointed ahead, where the road ended at steps that led up to another level of the grounds.

Their group headed toward it, flowing with the tourists.

Despite making it this far, they all remained anxious, pale-faced, and worried. They had spoken little on the four-hour train ride, only enough to share the strange coordinates that led them here. As a precaution, they had split up before boarding the train in Exeter, even taking seats separate from one another. They also switched lines at Bristol Parkway, to hopefully confound any hunters. Still, upon arriving in London, they had all rushed through the massive expanse of Paddington Station. With trains arriving every fifteen minutes from the direction of Exeter, any search for them would have proved challenging. Or so they hoped. Still, at the station, they had all departed by different exits, only reuniting outside at a coffeehouse several blocks away.

And now we've been directed to the Tower for some reason.

Sharyn's heart continued to pound, and her mouth remained stubbornly dry, but she felt oddly comforted by these thick walls that had stood for centuries. As much as this choice of location confused her, surely their pursuers would be equally baffled and never think to look in this direction.

"Wait." Duncan stopped them on the road. "There's a shortcut this way."

He lifted the tourist map and pointed it toward the newer brick wall. An archway cut through it. Past it, a set of steps led upward.

"Tower Green should be directly above us," he assured them. "Only a stone's throw from the King's House."

Our destination . . .

It had been formerly called the *Queen's* House, but that changed with the coronation of King Charles III.

Still, no matter the name, why were we sent here?

They crossed and headed up the stairs single file. As Sharyn followed, the raven led out a raucous caw. She ducked at the sudden outburst. The bird burst from the wall, circled once overhead, and vanished behind her. She followed its track, paranoid that its cry had been some sort of warning.

Still, there was no turning back now.

At the top of the stairs, Sharyn gathered with the others along the edge of a park. A stone walkway circled a wide expanse of lawn, which was shaded by massive trees whose leaves had crisped to a bright orange-yellow. Plenty of tourists wandered the lawn's edges, but Sharyn still felt exposed in the open.

"Where do we go?" she asked.

Duncan pointed across the green to an L-shaped set of row-houses that framed the far corner of the park. The red-brick homes had second stories timbered in the Tudor style, all with steeply gabled roofs.

"The King's House stands over there. Built in the sixteenth century by Henry VIII for his second wife, Anne Boleyn, who was held there before being beheaded on the Tower Green."

Sharyn stared across the peaceful landscape, which now took on an ominous cast. From the number of doorways, there had to be eight or nine houses. Towers flanked both ends, and a third fortification rose in the middle, behind the corner of the L.

She frowned at the spread of homes. "Which of those is the King's House?"

Duncan pointed to the one shadowed by the centermost tower. "That's the one with the black door."

Archie scowled. "You mean the one under guard."

Sharyn had noted the same. To the left of the door, a soldier of the King's Guard stood posted before a sentry box. He was dressed in a ceremonial red coat and tall bearskin hat. He also shouldered an assault rifle, tipped by a bayonet.

Archie frowned, clearly dismayed. "Do we just go up and knock?"

Tag shrugged. "We've been invited, haven't we?"

They circled the green, side-stepping through clusters of tourists gathered around traditionally garbed Beefeaters, who extoled their patrons with stories of beheaded queens and imprisoned traitors.

As Sharyn and the others approached the King's House, a roped stanchion blocked their way. A posted sign stated No Entry. The armed guard noted their group as they came to a stop. He firmed his grip on his weapon but remained silent.

"What now?" Naomi asked.

Anxious to get out of sight, Sharyn lifted an arm and called over. "We were told to come here! Could you check with whomever is inside?"

The guard shifted from his post, strode to the door, and rapped a fist on it, while never taking his eyes off them.

Duncan leaned toward Sharyn. "The King's House serves as the residence of the Constable of the Tower, an honorary title, given for recognition of distinguished military service."

"Do you know who holds the position now?" Tag asked.

Duncan shook his head. "Changes every five years."

The black door to the house swung open. A young woman, who looked to be in her late twenties, bowed her head out and listened as the guard whispered to her. She then eyed Sharyn's group, sizing them up.

Sharyn studied her in turn. The woman wore a thick gray turtleneck and jeans. Her red hair had been braided into an efficient tail.

Clearly not the constable.

The woman finally nodded and opened the door wider, but her eyes remained squinted with suspicion. The guard crossed to them, lifted the rope, and motioned them through.

Sharyn ducked past, wary of the weapon balanced in the soldier's other hand. The modernity of the black assault rifle contrasted harshly with the bright ceremonial clothing.

With each step toward the doorway, Sharyn felt a rising tension.

The woman shifted to the side and lifted an arm to welcome them. "My father is upstairs."

Anxious to get inside, Sharyn crossed the threshold first. The others crowded behind her into a foyer, where a marble bust of some historical figure stared at them, looking little impressed. Beyond the entryway, a larger hall opened, painted red and covered in framed art and formal photos. The space looked ready to receive dignitaries to the Tower.

Which is definitely not us.

The constable's daughter closed the door behind them, sealing them inside.

Sharyn turned to her. "Thank you for—"

A harsh cry, full of venom, cut her off.

"Traitors . . . Traitors all!"

18

3:51 p.m.

Duncan tensed at the angry outburst, which rose from the top of a staircase ahead. The five of them crowded toward the closed door behind them. They all had the same fear.

Did we walk into a trap?

The woman elbowed past them with a scowl and headed for the stairs. "It's only Hugh. Don't mind him. He's picked up on the day's tension. My father will calm him down."

Duncan turned to the others, trying to judge whether to hightail it out of there or not.

Sharyn let out a hard breath, then stepped after the woman, perhaps too curious to turn back. "Let's go."

They headed after the constable's daughter, who had stopped halfway up the steps after noting their hesitation.

"I'm Moira Kelly," she said as they joined her. "My father is General Sir Ronan Kelly. We were warned of your coming, of the hardships endured—and what you carry with you."

"Then you know about the book?" Sharyn asked.

"Saint-Germain's journal, yes. I had thought never to set eyes upon it."

Duncan frowned.

I wish I never had.

From everyone's pinched expressions, they must be thinking

the same. Throughout the train ride here, Duncan had questioned his decision to come along, reviewing events in his head, again and again. But he could not abandon Sharyn and the others. He cast blame not on them, but on their damnable professor, for forcing them down this path.

Contrary to Duncan's misgiving, Archie showed no such hesitancy. Or at least, never voiced it. Duncan suspected it wasn't *fear* that drove Archie to accompany him, but *friendship*.

Pray such loyalty doesn't get you killed.

Still, Duncan knew his reason for coming wasn't solely based on his concern for Sharyn or her friends. Nor was it the threat of being falsely accused of murder. Instead, during the train ride, he found himself dwelling on one aspect of the Frenchman's story. On the book's first revelation, its First Adage, and how it led to a cache of ancient coins unearthed in North Africa during World War II.

Where my grandad was stationed at the same time.

The coincidence had struck him then and weighed on him with every crossing mile of their flight. He could not dismiss this tingling sense of connection, of threads coming together.

Maybe this was meant to be . . .

Before going to Oxford, Duncan had briefly considered following in his grandad's footsteps and serving a stint in the British army. His father had forbade it. Duncan might have gone behind his back, but his mother's tears finally dissuaded him. Duncan's older brother had died at eighteen in a car accident. His mother could not survive another such loss. Even the fear of it threatened to break her.

And now I'm in danger anyway.

Duncan stared over at Sharyn, who kept a tight hold on the strap of her bag with a determined set to her lips. He again felt that strange tingling, of hidden gears turning, of history bearing on the present.

Maybe here is where I was meant to serve.

"Over this way," Moira said, drawing Duncan back, and guiding them down a white-plastered hallway. "The first floor below is mostly for ceremonial purposes and kept historically pristine. But Father and I live on the second, where we're allowed a degree of relaxed accommodations."

This became evident as the group passed a modernly appointed kitchen. A steaming kettle sat on the stove next to an open tin of biscuits. Duncan eyed them longingly, hoping for an afternoon cuppa.

Naomi merely gawked all around: at the age-darkened paintings on the walls, at the busts on pedestals, at the leaded windows that overlooked Tower Green. "I . . . I didn't know anyone lived in the Tower. I wish I had my phone to record all of this. It would make a great post." She glanced over to Moira. "How long have you been here?"

"My father for four years. Me, only a couple. Takes time to adjust. Like getting pizza delivered. Tell Dominos you live at the Tower of London, and they hang up on you. Still, at night, when the tourists are gone, when the grounds are empty and lamplit, the place turns magical."

Sharyn shifted closer to the woman. "And you live alone with your father?"

Moira nodded. "After my mother died, my father needed help. I was happy to join him. Especially with my degree in art history. What better place to work on my dissertation. I'll be sorry to leave next year when a new constable takes over."

Tag searched ahead, crooking his neck. "Where *is* your father?"

Before Moira could answer, another shout erupted from a doorway ahead, repeating the same accusation. "Traitors! Traitors all."

Despite the earlier reassurance, Duncan cringed at the anger in the voice, noting the deep baritone and northern accent.

Moira sighed and glanced at Tag. "It seems poor Hugh must be trying to answer your question, Mr. McKnight."

Duncan shared a look with the others, uncomfortable that the woman knew all their names. Of course, the Frenchman must have informed her and her father about their identities. Still, he steeled himself for any surprises.

"My father awaits us in the dining hall." Moira pointed to the doorway ahead. "The room where the traitor Guy Fawkes was interrogated after being tortured for his plot to blow up the Houses of Parliament."

Again, the same resounding cry warned them off, sounding Shakespearean in its outrage. "Traitors all!"

Sharyn cast a suspicious glance toward Moira. "I thought you said you lived alone with your father."

Moira turned to her as they reached the doorway. "That's true."

"Then who is—"

Duncan stepped across the threshold into a large timber-roofed hall. A long wooden dining table spanned its length. A broad painting over a massive fireplace depicted the execution of Guy Fawkes.

As they entered, a dark shadow burst from the far side of the room, where a silver-haired man sat before a tea service and an assortment of biscuits.

"Traitors!" shouted from above.

Moira lifted an arm. "That's enough, Hugh. Come here."

The black shadow swept across the rafters, over the dining table, and landed on Moira's arm. The large raven dwarfed the woman's head, dancing with sharp claws.

Moira turned to them. "This is Huginn. Though, we simply call him Hugh."

19

4:05 p.m.

Sharyn backed from the huge bird. The raven eyed her with a cold, black gaze. His neck feathers ruffled with warning. The bird kept his wings slightly parted, as if ready to lunge, which could prove dangerous. The creature's long black beak looked sharp enough to rip off a finger.

Moira reached up and rubbed the crown of the raven's head. "Quiet now, boyo."

The bird shook his body and leaned into her fingers.

The man at the other end of the table, no doubt the current Constable of the Tower, called across to them. "Moira, my dear, please return Hugh to his perch. I've set aside a couple biscuits to encourage him to behave."

"Yes, Father." Moira guided them alongside the table.

The raven chuckled, sounding eerily human, clearly happy in the woman's presence—or maybe he recognized the word *biscuit*. He then barked like a dog several times, sounding quite demanding.

"I didn't know ravens could talk," Naomi whispered.

Moira heard her. "Ravens are great mimics. Better than most parrots. And after twenty-one years, Hugh can swear up a bloody streak when riled or sing like an operatic soprano when truly enamored with someone."

Sharyn studied the bird closer, who was clearly old. One of his eyes was clouded over. A claw was missing two nails. "Is Hugh one of the ravens of the Tower?"

"He was once. But ailment—along with bereavement—has turned him into the sentinel of the King's House. His brother, Muninn, died a few years back, and Huginn slowly went into a decline. When my father arrived, he decided to take him inside. Turned a bedroom into an aviary, one with access to a fenced balcony. Of course, we still take him outside for supervised jaunts. But with the occasional fox roaming the Tower, an aged bird would make for easy prey."

Tag circled on Moira's far side, tapping his umbrella on the planked wood floor. "Muninn and Huginn? They were named after the two ravens that served the Norse god, Odin."

"Very good, young man," Sir Ronan Kelly called out, his voice rich and deep, made for command. "They were indeed. The loss of Muninn was mourned across Britain. But it struck his brother exceptionally hard."

"Ravens bond very deeply," Moira explained. "Even mating for life."

Sharyn glanced to Sir Kelly, who did not rise to greet them. He simply sipped from his cup, cradling its warmth in his palms. The reason became clear when they reached the far side of the table.

Moira's father sat in a motorized wheelchair. Still, no one would mistake him for an invalid. Broad of shoulder, with silver hair and goatee, he looked like an elder statesman. He was dressed casually in a navy V-neck and khakis. Still, he wore a crimson necktie, knotted squarely under his chin, with the tail tucked under the woolen sweater.

The constable cleared his throat and nodded to the raven as Moira shifted the large bird to a multibranched perch, festooned with dangling toys. "My dear, I left the biscuits sitting below. Best soak them first. You know what he likes."

"I do, Father."

Moira reached to a small plate of dry, brown biscuits. She dunked them in a porcelain cup full of a reddish-black fluid.

"Is that tea?" Archie asked, his voice sounding envious. "I wouldn't mind a cuppa, if you have any to spare."

"It's not tea." Moira lifted the dripping biscuit. "It's pig's blood."

Archie grimaced and backed a step. "Then no thank you."

Moira held up the soaked treat to Hugh, who snatched it with his large beak, while warbling a sound like a Swiss yodeler.

"That's my good boy," Moira said with a warm smile. She then wiped her fingers on a folded cloth and turned to them. "As to your arrival, I took a call from Monsieur Laurent. A worker's strike in Paris has delayed him, but he should join us in the next couple of hours. Once here, he'll take responsibility for Saint-Germain's diary, get it out of the country."

Sharyn shared a look with Duncan.

She must be talking about the Frenchman from the phone call . . .

Duncan raised another concern. "That's fine for the book, but what about us? We're still wanted by the police and hunted by an unknown enemy."

"The *Confrérie des Illuminés*," Sir Kelly intoned.

His daughter translated, "The Brotherhood of the Enlightened."

"That name," Archie groused. "Such a load of tosh. They sound proper full of themselves, don't they?"

The old man shifted in his chair. "Indeed. But they're not to be underestimated. Due to the speed of changing events, you've managed to outmaneuver them. For that you should be commended."

"But who exactly are they?" Sharyn asked. "For that matter, who is the alchemist who wrote this book?"

"The answer to both your questions are tied tightly together." Sir Kelly waved to the table. "Sit. If you might indulge me, I would very much like to see this notorious tome. I've only viewed it once, briefly, long ago."

Their group spread out to the chairs closest to the constable, while Moira moved to stand at her father's shoulder.

Before taking a seat, Sharyn tugged the crossbody strap and drew the bag into view. With a twinge of trepidation, she unzippered it and slipped the book out. She placed it on the table. The tome's copper bands shone dully in the weak light flowing through a bank of windows at the back of the hall. Still, the crystal orb gathered all that meager light and glowed on its own.

Sir Kelly reached for the book, but Sharyn placed her palm atop it and drew it closer to her. "First, tell us about who wrote this."

20

4:22 p.m.

Sharyn refused to hand over the book without some explanation, wanting to know about the man who penned a book that had led to so many deaths.

Sir Kelly leaned back. "You're right to inquire, Ms. Karr, and deserve an answer. Though, I must say the author—the Count of Saint-Germain—remains as much a mystery as the book itself."

"Then what can you tell us?" Sharyn pressed. "We had to toss all our electronics and never had a chance to search the internet for his name."

"If you had, you would've come across stories both historical and fanciful. In fact, even *where* he came from is fiercely debated. Some say he descended from a disgraced royal family, and to save face, he kept his past secret. Others that he was raised by the infamous Medici banking family. Or he might have been an Alsatian Jew or a Spanish Jesuit. No one really knows. Still, regardless of his origin, he arrived at the French court already a man of great wealth, always appearing in public with clothing adorned in jewels."

"Then what *is* known about him?" Sharyn asked.

"To best answer that," Sir Kelly continued, "I'll stick to what is substantiated by court records from the time, along with written accounts from luminaries of that era, including Frederick the Great, Mozart, Voltaire, even Casanova. The *London Chronicle* wrote of the man, along with newspapers in Italy and the Netherlands. For a time, throughout Europe, he was a celebrity in his own right."

Sharyn lowered to her seat. "What made him so famous?"

"Ah, first, he was a savant in many fields. He was a musical composer, a skilled violinist, a poet and painter. He spoke every language in Europe. He was also a well-studied historian, not just of Europe, but farther afield. As such, he served for a time as diplomat for King Louis XV. In fact, his politics were so astute that he predicted the French Revolution years before the Terror started, but his early warnings fell on deaf ears. Still, that all aside, his greatest fame lay in his scientific work."

"Scientific work?" Sharyn asked.

"He called it *alchemy*, a word synonymous with *science* at the time. Though, the two terms grew apart around the middle of the eighteenth century. But Saint-Germain still considered himself primarily an alchemist."

"Why do you say that?" Tag asked.

Sir Kelly reached over and tapped the symbol embossed on the book's cover. "It's practically his signature."

Sharyn frowned. "How do you mean?"

"I'll show you." He turned to his daughter. "May I borrow your phone?"

Moira handed it over.

Her father worked on it for a spell, then sighed, "Ah, here it is."

He slid the phone next to the old book.

"If you compare what's engraved into the book's leather, you can see how it matches *this* symbol."

They all gathered closer to look, studying the two side by side. The image on the phone showed a hand-drawn circle with radiating spokes, overwritten with words in Latin. Despite the differences, it was obvious Saint-Germain was inspired by this drawing to fabricate the signature atop his book.

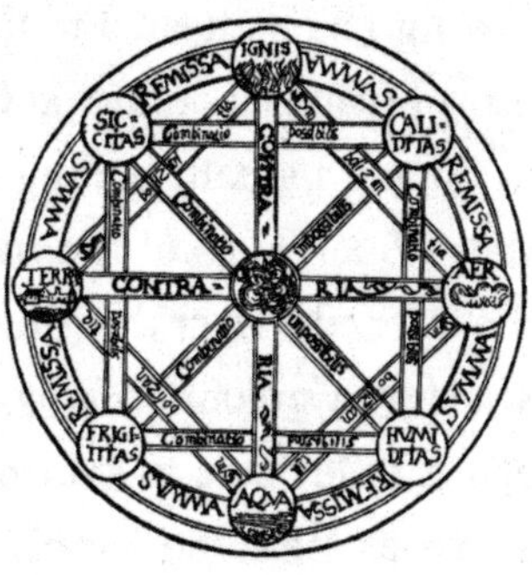

Tag pointed to the phone. "What's the symbol? Where did it come from?"

"It was drawn in the early eighteenth century by Gottfried Leibniz, a German polymath, who is credited, along with Isaac Newton, of inventing the field of calculus." Kelly turned to Sharyn. "And later in life, he became a librarian."

Sharyn straightened, intrigued despite the terrors of the past days. "And what does it mean?"

"It's Leibniz's representation of the universe, uniting together Aristotle's four elements: Earth, Air, Fire, and Water. It became the heraldic symbol of alchemy and the sciences that grew from it."

Naomi leaned forward. "That's all well and good. But whether Saint-Germain called himself an alchemist or a scientist, what field did he study?"

"Most everything, to be truthful. Like many alchemists of this time, he dabbled with the transmutation of metal, of turning lead into gold. But he also introduced new dyeing techniques, invented novel paints and oils. Over his lifetime, he consulted with physicists, astronomers, and mathematicians, both gaining knowledge from them and adding to it. Still, his most astounding accomplishments were in geology and mineralogy. Skills he learned in Arabia during his time spent at the Court of the Shah of Persia. Some claimed the man could melt diamonds and remove their flaws.

In fact, King Louis attested to this fact and eventually built Saint-Germain a private laboratory at Chambord Castle."

Moira made a small scoffing noise, which earned a frown from her father. "Such tales of the man must be taken with a grain of salt," she warned. "Over the centuries, his story has grown, bloated by mysticism, layered in infamy. Some say he had magical abilities. To teleport, to levitate, to control people telepathically. Many concluded he must be some Ascended Master birthed during the time of Christ and still influences the world today."

Sir Kelly scowled. "As you can see, it has become hard to separate truth from fantasy. But we must try our best to remain grounded."

Moira shook her head. "Like believing the man could remove flaws from diamonds?"

Sharyn looked at the orb shining atop the book. She remembered the astrological symbols embedded therein, a skill that defied comprehension, especially considering when it had been crafted.

Maybe such stories had a seed of truth to them.

Sir Kelly reached over and patted Moira's arm. "My lovely daughter, always the skeptic. Like so many others in the past. During Saint-Germain's lifetime, dozens of others tried to discredit the man—testing him, challenging him—but they all came away convinced otherwise."

"But not the Marquise de Maurepas," Moira added.

"No, not him," her father agreed dourly. "But *his* stubbornness was steeled more by jealousy."

"Who are you talking about?" Sharyn asked.

"Ah, of course, I'm getting ahead of myself. The Marquise de Maurepas was Louis XVI's minister of state and hated how the king had grown enamored of Saint-Germain. Fearing he might be displaced, the man set about to discredit Saint-Germain."

Sharyn frowned. "Why? Did he believe Saint-Germain was a charlatan who was fooling the king?"

"I can't say for sure. But the Marquise was deeply religious. As boisterously as he sought to dismiss Saint-Germain, he also vilified the alchemist as a blasphemer and Satanist. Eventually, the Marquise discovered that his enemy was crafting a grimoire of great power."

"You mean the book," Tag said.

Sir Kelly nodded. "Hoping to prove Saint-Germain's wickedness, the Marquise assembled a cabal of religious leaders, a crude start of the *Confrérie des Illuminés,* to hunt for the man and his grimoire."

"Which clearly failed," Naomi said.

"But they did set him on the run. Some believe he faked his death in 1784. Although, he was seen five years later in Paris and several times by others over the next decades."

"It was perhaps such events," Moira added, "that led to rumors of the Count's ability to defy death, with many believing he had discovered the key to immortality."

Sharyn remembered the phone conversation this morning. "Monsieur Laurent told us Saint-Germain claimed as much himself, writing it in the preface to his book."

Sir Kelly shrugged. "Some in our group take the Count at his word. Others assume it was merely poetic hyperbole. Either way, Saint-Germain had already gained a reputation for agelessness. Account after account stated how the man always appeared to be around fifty years old, with dark hair and an unblemished complexion. His regimen in life was very strict. He would never eat in public, avoided all meat and wine."

"So, the first vegan," Archie said.

While this was meant as a joke, Sir Kelly simply shrugged. "Quite likely, young man. Additionally, Saint-Germain studied with village healers, where he gained a great understanding of herbs and plants, and concocted medicines that he regularly consumed."

Tag sat straighter, eyeing the book with renewed interest, plainly drawn by his interest in ancient herbal remedies. "So he was both a vegan *and* a holistic pharmacologist."

"Perhaps. Whatever elixir he did develop, there are repeated accounts of him sharing his recipe. Like with a countess of his time, Madame de Georgy. It is said his elixir maintained her youthful look for twenty-five years. She eventually earned the title, the Everlasting Countess."

Moira maintained a stern expression. "Or his *elixir* could have been some new cosmetic regimen, one that would be the envy of the Paris fashion houses today."

"We cannot dismiss this possibility," Sir Kelly admitted.

"And what about the Marquise's *Confrérie*?" Sharyn asked. "How are they still plaguing us now?"

"Ah, eventually the Brotherhood changed with the times. Interest in the book waned as it remained out of their reach and became more legend than real. Still, power does not tolerate a vacuum. Over time, the Brotherhood grew stronger and wider, rooting across Europe and the New World. Its members eventually sought new avenues of power, pathways not found buried in some lost grimoire. Thus, the book was all but forgotten."

"Until World War II," Duncan noted.

Sharyn remembered what the Frenchman had told them about the discovery of a cache of gold coins.

Sir Kelly steepled his fingers at his chin. "After the First Adage was deciphered, aided by codebreakers during the war, we popped up on the Brotherhood's radar once again."

Duncan frowned. "Those codebreakers? Where were they from?"

"Bletchley Park, a team working under Alan Turing as he broke the code to decrypt Nazi communications."

Duncan's eyes pinched at this revelation. Sharyn recalled his story of his grandfather's involvement with a team of codebreakers.

Was it this same group?

Duncan noted her attention and must have read the question on her face. He gave her the smallest nod, confirming the same.

Before she could digest more, Sir Kelly continued. "Once Saint-Germain's diary proved itself to be of astounding value, the *Confrérie* renewed their pursuit of the book."

"Scooping us up in the process," Naomi noted.

Archie let out an exasperated sigh. "Even if you could make the book vanish, what about us? Those bastards framed us good."

"I understand. The *Gardiens* will do our best to clear your names."

Sharyn frowned. "*Gardiens*?"

Moira answered. "The *Gardiens du Livre*. The Keepers of the Book. The name given to those who sought to preserve Saint-Germain's diary and keep it out of the hands of those who would abuse it."

Her father nodded. "The First Keeper who took possession of the diary was Countess d'Adhémar, the former lady-in-waiting to Marie-Antoinette. She received the book directly from Saint-Germain in 1820, long after his supposed death."

"Unfortunately, she wrote about this encounter in her personal diary," Moira noted sourly.

"She did," her father confirmed. "But she must have suspected no one would read her words. Unfortunately, fourteen years after her death, someone found those journals and published them, which exposed the book to the *Confrérie* once again. By then, the book had moved on to its Second Keeper, someone the Countess had entrusted to continue her guardianship, giving birth to our organization."

Moira looked across at their group. "Your professor, Julian Wright, was the intended *Thirteenth* Keeper."

Sir Kelly turned to Sharyn. "A role you sadly had to assume, if only for a short time."

"So for two centuries," Duncan said, "your group has kept this book under wraps, while slowly piecing together its secrets."

"Indeed. It took us five decades to even discover how to safely open it. Saint-Germain had it booby-trapped, infusing the pages with an incendiary chemical."

Tag cast the book a wary look. "What do you mean?"

"Any mishandling or attempt to force the book open would ignite it on fire, burning it all to ash. Such was the level of Saint-Germain's fear that his knowledge might fall into the wrong hands."

"And after opening it," Sharyn said, "you've been attempting to decipher what was written."

"Painstakingly so, especially as we had to take care with whomever we reached out to for help. We solved the First Adage, but it took until the science of cryptology had advanced enough to eke out its meaning."

"Advancements made at Bletchley Park," Duncan noted.

Sir Kelly nodded. "Since then, while we've made progress on the Second Adage, its secret still eludes us. The code is vastly different from the first, one so daunting that it might take until science advances again to solve it."

"Maybe that was Saint-Germain's intent," Sharyn noted. "To only let his knowledge return to the world once humanity had matured enough to be ready for it."

Sir Kelly stared silently at her, his gaze thoughtful, before finally offering a bow of his head. "Very astute of you, Ms. Karr. In fact, Saint-Germain had warned Countess d'Adhémar that his diary would only return to the world after a long span of time, when it would be most needed, during a time of great tribulation."

Archie sighed. "That certainly describes our group's sorry state."

Sharyn remained focused on the book. "And what of the Third Adage, the last in the book? During our conversation with Monsieur Laurent, he believed that it might lead to the key to immortality."

"Again, the opening line to the diary might simply be poetic hyperbole. But many in our group, after decoding snatches from various pages, do suspect the Third Adage will point to a location of Saint-Germain's lost Elixir of Life."

"But that's not all," Moira added.

Sir Kelly frowned at her, as if scolding her for mentioning this.

Sharyn had enough of such guardedness and pressed him. "What *else* is supposedly hidden there?"

Moira crossed her arms and gave her father a hard look.

Sir Kelly closed his eyes and sagged a bit in resignation. "It may hold one last secret. A prophecy of sorts."

"Of what?"

He opened his eyes. "Of Earth's final destiny."

Before anyone else could react, Hugh burst off his perch with a flare of black wings. A scream burst out, sounding like a clarion call. "Traitors! Traitors all!"

Moira turned to the bank of windows, now gone dark. While they had talked, the sun had set. Lampposts glowed across the Tower Green, now empty of tourists.

"Someone's coming," she warned.

21

5:18 p.m.

Duncan hurried with Moira to the window overlooking the park. Through the twilit gloaming, three men approached the front door. From their bright Beefeater uniforms, they all appeared to be Yeoman Warders. The trio led a fourth man, who carried a satchel over a shoulder and kept his face lowered.

"Is that the Frenchman?" Duncan asked Moira. "Monsieur Laurent?"

"Possibly. He must have caught an early train."

The King's Guard crossed from his sentinel box and confronted the group, lowering his rifle threateningly.

Moira stiffened. "Why is he . . . he knows all the Warders."

A muffled cough and the guardsman's head jerked back, followed by his body. He struck the front door with a clatter and the others closed in on him.

Hugh screamed the obvious. "Traitors!"

Duncan rushed away from the windows. "They're here . . ."

Moira crossed to her father. "The Brotherhood."

The front door—left unlocked as it had been under guard—crashed open. Duncan pictured the assailants dragging the dead man inside with them. It would not take them long to search the house.

Sir Kelly must have realized the same and slipped a pistol from a hidden holster. It seemed the constable intended his role this night to be more than ceremonial. "I'll hold the bastards off. Moira, take the others out the back."

Duncan frowned. *Out the back?* Behind the row of Tudor houses was only a ten-foot-thick wall.

Moira looked similarly dismayed, but for a more personal reason. "Father—"

"This is my duty. To the Tower, to the *Gardiens*. Now go."

The last words cracked with command, but grief deepened the lines on the old man's face. He pushed Moira away, which clearly took all his strength.

Moira stumbled to obey, turning to the table. Sharyn had already grabbed the book and struggled to shove it into her crossbody bag.

"This way!" Moira called to them all, her voice tight.

They hurried toward the door. The hum of a motor trailed after them as Sir Kelly followed in his wheelchair. Out in the hall, Moira led them away from the main stairs.

Duncan paused at the threshold and turned to Sir Kelly. "I can stay. Help hold them off."

Kelly drew his chair to a stop, half-sheltered by the stout door. He lifted his pistol toward the stairs. "Son, I have the only weapon. You'll do more good getting everyone away."

Duncan hesitated, hating to abandon the old man.

Boots pounded up the steps.

Kelly barked at him. "Go! Help the others!"

Duncan turned and spotted Tag hobbling to keep up, reminded that the old man was not the only one compromised. Past Tag, Moira vanished into another room off the hall, drawing the others with her.

Duncan bit down a curse and rushed after them.

He reached Tag and scooped the man under his shoulder. Together, they followed the others into the next chamber. A gunshot exploded behind them. A glance back showed a shadow ducking out of view into the stairwell.

Duncan lunged with Tag out of the hallway and into a small bedroom. An old stone fireplace filled one wall, large enough that two chairs stood inside it. Despite the age of the space, it had none of the formality of the rest of the King's House. A tangle of blankets and sheets covered a four-poster bed. The bureau held a densely packed assembly of cosmetics and brushes of various sizes. A wardrobe stood open, overstuffed with sweaters, blouses, and jeans.

Moira's bedroom, Duncan realized, which only stoked his panicked confusion.

Tag voiced it aloud. "We're trapped in here."

A flurry of gunfire erupted out in the hall, a mix of deafening blasts and muffled pops.

"Hurry!" Moira rushed toward a closed door at the back, either a closet or private bathroom. She yanked it open and ducked through.

The others piled after her—and into the past.

Beyond the doorway, the plaster walls turned to rough stone. They all rushed into a vaulted space, crannied with crumbling cubbies and cut through by cross-shaped window slits. Shocked by the sudden change of venue, Duncan stumbled on the roughhewn floor. Archie caught and steadied him, taking Tag from him.

Archie gawked around. "We're in the Bell Tower."

Duncan pictured the fortification that rose behind the corner of the row of Tudor homes. He had no idea the King's House had its own entry into this twelfth-century tower. On the walls were hung the images of its former prisoners: Lady Jane Grey, Elizabeth I, Sir Thomas More. In more contemporary times, the Nazi Rudolf Hess had also been held here. Somewhere off this chamber, Duncan had read a flush toilet had been installed—not for Hess, but for another Nazi whom the Brits had hoped to imprison here: Adolf Hitler.

"Keep moving," Moira urged them.

She led them down a short tunnel, past a stairwell that led up to the belfry and down to a possible exit. Duncan glanced at the dark spiraling steps. They were clearly not leaving that way.

Moira shouldered open a door and a cold breeze buffeted into the cramped space. They ducked against the chill and exited onto an open battlement. Ahead, a narrow path ran behind the brick rowhouses. Crenellated parapets lined the walkway's other side, overlooking a long drop to a shadowy stretch of Mint Street, which separated the inner curtain wall from the Tower's outer rampart.

Naomi kept next to Sharyn as they hurried after Moira. "This is Elizabeth's Walk."

Duncan finally recognized it, too. Atop this battlement, the imprisoned princess had been allowed to stretch her legs while being held captive at the Bell Tower. Ahead of them, the path led to another fortification, the Beauchamp Tower.

Archie trailed behind with Tag. "Moira's clearly not taking any chances that the bastards might have the Bell Tower watched."

Duncan nodded.

Smart . . .

He searched ahead. A black door beckoned at the end of the walkway. Moira's plan must be to escape down through the Beauchamp Tower, which sat on the green about fifty yards from the King's House.

With the cover of darkness, we might be able to—

The black door shoved open ahead of them.

A shadowy figure strode out onto the battlement, a sliver of moonlight illuminating the bright red garb and cap. Another Beefeater. But this was no Warder of the Tower.

The bastard yanked up a pistol and fired.

Moira gasped and fell back into Naomi and Sharyn.

Duncan struggled to draw them away, but the confines of the battlement confounded him. The Beefeater strode forward, centering his aim. The surprise of seeing their group rushing at him must have thrown off the bastard's first shot. Now, he intended to correct that mistake.

Behind him, a second gunman appeared at the threshold, blocking any escape.

Moira breathed hard, clutching her side.

Duncan shoved forward, sheltering the others behind him.

It was all he could do.

22

5:30 p.m.

With Duncan guarding over them, Sharyn struggled for her folded knife. She had zippered the karambit into an inner pocket of her crossbody satchel. She had managed to slip the blade past security during the bag check at the entrance. The strange book, with its copper bands and crystalline orb, had drawn eyes away from the hidden weapon.

She pulled the blade free and flipped it open, hearing her father's admonishment.

Never bring a knife to a gunfight.

Still, she refused to simply give in.

She also chose to defy her father, too, proving one didn't need a gun.

Not when armed with razor claws and a sharp beak.

A dark shadow swooped overhead and dove down like a feathered arrow. A screech of fury burst from the raven's chest.

Hugh must have trailed after them, either on his own or sent by Moira's father. Ever smart, ever protective, the raven crashed into the first Beefeater, ripping at the man's face with talons and driving his beak like a battering ram again and again.

The man bellowed at the savage mauling and batted wildly. In a panic, he accidentally fired his weapon. The recoil knocked the pistol loose, where it clattered to the stone path.

Duncan rushed forward and slammed into the gunman's belly like a linebacker, lifting him off his feet.

Sharyn reacted with a reflex ingrained into her from countless jiujitsu bouts.

Take every advantage offered.

She followed at Duncan's heels. As he shouldered the gunman up, she pocketed her knife, slid on her knees, and snatched the abandoned pistol—a Glock 17 threaded with suppressor. Cradling the pistol in both hands, she fired at the second man in the doorway. She squeezed the trigger three times, until a round struck his face.

As her target fell backward into the Tower, Duncan turned and tossed his attacker over the edge of the parapet. Arms flailing, the man fell away. His body struck with a wet slap on the dark cobblestones far below.

The battlement's third defender landed on the path. Hugh limped, holding a wing askew, plainly injured.

But he was not the only one.

"Guard the door," Sharyn ordered Duncan as she rushed to the others.

Tag sat on his knees next to Moira. Blood welled through the side of her sweater. "Bullet went through and through, I think," Tag assessed.

Moira tried to push to her feet. "I can manage."

She could not and fell back to her bottom.

Tag shrugged off his jacket and hurriedly bunched up the lower half. "Lift your arms. This is going to hurt."

"Do it," Moira seethed between clenched teeth.

Tag pressed his wadded up jacket against her wounded side. Moira moaned, her eyes squeezed tight. He then quickly tied the coat's sleeves around her thin waist and knotted them tight.

"Help her get moving," Tag said, struggling to gain his feet himself.

As Archie hauled her up, Moira cursed a bloody streak, which was echoed by Hugh, who came limping up. It was plain *where* the raven had picked up this foul habit.

"Stay, my boyo," she groaned to the bird, recognizing he was hurt. "Extra biscuits when I get back, I promise."

Hugh clucked at her, sounding like a chicken, which he certainly was not by any definition of the word.

They set off toward the open door into the Beauchamp Tower, trying for as much speed as possible. Sharyn glanced back along the battlement.

Hugh leaped to a perch atop the parapet, casting his gaze in all directions, continuing his role as the Tower's guardian, likely still worried about Moira.

"We'll take it from here," Sharyn whispered, clutching her pistol.

She then rushed after the others, stepping over the man she had shot. She kept her gaze away. She had dropped many an opponent, but she had never killed anyone. While the death was justified, a darkness weighed on her. She knew she would need time to come to terms with this.

Just not now.

She hurried with the group down through the depths of the dark tower, where plaster still covered sections of raw stone. Tour exhibits dotted their path. As she ran a hand along a wall for support, she felt the scars of ancient graffiti carved into the stone, left behind by either guards or prisoners.

They finally reached the exit, where the door had been left open. They paused at the threshold. It lay a full landing below the level of the Tower Green.

Sharyn edged up, climbing the steps with Duncan, who had collected the pistol from the man she had shot. She hunched with him at the top step. She noted the tremor in Duncan's hand as he held the weapon. She didn't know if it was from terror, adrenaline, or, like her, the knowledge that he had killed someone this night.

She pushed this all down and forced her focus ahead.

After failing to encounter anyone else inside the Tower, she hoped this meant the enemy had limited numbers. If so, she could guess why that was. The Tower's thirty-two Warders must be a close-knit group. The enemy's masquerade risked exposure if the bastards brought too many impostors into the Tower. The attackers must have used the cover of nightfall before changing into their costumes, and they had planned on escaping with the last tourists after acquiring the book.

Praying she was right, she huddled low and searched the grounds.

By now, twilight had darkened to a moonless night. A heavy layer of mist had settled over the parklands, where a few lamps glowed. The flight across the battlement had dropped them halfway along the Tower Green. A well-lit path stretched directly ahead, bisecting the lawn in two. It led to the bulk of the White Tower castle, which was brightly illuminated, like a turreted birthday cake sitting at the center of the fog-shrouded grounds.

She spotted no one moving out there. From the rowhouses to her right, she heard the occasional soft pop of a pistol. But she had to strain to hear it. The noise was barely discernible, muffled by the house's thick brick walls.

Still, one thing was evident . . .

"Kelly is still holding ground," Duncan noted quietly.

But for how much longer?

She dropped down to the others, intending not to waste the constable's efforts. "We must go," she warned. "But cautiously. No telling if more of the bastards are out there.

Moira nodded, pain clipping her words. "To get out, we'd best avoid the main West Gate and Middle Drawbridge. If we circle behind the White Tower, we can make for the eastern exit. It's smaller, mostly a service access and emergency route."

"I think this counts as an emergency," Archie mumbled.

Sharyn recognized a significant flaw in this plan. "The enemy will surely have *all* exits watched."

And outside, there would be no restrictions on their numbers.

"You may be right." Moira waved ahead. "But we'll have to cross that bridge when we get to it."

They got moving again. At the top of the steps, they circled the edge of the green, sticking to the deeper mists and shadows, and headed away from the rowhouse corner. Occasionally, vague shapes stirred in the distance. From their silhouettes, they were mostly Beefeaters, who appeared to be herding late-straying tourists toward the exits.

Whether these Warders were friend or foe, it was impossible to tell.

23

5:55 p.m.

Every step across the dark grounds tightened the tension across Sharyn's shoulders. The mists continued to thicken with the falling temperatures. The night dissolved into glowing patches of fog and deeper shadows. While this offered their group ample cover, it also strained her eyes as she searched for any threat.

"Shouldn't there be more security out here?" Tag whispered.

Moira grimaced. "You'd think so, but it's closing time. The witching hour. Most security congregates around the Crown Jewels building. Everyone else is closing places or scurrying out the last tourists."

Sharyn continued to watch for any of the above. She held her pistol at her hip, hidden under the fall of her jacket. Duncan did the same with his weapon. At any moment, she expected to hear the crack of a sniper's rifle, to see one of her friends fall.

Still, their group safely cleared the green and headed behind the massive rise of the White Tower. They kept tightly clustered, trying to hide that Moira was propped up by Archie.

"Oy, there!" a voice shouted behind them.

They all turned as a Beefeater stepped from the misty stairwell, jangling a set of keys.

"Tower's well closed," he called over. "Shouldn't still be about."

Moira shifted forward, hanging on Archie as if he were her boyfriend. "It's just me! Moira Kelly. Getting a late start with some friends." She motioned with her chin. "Heading to the Hung, Drawn, and Quartered."

"Good pub, but not as nice as The Keys right here at the Tower. With this pea-souper dropping on us, you and your friends are welcome, if it suits you."

"Cheers for that, but we have others waiting for us." Moira waved a goodbye that nearly took her legs out from under her.

Archie kept her going. "A pub? Here? I could use a pint about now."

"Not a good idea," Moira wheezed out. "The Keys is a private Warder's pub, friends and family only. Either way, we don't want to be caught there."

"Why?" Naomi glanced back to the Beefeater as he headed off into the fog. "When all hell breaks loose, which will happen before long, what better place to be?"

"And you need medical attention," Duncan reminded her.

"No." Moira continued on. "Don't let the Beefeaters garb mislead you. All the Warders have at least twenty-two years of military service. They're no nonsense when it comes to security of the Tower. Once they realize something is awry, they'll lock this place down—and us."

"Wouldn't that be a good thing?" Tag asked.

"Not if they confiscate the book, which they'll certainly do. Afterward, it will no doubt vanish into the Brotherhood as they pull their strings."

Archie added the other concern. "And don't forget, we're all framed for murder. The deaths here will not help our case."

"Good riddance to the book, I say," Duncan muttered.

Moira glared at him. "My father risked his life . . . possibly gave it . . . to get the book to safety. I will not fail him. And neither will you. You owe him that much."

Naomi glanced back to the Tower Green. "What about your father?"

"He . . . he's a soldier. Once you're away, I'll raise the alarm, try to get help to him before they . . . before he . . ." She shook her head, unable to finish the grim sentiment. Instead, she hobbled faster. "Which means I need to get your butts out of here as quickly as possible."

Sharyn kept next to her, gripping her pistol.

Moira continued. "I'll reach out to Laurent. Let him know about the ambush. Arrange a new rendezvous. He said you had a burner phone."

"We do," Sharyn agreed.

"He also told me that he had made arrangements to get you all out of the country until matters could be sorted. It's another reason he was delayed. To secure forged papers for you all. Papers at least good enough to get you into France."

"France?" Naomi said.

"The *Gardiens'* main quarters are in Paris."

Sharyn raised a concern that they all likely shared. "Can we trust this man? He was the one who sent us here."

Into a trap.

"I . . . I don't know," Moira admitted. "I would've never suspected him before this. But if he had meant to betray you, he could've sent you *anywhere,* certainly to a location far easier to set up an ambush than the Tower of London."

Sharyn recognized this made sense, but she could not shake her paranoia. Professor Wright's warning blazed behind her eyes.

Trust no one.

The group continued and cleared the corner of the White Tower. They followed along the castle's eastern façade, hurrying past the hulk of a cannon, turned a rich verdigris by age. On the other side, a parked white service van unloaded crates and supplies toward the open doors of a café.

Sharyn's stomach stirred at the smell of baked bread.

When was the last time I ate anything?

Still, she kept going, drawn by the arched tunnel through the Tower's inner wall.

Almost out.

As they headed into the tunnel, the outer curtain wall appeared. The bulwark rose on the far side of a street that ran between the Tower's two walls. An archway cut through it and led to a narrow wooden bridge that spanned the castle's dry moat. It ended at a park that bordered the Thames.

Sharyn stared longingly at the misty river as it glowed, illuminated by the shining bulk of Tower Bridge that crested high over the water.

Freedom lay so close.

And so far.

Tag groaned, clearly recognizing this, too.

A pair of police vehicles blocked the bridge's far side, along with a gray-paneled truck that looked military. Blue lights flashed and spun everywhere. Uniformed figures stirred amid the chaos.

Archie shook his head. "Seems we're not getting out of here any time soon."

24

6:14 p.m.

This plan is daft.

Duncan waited with the others inside the Cradle Tower. The square fortification dated to the fourteenth century. It had been built by King Edward III along the outer curtain wall, to serve as his private water gate into the castle, back when the Thames once brushed against these walls—and later, when the moat took its place.

Duncan stood with Sharyn before the black iron portcullis that overlooked the dry moat and, beyond it, the north bank of the Thames. The welded gate was barely wide enough for the two to stand shoulder to shoulder.

Sharyn leaned closer to the gate, studying the challenge ahead. The Cradle Tower rose to the right of the exit they hoped to use, so it offered the perfect vantage to spy upon the police force gathered at the foot of the Eastern Drawbridge. Moira had directed them to shelter inside the tower, while she and Archie left to ready matters, taking one of the pistols with them. To enter the tower, it had required slipping a few steps down the street that ran between the castle's two walls.

Luckily, the heavy fog aided them, keeping them out of sight.

Sharyn raised another bit of fortune. "Thank god, all the Tower's exits aren't already locked up."

"Don't thank *god,*" Duncan corrected. "Thank *tradition.* The place isn't officially shuttered until 9:52 p.m. during the Ceremony of the Keys. Which happens every night like clockwork. The ritual has gone uninterrupted for seven hundred years."

"Then we have some time to spare," Sharyn noted. "But I don't think the police blockade will be coming down before then."

Duncan stared out at the two bulky cars with flashing lights. They were stationed at the foot of the drawbridge. Both were ARVs—Armed Response Vehicles. The pair looked official, as did the armored riot van parked behind them. No doubt the enemy had manipulated this force to aid them in trapping Duncan's group.

Tag spoke behind him. "I wouldn't mind some rope right about now. Certainly helped these chaps."

Duncan turned to where Tag and Naomi had been studying a tourist placard. It told the story of a famous escape from the Tower of London in 1597. Two men—a Jesuit priest named John Gerard and fellow prisoner John Arden—broke a lock to the Tower roof and slid down a rope to a waiting boat, then fled under the cover of night.

"We're missing a boat, too," Duncan reminded Tag and returned his attention to the drawbridge.

And water, for that matter.

He stared across the stretch of foggy moat, which had been drained long ago. Over the centuries, the green space had been used to grow vegetables and graze livestock. Soldiers had also camped there many times. Then for several summers, including this past one, the moat had been transformed into a flowering paradise, with twenty million seeds planted. It drew thousands every year, to wander its fragrant paths.

Such wasn't the case now.

The Superbloom—as the exhibit was called—ended a month ago. Since then, gardeners and landscapers had set about cleaning, digging, trenching, and raking. It now looked like a minefield of mounds, dotted with wheelbarrows, tractors, and other bits of equipment. Presently, a thick fog spilled off the Thames and filled the moat, as if Mother Nature were trying to hide the desecration of Her wonderland.

The rapid slap of shoe leather on cobbles drew Duncan's attention around. Archie burst into the doorway and stopped. "Get crackin'! Moira's coming in hot!"

Finally . . .

Duncan herded his group to the exit. "Let's move."

They all fled outside and flattened against the stones between the tower door and the archway that led to the drawbridge.

With his back to the rocks, Duncan stared across the street to the tunnel that pierced the inner wall. The Tower's main courtyard lay on the far side. As he waited, he strained for any sign of Moira. He searched for her lights, but the fog blanketed everything.

Then he heard the rumble of an engine. It ratcheted louder with his every strained breath. A glow grew in the fog, then separated into two lights.

A van swept into the tunnel, shedding some of the fog. It was the service vehicle he had spotted earlier, the one offloading supplies into a café.

Only, Duncan knew its driver had been swapped out, likely at gunpoint.

The large white truck burst out of the tunnel, sped across the narrow street, and drove headlong into the archway leading to the Eastern Drawbridge.

Moira did not slow for them.

Once the vehicle flew past, Duncan and the others chased after it, sprinting into the tunnel. Ahead, the van sped out onto the wooden drawbridge. As it barreled into the fog, its brake lights flared an angry crimson. The truck fishtailed hard. Its front end struck a sentry booth to the left of the bridge, then spun sideways and slammed broadside into the police vehicles.

The two ARVs were knocked backward into the riot van.

Chaos ensued, lost in the mists, heard more than seen.

Shouts and screams.

Shattering glass.

Crunch of metal.

A spatter of gunfire.

By then, Duncan and the others had cleared the tunnel and dashed to the left, to the bridge's railing that overlooked the dry moat. Without pausing, Duncan hurried their group over the side. It was a drop of less than ten feet, which was lessened and cushioned by a mound of dirt and raked debris.

Duncan followed last, praying that Moira was okay. She swore she could handle this task, telling him she had watched plenty of *Top Gear.* She had also wanted to rouse the Tower in a spectacular fashion, to stir everyone to get to her father as soon as possible. Her wounded state should further facilitate a prompt response.

In the meantime, using the distraction, the fog, and the darkness, Duncan dropped and slid into the moat. The others were already moving, following a path picked out from their spy post. They kept the mounded piles and landscaping equipment between them and those up top.

As they fled, Archie helped Tag, all but carrying him.

Sharyn and Naomi raced in tandem.

Duncan followed last, gripping his pistol, ready to use it if needed to help the others escape. But it proved unnecessary. They made it around the corner of the Tower's wall and fled to the north, toward the rear of the massive edifice.

Once far enough away, they finally slowed, too exhausted and adrenaline-worn to keep up the pace.

"We need a way out of this bloody ditch," Archie panted.

Duncan searched around. To his right, a tall brick bulwark led up to the elevated A100 that crossed the Tower Bridge. Up ahead, one last piece of the Superbloom exhibit remained, likely left to aid workers into and out of the moat. A constructed set of steps led to the top of the brick dike that enclosed the moat.

Duncan pointed. "Over there."

Scraped, bruised, and half-beaten, they rushed the last of the distance and climbed the steps. A barricade up top closed off access to the sidewalk, but after escaping the Tower of London, this was no obstacle. Duncan helped them scale the fence and drop on the far side.

A few passersby gave them looks that ranged from amused to disgusted. Still, no one made any fuss.

This was London.

"What now?" Sharyn asked as they gathered under a row of trees at the edge of a small park.

"Pizza and pints," Archie offered.

Duncan had no argument against this plan. But before he could agree wholeheartedly, the pocket of his jacket shivered.

With a grimace, he pulled out his burner phone.

He checked the number and lifted the cell. "We may have to hold off on that."

FOURTH

25

November 2, 12:18 a.m. GMT
English Channel

Sharyn stood alone on the open stern deck of the forty-foot fishing trawler, wondering for the hundredth time how she ended up here. A bright *V* of churned wake spread out behind the boat as it cleaved through the nighttime waters of the English Channel. Stars shone overhead, which made her feel smaller and more lost.

After escaping the Tower of London, the mysterious Laurent had phoned them. The Frenchman had been about to board a Eurostar train for London when word had reached him of a police force closing around the castle fortress. Fearing the worst, he had called to check on their status.

Upon learning of the ambush—and after much cursing—he had expedited a plan to smuggle them into France. Sharyn's group had boarded yet another train, paying cash at the Waterloo station, which lay only a short distance from the Tower. Laurent had directed them to travel to Portsmouth, a city at the edge of the Channel, where he arranged for a boat to ferry them across to France, to the town of Le Havre at the mouth of the Seine.

She checked her wristwatch.

They had boarded the boat three hours ago and still had

another four to go. Traveling by Eurostar through the Channel Tunnel would've been far faster, but that would have also meant going through passport control, which they dared not do. They could not risk their names pinging on some authority's database.

Laurent had also encouraged them to take advantage of the longer transit and get some sleep. Once at Le Havre, he would meet them with a car for the last leg, an overland trip to a spot outside Paris. He would not say exactly where—which still troubled Sharyn.

Can we truly trust this man?

The worry settled like a stone in her chest. Even if he had not betrayed them, where did his true loyalties lay? He was clearly more concerned about the damnable book than about their well-being. For now, the two were bound inexorably together, but what about afterward? Once he had secured the book, how important was their safety?

Sharyn sighed and pushed off the stern rail. This fretful worrying was doing no good.

And I do need to get some sleep.

The boys were all below deck, sharing a set of stacked bunks in the crew quarters. The captain—a Swede with a wind-scoured face and gnarled beard—had offered his cabin to Sharyn and Naomi. Otherwise, the man remained reticent and showed little interest in them, neither did his two crewmen. The three had likely been well paid for such apathy. She suspected this was not the first time the trawler had been involved in human trafficking.

As she headed for the door below, a cold breeze, heavy with salt, blew her hair about her face. Still, it was better than the reek of algae and fish blood that permeated the curled ropes and folded nets that crowded the deck. She reached the hatch and ducked through. The wind slammed the door behind her with a resounding clap. As she descended a steep stair to a short passageway, voices murmured from a tiny galley at the end of the hall. She recognized Tag's wheeze and Naomi's sarcasm.

Clearly, I'm not the only one suffering from insomnia.

She considered joining the others, but she had escaped to the open deck to be alone, to collect herself, to balance the bloodshed and danger against their survival. Before she could reach the door to the captain's cabin, a large shadow stepped out into the passageway from the galley.

"Thought I heard you return." Duncan closed on her and held up a mug. "I made you some tea. Chamomile."

"Thanks," she said.

He lifted a flask. "Archie also paid one of the crew for something stronger. It worked for him. He's snoring away in his bunk."

"Tea's fine. And we should all try to catch some sleep."

He sighed. "Trying and doing are two different things."

She smiled, but it was a weak effort. "That's certainly true."

As she stepped toward the cabin door, she became all too cognizant of Duncan's presence. He didn't block her, but he still filled the narrow passageway. She smelled the damp wool of his sweater, the hint of muskiness behind it. In the dimly lit space, his face was shadows, darkened by stubble.

Before she could reach the door, he touched her arm. She flinched, still too tense after all that had happened. He dropped his hand. "Sorry."

"No, it's not anything," she stammered, feeling foolish. "Truly."

"I just wanted . . . hoped to talk to you about something. In private. While we had a moment."

"Of course." Though tired and heart-worn, she could not deny him. "In here."

She opened the door and led him into the captain's quarters. Due to the economy of space, the cabin was no bigger than a walk-in closet. It held a narrow desk, cluttered with papers, charts, and logbooks, all crammed next to a double bed. The scent of cigar smoke clung to every surface and fabric.

She squeezed to take a seat on the bed, while Duncan dropped into the desk chair. "What is it?" she asked.

"I . . . I feel stupid bringing this up." He shook his head, then let it hang. His voice dropped to a pained whisper, nothing like his normally cavalier demeanor. "But I didn't know who else to talk to."

"About what?"

"I shouldn't feel this way, but I can't shake it." He lifted a hand, which tremored slightly, then lowered it again.

She recalled the same tremble as he held his pistol at the edge of the Tower Green. She suddenly suspected the source of his angst and distress. They had seen too much death over the past twenty-four hours. And now, with ample time to ponder, Duncan clearly struggled with his own actions of the past night, especially in regard to the life he had taken.

And not just him.

She pictured her assailant's body falling backward through the tower doorway, the ruins of his face after being shot. She also heard the wet smack of bone and flesh on stone after Duncan threw his man over the parapet.

While she had downed many an opponent during her training, she had never killed anyone.

And no doubt, neither had Duncan.

"I mean what we did . . . it was warranted, of course," he whispered as if sharing a piece of his heart. "We had no other choice, right?"

She wanted to offer him absolution, but she struggled to do the same for herself. Instead, she had crammed that guilt and ache down deep, an emotional crutch that had served her in the past.

Bury it and deal with it later—or never.

Still, that seldom worked. Pain always churned back up, often in harmful ways. And for Duncan, who had seemingly led a charmed life, he had not developed the scarred walls to hold in that much guilt and emotional ache.

To help him, she let her own guard down and placed her hand on his knee.

Her father had warned her how taking a life, even when justified, wore on a soul. With too much time on hand, she could not help but wonder: *Did those men have family? Wives who loved them? Children who needed them? Parents who took pride in them? Ultimately, did they believe their cause was as righteous as our own?*

She knew cops got counseling after a shooting. Soldiers masked their actions with veiled jargon—engaging, bagging, dropping—avoiding a term far more weighted.

Duncan voiced it now. "Does this make us murderers?"

After her upbringing, she had gone through therapy and countless talks over coffee with her Al-Anon sponsor to address the guilt that came from walking out of a fire, maybe burned, maybe scarred, but alive.

She reached to Duncan's bowed head and lifted his chin, to force him to stare her in the eyes, then answered his question. "No, it makes us survivors. Nothing more, nothing less."

She read the pain shining there, knowing no words could truly lessen it. Only time held that power. Still, he swallowed hard and nodded. She leaned her brow to his, two survivors, grieving what it took to stay alive.

"I . . . I remember," he said softly, "my grandfather shared wartime stories. They were accounts of misery in the trenches, of the sounds and terror of battle, of happier moments captured in between. But he never . . . he never . . ."

"Told about the deaths at his hand. My father was the same way."

"When I was twelve or so, I once asked him how many Nazis he had killed."

"What did he say?"

Duncan sighed. "He mumbled that the enemy weren't Nazis,

mostly just boys as terrified as he was. When I pressed him again, he claimed to have killed no one. But I knew he was lying. And he knew I knew it. And I never asked him again."

"You let him keep his secret, his dignity. He no doubt fought bravely, but it's hard to take pride in killing another."

Duncan lifted his face, still keeping close. She caught a hint of whiskey on his breath, then a moment later, she tasted it on his lips, his tongue. She could not say who initiated the kiss, only that it was necessary.

He shifted to the bed and sat beside her, pulling her closer, drawing her fully to him. They fell into the blankets, finding a language, a comfort, that could only be spoken without words. Their hands and mouths sought out the tenderest spots. He hardened in response, but even then, it was less passion than compassion. They needed to feel, to accept a truth that lay beyond guilt.

We're still alive.

26

5:02 a.m.

A firm knocking shattered Sharyn out of a deep sleep. She struggled to understand where she was, only gaining clarity from the muscular arms embracing her. Blankets tangled them together. Clothing lay strewn about.

She pushed up to an elbow, shocked to discover she had fallen asleep.

With a groan, Duncan rolled over and lowered his feet to the floor. His hair was mussed and sticking boyishly askew. But as he stood, his firm buttocks and what swung between his legs at half-mast belied any such youthfulness.

She turned from the sight and fought through the blankets to search for her clothing.

"We've dropped anchor!" Naomi called through the door to them. "The crew are prepping a dinghy to ferry us to shore."

"We'll be right out," Sharyn answered.

Duncan turned to her and leaned in close. "Sure about that?"

His mast had grown firmer, adding conviction of this question.

She tipped up on her toes and gave him a quick kiss, noting the bruised tenderness to her lips and a deeper ache that warmed the chill from the cold cabin.

"I said nothing about this being a *regular* occurrence," she reminded him, refusing to assign anything more to this night than two people needing to comfort each other. "Maybe for now, what happens on the English Channel stays on the English Channel."

He frowned and pulled on his clothes, tucking himself away with some effort. "We're still *on* the English Channel, I might remind you."

"Hopefully, not for long." She finished dressing and pushed him toward the door. "Until then, let's see if this boat's send-off includes coffee."

As they exited the cabin, Naomi waited in the passageway. She eyed them both with raised brows and an amused smirk. "Archie and Tag are already up on deck."

Duncan tried his best to smooth his clothing and his dignity. "I'll go see if anyone needs help."

Naomi scooped an arm around Sharyn's waist. "I will want details later. I deserve it after being driven away last night by the commotion going on inside the cabin."

"Where did you—"

"I bunked with Archie and Tag. Not exactly the three-way—or *ménage à trois,* I should say, as we're now in French waters—that I was hoping for."

The two of them climbed the narrow steps single file. Duncan held the door open, fighting a stiffer wind that had blown in overnight, clearing the clouds. Stars and a bright moon hung over the dark waters. While sunrise was still a couple hours off, a slight pinkening to the eastern skies promised a new dawn to come.

Hopefully on a better day.

Atop the deck, the captain oversaw his two crewmen, rushing them with urgent commands in Swedish. He clearly did not want to tarry long in these waters. According to Laurent, French authorities regularly patrolled the coasts, but they would likely give little attention to a fishing trawler.

Still, no one was taking any chances.

The crew had already rigged nets as if readying for a new day of fishing. The pair now worked to lower a dinghy into the water, fighting the strong gusts. The little craft looked more rust than metal, but at least it had a motor, and they wouldn't have to row to shore.

Duncan and Archie, even Tag, sought to be of assistance, which proved to be mostly useless, but such was the conceit of men. Sharyn crossed with Naomi to the stern rail. With the trawler anchored, the windblown seas rocked the boat with large swells. Sharyn feared, if they delayed much longer, her stomach would be churning just as fiercely.

To ward off nausea, she focused on the horizon. The coastline was only discernible as a bright line of sand or rock against the black water. A few lights glowed farther inland, marking a few homes. Farther to the west, a constellation of lights marked the city of Le Havre, split down the middle by the Seine as it carved a path from the Channel and headed toward Paris.

A loud splash and rattle of metal drew her attention. A loose rope ladder with plastic rungs was tossed overboard to the dinghy.

The captain waved to them. "*Dags att gå!*"

Though she didn't understand Swedish, they were clearly being dismissed. Helped by one of the crew, they scaled down the ladder. The dinghy rocked and battered against the trawler's hull. Once weighted by the five of them, along with the crewman who would be tendering them to shore, the little craft became somewhat tamed.

The captain called final orders to the man below, then lifted an arm toward them. "*Hej då! Lycka till!*"

The guttural and hard words sounded like a curse, but the crewman at the stern translated. "He say goodbye. And good luck."

The little motor growled into an angry buzz, and the dinghy heaved toward shore, bouncing roughly at first, then growing smoother, skimming over the swells.

Sharyn glanced back to the trawler. She had thought the captain had been perturbed with them, but maybe it was just his cultural mannerisms and language. His orders and admonishments in Swedish reminded her of the conversation she had overheard when Professor Wright took a call back at the Old Library. She suspected now it wasn't German he had been speaking, but one of the Scandinavian languages.

She did not know if this was significant, but a gloominess settled over her. That urgent call had set everything in motion and led to so many deaths.

Back aboard the trawler, she had kept Saint-Germain's book secured in her crossbody bag. She was more than ready to hand off its responsibility to another.

I'm done with being its accursed Thirteenth Keeper.

The last of the ride across the Channel left her cold, bitter, and sprayed with salt, which stung her lips, as if scolding her for her brief moment of relief. The dinghy finally nosed into a stretch of empty sand. Across the beach, a small restaurant stood dark and abandoned, looking long shuttered for the winter season.

But as they climbed out of the skiff, a pair of headlights flared to the side, revealing a black van parked there.

Sharyn and the others drew tighter together, wary and fearful. She dropped a hand to the Glock she had tucked into her waistband. Duncan drew his pistol fully out, proving he was not as adept when facing a threat.

Never show the enemy your cards, her father had instructed her. *Surprise can be as powerful a weapon as any gun.*

27

5:44 a.m.

Suspicious and worried, Sharyn waved everyone back from the parked van, but there was nowhere to retreat. They were fully exposed on the beach. Even the trawler's crewman had not wasted any time. He had shoved off and was headed away with the dinghy, abandoning them to their fate.

Finally, the door to the van popped open. The interior lamps silhouetted a tall shadowy figure as he exited, dressed in an ankle-length coat. He appeared to be alone. Still, she prayed it was not another ambush.

"I'm Malick Laurent!" the man called over, keeping his distance, likely noting Duncan's raised weapon. "I see you've reached our shores safely."

Recognizing the man's voice, Sharyn swallowed hard and responded. "I don't know if I'd use the word *safely*, Monsieur Laurent."

If that's who you are.

After all of this, she refused to take anything at face value.

"Fear not, let us get you all aboard and put more distance between you and any further threat."

Duncan turned to her, slightly lowering his weapon. "What do you think?"

She weighed the risk and came to a decision. "We've trusted

him this far. We might as well finish the journey." She waved to the others. "Let's go."

As they crossed toward the vehicle, Sharyn studied Laurent. From his accent, from his sense of authority over the phone, she had expected an older gentleman, picturing some pale French aristocrat. But Laurent was Black, possibly West African, with stubbled hair so dense that it appeared like a dark skullcap. His physique was muscled, and his complexion hard, roughened by a scar at his chin and one brow. Still, he looked to be no older than his mid-thirties.

Naomi also eyed him as they approached and whispered, "Who knew Idris Elba had a son?"

"Be on your guard," Duncan warned them.

Laurent slid open a large hatch on the side of the vehicle. It was a black Mercedes Sprinter van, some executive model with darkly tinted windows. Inside, leather seats welcomed them, as did a well-stocked bar to one side, glittering with bottles on ice.

"At least the bloke brought us a party bus," Archie commented, wincing as he climbed aboard, holding the elbow of his wounded arm. He crossed over, grabbed a bottle of scotch, cradled it to his chest, and dropped heavily into a rear seat.

Tag took a spot opposite him. "Hope you're planning on sharing that."

"No promises, mate. I need it for medicinal purposes."

Naomi surveyed the bar, then passed Sharyn a bottle of Perrier before joining her near the front. Duncan tucked away his Glock and took the passenger seat next to Laurent.

The Frenchman climbed behind the wheel, started the engine, and called back to them. "Settle in. We still have a two-hour drive ahead of us."

"To where?" Sharyn pressed him.

"To Meaux, a small village forty kilometers outside of Paris."

"And we'll be safe there?" Duncan asked.

Laurent sighed. "As well as can be managed," he answered, offering no real reassurance.

Despite this lack of guarantee, Sharyn appreciated his candor.

Laurent bumped the large van out of the beach parking lot and headed down a dark country road.

Once underway, the Frenchman continued, "I understand your worry. We plainly have a mole in the *Gardiens*. Someone who has been leaking intelligence to the *Confrérie*. I fear—in making arrangements to rendezvous at the Tower of London, along with acquiring new papers for you all—word must have reached the wrong ears."

"Does your group have any idea who this traitor might be?" Sharyn asked.

"Not as of yet."

As his gaze flicked to the rearview mirror, she noted the slight narrowing of his eyes. He must be wondering if one of them could be complicit. While Sharyn refused to believe this, she could not help but consider it. Their small group had separated multiple times during their escape to London. One of them could have secured another burner or borrowed a stranger's cell to alert the enemy of their destination.

Still, she pushed down such doubts before they unnerved her. Instead, she raised a worry that had troubled her all the way to this shore. "Have you heard anything about Sir Kelly or his daughter?"

"Ah, *oui*. Of course. I should have told you at the outset. Moira Kelly is being cared for at the hospital and faring well—though worried. Last I heard, her father was in surgery. He suffered sorely but still lived, managing to take out all but one combatant, who was killed when the Warders, alerted by Moira, went to his aid."

Sharyn sank deeper in her seat, relieved to the point of tears.

Thank god . . .

She could not bear any more deaths on her shoulders.

"Moira informed the authorities of the attack," Laurent continued, "while denying any knowledge of five students who were being sought by the police."

"Still, the Brotherhood will not stop hunting us," Duncan said.

"No. Not as long as you carry the book."

"What about now?" Naomi shifted forward. "How many know we're headed to Meaux?"

"Only those inside this vehicle. Even the trawler who carried you here, I arranged personally, using my former contacts with military intelligence."

Duncan frowned. "Military intelligence? Did you once serve?"

"*Oui.* With the First Marine Infantry Parachute Regiment."

From Duncan's raised brows, Sharyn assumed it must be a significant battalion. He turned to her and explained. "They're the French equivalent of the SAS."

"But I took leave of them four years ago," Laurent said. "After finishing my graduate work."

Sharyn eyed the man, framing him in this new light. "Graduate work? In what field?"

"Archaeology."

Naomi sat straighter, clearly intrigued, as this was her field, too. "Why archaeology?"

"A passion, of course. Generational. Following in the footsteps of my father and grandfather. The latter served with the Free French Brigade in Libya, while also being a part of the *Gardiens.* He had been involved with the search for the cache of King Solomon's gold, only to lose it to betrayal."

"And you've picked up that torch," Sharyn said. "Continuing with the *Gardiens.*"

"How could I not? I've been working with a team to decipher the Second Adage, to discern where its treasure is hidden."

Sharyn wondered if the man's desire to achieve this goal was driven by an effort—consciously or not—to redeem his grandfather's failure, to right that wrong.

Archie called from the back, where he had been silently nursing his bottle. Still, he raised an issue that Sharyn had never considered. "Mate! If you've been working on that puzzle, it means your group's already made a copy of the book."

"True, Monsieur Bailey. The entire volume has been digitized and locked behind firewalls and doubly encrypted using AES-256 and a quantum key."

Duncan looked at Archie, then to Laurent. "Wait. If you've preserved its content, why is the physical book so important?"

Sharyn's face heated up. "That's right. Why haven't you already destroyed it? Then there would be no need to hide it or risk the lives of its Keepers. It would also assure that the *Confrérie* never got their hands on its contents."

Laurent answered, while concentrating on the curves of the dark road. "For three reasons. First, one does not destroy such a rare artifact out of hand. As a librarian, you must recognize the necessity of preserving historical treasures, especially one this unique."

Sharyn found it hard to argue against this. She pictured the fiery destruction of the Old Library at Exeter and remembered the pain of that irreplaceable loss.

"Second, back during World War II, the physical book acted as a key to unlock access to the treasure in Africa. So, we must assume it will be needed for the others."

Sharyn grimaced, appreciating now why protecting it had been so important, but Laurent was not done.

"Third and most important, Saint-Germain was adamant about preserving his book. And the *Gardiens* swore to do so. Still, regardless of that pledge, many believe there are yet secrets hidden in Saint-Germain's book, mysteries *beyond* what is inscribed on its pages or its use as a physical key. If the volume was destroyed, we do not know what might be lost forever."

"So better to be cautious," Naomi said.

"A wisdom we'd best heed from here," Laurent warned. "Which is why no one knows where I'm taking you."

Sharyn furrowed her brow, finding little comfort in those last words. She stared out at the passing countryside, at the rolling orchards and windswept fields, tilled over and dark.

Where the hell is he taking us?

28

7:09 a.m. GMT
London, England

From the top of the Shard, Keir Marchand had an eagle-eye view of the Tower of London—and most of the city, for that matter, as it woke to a new day.

The seventy-two-story pyramidal skyscraper climbed more than three hundred meters, piercing the low clouds. It was the tallest building in the United Kingdom. Due to its prominence, along with its convenient location within the financial hub of the city, Keir's company—NeuVentis Pharma—had leased the entire sixtieth floor.

Keir stared below at the bustle of vehicles that had locked down the Tower grounds. Lights flashed and blinked all around the fortress. Roads had been barricaded. Interrogations continued, while teams still painstakingly searched every corner of the Tower for any hidden assailants.

As of now, the belief was that the interlopers had sought to subdue the Constable of the Tower, all in an attempt to gain access to the Crown Jewels. Of course, the *Confrérie*'s contacts both within MI5 and the Metropolitan Police had bolstered this misconception. And with no survivors of the assault, it would be hard to claim otherwise.

Ultimately, all the commotion below was just noise.

Useless bluster.

The *Confrérie*'s true targets had escaped the ambush.

Keir glanced across the conference room to where Cardinal Tissot clustered with four of the Brotherhood, those who were within his inner circle. Even after this failure, the man continued to remain cagey, refusing to reveal his source inside the *Gardiens.* If anything, this fiasco only served to make Tissot more guarded. The man needed to keep this knowledge under wraps to prevent himself from being booted aside.

Which he deserved.

The cardinal had orchestrated the botched ambush within the Tower grounds. Still, Keir knew Tissot was not solely at fault. Some of the blame fell on the shoulders of Saanvi Burman, who had manipulated her resources within the policing forces to cordon off all exits from the fortress.

Both had failed.

As of now, two questions remained:

How did the bastards slip our noose?

And where did they go?

All of the *Confrérie* assets were engaged to figure out those answers.

As Keir waited—frustrated with the book having been so close at hand—he wondered for the thousandth time what miracles were hidden in the pages of Saint-Germain's book. Still, one remained tantamount in his mind's eye, a treasure beyond all others:

The key to immortality.

Such a discovery held the promise to catapult NeuVentis into the stratosphere, transform it into a trillion-dollar business.

And better yet . . .

With the key in hand, I will live to see it happen.

Before he could ponder this further, Burman called over, her voice ringing with triumph. "We've found them!"

Keir clenched a fist.

At last . . .

He swung away from the window and crossed to the room's conference table, a custom Hermès masterpiece in wood and leather. Burman stood amid her own team, where laptops had been lined up, drawing intelligence from hundreds of sources.

"Where are they?" Keir demanded, pushing next to Burman.

She leaned over a screen that showed an overhead view of the Tower at night. "It took much effort to gain this footage, though it's a few hours old. It came from a MINERVA military satellite, one equipped with high-resolution ISR—Intelligence, Surveillance, and Reconnaissance."

Keir could not hide his disappointment, which turned his words bitter. "So, this is from last night? Not a current feed?"

"That's correct," Burman admitted. "Still, it shows *how* the others escaped, the route they took."

Keir bit back an angry retort. While this was progress, it didn't answer the fundamental question of their targets' location now.

"Show me," he said.

Burman zoomed the image down onto a drawbridge near the Tower's eastern corner. She allowed the footage to run, which remained poorly lit and frosted over by thick fog. "The MINVERVA satellite was designed for daytime reconnaissance, so this was the best that could be managed. But it proved good enough."

As Keir watched, a large white van burst across the bridge and slammed into the vehicles blocking the way. Commotion ensued, but he failed to see anything unusual.

"What is this?" he asked. "Were the students inside the van?"

"No. The crash was meant as a distraction." Burman rewound the footage and froze on an image. She tapped the other end of the drawbridge, which was shrouded in mist. "Look right there."

Keir had to lean in close to spot a thin break in the fog. A cluster of figures were caught in midleap, dropping into the dark moat below.

"That's them," Burman insisted. "That's how they slipped away."

"But where did they go?"

"We caught them in glimpses, fleeing around the Tower and climbing out again to reach the A100. We're still compiling CCTV feeds to continue to track them. Still, it may take another hour or so."

Keir nodded, though it took all his strength to bend the steel that had hardened in his neck. *Another hour or so?* After all this time, there was no telling how far the others had gotten.

"We can't lose them . . ." he muttered.

"We'll do our best. London is one of the most surveilled cities in the world. But the foggy night will make this challenging."

"Just find them."

He stalked away. Rather than returning to the window, he circled the table to close upon Tissot and his group, three of whom had cell phones pressed to their ears, speaking different languages.

Keir ignored them and confronted the cardinal. "Has there been any further word from your mole? Any hint where the students might have fled to?"

Tissot clutched the large pectoral cross that hung at his chest, as if ready to ward off Keir. "Not as of yet, I'm afraid. They've gone silent, likely fearing discovery after last night. By now, the *Gardiens* must know someone betrayed them. The group will be wary. If I press our contact too hard, it'll risk exposure. And right now, the mole remains our best chance of regaining the book's trail."

"Yet, you still won't tell us *who* that is?"

Cardinal lifted his open palms. "I've sworn an oath of secrecy. Which was necessary to gain their trust. Any approach by another will burn that bridge forever."

Keir had to fight against throttling this faux-pious bastard. Over the years, Keir had gathered intel on Tissot—as he had with many high-ranking members of the *Confrérie*. And no doubt those others had the same on him. It was a form of mutually assured destruction.

In his case, one couldn't build a multi-billion-dollar enterprise without breaking rules. NeuVentis operated a dozen black labs in countries known for lax oversight. He felt no remorse for the many deaths and disabilities that had resulted from the company's illicit human trials. It was a practical necessity if one wanted to beat a drug to market, and his efforts ultimately served the greater good. Like how NeuVentis's latest chemotherapy drug would undoubtedly save countless lives. So what did it matter if a few eggs were broken to achieve this goal? In the end, the net gain would be a positive one—which was the crux of the Brotherhood's new adherence to longtermism, where hard choices made today were judged against the greater good to humanity's future.

Still, even Keir had his limits when it came to breaking rules.

He turned from the cardinal and paced away in disgust. He knew *what* his investigators had turned up on Tissot. The vile photographs. The videotapes. The autopsy results of a young Swiss boy from a mountain parish where Tissot had once served before gaining his crimson robes.

Keir had considered using this material to coerce Tissot into revealing the mole, but he decided against it. He recognized Tissot was correct in one regard:

We dare not spook his mole.

That resource remained the best hope of finding where the book had gone.

Burman called Keir back to her group. With a grim expression, she reported on what she had learned from reviewing all available CCTV footage.

"We tracked the group to the Waterloo station, but we lost them there. With the crush of passengers at that hour, they hid themselves well. And with trains leaving every few minutes, there's no telling where they went."

Keir closed his eyes. "Then how do we find them?"

Burman looked across the room toward Tissot.

Of course . . .

Keir shook his head and bit down a curse.

Still, Burman offered an additional possibility. "After a decade in MI5, I've learned to place my trust in one certainty. It's proven true countless times."

"Which is what?"

She turned to the windows overlooking the city. "No matter how careful . . . someone always makes a mistake."

29

8:38 a.m. CET

Meaux, France

Where are we?

Duncan stretched a kink from his back as he climbed out of the van with the others. He frowned across the winter gardens to the façade of a large French estate. The centuries-old building, flanked by two pointed towers, rose in archways and ornate iron balustrades to a slate-tiled roof frosted with moss.

What is this place?

After hours of driving, they had arrived at the picturesque commune of Meaux. The village clustered around the snaking course of the Marne River. A large cathedral—Saint-Étienne—anchored the town with its fanciful Gothic spire. They continued past it and followed along the green river, which was bordered by buildings both modern and old. Finally, they climbed a hill to this walled and gated estate at the commune's rural edge.

"Welcome to Château de Barbier," Laurent introduced. He hauled out a large hardshell case and led them down the gravel drive toward the château's porch. "The home was built in 1610, though part of the home was set afire during the French Revolution and reconstructed in 1844."

"Why have you brought us here?" Sharyn asked.

"I have deep roots locally, though few know of it, which is one of the reasons I chose this spot."

He hurried them forward. While the château was old, it was certainly well-kept. The expansive gardens were lined by boxed shrubbery and raised bricked flowerbeds. A grove of ancient-looking lime trees surrounded a languid emerald pond that reflected the cloud-scudded sky.

"Did this place once belong to your family?" Tag asked.

Laurent scowled. "No. Never. The château has been with the Barbiers since it was built and remains so today."

Naomi frowned at their guide. "Then what's your connection here?"

"My ancestors were brought to France from Senegal in the mid-seventeenth century. As slaves. We were purchased by the Barbiers, who freed us a century later."

Duncan stared aghast at the man. "That's your connection to this place?"

"After so much time, my people became enmeshed with the Barbier family. While certainly not treated as blood, we were respected and cared for enough. They kept us employed, paid for our education. They did their best, especially for people of that time. In fact, it was my great ancestor, Malick—whom I was named after—who helped put out the fire during the Terror, battling the flames alongside the master of the house, Gerard Barbier, to save the estate."

"And that's reason enough to bring us here?" Archie scoffed.

"As I said, it was only *one* of the reasons."

Duncan scowled, tired of this trickling of information. "Then what's the other?"

"Because Gerard Barbier was the great nephew to Countess d'Adhémar."

Sharyn cast the Frenchman a hard look. "The woman who was entrusted with the book by Saint-Germain himself?"

"The same. It was the Countess who passed the responsibility of guardianship to her great nephew, a distinguished scholar of his times, with a library of great depth and size."

Duncan stared ahead at the stone façade. "Then this home, it's—"

"The home of the Second Keeper," Laurent concurred.

Duncan eyed their guide, beginning to understand the deeper connection here. "Is that how your family first became involved with the *Gardiens*?"

"Indeed. From its very outset. In fact, it was my great ancestor Malick who christened the group with its name."

Ahead of them, the door to the estate opened. Two huge dogs—easily half Duncan's weight—bounded out, bawling at the intruders. Their brown coats were sleek, their muzzles wrinkled and flattened. Some might mistake them for boxers, but from Duncan's years in the fields and marshes, he recognized these mastiff-size creatures to be French hunting dogs, Dogue de Bordeaux.

The pair flew at the group, throwing slather from their curled lips.

Duncan pushed the others back.

Laurent held his ground. "*Tristan et Isolde, calme-toi!*"

The dogs ignored him and ran up, bowling into the man sideways, then circling merrily. Laurent barely kept his feet, holding his case high, but a rare smile broke through at their antics. He patted their flanks in an attempt to sway them to obey but to no avail.

Finally, a young man appeared at the door. "*Triss! Izzy! Retour au porche! Tout de suite!*"

The dogs gave Laurent a final pass, then ran back to the flagstone porch, where they dropped to their haunches, flanking the young man, who lifted an arm in greeting.

"*Salut!*" he called over. "*Entre, s'il te plait.*"

Duncan's French was rusty, but he understood enough to know they were being invited inside. Laurent led them to the porch, clapped the young man on the shoulder, then gave him a one-armed hug, still never relinquishing his hardshell case. The two spoke in French, clearly affectionate and known to one another.

Laurent turned to them. "This is Gabriel Barbier, the current master of the house."

The young man huffed and politely switched to English. "Try telling that to my mother or two older sisters. They'll bite your head off." He stepped aside and motioned toward the door. "Please be welcome."

The dogs took him at his word and crashed headlong through the doorway, bumping against each other to enter first.

Gabriel sighed and shook his head. "Now after you all."

Duncan sized up the master of the house, who looked no more than twenty. Gabriel wore jeans and a flannel shirt under a leather vest. His boots were slightly muddy, smelling of manure, as if he had just come from the fields that surrounded the estate.

Apparently, the Barbier family no longer had slaves for such labors.

As Duncan headed inside, he noted the tight curl to the man's close-cropped hair and a slightly olive complexion, all suggesting a mixed heritage. He glanced to Laurent, wondering if in the past the two families living here had shared more than just an interest in guarding an old book.

Whatever the case, Tag stared a touch too long at the young man, who, no matter his heritage, or maybe because of it, was undeniably handsome, with eyes so blue they looked nearly white. Tag's attention drew a shadow of a smile on the man's lips and a flush to Tag's cheeks.

Even Archie gave Gabriel an appreciative once over, straightening his back as he passed, trying to match the young man's height.

Once they were all inside, the entry hall proved to be warmer and homier than the château's stately façade. A crimson-and-green Turkish rug, well-worn by passing feet, covered a floor of wide-plank French oak. Tapestries draped the plaster walls, which showed aged cracks that looked less like disrepair and more like the wrinkles of an old man's wizened face. A large stone fireplace filled one corner, flickering with a few flames from a glowing bed of embers.

"Mother's in the library," Gabriel informed Laurent. "She should have everything ready. If you'd texted us sooner, we could've been better prepared."

Duncan knew Laurent had waited until only an hour ago to reach ahead to the estate and alert them of their arrival. The man was clearly taking no chances of word getting out. He had even borrowed their burner phone to send the text, fearing someone might be monitoring his own cell, which he had disabled to keep anyone from tracking him.

Gabriel continued across the hall, keeping close to Laurent. "We've not seen you in more than three years. When word came from that unknown number, we questioned if it was truly you. But after you gave such specific instructions, it left little doubt."

"*Je suis désolé,*" he apologized. "I had to be cautious. And you told no one, *est-ce exact?*"

"*Bien sûr.* No one. And we dismissed our cook and maid, as you instructed. It is only us here."

Sharyn overheard all this, too. "I still don't understand. Even as remotely connected as this place is to you, it *is* the home to the Second Keeper. The *Confrérie* might know about this estate, especially if there is a traitor in your group."

Duncan nodded. "Is your plan to hide the book here? Like in the past?"

He pictured the alchemist's diary shifting from Keeper to Keeper, until finally returning to the château, making nearly a complete circle. As he thought of this, he again felt that inkling of fate, of turning wheels, drawing them all to this place.

Still, he was mistaken in one regard.

"No," Laurent said. "The book must move on. It will not stay here any longer than necessary."

"Necessary for what?" Sharyn pressed him.

Laurent turned to their group. "I brought you all here for one *final* reason. Something that can only be done at this location."

"Which is what?" Duncan asked.

The Frenchman's hard gaze fell upon them. "We must open the book—and decrypt the Second Adage."

30

9:23 a.m.

I've had dreams like this . . .

Despite the tension, Sharyn gaped at the breadth of the château's library. It filled two floors, each towering fifteen feet in height. The second story, accessible by a spiral wooden stair, was broken into alcoves filled with more shelves. Higher still, centuries-old frescoes adorned the arched roof.

From the upper level, a massive antique grandfather clock loomed down at them, its mother-of-pearl face shining from a polished walnut case. Below, a small hearth crackled with flames, flanked by two deeply cushioned captain chairs, whose leather looked warmed by age to soft butter.

Sharyn inhaled deeply, trying to draw the space inside her. The air had a musty smokiness to it, tinged with notes of vanilla, the familiar balm of old books. She wanted nothing more than to wander these stacks, select a volume, sink into one of the chairs, and be transported away by the magic of ink on paper.

But that was not why they had come here.

"Be welcome," an older woman greeted them, waving them all deeper inside, to where a walnut library table, stout-legged and circular, stood at the room's center.

She placed down a platter of cheese next to a basket of baguettes, then wiped her hands on a blue toile apron tied over a simple white blouse and khaki slacks. Her dark hair, streaked with gray, was partially hidden under a headscarf of the same toile fabric. She struck Sharyn as a no-nonsense woman, someone who likely raised and killed her own chickens to make *coq au vin*.

Laurent crossed to her and kissed both cheeks. "*Merci, Anna.*"

"*Ça fait trop longtemps, Laurent,*" she scolded, then switched to English. "You should visit us more. Charlotte and Amélie miss you."

"Where are your girls?"

"*Women* now, Laurent. That is how long you've been gone." Anna waved toward the roof. "They are already in the towers, watching the hill with binoculars. None will approach without fair warning. As you instructed."

"*Merci.* We will hopefully not overstay our welcome."

Sharyn frowned at this statement but kept silent.

"I made your other arrangements, too." Anna nodded to the spread on the table, which included tea and a mix of strawberries and grapes and a carafe of white wine. "You did not ask for this, but I will not tarnish the château's reputation with a lack of cordialness."

"You are too kind." Laurent turned to them and urged Sharyn and the others closer. "We should take advantage while we can."

Anna pointed to the wheels of crusted cheese, sliced open to reveal a tender softness. "*Brie de Meaux.* Produced locally. Also, that small pot holds a mushroom spread that's a longstanding family recipe. But be warned, it does contain cognac."

Archie shifted that pot closer to him and sat down. "I'll take my chances."

Sharyn and the others joined him. As she sampled what was offered, she grew to recognize how hungry she was. The same must have been true for the others. They fully partook of the château's *cordialness.*

Finally, though, Laurent drew them back to the task at hand. "We should get to work."

Upon this signal, Gabriel and Anna cleared the table, leaving only the tea service, then left, closing the door behind them. They must have been told to give them privacy for what comes next.

"You truly know how to open the book?" Tag asked.

"I will show you. It is a closely kept secret within the *Gardiens*, but if we wish to make headway, I have no choice."

Sharyn still didn't understand why this was necessary, but she had no intention of discouraging this revelation. Regardless of the terror and bloodshed that had brought them all here, she could not dismiss the raw curiosity that ached through her. Aboard the van, they perused a detailed biography on Saint-Germain that Laurent had printed out, which filled in much more of the alchemist's history—or at least, what was known. She had spent the long drive lost in the man's story, which only whetted her desire to know more.

Laurent leaned down, retrieved his case from the floor, and placed it on the table. "Ms. Karr, if you could pass me Saint-Germain's diary."

"Of course."

She stood and shifted her crossbody bag around. She yanked the waterproof zipper and slipped out the book, still wrapped in the original cloth from when Professor Wright had thrust this responsibility upon her. As she set it on the table, the others gathered close. She drew back the folds of cloth to reveal the book's scarred leather binding, the bands of copper, and the locking box embedded with the crystal orb.

As she did, Laurent dialed in a code on his hardshell case, then snapped it open. He lifted the lid to reveal a built-in computer, with keyboard and screen. Smaller leather boxes were aligned to one side, one of which Laurent took out and placed on the table.

The Frenchman then dropped both palms to either side of the book.

"It took five decades of study to learn how to safely open this, especially after Saint-Germain's warning about its incendiary nature."

Duncan frowned. "You said the alchemist soaked the pages in some flammable oils. Was this ever confirmed?"

"Indeed."

"What sort of compound was it?" Tag asked, clearly intrigued from his biochemistry background.

"We don't truly know," Laurent admitted. "It's a bit of alchemy that still defies us. After opening the book, an archivist took a small sample of a page, no larger than a pea. It was run through spectroscopy, electrophoresis, chromatography, and other methods of study. All that could be determined was that the chemical was somehow inseparably bonded to the very fibers of the page, which made elemental analysis so challenging."

Naomi squinted down at the mystery sitting on the table. "Did you perform any other tests?"

"*Oui*. A few. But we had to be very cautious. The group once tried to x-ray the book, to better understand how it was constructed. When we did, the volume started to heat up. We believe the radiation excited something within its structure, as if this attempt to peer inside without permission risked setting it afire."

Sharyn inwardly cringed, picturing all the jostling and abuse the book had taken to bring it here. They could've inadvertently destroyed it.

Laurent continued. "This brief attempt did offer some insight into the diary's structure. We learned how its binding is run through with fine metallic filaments, a copper amalgam. Again, a strange fusion we don't quite understand, one involving mercury. We've been unable to replicate it in our labs. Still, we're fairly certain the filaments are involved in igniting and destroying the volume. In fact, microscopic fibrils of the same metal run through many of the book's pages."

"*Inside* the paper?" Duncan asked.

"At the molecular level."

Archie frowned. "How could they have done this in the past, with the level of tech at the time?"

Sharyn pictured the astrological symbols—formed of gold and silver—embedded within the crystal orb. She suspected those metals were similarly unique.

Though, I'm fairly certain of one detail concerning them . . .

Laurent continued, addressing Archie's question. "Do not dismiss the technological capabilities of our forefathers. Even today, we continue to debate how the Egyptian pyramids were built. Or how the Mayans developed such a sophisticated calendar. My master's thesis when I pursued my degree in archaeology was on early scientific innovations of ancient peoples. Many examples of which show how knowledge can be discovered, only to be lost again."

"Like with Damascus steel," Naomi noted.

Laurent pointed at her. "Exactly."

Sharyn turned to her friend, who had clearly studied along similar lines in pursuing her own degree.

"Damascus is an exceptionally hard steel," Naomi explained. "It had been produced for more than eleven centuries. Then in one generation, the method of its manufacture was lost."

"And there are many other examples." Laurent ticked them off. "The recipe to make Greek Fire, an incendiary weapon used in ancient times, remains a mystery. We still don't know how to produce the resilient Roman concrete used to build the Colosseum and Pantheon. There is an iron pillar in Delhi that refuses to rust, but we don't know why and attempts to replicate its properties have all failed."

"The Lycurgus Cup," Naomi blurted out, adding to the list herself. "A fourth-century Roman glass vessel made of dichroic glass.

You can see it at the British Museum. It changes color depending on how light strikes it. This feat is caused by silver and gold nanoparticles trapped within the glass."

Duncan looked both bewildered and awed. "Like a form of ancient nanotechnology?"

Naomi nodded. "Even today, the method to manufacture such glass remains unknown."

Laurent hovered a palm over the book. "So while some of this may seem miraculous, it's likely just another example of technology that was lost."

"But it's not magic." Naomi cast her gaze over their group. "Remember the program we're all enrolled in. Women were burned as witches for using herbal healing techniques that defied the science of their time. Magic is just knowledge that remains inexplicable to us today."

Sharyn pictured the placard engraved with the names of four women, forever condemned to be the Devon Witches.

Archie finally relented, waving at the book. "Enough flogging of this horse, let's get on with opening the bloody book."

Laurent nodded and shifted a hand to the small leather box in his hardshell case. Still, he hesitated, as if suddenly wary, maybe second-guessing himself about what he was about to reveal, a secret protected by the *Gardiens* for centuries.

Sharyn saved him the trouble. "You have magnets inside that box, don't you?"

Laurent turned to her, his eyes wide, as if suddenly fearful she might indeed be a witch.

Not a witch. She unflinchingly met his gaze. *Just a librarian with knowledge.*

31

10:34 a.m.

"How . . . how did you know?" Laurent asked, looking stunned.

Sharyn waved in the direction of the van outside. "You shared a detailed brief on Saint-Germain. And I fear some of your bias showed, which helped me make this leap."

"What do you mean?"

"Back at the Tower of London, when Sir Kelly told us about Saint-Germain, he stuck to the factual versus fanciful. As did you. Most of what you gave us pertained to Saint-Germain's scientific pursuits, concentrating along the lines of your own archaeological study, the subject of arcane knowledge lost in the past."

"Still, you made quite the leap to reach an answer that had baffled the *Gardiens* for decades."

Sharyn shrugged. "While you included a long list of scientists, physicists, mathematicians, and doctors whom Saint-Germain had consulted, I skimmed through most of them. I concentrated on the section of Saint-Germain's dossier that pertained to his study of *astronomy*." She pointed to the shining orb. "If there was a clue to the book's key, it had to lie in that pursuit."

Sharyn pictured the tiny astrological symbols trapped within the crystal.

"I see," Laurent said.

"Again, even in this regard, I think you inadvertently showed your hand by including a large volume of information on *one* particular astronomist, someone who was also a well-respected physician of his time."

Duncan leaned closer. He had spent little time reading the supplied pages, drowsing instead, clearly exhausted from their night together. "Who are you talking about?"

"Franz Anton Mesmer," she answered. "A German physician who spent time in Vienna and Paris and gained the attention of Saint-Germain. The two spent considerable time in each other's company, pursuing an unusual angle of study: how the movements of the sun and moon affected the human body. Mesmer believed there were unseen gravitational forces that could shift the energies of a body."

"What he dubbed *animal magnetism,*" Laurent explained. "Later known as *mesmerism.*"

"Sounds more like *astrology,*" Archie scoffed.

"Do not be too dismissive of Mesmer's claims," Laurent warned. "His belief in a flowing process through our bodies that can be influenced by outside energies is similar to qi of traditional Chinese medicine."

"Or like Qigong practices," Tag added, drawing on his knowledge of alternative forms of healing. "Which treats illnesses as blockages in a body's flow."

Sharyn nodded. "It was this pursuit that interested Saint-Germain. There is an account in Laurent's papers from 1774. Saint-Germain attended Mesmer's treatment of a woman. Someone suffering from what sounded like schizophrenia. The doctor gave the patient a slurry containing iron, then attached magnets to specific points on her body and shifted them around. Within hours, her delirium cleared and her symptoms disappeared."

Duncan stared down at the crystal orb. "And that's why you thought *magnetism* might be the key?"

"If Saint-Germain believed the movement of the heavens and

unseen forces was vital to revealing the mysteries of the world, then, knowing his fascination with Mesmer, it was not difficult to assume magnetism might be involved. In fact, I wager there must be iron fused into those gold-and-silver symbols."

"Very astute, Ms. Karr. Clearly, your professor chose well in picking you to be the Thirteenth Keeper."

Laurent opened the small leather box, which contained two dark sticks that had to be magnets. The container appeared lead-lined to keep its energies from affecting the case's computer. He removed the rods and shifted the book closer.

"Even with such insight," the Frenchman attested, "it took some effort to learn how to use the magnets as a key to this crystalline lock. Let me show you what was eventually determined."

He positioned the end of each magnet to the top and bottom of the orb—its north and south poles. The orb shivered in its cradled socket, spun slightly, then aligned itself to the magnetic field.

Sharyn imagined that the constellations inside now mirrored their correct positions in the sky, matching some season or another.

They all leaned closer, but nothing happened.

"Did we break it?" Archie muttered.

"No. We must let time pass. Specifically, the turning of a year."

With great care, Laurent slowly rotated the two dark rods, bringing north to south, then around again, rotating the orb one full turn.

"We believe this represents the journey outward and back again, of venturing forth to grow and returning to share what was learned."

As he completed the circle, an audible click sounded as the energies of the magnet and the alchemy of the orb stirred something deeper inside the copper tin that cradled the crystal. Laurent lifted the tiny box with its orb, parting the two metal bands that had clasped the book closed.

He stared at their group. "Welcome to the true mysteries of Saint Germain."

32

11:04 a.m.

Duncan gathered with the others around the table. Laurent opened the cover and revealed yellowed pages, age-crinkled and slightly splotched in places, as if Saint-Germain's incendiary chemical had pooled in spots.

The title page held a single line of introductory script, written in French with a bit of flourish. Despite having already shared these words, Laurent read them aloud again.

"C'est là que réside le secret de mon immortalité. Viens me trouver si tu l'oses."

Sharyn whispered the translation. "Herein lies the secret to my immortality. Come find me, if you dare."

Laurent turned several pages with great care. They showed dense lines of writing, inscribed in neat rows, demonstrating the precise work of a man of science. Even a casual perusal showed it contained a mix of many languages, mostly European, including Latin, but also sections of cursive Arabic.

Archie, ever the linguist, noted the same, pointing to one such section and raising a concern. "There are no diacritical marks in the Arabic, which normally represent the vowels in their written language. It's like he's making it a more challenging read, forcing you to fill in the blanks. It's also written backward. Normally Arabic is written from right to left. This is running in the opposite direction."

"Which was likely done—along with the jumble of languages—as a means of simple encryption," Laurent explained. "We believe this opening quarter of the book was meant to be a minor challenge, requiring the reader to prove his fluency in many tongues, while adding obstacles, as you've noted."

Sharyn pointed to another passage as he flipped through pages. "That's mirror writing, where he's reversed his cursive. I saw examples of the same in a seventeenth-century text back at the Old Library at Exeter."

"Da Vinci used it, too, in his own journals," Duncan noted.

"Again, another crude form of encryption. And perhaps a nod to Leonardo himself."

As Laurent skipped ahead, Duncan noted the manuscript was also illuminated with beautiful sketches: of people, of animals, both real and fanciful. Sharyn forced Laurent to stop at several, so she could appreciate the vibrant colors and brilliant pigments.

Duncan remembered Sir Kelly's account of the alchemist's skill with drawing and painting, including his introduction of novel oils and dyes.

Naomi finally raised a question that had surely grown in all their minds. "If this opening section was so easy to decipher—nearly a quarter of the book from the looks of it—what does it say?"

Laurent leaned back and cracked his neck after hunching for so long. "All these neatly inscribed and illustrated pages tell the story of the man's life, of his travels. Though, they still leave his origins cloaked. Very frustratingly so, I might add."

"What *did* you learn?" Sharyn asked. "From those illuminated drawings, it appears he traveled to many corners of the globe. There was that African lion, captured in mid-leap. A sketch of Stonehenge. Another nearly architectural model of the Taj Mahal. And a painting of an Egyptian merchant ship." She turned to Naomi for her expertise. "Right?"

"A felucca," Naomi agreed.

"It is indeed an account of his many travels," Laurent agreed. "A true travelogue, if you will. It starts with his youth, in his late teens or early twenties, when he spent a chunk of his life journeying throughout the Arabian Peninsula. From the palaces of shahs to landmarks across the Holy Lands. And, yes, he did spend a year in Africa, where he must have seen that lion. But as he grew older, his travels expanded. He moved on to serve in the court of Catherine the Great in Russia. Then to India, even the Orient, following the Silk Road."

"So he stamped his passport well," Archie noted. "But what did he gain by all of this?"

Laurent turned to him, his expression incredulous, as if the answer were obvious. "Knowledge. That is what he acquired. From a hundred ports. From a thousand roads. From many times that in the people he met. Similar to his time spent in Paris, he consulted with scientists and alchemists of every ilk, at every stop. But more importantly—and I think this is the most critical—he built a network of the same. Savants and scholars from all fields of study."

"Why is this so critical?" Duncan asked.

"Because ultimately the myth of Saint-Germain was larger than *one* man. He represented an enlightened *movement*, one that spread wider in his wake, grew ever larger with time. When he eventually arrived in Paris, he brought that knowledge with him. But he also maintained his connection to this network and leaned on them. There are many accounts where Saint-Germain would disappear for long spells of time."

"You think he went off to commune with this larger organization," Sharyn said.

"I do. Even his warning about the French Revolution, which came a full decade before it broke out, came not from any prophetic foretelling, but from a reading of political and societal trends that he had gained from his network. Many of his contemporaries believed Saint-Germain founded the Freemasons, maybe even the Rosicrucians, but this was more likely born from some sense of the greater network tied to him."

Naomi frowned. "That's all well and good, but what does it have to do with this book on the table?"

Laurent hovered a hand over the splayed pages. "While many in the *Gardiens* will argue otherwise, I think Saint-Germain's opening line to his diary was a nod to this network. It is this *movement*, not the *man*, that is immortal."

Sharyn's eyes grew larger. "And you think that's what he wants us to ultimately uncover. This network of the enlightened."

"To bring them out of the shadows and into the light."

"Does the diary reveal anything else about this mysterious group?" Tag asked.

"Very little. It tells of its start, some of its growth, but not its end."

Duncan frowned. "Why did he stop?"

"I know why." Laurent flipped through to the deeper sections of the book, where the writing became more erratic, the drawings more skeletal and sketchier. Even Duncan could recognize the haste and urgency depicted. "It was fear. Maybe of premature discovery. Maybe sensing the ignoble forces closing upon him."

Laurent stopped at a page that showed the rough sketch of a pointed star, a crude version of the symbol embossed on the cover.

Only here, it featured a skull at the center, as if giving form to Saint-Germain's anxieties.

"This thin section relates to Saint-Germain's construction of this book itself. He likely bound the opening diary section into his new construction or rewrote it inside. Either way, the man's goal abruptly changes afterward, and he starts to lay out his three Adages, his three encrypted messages that could ultimately lead to this hidden group."

Laurent continued through to the title page of the next section, where the Latin words *Adagium Primum*—the First Adage—were crisply inscribed. The writing was also encircled by a ring of animals: monkeys, hippos, giraffes, etc. All the beasts were from Africa. This was further confirmed as Laurent turned more pages, revealing beautifully illuminated maps of the continent, along with illustrations of flora and fauna. Written around and across much of the drawings were lines and patches of the same urgent writing, all in an unknown language—or at least unknown to Duncan.

He glanced to Archie, who merely shrugged, just as mystified.

Sharyn made Laurent slow down. "This is the section that the *Gardiens* eventually decrypted? Leading to a site in Africa—"

"In Libya," Laurent clarified.

"Where you uncovered the cache of Solomonic gold."

"And lost it."

Duncan pictured his grandfather—who had served in that same desert and later moved on to guard Bletchley Park and its team of decoders, which included his grandmother.

And now I'm here, continuing where they left off.

Laurent turned the pages with more haste, as if too angry or ashamed to linger. He finally reached a page inscribed in a similar pattern as the First Adage. Again, the same handsome lettering spelled out words in Latin, *Adagium Secundum.*

Only this spread of pages was adorned by a garden of flowers, painted in hues of blue and purple, with brilliant green leaves. They looked so real one was tempted to pluck them from the paper.

Laurent stopped there and stared at their group. "In the past, the *Gardiens* lost the *first* treasure. We must not lose the *second*. Right now, we find ourselves in the same straits as Saint-Germain when he delivered his book to Countess d'Adhémar, with the same enemy closing in on us."

"And you expect us to decrypt this section?" Duncan challenged him. "Something your group has struggled to do for decades."

"I do."

The doors to the library opened. Gabriel and his mother Anna entered, but they did not bring in lunch. They both cradled shotguns, covering the only exit.

Laurent never took his eyes off their group. "You must . . . if you wish to live."

33

11:39 a.m.

Sharyn grabbed for her pistol, less with any hope of escape and more to grip steel in her hand, to anchor herself. The two huge dogs drew into view, flanking the armed pair.

Anna called over. "Laurent! Amélie radioed from her tower. There's a commotion at the bottom of the hill. It appears to be an accident, but from the flashing lights, the *gendarmes* are coming."

Laurent shoved to his feet, only now seeming to notice the two's arrival. "*Que ferez-vous?*"

"I will take Izzy in the truck and get a closer look. Gabriel will move your van into our garage, then patrol out front with Triss. Charlotte and Amélie have rifles in the towers. I will radio when I know more."

After this clipped report, she swung away, drawing her son with her.

Laurent remained standing, breathing harder.

He was not the only one.

Archie backed a step, his face pale but with a rising flush to it. "Bugger all this! I thought this was a trap."

Sharyn lowered her hand from her Glock. After all that had happened, their group's paranoia had been honed to a razor's edge.

Laurent finally recognized their distress. "I'm sorry. But you have nothing to fear from the Barbiers. They are loyal to a fault.

During World War II, their family fought with the French Resistance, losing many members. They will not betray us."

"But what about that commotion down the hill?" Duncan asked, keeping a hand on his pistol.

"Anna will assess the situation. It is likely nothing, but we must be ready to move if that's not the case." Laurent cast his gaze around their group. "Still, this serves as warning enough. While I've been cautious, I can't discount that the *Confrérie* know about this place. They attacked the Twelfth Keeper's home in Norway. They may know about the handful of others that still exist."

Duncan grimaced. "Which means they could have them *all* watched."

"A possibility, but a slim one," Laurent admitted, clearly trying to downplay the risk.

"Then why bring us to this château?" Sharyn pressed him. "You said earlier that there was something you could do only here. What were you talking about?"

Laurent turned to the table and stepped to his computer case.

"While Saint-Germain's tome may move on from Keeper to Keeper, a seed is always left behind, both as a reward and as a means for the guardians and their heirs to still aid in the study of this treasured volume. Currently that seed is a quantum key, which decrypts access to the mainframe over at the *Gardiens'* headquarters in Paris. It also connects to a series of VPNs linked around the globe to further mask our research. It's why we had to reach this château for any hope of uncovering the secret buried in the pages of the Second Adage—to use its quantum key."

Sharyn slowly sank into her chair. "But considering the danger we're in, why does decrypting it even matter?"

Tag returned to a neighboring seat, trembling, clearly still shaken by the false alarm. "And why do our lives depend on this?"

Laurent sighed, nodding. "Because knowledge is power. And at this point, I cannot trust anyone in the *Gardiens*. I don't know who are—or even the number of—the traitors in our midst. If we can solve the mystery of the Second Adage, we can take the book—and ourselves—to a location unknown to both my people and the enemy. It is the best way to safeguard your lives and the book, while also securing a treasure that must not fall into the wrong hands. Especially if we ever hope to decipher the Third Adage."

"Why is that?" Sharyn asked. While not fully accepting Laurent's explanation, she was intrigued nonetheless.

"Many of us in the *Gardiens* believe the gold lost in Africa held a clue to solving the Second Adage. Losing that knowledge stymied our efforts going forward." Laurent stared at them with pained eyes, likely dwelling on his own grandfather's culpability for that loss. "For this reason, we must not lose this chance to secure the treasure hidden by the Second Adage."

"But what *chance* do we have?" Naomi pressed him. "What makes you think we could solve this mystery—something that has stumped your group for decades?"

"As I mentioned before, we *have* made significant progress over these past decades. We've learned much. Still, there remains a missing key, likely lost with the Solomonic gold. But now—whether due to fate or circumstance—the answer may be within our grasp."

"Why is that?" Duncan asked.

Laurent turned to him. "Because of your work, Mr. Maxwell."

34

11:52 a.m.

Duncan stumbled away. "My work?"

Laurent nodded. "Your graduate thesis at Oxford. After learning *who* had taken possession of the book, I prepared dossiers on all of you. In doing so, I read your research paper. I might have ignored it, but your work built upon methods devised by your grandmother and others at Bletchley Park. All of which was critical in helping Turing build his Bombe machine, an early computer that broke the Nazi communication codes."

"You said those same methods helped you solve the First Adage," Duncan noted.

"They did."

Duncan swallowed down his shock. He had chosen this angle for his research to honor his grandmother's efforts during the war, to demonstrate how one can build on the past, to use its foundation for greater achievements.

"Your paper proposed a unique method of advancing the abilities of Turing's Bombe machine. To use AI machine learning to boost its functioning, to make it a millionfold more powerful. You even referenced how AI methodologies had been used to decipher the Voynich Manuscript."

Tag frowned at Duncan. "What is that?"

"A fifteenth-century text. Crammed with strange drawings and written in an unknown language. Some believe it to be an encoded treatise that holds the secrets to lost knowledge."

Naomi scowled at Saint-Germain's book. "Sounds familiar."

"Or it could've been a total fraud," Duncan admitted. "But that didn't stop cryptologists from using AI to try to decipher it. Applying machine learning to enhance Word Recurrence Intervals, N-Gram relationships, enhanced image processing. Plus, a slew of other methods that I'll skip over."

"Thank god," Archie mumbled.

"And that worked?" Tag asked.

"No, it failed. Like I said, the whole thing might've been a hoax, but the manuscript proved to be a great sounding board to test new AI decryption methods. Several of the most promising I outlined in my thesis."

Sharyn turned to Laurent. "And you think one of these might solve the Second Adage."

"It's worth attempting. I find it perhaps providential that this technique builds upon the methods from Bletchley that solved the First Adage."

"But my paper was mostly theoretical," Duncan warned.

"Still, you offered methods we had not considered. The *Gardiens* had already been working with AI. It's why we have made progress of late. But your techniques offered a unique tweak to it all. I reached out to a cryptologist in our group and had him adjust our methodology, recoding it accordingly. While waiting for your boat to arrive at Le Havre, I received word that he had revised our module and left it buried on our mainframe, accessible only to him and myself."

"You're saying you turned my theory into a practical reality?"

"Hopefully well enough." Laurent drew Duncan toward the computer case, while glancing toward the library door. "With the dogs on our heels, we only have a narrow window to test it. But I'll need your expertise to truly judge if this will work."

Duncan found his heart thumping harder. "Show me."

Laurent nodded, powered up the portable device, and set about connecting to the estate's encrypted VPN network

Sharyn raised a concern. "Will reaching the mainframe expose us?"

"*Non.* Anyone monitoring the headquarters' array will know someone has accessed it with the proper key, but they will not know who or where we are. In fact"—Laurent shifted and removed a pair of small iPads from a pouch in his case and slid them across the table—"you can follow our work on these, or even safely get on the internet."

Naomi grabbed one, which she shared with Archie. Tag took the other, but Sharyn remained focused on the book.

Laurent instructed them on how to link to the estate's network. "With the encrypted VPNs, you'll be insulated from anyone following your digital trail. Still, I suggest you avoid checking email or anything that requires personal passwords."

Duncan ignored most of this, concentrating on the computer. Laurent set about creating a handshake between his device and the *Gardiens'* mainframe.

Finally, after they passed through several layers of firewalls, an eerie phantom of Saint-Germain's diary glowed on the screen, rendered in 3D. Laurent typed a number into a blinking box, and the book opened on its own, cascading through pages to land on the title page to the Second Adage.

Laurent turned to Duncan. "Ready to get to work?"

35

12:18 p.m.

Sharyn initially tried to follow the efforts of Laurent and Duncan, but their arcane language and the flowing algorithmic screens defied her.

Instead, she drew the physical book closer to her. As the two men delved deeper into its digital version on the screen, she moved forward on her own. The next few pages showed views of jagged mountain tops. Their sharp-edged slopes flowed with lines of cryptic text, strange symbols, and bewildering passages.

She flipped between a couple pages, trying to judge if what was drawn was the same peak, sketched at different angles.

She frowned, still unsure.

No wonder this proved to be so challenging.

Laurent had claimed some progress, even saying he knew roughly *where* the Second Adage's treasure might be hidden. As the Frenchman stepped back from the computer to allow Duncan to work, Sharyn pointed at the page and challenged him.

"You said this location might be in the Alps. Why do you think that?"

Laurent turned toward her. "If you look through the rest of this section, you'll see many mountains depicted. We were able to compare this to peaks around the world, but we didn't have to look far. Several of the sketched mountains are perfect matches to those found in the Alps. But which of the peaks—if any of them—might hold the treasure still confounds us."

Sharyn flipped through more pages and saw he was right. She counted at least two dozen mountains scattered through the fifty pages of this section. When she reached the end, a turn of the last page revealed the greater challenge ahead.

The Third Adage.

A cold shudder passed through her.

The title page—inscribed in Latin, like the others—was similarly illuminated, in brilliant whites, ochres, and darker inks. They ominously rendered a large skull and a scatter of bones.

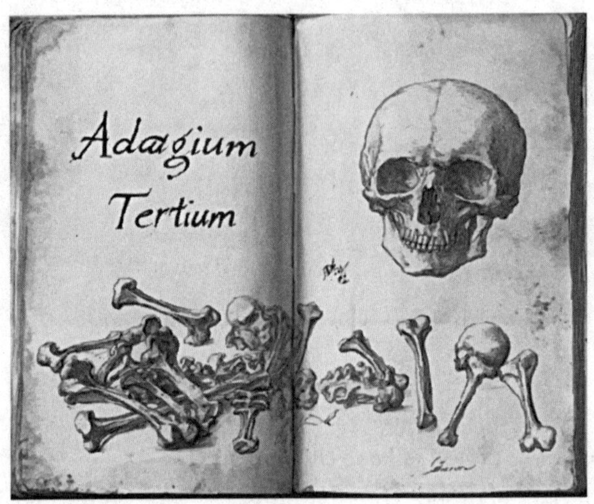

Despite the disturbing imagery, Sharyn could not help but skip ahead. Laurent had said many of the *Gardiens* thought this final Adage might hide the key to immortality, a way to conquer death.

No wonder they believed this . . .

She opened only a few pages to see what else might be depicted in this section. She wished she had shown more caution. The sketches inside looked like something from a macabre anatomical textbook.

They showed gruesome images of bodies stripped of skin, some down to their bones. Many disarticulated or decapitated. Yet, there remained a clinical detachment to the horrors shown within. Again, passages and lines filled the empty spaces, along with arcane symbols that looked like measurements. It all boiled down to an obvious conclusion, an indication of the research being recorded:

Human experimentation.

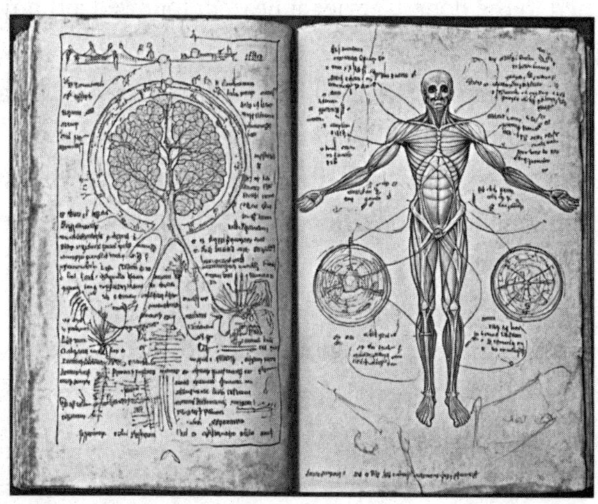

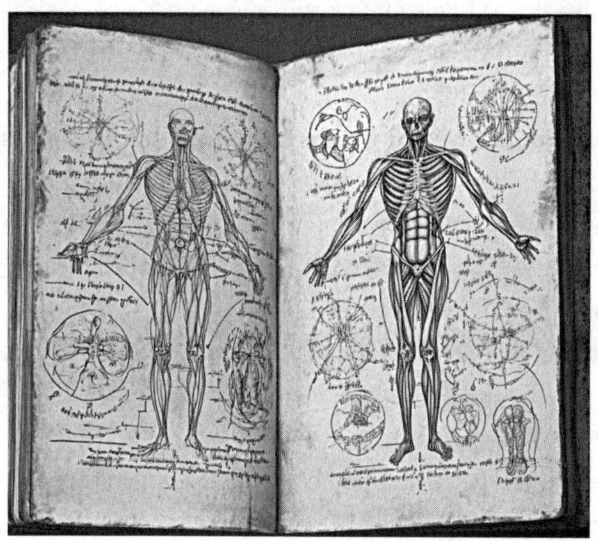

Sharyn shook her head, wondering if this book should be burned. This was a path no one should pursue. She quickly flipped back to earlier in the book, returning to the title page of the Second Adage, leaving the horrors ahead to others.

As she sat back, a rush of footsteps set her heart to pounding.

She turned to the door. Gabriel appeared, followed a moment later by the panting bulk of Tristan.

The young man, breathless, skidded to a stop. "Update from below. From my mother. *Gendarmerie* arrived on scene, but they look to be staying at the crash site, where arguments continue. Still, Mother remains suspicious. She keeps to a nearby field, pretending to hunt rabbits with Izzy."

"*Merci, Gabriel,*" Laurent said.

"But I know Mother. Without saying so, she implies you'd best not tarry here much longer."

"Understood," Laurent noted.

Gabriel gave a nod, turned, and set off to return to his patrol.

Laurent frowned. "We should heed Anna's good senses. If we can't solve this riddle soon, we will move on."

"To where?" Sharyn asked. "The more we move, the more likely we'll be discovered."

Naomi groaned, as if fearing the same, but her attention was focused on her small iPad. Archie looked equally ill as he peered down at the tiny screen.

"What is it?" Sharyn asked, waving for Duncan to keep working after he looked on with concern.

"I got on TikTok," Naomi said. "I didn't log in to my account, but I ghosted onto my site."

Her WitchTok page . . .

"I wanted to get a feel for the general temperature. Of how the public is taking the deaths in Exeter and the accusations against us."

"It's not going well," Archie muttered.

"Even my followers have turned against me. And why would they not? When one of their own is accused of a ritualistic murder. Only a few came to my defense, declaring it a false accusation, a digital burning of a witch."

Archie looked up from the screen. "There are also memorial

messages on the site for Professor Wright. With links to the latest news out of Exeter."

"What are they saying?" Tag asked.

"Though the professor's body was badly burned, the coroner has confirmed his identity from medical records."

Sharyn closed her eyes and took a deep breath. Anger at the man still burned inside her, but he did not deserve such an end.

"The police have stepped up their efforts to look for us," Naomi added. "Expanding to include Europol and intelligence agencies across the Continent."

"Then we must work quickly," Laurent said. "If we are forced to leave, I have new ID papers for the lot of you."

Sharyn felt little relief at this.

"I may have something," Duncan blurted out, glancing to Laurent, then back to the computer. "While you succeeded in decrypting the large section at the beginning of the Adage, I think it's wrong to apply the same methodology to the rest. I believe the encryption of the mountain's location is entirely *different* from the rest. So, I'm going to erase the prior dataset for the next pass, then apply MDA—Multiple Discriminant Analysis—and start fresh."

Laurent pushed him closer to the computer. "Don't explain. Just do it."

As they worked, Sharyn found herself bothered by what Duncan had just said. She eyed Laurent, who stood with his arms crossed, casting frequent glances toward the library door.

Sharyn raised a hand to draw the Frenchman's attention. "Duncan said you had already decrypted a chunk of the writing, and that it had nothing to do with the location of the hidden site. If so, then *what* was deciphered in that first section?"

Laurent looked at her, his expression hardening, clearly reluctant to divulge this information. It must be something kept tightly guarded.

"I think we're well beyond secrets now," Sharyn stressed. "What did you learn?"

He unfolded his arms, giving in. "It is something we do not want the *Confrérie* to know. Not after having the Solomonic gold stolen from us. Though, with a traitor amongst us, such guardedness might be moot."

"What are you holding back?"

He sighed. "The passage we deciphered. It revealed *what* is hidden out in those mountains, what the Second Adage was meant to protect."

Sharyn stared aghast at him. "You know what the treasure is?"

36

1:07 p.m.

Shock shoved Sharyn to her feet. "All this time, you've known what's out there?"

"For less than a year," Laurent amended. "We had to protect the secret. It's a treasure that could shake the Western world."

Naomi stood up, challenging him, too. "What is it?"

"Similar to the cache of gold coins from the First Adage, the second treasure is tied to King Solomon. They are artifacts of immense value—not just in monetary worth, but also of great archaeological, historical, and religious significance."

"What the bloody hell are you talking about?" Archie pressed the man.

Laurent stared around the room. "Are you familiar with the story of Jerusalem's Second Temple, the most holy site of the Jewish people?"

Sharyn knew some of its history, but Naomi was far better versed from her own studies. Her friend's eyes narrowed, as if she already suspected where this was leading.

"The temple was destroyed in AD 70." Naomi picked up her iPad and tapped at its screen. "By the Roman general Titus who ransacked the temple, then his soldiers set it on fire. But not before his army stole many of the temple's most sacred relics and hauled them to Italy."

"What did they take?" Tag asked.

"Everything they could get their grubby hands on." Naomi slid her iPad to the center of the table for all to see. "But *this* was the most significant artifact, something of inestimable value. An object as revered and important as the Ark of the Covenant."

Sharyn leaned over to view the image on the iPad. It was a carving in stone, etched deeply and scarred by age, of a group of men holding aloft a large menorah.

Naomi continued. "The bas relief depicts the raid, memorialized in the Arch of Titus, which can still be seen in Rome. It shows the parade of the temple's golden menorah—the most holy relic of Judaism—across the city."

"What became of it?" Tag asked, wheezing a bit and taking a blast from his inhaler.

Naomi glared accusingly at Laurent. "It vanished into history. Around AD 410, or maybe AD 455. Following the sacking of Rome by the Visigoths, then the Vandals. Some believe the invaders melted it down or lost it at sea. Others say it was tossed into the Tiber River to protect it from those raiders. Then there are those who claim it's still somewhere in the Vatican."

Sharyn turned to Laurent. "Is that what's hidden in the Alps, the *true* location of the menorah?"

Laurent remained silent for a breath. "That would be enough, of course. But what lies out there is far greater. It ties directly to what was described in the Biblical Book of Kings. In fact, Saint-Germain quotes from that text, where King Solomon ordered the sculpting of not just *one* golden menorah, but many. Ten or eleven in total."

Sharyn felt a chill pass through her.

Laurent gave their group a stern look. "Saint-Germain claims *seven* of the original Solomonic menorahs are hidden out there, including the most sacred of them all. There are also golden incense burners and trumpets. Along with a monumental gold stand, the original Table of Showbread from the Holy Temple."

Sharyn took a deep breath at this revelation, beginning to understand Laurent's haste to secure such a find.

It's beyond priceless.

Still, Laurent hung a price tag on it. "From the dimensions and measurements recorded in the Bible, the *Gardiens* estimate the value in gold alone to be upwards of three hundred million."

Silence settled over the room, weighted down by this revelation.

Duncan finally broke the stillness with a gasp. He had never stopped working through all of this. Only now, he stumbled away from the computer and raised his hands. "I . . . I don't know what I just did."

Sharyn shifted closer, as did the others. Only Tag remained seated, clearly having reached his limit.

"What is it?" Laurent pressed Duncan.

He pointed at the computer. "Look! It's just started doing this, like the AI program took over on its own."

On the screen, Saint-Germain's book lay splayed open, rotating gently in place. Like smoke rising from a fire, a cloud of grayscale pixelation formed above the pages. As they watched, the haze distilled down and formed a three-dimensional image of a pyramidal peak, which slowly spun with the book.

Duncan turned to Laurent. "Could this be the answer?"

Along one flank of the mountain, a small blip blinked steadily from the shadowy outline, appearing and disappearing as the image revolved.

"Possibly . . ." Laurent murmured, his voice tremulous, then firming up with conviction. "It must be it."

Sharyn peered closer. "You said you had already identified all the peaks sketched by Saint-Germain. Do you know which one this is?"

"I should . . . I do."

He reached to the table and picked up Naomi's iPad. He pecked vigorously at it, mumbling under his breath. Finally, he nodded and showed them a topographical map of northern Italy, where it bordered Austria. A red triangle marked a location in a deeply mountainous terrain.

"It's Monte Antelao. The highest peak in the eastern Dolomites—which is what the Alps are called in this region of Italy. In fact, this mountain has been dubbed the King of the Dolomites."

Duncan looked at the spinning image on the screen with a mix of fear and doubt. "But can we be *sure* this is the right place? Could such a massive treasure be hidden there?"

Archie offered a bit of confirmation. "When my father served in the British embassy in Rome, we spent time up at Lake Como. I did some biking into the Dolomites. Those mountains are riddled with caves and hundreds of old World War II bunkers. If you wanted to hide something, it's not a bad spot."

Duncan rubbed his chin, still plainly unsure.

A firmer conviction came from an unlikely source.

"I can't say this is the exact mountain," Tag noted, "but the location is certainly somewhere in the Dolomites. So, Duncan's decryption is most likely accurate."

Sharyn turned to Tag. "Why do you say that?"

Her friend shifted his iPad and placed it under the Saint Germain book, which was still open to the title page for the Second Adage. On the iPad's screen, he had pulled up a photo of a clutch of bright blue flowers with emerald leaves.

Tag motioned between the book and the iPad. "As you can see, this is the plant that Saint-Germain sketched at the start of the section. I thought I had recognized it. *Campanula morettiana.* Also known as Moretti's bellflower. It only grows in the limestone cliffs of the Dolomite mountains."

She stared closer. *He's right* . . . The unusual base of the flower, the number of petals, the shape of the leaves—they all matched what Saint-Germain had drawn.

Naomi frowned at Tag. "How did you even recognize it?"

Tag shrugged. "From my studies. In medieval times, this plant was used as a cure for tuberculosis."

Sharyn breathed harder, recognizing how each of them had contributed to this discovery: her delivery of the book, Duncan's AI modification, Naomi's archaeological knowledge of the treasure, Archie's past in the region, and now Tag's herbology expertise.

She sensed the coming together of the threads of fate, which cemented her own conviction. "This *must* be the right location."

"Even so," Duncan said, "what do we do with this information?"

The answer came from outside the library. Gabriel rushed across the entry hall and burst into the room. "The *gendarmes* are coming up the hill, lights flashing. Others are racing from the city proper. Mother follows behind the first, but—"

A thumping roar cut off his words, sweeping over the château.

"A helicopter," Archie warned, ducking from the threatening noise.

Worse, a ringing klaxon burst from the computer. On its screen, the mountain vanished away, replaced with an angry red box, flashing with words in French.

Laurent rushed to the keyboard and typed rapidly. "Someone's hacking us. From *inside* our headquarters."

Gabriel waved. "We must go. Now!"

"Not until I scrub our work," Laurent gasped out. "Before they gain access."

Sharyn snatched Saint-Germain's book, closed it, and fumbled to lock its straps. Naomi slid over and helped.

Laurent tapped a few last instructions, then hit a button alongside the computer. A loud snap jolted the case. Smoke billowed out a moment later, accompanied by the smell of frying electronics.

Laurent grabbed a few items from his case, along with the tiny leather box holding the magnets. "Go!"

"This way!" Gabriel urged them.

37

2:10 p.m.

Struggling to tuck away the book, Sharyn followed at Gabriel's heels. Rather than leading them to the library door, he rushed toward the room's fireplace, to an alcove in the shelving next to it, full of dusty leather volumes.

As he shoved into the narrow space, a blare of sirens drew her attention toward the front of the estate. A moment later, a horn burst out in furious honks. Then Anna's voice called out sharply, scolding in French, clearly angry. Dogs began barking—Tristan and Isolde—sounding as irate as their mistress.

Gabriel used this distraction to reach to a shelved relic—a small, tarnished oil lamp, like out of the story of Aladdin. Unlike that tale, no magic words were needed. Gabriel tilted the lamp, and a back section of shelving snapped open, swinging on a hidden hinge.

"Inside," he ordered their group, pushing the opening wider.

They piled through, one after the other due to the narrowness. Sharyn entered behind Duncan, who kept looking backward. A muffled rifle blast made her flinch. It sounded like it came from one of the towers. A single round, likely a warning shot to discourage trespassing.

"Keep going!" Gabriel crowded after Naomi and closed the door behind him.

Past the threshold, a short landing led to steep stairs heading downward. The path was lit by a series of caged bulbs wired across the roof. The walls appeared to be raw limestone, chiseled roughly.

"Wh . . . Where does this go?" Tag coughed out from ahead, struggling with the steepness, aided by Archie.

"Our family and allies used this hiding place during the Resistance," Gabriel called forward, forcing them all onward.

They hurried down the steps. Laurent, who led them, finally reached a stout steel door, barricaded tightly on this side. He yanked the bar, flipping it aside, and opened the way.

Sharyn noted there was no hesitation on his part.

He knew about this exit.

She understood now why he had felt so confident about coming to the château. Angered by his silence, she shoved past him. Beyond the door, a cavernous space opened. Its dimensions were hard to discern due to the scarcity of lighting. Only a few lamps hung from the stone roof.

Still, it was clear this was no natural cavern, but a quarried space. The walls were too straight, the ceiling flat. Yet, like all true caves, the place was dank and humid. Only here, the air reeked strangely of manure.

Horse dung . . .

Earlier, she had noted a similar ripeness from the dried mud on Gabriel's boots. He must have been down here before they arrived, preparing for this contingency.

The source of the smell was evident. The few lamps illuminated wide, raised trays full of manure and hay. Pale growths grew thickly over the surface. Farther on, she spotted plastic-wrapped bales that sprouted thick white fronds from their sides.

"Mushrooms," Duncan mumbled.

Gabriel explained. "Part of the family business. It was from these old quarries that limestone was mined for the hundreds of châteaus in the region. Abandoned and nearly forgotten, they proved the perfect place for growing mushrooms."

As he hurried through the labyrinth of interconnecting caves, he extoled on their inventory. "While other regions are famous for *champagne*, we are known for our *champignon*. Or mushrooms. In these *meules*," he waved to the wide trays, "we grow oysters and our legendary buttons. The bales all around are beds for shiitakes."

He spoke in a rush, fear making him ramble, which was clear from his frequent glances back. He must hate leaving his family behind, but like all Barbiers, he knew his duty and the risks involved.

Naomi searched around. "Is the plan to hide down there?"

"The locals certainly did that during the Napoleonic Wars," Gabriel said. "But no, I've made other arrangements."

"We're leaving again?" Tag asked, his face pale.

"We can't stay," Laurent explained. "Many know of this place. Both for its refuge in the past and its farming use today. Authorities will eventually think to search down here. None of us can be found."

Sharyn understood why, and it no longer centered on murder charges. "We know where the Second Adage points."

Lawrence nodded. "If captured, they'll force it out of you."

"What about the Barbiers?" Duncan glanced to Gabriel. "While his family doesn't know what we learned, we've put them in danger."

Gabriel shrugged. "With you all gone, we can claim ignorance. Laurent had already rented your van under our name. And my mother and sister's defense of the château would be taken as nothing more than protecting our land. We rural French folk are a notoriously irascible lot, easily provoked to overreact. Plus, our family is well-respected in the area."

After hiking another few minutes, they reached a cavern that held farm vehicles and equipment. A hangar-like steel door towered on the far side.

Gabriel led them to an old truck whose wide bed was stacked with hay bales. Likely the supply was meant for the dark garden inside here, but as Gabriel led them to the rear, it was clear that was not its purpose now. The stacked hay held a hollow pocket inside, clearly meant to hide them.

"We learned many tricks during the Resistance," Gabriel offered and waved for them to climb inside. "You'll find a *périscope* at the back. To allow you to peek out as we travel. I'll get you to the train station a few villages over. From there, I must wish you all well."

Despite his brave words, the strain in his voice spoke to his anxiety to rejoin his family. To avoid delaying him any longer, they all clambered up and ducked into the cavity, which smelled of an earthy grassiness.

Tag kept his inhaler in hand, staring at the confinement with concern. None of them looked any less worried. Especially as Gabriel and Laurent lifted the final bale from the stone floor and filled in the remaining gap, trapping them inside. Plainly, Laurent intended to travel in the truck's cab.

The reason became clear as the man pressed their host. "You have my rifle?"

"Up front," Gabriel assured him.

Moments later, the trundling rumble of the hangar door reached them, followed by the roar of a diesel engine. With a jolting shake, the truck headed out. The only sign that they had exited the cavern was a slight increase in the meager light seeping between the hay bales.

Sharyn stared around at their shadowy shapes, all huddled together.

"I think we made it," Tag whispered.

Archie cursed him. "Bollocks, mate, never say—"

The thumping of a helicopter cut him off, growing louder, closing on their location. It was impossible to say whether the truck had been spotted or the aircraft had made a poorly timed pass in their direction.

Sharyn reached up and pawed around her shoulders. Her hands struck something other than hay. She grabbed the end of the periscope that Gabriel had mentioned. She twisted to get her eyes to its goggled end. At first, there was only darkness, but her thumb found a lever and pushed it to the side.

A blinding light flared through the lenses.

She squinted against it and spied a bumpy view of woods to either side of a gravel road. The truck sped up as those in the cab recognized the threat, too.

Sharyn fought the scope to search the skies. Beyond the shoulder of the hill where the château sat, a black helicopter swept into view. Its flight momentarily bobbled, likely catching sight of the retreating truck. It angled for a closer inspection.

"They spotted us," Sharyn warned.

Her words were meant for those trapped in the hay, but another still responded.

The crack of a rifle exploded from the cab. She pictured Laurent leaning out the window with his weapon. From the accuracy of his shot, the rifle must have been fitted with a sniper's scope. The helicopter's tail rotor shattered, sending the bird into a hard spin. It twirled in midair, then plummeted precipitously toward the forest. Leaves and branches exploded around it as it struck.

She held her breath, but no fiery explosion followed. She prayed those aboard had survived, as they were likely only local forces. She also hoped the pilot had not radioed ahead about the fleeing vehicle.

Their truck reached a main road, bumping from gravel to pavement, then picked up speed. They rode in a tense silence, having to trust that Gabriel knew the backroads well enough to make their escape.

After another fifteen minutes, Sharyn allowed herself to breathe more fully.

"Don't say it," Archie warned Tag this time.

Though their shapes remained shadowy, Sharyn recognized Duncan as he put his arm around her and drew her closer.

"What now?" Naomi asked.

No one answered.

Not even Archie offered a quip.

Sharyn leaned into Duncan's embrace. She knew they must head into the Alps. Laurent had given them little other choice, especially with the knowledge they now possessed. She felt trapped and wondered if Laurent had done this purposefully, forcing their cooperation, especially as another question troubled her:

How did the Brotherhood know where we were?

She found it odd that the enemy had crashed upon them shortly after they had deciphered the Second Adage. It was as if their adversaries had been waiting for this threshold to be passed before attacking.

She pictured Laurent, who continued to hold too many secrets. Like the backdoor out of the château. Could he have co-opted their group for his own ends or in service to the *Confrérie*?

And maybe not just him.

She stared across to Naomi, Tag, and Archie. All three had had hold of an iPad at one time or another. Even Duncan had ample time at the computer.

She took a deep breath and let it out slowly, accepting a hard truth, something ingrained into her by now. Going forward, she intended to adhere to it.

Trust no one.

FIFTH

38

November 3, 8:02 a.m. CET

San Vito di Cadore, Italy

Sharyn soaked in the hot shower, trying to warm the knots from her body after the long trip. It had taken more than fifteen hours to travel from Reims, France—where Gabriel had dropped them off—to this sleepy Alpine village.

To reach here, they had ridden a series of trains. The journey could have been shortened by adding an airplane leg, but Laurent had worried how well their new French identity cards would stand up to close inspection. The forgeries had certainly worked well enough aboard the trains, where scrutiny had been minimal. They had safely made it across four borders to reach Italy. Laurent had assured them the plastic cards would allow them to travel anywhere within the EU without the need for passports.

Still, Sharyn had appreciated the slower means of travel. The longest leg had taken them through the Swiss and German Alps at night, allowing them to finally get some real rest, with the six of them spread across three sleeper cars. Sharyn had shared her space with Naomi, which had disappointed Duncan. But she had been too tired to assuage his crestfallen look.

While she wanted nothing more than to find refuge in his arms, she could not shake a deep-seated unease, a mistrust that she could not dismiss as mere paranoia. Men in her past—those she met online or was set up with by friends—had always started out kind, funny, even gallant, only to later prove themselves to be on a spectrum from dishonest to treacherous.

Including my father.

Then again, she knew she likely colored any suitors in her father's light. Over the years, she had found herself eventually looking for ways to kick men to the curb, guarding her heart, not willing to trust a relationship as anything more than casual.

Am I doing the same now with Duncan?

This question had plagued her on the trip through the Alps. Sprawled on the top bunk, she had stared out the train window at the passing moonlit peaks, their tops dusted with snow. The mountains had looked romantically picturesque. Something out of a storybook. But at the same time, there was a cold inhospitality to them, a dark beauty that could not be fully trusted. Still, after an hour, the train barreled into an unseasonably strong snowstorm, which erased the view and finally allowed her to fall asleep.

Standing in the shower now, she closed her eyes and luxuriated in the steam. She tried to draw in the heat, knowing it might be a long time before she felt this warm again. Two hours ago, their group had arrived in the mountain village of San Vito di Cadore. Laurent had rented rooms in a small chalet at the edge of a pine forest, backdropped by the sheer massif of the neighboring Dolomites. Their goal—Monte Antelao—towered a few miles to the east.

To prepare for the trek, Laurent had left the hotel with a wad of Euros. He had gone to purchase gear for them: winter clothing, hiking poles, flashlights, ropes. He had also planned to search for a mountain guide, someone familiar with the Dolomites, especially its more desolate, inhospitable regions.

A knock on the door forced Sharyn from the shower.

"The boys are already down at the buffet." Naomi popped her head inside. "If we want them to leave us anything, we'd better get down there."

"Okay. I'll be right out."

Now warmed all over, she recognized how hungry she was, something that surprised her. It seemed a body's demands superseded the tensions and terrors. Plus, there was no telling when she might get another hot meal.

She quickly dried off and dressed. As she pulled on her sweater, her nose caught the grassy hint of hay, reminding her of their escape from the Barbier estate. She hoped Gabriel had gotten back to the château safely and that the repercussions for his family would not be too severe. Despite his earlier assurances, a downed helicopter would be difficult to brush away. Still, Gabriel had said he trusted the loyalty of the locals to his family and, if questioned, planned to blame the crash on a mechanical failure, not on a sniper's well-placed shot.

No matter the outcome in France, Sharyn had greater worries of her own. As she followed Naomi down the hotel stairs, she stared past a row of windows. In the distance, sheer gray cliffs towered above a dense pine forest. Higher still, a line of snowy peaks cut a jagged line across the blue sky. The thought of journeying into those mountains tightened her chest.

How can we hope to find anything out there, something hidden for untold centuries, maybe millennia?

Laughter—an impossible noise to her ears—drew her attention to the trio seated at a table, only steps from the spread of a morning buffet. Archie chatted up a server, a buxom, dark-haired young woman. His Italian sounded flawless, accompanied by an authentic accent.

Duncan noted Sharyn and Naomi's arrival. He lifted an arm. "About time!" he said with a grin. He looked freshly scrubbed, his hair still damp. "I got a pot of coffee for the table. And ordered you both cappuccinos. But you'd better grab what you can. They close the buffet in fifteen minutes."

Tag turned to them. "And Laurent called. He's on his way back."

Sharyn crossed and picked up a plate. The spread of cured meats, breads, and jams drew her, especially a selection of pastries, which ran the gamut from delicate eclairs and Swiss cream puffs to the more familiar jelly-filled doughnuts. She centered two of the latter on her plate—an indulgent reminder of home—and surrounded the pair with scrambled eggs and thick-slabbed bacon.

She and Naomi joined the men as the server returned with the promised cappuccinos.

Archie nodded to the cups, whose froth had been inscribed with designs of a pine tree. "Only the Italians know how to make a proper coffee."

After a sip, Sharyn could not argue against this. As she settled into her breakfast, Archie and Duncan left to refill their plates.

Tag looked out the windows at the sleepy little resort town. "The ski season doesn't start here for another month, but the waitress said, after last night's heavy storm, the resorts might open early. If so, this place will soon be bustling."

She nodded, remembering the small blizzard that had swallowed the train. The same storm had dumped several feet of snow over the top of the Dolomites and left a dusting at this elevation.

"Another storm is forecast for tonight," Tag warned. "Which means you'll all need to get up there before it strikes."

Sharyn searched the blue skies but saw no evidence of this threat. Still, mountain weather was notoriously unpredictable. She also noted the worried cast to Tag's eyes, along with the hard set to his lips, which had a bluish tinge to them.

Tag would not join them on the trek into the mountains. Already the elevation here challenged her friend's breathing. The steep climb into the highlands would certainly prove too daunting, even dangerous, for him. More worrisome, he had run out of his supply of Zanaflex, a strong muscle relaxant needed to counteract the crippling spasms from his palsy.

All of this frustrated him. He clearly hated to be left behind.

But what bothered him most was that Naomi had been consigned to stay with him. It mortified him that he required babysitting, especially as it would keep Naomi from participating in the possible archaeological discovery of the ages.

Still, the two left behind were vital to the efforts ahead.

Laurent had assigned them to be a point of contact if the group should run into trouble in the mountains—or if they discovered anything up there. The best way to protect an archaeological site of this magnitude was to shine a large light on it as quickly as possible. To alert local authorities, the media, even the military. They needed to employ any and all means to keep the *Confrérie* from being able to whisk this golden fortune off when no one was looking.

It was a treasure that belonged to the world.

Such a discovery also potentially served another purpose, one more personal.

Tag raised this possibility, lowering his voice to a whisper. "Do you truly think finding those relics will help clear our names?"

"It had better," Naomi said bitterly, still angry at being pushed aside.

Her words made Tag wince, clearly wounding him.

Sharyn frowned, knowing how much hinged on this discovery. "It'll be easier to prove we've been framed if the reason behind it is a fortune worth hundreds of millions versus a single old book of questionable value."

The boys returned with full plates.

Duncan dropped heavily into his seat. "First, though, we have to find out if I was right about the location. Otherwise, none of this will matter."

Naomi shrugged. "At least no one will think to look for us way out here."

"Maybe," Sharyn said, unconvinced, too suspicious to think any differently.

Duncan agreed. "We still don't know if whoever hacked into the

Gardiens' mainframe was successful. They might have breached it before Laurent could destroy our work."

Sharyn pictured the smoking computer at the Barbiers' library. "And Laurent can't reach out to his group to find out, not with an unknown number of traitors in their midst."

"So, we're on our own again," Tag said.

Archie shrugged. "Not much we can do about it. If the hack failed, then Naomi's right—we've shaken the enemy for now. If the bastards successfully broke through, then it leaves us no other choice."

Sharyn turned to the windows. "We must get there first."

A gush of frigid air from the chalet lobby drew her attention. Laurent entered, hauling two large shopping bags, along with a heavy backpack slung over his shoulders. He searched, breathing hard, then spotted them.

He crossed in stiff steps to the table. "We must go. Now."

Duncan stood, abandoning his plate. "Why?"

"Weather's turning quickly. We must duck the storm if we hope to reach the site. If it gets buried in snow, any search may have to wait until spring."

"There's no way we can keep this secret for that long," Sharyn noted.

"No, we can't. It's now or never."

From the worry in his eyes, Sharyn knew what he had left unsaid:

Especially if the enemy knows about this place.

39

9:06 a.m. CET
Airborne over Switzerland

Keir sat next to Saanvi Burman aboard the Citation XLS as the jet raced over the Swiss Alps. They both leaned beside a laptop that rested on a polished African wenge table, one of the many luxuries customized into his private plane. The cabin had cashmere carpets and had been appointed with saddle-soft leather, all stitched with the NeuVentis logo.

Behind him, the seven cabin seats were all occupied. Two by Cardinal Tissot and one of his associates. The remaining spaces were packed with the leader of a mercenary force and four of his crew. The group served both as Keir's personal security team and, when needed, to stamp out problems at the corporation's black sites. The men had also participated in the raid on the Twelfth Keeper's estate in Norway.

Another jet trailed behind this one, carrying an additional dozen soldiers, bringing the total number of his armed force to seventeen. After the prior failures, Keir had decided to take matters into his own hands, trusting no one else at this critical juncture.

Especially now.

He studied the image on the laptop.

Could the others have truly uncovered the location of the Second Adage's treasure?

The screen showed the outline of a dark mountain hovering over open pages. The data had come from a hack of the *Gardiens'* systems, orchestrated by Tissot's mole.

Still, such a boon was not solely the triumph of the cardinal.

Keir glanced to Burman. Her words yesterday had proved providential:

Someone always makes a mistake.

In this case, after the students fled the Tower of London, the mole had reached out and warned them to spy on several locations—the estates and homes of the *Gardiens'* former Keepers. Unfortunately, this warning came late. Confounding matters further, there were eight different sites spread across six countries and two continents. Even when Burman concentrated operations on the five closest to London, their people had been spread thin, especially as most of the spots were remote. It had required Burman to co-opt local forces and lean on Europol. Even then, they had to be cautious, so as not to expose themselves.

In the end, a location in Meaux had raised a red flag—marking the first mistake by the others as they needlessly exposed themselves by going to a known *Gardiens* location. The local gendarmes had spotted a large black van entering one of the compounds. Still, no one could be certain it was their targets. Afraid to prematurely show their hand if this proved to be wrong, they had kept a watch on the place, both on the ground and by satellite, looking for verification.

Then another call had come from the mole. They had been informed that someone had reached out shortly after the van had arrived and was operating a deeply encrypted program on the *Gardiens'* mainframe. Their contact could not say if this was coincidental or significant, especially due to the scrambled VPN network hiding the source. Still, the mole had warned the cardinal to hold off on raiding the estate until a hack could be attempted, to hopefully secure the data. The belief was that their targets were attempting to decipher a section of Saint-Germain's book.

Keir had grudgingly agreed, adhering to a philosophy that had served him well in the past—as it had with the *Confrérie* during World War II:

Let others do the heavy lifting, then sweep in and steal the prize.

After making this decision, Keir had paced away those long ninety minutes, flipflopping back and forth on whether or not to drop the hammer anyway.

In the end, his patience was rewarded.

A text had been dispatched to Tissot. His contact had found a weakness, a hole to breach the encryption. The mole ordered the raid on the château to commence, to put pressure on their targets while he forced his way inside digitally.

The result ended up being a mixed bag, mostly due to the threadbare forces at their disposal, all of whom had been local and likely had a degree of loyalty to the family at the château. Once again, their targets had escaped. Only this time, they had left behind a large breadcrumb—a mountain-size one.

Before the hack could be stopped, Tissot's mole had successively broken through the encryption and discovered an effort to decode the Second Adage. Unfortunately, the abrupt interruption had wiped away vast amounts of data and corrupted the rest. It had taken the mole half a day to recover and compile enough to present the *Confrérie* with this prize.

Still, the delay had allowed their targets to get a jump on Keir's team.

But hopefully not enough of one.

Burman lowered her phone. "I've alerted Italian authorities. Forwarding photos and names. But that area of the Dolomites has dozens of villages and towns, not to mention small farms that serve as Airbnbs."

"And you told them to concentrate around Monte Antelao?"

She scowled at him for questioning her skills. "Don't worry about the Italians. We have our own *search* to worry about."

"True . . ."

He frowned at the mountain on the screen, a dark mystery that still challenged them—and he prayed the same was true for the others. While this peak had been identified, the fractured data failed to pinpoint *where* on this mountain the Second Adage's treasure might be located. Even worse, his mole had expressed fear that this information—the true site—had been successfully ascertained by the others.

If so, it meant the *Confrérie* still needed to find the missing students. His team had to either force the location out of them or eliminate them and begin a search on their own. The latter would be a daunting task. Monte Antelao—the King of the Dolomites—towered higher than ten thousand feet, with slopes encompassing hundreds of square miles, most of it challenging terrain.

Keir exhaled heavily. "We must find those students—along with whoever is helping them."

Burman looked over her shoulder. "Between the local police and your small army, even a mountain as large as Antelao will offer our targets little refuge."

"Yet, they escaped us before."

"With the aid of the *Gardiens*," she reminded him. "A resource that is no longer available to them. At the moment, they are cut off and alone."

"If so, it also means Tissot's mole will be of no use to us."

Burman shrugged. "One never knows, so it's best you brought the cardinal along."

"I still don't trust the bastard."

"You don't need to. Instead, put your trust in what has proven true already."

"What's that?"

"The others made one mistake." She turned to him. "They'll do so again."

40

10:10 a.m.
San Vito di Cadore, Italy

Duncan climbed the steep path toward a timbered cabin buried at the edge of a pine forest. The home's wood shingles carried a heavy growth of moss, as if the place had grown out of the woodlands.

Laurent had hired a small bus—normally used to shuttle skiers to the resorts—to take them to this remote cabin. But the driver had refused to haul his bus up this precipitous entry road. So, they had to trek the last quarter mile on their own.

"Our guide lives way out here?" Archie asked, already huffing from the thin air.

Laurent trudged on. "Yes. I've made all the arrangements."

Duncan squinted ahead. "How did you hear about this person?"

"Locals in town. They said no one knows the highlands better. Though, their recommendation came with a warning."

"What do you mean?" Sharyn asked, adjusting her coat.

Like the rest of them, Sharyn had donned a ski parka, Gore-Tex boots, and a thick cap with furred ear flaps. They each had been given a stuffed pack, holding gear that included rope, a collapsible shovel, a flashlight, and, strapped to the outside, a pair of snowshoes.

Laurent carried the largest pack, crammed with camping equipment and a four-season tent. He turned to Sharyn. "I was cautioned that our guide can be a bit eccentric. Likely from spending too much time alone in the backcountry. The woman is a wildlife biologist. She's well known for—"

"Wait. The guide is a *woman?*" Duncan was unable to keep the shock from his voice. Unfortunately, the words were out of his mouth before he could stop them.

"And that's a problem?" Sharyn challenged him pointedly.

Duncan's face heated up, defying the cold bite to the air. "Of . . . Of course not. I was just surprised."

"I could tell."

Archie clapped Duncan on the shoulder. "Keeping digging that hole, mate."

Duncan had already pissed Sharyn off. After arriving in town, he had suggested she should stay behind with Tag and Naomi. She had not taken this recommendation well, questioning why he thought he was any better fit for the trek ahead. She was certainly aerobically stronger than him, what with all her marathon runs. In fact, it was how Sharyn had first caught his attention, lapping around the Exeter campus in running shorts and a T-shirt. Days ago—which felt like a lifetime—his arrival at the Old Library had not been happenstance. While he had needed to pick up the book he had ordered from the British Library, he had timed his visit to be there when she was.

Not that I'd ever admit to such stalking behavior.

Still, Sharyn's adamance had little to do with her fitness. Under her parka, she still carried Saint-Germain's book. She refused to give up the volume, not even allowing Laurent to take it. She had been clear why: *Wright gave this to me, sacrificed his life to protect it. I'll be the Thirteenth Keeper until I'm no longer needed in this role.*

Archie raised a question, diverting attention from Duncan. "What's so *eccentric* about this guide of ours?"

Laurent waved ahead. "Like I said, she's a wildlife biologist.

She's been involved with a project to repopulate Alpine species that were decimated over the past centuries. It's why she spends so much time in the backcountry. From what I've heard, she can be bristly. Preferring animals over people."

"After all that's happened," Archie muttered, "I'm beginning to agree with her."

"In fact, I should warn you that—"

From out of the tree line, a gray-haired woman stalked into view. She carried a bucket sloshing with milk, along with a shotgun resting on her opposite shoulder. Only now did Duncan spot the outline of a barn deeper in the woods, in a small clearing with a few penned goats nearby. The woman's eyes pinched at the sight of them.

"*Signor* Laurent?" she called over.

"Yes. And the companions I told you about."

"You should've been here an hour ago," she scolded. "The storm will be upon us before nightfall. We will be hard pressed to reach the mountain's northern approach before then. If that's still your goal. Like I told you before, there is little worth seeing out there."

Duncan knew Laurent had refrained from sharing too many details with their guide, certainly not the exact location of their goal. Before leaving the Barbier estate, Laurent had grabbed everything he needed from his hardshell case, including a thumb drive that held a copy of their decryption. On the long journey here, using topo maps of Monte Antelao, he and Laurent had managed to assign rough coordinates to the glowing blip on the pixelated mountain.

The woman crossed to the cabin's wooden porch and set down her shotgun. "Let me get this goat milk in the icebox and we'll be underway."

She vanished into the cabin, the interior of which was softly firelit. She closed the door, not bothering to invite them inside to warm themselves.

As they waited, Duncan stamped his feet to stir circulation. "She's a bit gruff, like you said."

"And what's with the shotgun?" Archie added.

Laurent shaded his eyes to stare up at the towering peaks, snow-crested and deeply valleyed. "The Dolomites are not without their dangers."

A low rumbling growl confirmed this.

From the dark woods, a shape slinked into view. The massive cat crept low, shivering its tawny hackles, baring long fangs. Its shoulders stood as tall as Duncan's thigh. As it crouched, its raised haunches revealed a bobbed tail. Long tufts trembled atop its ears, which flattened against its skull in a threatening manner.

"No one move," Laurent whispered.

The door opened and their guide returned, having only donned a mid-length coat, still loose and undone, along with a pack over one shoulder. She also had a large pistol strapped at her waist.

Duncan opened his mouth to warn her, but she spotted the cat first.

Unfazed, she retrieved her shotgun. "*Maledizione,* Katch, were you off stalking the goats again? You had better not have scared them and soured their milk."

As the woman crossed to join them, the mountain cat circled to follow, maintaining a wary distance.

Their guide shook each of their hands in a perfunctory manner. Her grip was iron with nothing friendly about it, just professional. "I'm Dr. Bianca Russo."

"And . . . And that big cat?" Archie asked.

She glanced at the beast. "A former breeding stud. For a project to return the Eurasian lynx to these mountains. Unfortunately, after six years with the program, he's been deemed too dependent on humans to survive on his own in the wild."

Duncan gaped as the huge cat stalked back and forth. Its pads were larger than his palms and tipped by black claws. Only now did he note the thick leather collar around its neck, supporting a knob of metal, some sort of a wildlife tracker.

"So, you keep him as a pet now?" Duncan asked.

"Not a pet. Never forget that. While Katch will mostly mind me, he's still a wild animal. A Carpathian lynx, to be exact. I've been working with him out here. A case study. To judge if it might be possible to return him to the wild after all."

"And you named him Katch?" Sharyn asked.

"Short for *cacciatore*, though spelled with a capital K."

Archie frowned. "Like the stew?"

"No, *cacciatore* means *hunter* in Italian." Russo shrugged. "It seemed fitting enough."

Duncan looked between the woman and the cat. Even the lynx's name spoke to the biologist's cold manner. She had not picked out anything overly affectionate, just practical.

"Let's get going," Russo ordered. "I've a truck parked around back. We'll take it as far as we can. Then it'll be on foot from there."

As they headed off, the lynx tracked them.

Sharyn noted this, too. "Is Katch coming with us?"

Russo didn't turn around. "He needs training time in the wild. Plus, he'll keep any other threats at bay."

"Other threats?" Duncan asked.

She nodded toward the peaks. "Over sixty bears have resettled this corner of the Dolomites. There've been a few altercations. A hiker was mauled a few years back. Then there are the wolves slowly returning, which is a great show of the progress we've made."

"Wolves?" From Sharyn's pinched brows, she clearly did not share the biologist's enthusiasm.

"Packs are mostly in the French Alps, but they've been successfully extending their territory across the mountains. A lone specimen was spotted in the western Dolomites about six months ago."

Duncan looked at the large cat trailing them. While Katch might ward off such threats, he found little comfort with this furry danger at their back.

As if making this clear, a low rumble—sounding like distant thunder—rose from the bristling beast.

Duncan stared ahead at Russo, questioning Laurent's choice of guides.

Eccentric did not begin to describe this woman.

He settled on a more fitting word.

Dangerous.

41

10:55 a.m.

Sharyn dropped out of the rear cab of the truck. Per the number of dents and a mismatched door, the older-model pickup had clearly seen some rough travel. Still, the interior had been clean and, more importantly, warm.

She rubbed her palms and pulled on a pair of insulated gloves.

Archie and Duncan climbed out the other side, stamping and gasping at the cold. The three of them had shared the back seat, sitting on top of one another. But none of them had volunteered to travel in the truck's bed, where a large aluminum cage confined the massive lynx.

Laurent had grabbed the front passenger spot and used the drive to review topo maps with their guide. Russo had scowled—or maybe it was just her resting face—throughout the discussion of routes and options. The pair spoke in Italian, which Laurent proved himself to be fluent in. As was Archie, who whispered a translation for her and Duncan.

The truck traversed an ever-narrowing road that went from broken pavement to gravel to a rutted dirt track clogged with frost-deadened weeds, until eventually they traveled a path of unblemished snow. The forest to either side dwindled from dense Norway spruces and Swiss pines to scraggly versions, contorted by wind and snow and pushing straight out of the icy rock.

They had finally come to a stop where a shoulder of the mountain blocked the way, rising in a sheer cliff. The precipitous face was surely a delight to rock climbers. But, for Sharyn, it appeared ready to topple over on top of them. The latter impression was reinforced by the tumble of boulders at its base.

Sharyn craned up. "How far is it to reach the northern approach from here?" she asked Russo.

The woman crossed to the back of the truck and opened the crate. "Not far. Twenty kilometers. During which we'll gain a thousand meters in elevation."

Sharyn winced at the challenge ahead.

Russo offered a bit of consolation. "We'll be mostly hiking on the leeward side of the mountain, so the snow underfoot—at least for now—should be manageable."

It was the *at least for now* part that worried Sharyn. She searched the late morning sky, which remained achingly blue and continued to show no evidence of a threatening storm.

Maybe it'll pass us by.

To the side, Katch leaped from his crate, landed on his huge paws, then stretched his back into a spine-breaking arch, extending his forelegs—along with those huge claws.

Sharyn kept well back.

Russo scratched the lynx's ruff, digging deep, which earned a contented rumble from the beast, followed by a head butt that was both affectionate and dismissive.

Despite his massive size, Katch was still all feline.

With the crate now empty, they collected their packs from the truck bed. Russo sized their group up, her face unreadable. Once they were ready, she simply turned and headed off into the woods, following a snow-dusted trail only she seemed to be able to pick out.

Archie kept close to their guide, eyeing the shotgun slung across her back. "You mentioned bears. Are there any near here?"

"*Certo.* They're definitely around. The cold snap and snow will likely have them foraging hard and seeking caves to hibernate out the winter."

Sharyn stared over at the boulder-strewn cliffs that paralleled their path. "Those caves? Are there a lot of them in this area?" She gave Duncan a meaningful glance. "Do any of them go very deep?"

"*Sì*. Of course. Some burrow far into the mountains. These peaks are mostly formed of limestone, specifically a variant called dolomite, which is why there are so many caves out here." She glanced to Laurent. "Is that what you came here to find?"

Laurent must have decided it was safe enough to let his guard down somewhat. "Yes. We've heard rumors of a cavern system that might yet be undiscovered."

Russo made a scoffing noise. "I would not place much faith in *rumors* when it comes to the Dolomites. There are hundreds of tales and legends about these mountains. Of the discovery of elephant bones from Hannibal's crossing. Of lost Roman outposts. Of strange energies. Even of nymph-like witches—the *anguana*—who guard the mouths of highland caves."

Archie sighed. "Well, we shouldn't have too much worry about them as we're practically study partners."

Russo frowned at this. "I wouldn't suggest venturing into their caves."

"Why's that?"

"They are known to cast spells that cause trespassers to fall into a deep sleep."

Archie shrugged. "That doesn't sound so bad."

"Then the witches drain your blood or drown you in a mountain spring."

Archie lifted a palm. "Okay, I retract my statement."

Laurent sighed and waved her onward. "What other stories have you heard?"

"Plenty. About all manner of creatures. Like Mazaròl, a mischievous red-capped gnome who lures people astray. Or the wild men of the mountains, called *salvanel*, immortal beings who roam its remotest regions."

Sharyn's ears perked at the mention of such men.

But Russo quickly cast cold water on all of this. "I've been throughout the Dolomites. For more than fifteen years. I've never encountered anything beyond its natural beauty. These mountains and valleys need no tall tales to embellish their true wonders. As you will see."

They continued onward, heading ever higher. The quiet murmuring among them died as the cold, thin air and exertion took their toll. After three hours, they eventually left the main forest below and crossed into a terrain of bare stone, treacherous loose shale, and rock-hugging scrub that scribed frosty emerald lines across the slopes.

As their guide predicted, the snows proved scant on this side of the mountain, but the slopes remained icy. Katch continued to roam around them, his wide pads finding secure footing on rock, snow, or ice. He certainly belonged in these mountains.

Upon reaching a flat expanse, Russo called for a stop. "We'll take a short break. No more than twenty minutes. We've made good time, but the next half will tax us harder."

"Wait. We're only halfway?" Archie blew out a tired exhalation and dropped his butt to the stone.

Duncan looked no happier as he joined his friend. "Wish I'd had more time to break in these new boots."

Russo turned to Laurent. "I hope the cavern system you're looking for is out there."

"Why is that?"

Russo pointed to a dark line across the southeastern sky, which rose behind Antelao's craggy summit. "The stormfront looks worse than predicted. We'll eventually need to find shelter to weather it out."

"I brought a large tent."

Russo cocked a leery eye at him. "You may need something stronger than canvas. I know of a couple caves, where we can light a fire. Both are closer. Maybe we should overnight in one of them and continue in the morning."

Sharyn stepped forward. "Does that mean we can't make it before the storm hits?"

"I could answer that if you'd be more forthcoming about *exactly* where you're going."

Sharyn turned to Laurent. "You'd better show her."

He nodded, needing no further convincing. He pulled out the topo map, one he had not shared with their guide, and spread it on the rock. The location's coordinates had been marked with a series of concentric blue circles, radiating out from the most likely location. But they could not rule out that their goal might be anywhere within the scope of those rings.

Russo stared for a long moment, then let out a slow breath. "That's where you want to go?"

"We do."

She shook her head. "If you had been forthright, I could've saved you a long trek."

"Why?" Sharyn asked.

"I know that spot. There's no major cavern system in the area. Only an old bunker, a fortification from World War II. Locals call it the Castello. It's a dead end, too. Teenagers camped and partied there for decades, until it was eventually gated and chained."

Duncan overhead this. "Maybe there's a cave opening you don't know about?"

Russo glared at them. "There's nothing there. You're all wasting your time."

Sharyn turned to Laurent. "We still have to look, right?"

He nodded. "We go on." He then repeated Sharyn's earlier concern. "Can we reach there before the storm hits?"

"It'll be close. I'll have to set a hard pace. And the last stretch is exposed and treacherous. We don't want to be caught in the open when the storm hits."

To lessen the chance of that happening, Russo shortened their break to five minutes, then set off again. After another hour, they cleared a shoulder of the mountain, and the lights of San Vito appeared far below, looking small and buried in the surrounding dark forest.

Sharyn had not imagined they had climbed so high. As she stared below, a light snow sifted out of the sky, likely blowing off the front edge of the incoming blizzard.

"We'd better move faster," Russo urged, holding a palm up to the icy flakes.

Before Sharyn could turn away, movement below caught her eye. A trio of large helicopters, illuminated by bright lights, swept over the black pines. They circled and descended toward the village.

She shared a look with Duncan, the worry on her face matching his own.

"We'd better move faster," he said, parroting their guide.

She glanced back as they set off. Maybe the helicopter only carried skiers—those hoping for an early season and fresh powder—but she feared the worst. Her gaze lingered on the lights of the village, knowing who they had left behind.

Be careful, you two.

42

3:18 p.m.

Naomi cringed as Tag coughed harshly on the room's sofa. Her friend lay curled on his side, wracked in a tight spasm. Sweat pebbled his brow. His inhaler was empty, but he still clutched it like a lifeline.

Naomi paced the room, looking past the chalet's balcony to the mountains beyond. She wished the others were still here. Tag had taken a turn for the worse an hour ago, complaining of a crippling headache that left him sprawled across the sofa. He had warned her that abruptly stopping his Zanaflex and its sudden withdrawal would hit him hard.

But I never expected it to be this bad.

She weighed the risk of attempting to refill his meds, knowing it might expose them if his real name popped up on a database. But seeing him suffer now, she questioned if such caution was necessary.

Is he suffering for no reason?

She crossed to him and dropped to her knee. "Is there anything I can do? Get you? Something over the counter?"

With a trembling arm, he wiped a drape of drool from his lips. His expression was pained, looking as much embarrassed as agonized. "Pain relievers . . . sometimes they take the edge off."

"Like what?"

"Maybe Archie left some ibuprofen. But naproxen usually works better. Even soaking in a hot bath with Epsom salts relieves some of the pain. But we don't have either."

She turned to the French doors off the balcony, picturing the small village beyond. "When we got into town, I spotted a pharmacy a few blocks off. I should be able to pick stuff up there."

"We're not supposed to leave the hotel," he reminded her.

"Then I'll have it delivered."

"Not without a credit card."

She cursed under her breath.

He's right. And we only have a little cash left.

"Actually," Tag gasped out, "what works best is marijuana."

She raised a brow toward him. "Weed? You? Mr. Holistic?"

He smiled wanly. "It's herbal and medicinal. Right up my alley."

"That's true."

He swallowed, which clearly took great effort. "The cannabinoids in marijuana have efficacy in both relieving pain and relaxing muscle spasms."

She frowned at him. "You don't have to get all scientific to explain why you want to get high."

He started to laugh but curled into a hard jag of coughing. When he could finally breathe, tears coursed from his eyes.

Screw this . . .

She headed toward the door, grabbing her jacket.

Tag grunted at her in concern. "Naomi . . ."

"Weed is illegal to buy in Italy," she said. "So, no prescription is needed, making it technically over the counter. And this town is full of shiftless ski bums, waiting for the season to start. Someone out there has to be holding."

He called after her. "If you can score some Valium, I wouldn't object."

She turned to him.

He forced a painful shrug. "Sometimes Western medicine has its advantages, too."

You got it.

Naomi headed out, hurried down the stairs to the lobby, and made a discreet inquiry with the woman who had been their server earlier. Twenty minutes later, she found herself crossing into an icy park.

She kept bundled, not just from the cold, but to keep her features hidden. She wore a cap with its bill tugged low and a scarf covering her nose and mouth. She searched the neighboring streets but spotted no one staring suspiciously at her.

Satisfied, she crossed through the park to a fountain. Its basin had been drained for the season. The statue of an angel rose at the center, encrusted with ice and crowned by snow.

Off to the side, a pair of figures lounged on a nearby bench.

Just like the waitress told me to expect.

Naomi looked around once more, unable to suppress a tremble of unease, this being her first drug deal. As she approached, one of the pair stood and confronted her. He wore a puffy Moncler parka and boots, topped by a Bogner cap, all expensive gear. It seemed drug dealing must be very profitable in this ski town, or this was some rich kid slumming it for extra change.

"*Cosa vuoi?*" he challenged her brusquely.

She hoped he spoke English. "I . . . I'm looking to buy some weed."

He smoothly switched to match her. "Are you a cop?"

She fought not to roll her eyes. *Guy's definitely an amateur. Or stupid. Or likely both.* Despite what was portrayed in procedurals on TV, the police didn't have to admit to being a cop when confronted.

"I'm not. I have a friend who's hurting."

The dealer's outthrust chest relaxed. "Okay. How much do you want?"

"A couple grams."

"That all?" He cast his gaze up and down her in a dismissive manner.

"Funds are limited. I could also use a few tabs of Valium if you have any."

The dealer shrugged and waved to his partner. As the figure stood, Naomi saw it was an older woman, as heavily bundled as herself. If nothing else, it was nice to contribute her Euros to a female-run business.

As the negotiation started, Naomi noted a chain round the woman's neck. A clear vial, full of a crystalline powder, hung from it. Naomi suspected it was not a drug on display, but instead served as an amulet of some sort.

Naomi pointed at it, guessing its contents. "Is that salt in there?"

The woman clutched the vial. "*Sì. Sale.* You know?"

"I do. It's to ward off evil."

The woman nodded, her cold demeanor softening. According to tradition, a malevolent spirit could not attack someone until they finished counting every grain of salt in a protective charm.

Naomi was not overly surprised to find such an ornament on this woman. She had recently read a journal article on the high prevalence of superstitious beliefs among criminal elements. Hispanic gangs would never steal from a church, believing it would curse them. As contradictory as it might seem, mafia members adhered to the religious practices of the Catholic faith with a fervency that surpassed most of the devoted. The thesis of the article was that criminals knew they were doing wrong and sought a higher means of absolution and protection.

"You know the *stregheria* ways?" the woman asked.

"I'm acquainted," Naomi admitted, recognizing the archaic term for an Italian form of witchcraft.

"Then I will make you a good deal, *sì?*" She nudged her large companion. "Antonio, show her our best."

Naomi didn't know if she was being conned. Maybe this was a faked camaraderie to make her drop her guard. Still, after some back and forth, she completed the transaction. She had to settle for a single gram of cannabis and three tabs of Valium. She hoped it would be enough to stem Tag's agony—at least long enough for the others to get back, which likely wouldn't be until tomorrow.

She said her goodbyes and crossed out of the park. As she headed for their tiny hotel, she fought to walk nonchalantly, which only made her gait more stilted. She also looked around far too often, even for a tourist. Recognizing this, she tried to use reflections in passing windows to watch if anyone suddenly turned and stepped after her.

No one did.

Then up ahead, a sleek black car topped by a bar of blue lights turned a corner and passed slowly down the street. Emblazoned on its side in silver letters was the word *Carabinieri*. She tripped a step, recognizing the more militarized version of the Italian police. She quickly turned toward a ski shop and pretended to show keen interest in a display of snowboards.

Reflected in the glass, the vehicle slowly idled past—then continued on.

She let out the breath she had been holding, hunched her shoulders, and headed again down the street, her pace quicker now.

As she reached the hotel, she glanced back. A few blocks away, the brake lights of the Carabinieri sedan flared brighter. She cringed and waited until it turned a corner and vanished.

She must have looked suspicious at that moment, drawing the eyes of a couple bystanders across the street. Or maybe they were simply inspecting the hotel's chalkboard, which displayed the restaurant's specials.

Enough of this . . .

She headed inside.

I'm just being paranoid . . . and I've not even partaken of the wares I just bought.

As she headed across the lobby, the waitress from earlier gave her an inquiring look. Naomi answered with a thumb's up, then hurried to the stairs and climbed to the second floor. She crossed to her room, unlocked it, and ducked inside.

Tag coughed, then croaked to her. "How was—"

"Got everything," she gasped out, relieved to be back.

She paused at the closed door, resting her forehead against it. She flipped the deadbolt. As an extra measure, she fumbled the privacy chain across the frame. She trembled there, her heart pounding, not fully trusting that she hadn't exposed herself. She pictured the flash of the brake lights, the faces staring toward her.

From here on out, she decided to proceed with more caution and adhere to the wisdom she had once read:

Just because you're paranoid doesn't mean they aren't after you.

43

5:33 p.m.

Sharyn slogged through the snow. At this elevation, the depth remained manageable, only reaching her ankles. But that would change. Flurries and spats of heavier snow battled them. And the heart of the storm had yet to reach the mountain.

As the group climbed out of a rocky bowl, they walked in a hunched line. Higher up, the clifftops and summit of Monte Antelao carried heavy cornices of snow, which the winds had blown into huge flumes.

She prayed they were close to their destination, especially as the sun was only a cloaked glimmer to the west. The sky above had become a gray blanket that darkened to an ominous black off to the east. By now, her face and feet had gone numb. The scarf over her lips had frozen at its edges.

Russo called back and pointed her flashlight. "There's a plateau ahead. Once there, we must find a place to shelter for the night."

They were all too exhausted to respond. They simply followed her. The only one who seemed unbothered by the weather and exertion was Katch. The large lynx kept an easy pace with Russo. A layer of powder coated his spotted fur, offering perfect camouflage for this environment.

The steep slope finally evened out into a wide shelf, as large as a football field. As they trekked onto it, the winds struck harder. But those same gusts had cleared the rock of most of the snow, which swirled in icy devils around them.

Ahead, a sheer wall of icy rock climbed into the clouds. Sharyn searched its face as far as the gloom permitted. She spotted no breaks in the cliff, no shadows that might hide a cave entrance.

"What now?" Archie grumbled.

Russo waved them into a cluster. "We've reached the circle you marked on your map. Like I warned, there's nothing here."

"We can't say that with certainty," Laurent warned, his breath steaming through his frosted scarf. "It's gotten too dark. We'll find a place to camp and search at daybreak, after the storm clears."

"Where do we go?" Duncan asked.

Sharyn looked to Russo. "What about that World War II bunker you mentioned? Is it close?"

The woman pointed to the right. "A path hugs the cliffs over there. The last approach is narrow with a steep drop, but it's the only way to reach the Castello. And like I told you, it was gated and chained years ago."

"I have a bolt cutter in my pack," Laurent said. "Will that get us inside?"

Russo shrugged, plainly noncommittal.

Laurent shared a weighted look with the others.

Back at the Barbier château, Archie had told them about his bike trip through the Dolomites and the number of caves and World War II bunkers that riddled the peaks. Knowing such places might have to be searched, Laurent had come prepared. He also carried an ax slung atop his pack, ready to do some breaking and entering if need be.

During the long climb, the group had discussed—out of earshot of Russo—the possibility that the Castello could be blocking the lost cavern system. *Like a thumb in the dike,* as Archie had put it. If Russo was correct about nothing else being up here, the bunker seemed like a good place to begin their search.

And if nothing else, it'll get us out of the weather for the night.

"Take us there," Laurent ordered.

Russo got them moving again. She led them across the plateau, angling toward the cliff. As they neared it, the footing under them steadily narrowed. It dwindled down to a path barely wide enough for two people, with a sheer drop along one side. Ahead, piles of windblown snow covered the icy trail. Above it, snowy cornices hung like frozen waves. Whatever lay at the end remained lost in the gloom.

Russo turned to them. "Are you sure you want to chance this? Before we lose the light entirely, I can find an outcropping we can stake our tents under. It'll be cold but manageable."

Laurent did not bother checking with the group. He freed his flashlight and clicked it on. "We should check it out. If we can't get inside, we'll camp out here somewhere."

Russo shrugged and set off. "*Va bene.* Stay close, go slow, and watch your footing."

One member of their party balked at this plan. Katch stopped at the trailhead and tested the air, chuffing softly into the wind.

"Maybe he smells one of those witches that his boss mentioned," Archie said.

Russo noted the cat's hesitation and patted her hip. "*Venga, Katch, venga.*"

With clear reluctance, the lynx followed his mistress onto the cliffside trail. Katch stayed low, taking cautious steps.

Sharyn wondered if they should all heed the feline's keener senses. Still, as Laurent followed, she got pulled in his wake. Archie and Duncan came after, with their flashlights drawn to better illuminate the path.

They kept to a single file, keeping well clear of the drop. Ice and snow made every step treacherous. Worst of all, the winds came in unpredictable gusts. After ten yards, Sharyn's legs trembled from the tension.

Then, out of the gloom, a hulking shadow appeared. It blocked the trail. As they drew closer, the path widened into an apron in front of it.

Sharyn gaped as the sight fully revealed itself.

No wonder it had been named the Castello.

The fortification had been constructed of large concrete blocks and smaller bricks, all of which climbed into a tower topped by a parapet. Clearly it was a bit of fanciful embellishment by the Axis forces, who had built this mountainside bunker. Frosted with ice, crowned by snow, this castle looked a part of the mountain, as if it had always been there.

Once Sharyn reached the wider apron, she noted the bunker's arched entry had been sealed by a gate of iron bars, wrapped tight with chains and a lock. This close, the mystique of the place dimmed. Its façade was scarred and pocked by missing bricks. Its surface was heavily stained by splashes of graffiti, which spilled onto the neighboring cliff.

Sharyn felt a sinking in her gut, fearing Russo's assessment of this place was likely correct. The bunker had been harshly abused. The possibility of finding anything inside seemed hopeless.

Still, Laurent dropped his pack, fished out his bolt cutter, and in short order broke free the chain. The gate itself—frozen, iced over, and corroded—proved more stubborn. Laurent and Archie shouldered into it, trying to force it.

While they struggled, Duncan drew Sharyn's attention to the expansive view of the valley below. The storm had momentarily let up, clearing the skies of snow. Off in the distance, a scatter of lights glowed.

"I think that's San Vito," he said, his voice muffled by his scarf.

She nodded, remembering the helicopters she had spotted hours ago. "I hope Tag and Naomi are okay."

"Right now, I wish I was down there with them."

Sharyn hugged her arms around her chest, shivering against the cold. "And miss all this fun?"

Archie boomed out in triumph. "Take that, you bloody bugger!"

As she turned, the two men shoved the gate the rest of the way open, accompanied by a grinding complaint of its hinges.

With Archie's face still masked over, she could only imagine his grin. He pointed toward the dark entry. "Who's for storming the castle?"

As they gathered closer, a harsh wailing rose, coming from everywhere, rising quickly.

"Inside!" Russo warned.

As they stumbled forward, a burst of gale-force winds ripped over the mountaintop. Snow followed, pouring heavily, whipped into a blinding frenzy. A gust nearly tore Sharyn off her feet, but Duncan caught her. Together, they huddled low and dove for the entrance.

Once out of the blizzard and far enough inside, Sharyn shook snow from her body and pulled down her scarf. She turned and stared at the growing storm. "At least we should be safe in here."

Another disagreed.

Katch kept sheltered in the doorway, crouched low and hissing menacingly. But the cat did not face the storm. Its eyes glowed, reflecting their lights—and stared into the dark depths of the bunker.

44

6:07 p.m.

Propped up on the sofa, Tag clutched the smoke in his chest, struggling to let it steep into his lungs' alveoli. He pictured the tetrahydrocannabinol dissolving into his bloodstream. The natural compound had both psychoactive and anti-inflammatory properties, perfect for easing tensions and dulling pain. But more importantly for his condition, the drug had an anti-spasmodic effect on a body.

Unable to hold the smoke in any longer, he let it sigh out his lips.

By now, the tremoring strictures in his limbs had already lessened. His breathing, while still tight, had eased. Of course, the tab of Valium he had swallowed a short time ago certainly helped, too.

During her drug run, Naomi had also purchased rolling papers and a lighter from the dealer. Once back here, she had helped Tag divide the single gram of weed into three joints. He planned to parse them out for as long as possible. It was why he had waited ninety minutes after taking the Valium before lighting his first joint. Unfortunately, this one had already winnowed down to a tiny roach clutched in a set of tweezers.

His plan was to alternate between Western medicine and natural herbology, to bide his time while he and Naomi waited.

"Is it helping?" she asked him.

She stood by the French doors out to the balcony. She had left the jamb open after he lit the joint, to help dispel the smoke and skunky odor. Even the small gap had dropped the room's temperature precipitously. To keep warm, she had donned her coat and a wool hat and dragged a blanket from the bed and draped it around him.

Outside, the blizzard had finally struck the village. Winds blew in fierce gusts. Heavy snow obscured the view, lowering visibility to only a few feet past the window. A half foot of snow had already piled on the balcony.

"How are you feeling?" Naomi asked.

He grinned, far more relaxed, enough to offer a sarcastic "Bitchin'."

He took another long pull on the joint, until it finally snuffed out and turned to ash. He held the smoke inside his chest longer this time, then slowly released the precious traces from his lungs.

As he sagged deeper into the pillows, Naomi waved the pall toward the open door, then closed it. "Done, my little pothead?"

"For now. Thanks. You're a lifesaver. If you hadn't—"

Behind him, the door to the room exploded open with a splintering crash. He jerked around, earning a stabbing pain in his neck. Armored men burst through, following a gray steel battering ram. They rushed inside with weapons raised, screaming for them to drop to the floor.

Tangled in his blanket, Tag struggled to obey. He rolled awkwardly off the sofa to the carpet, bumping into the coffee table and knocking aside his cane.

Naomi simply collapsed to her knees and raised her palms.

"Down!" a huge man bellowed at her, driving forward with a pistol leveled. He wore black armor and a matching helmet with a lowered face shield, all with no insignia.

She obeyed, sprawling flat, but not before Tag noted her agonized expression, her eyes sorrowful and pinched, wracked by guilt.

He felt a stab of the same.

They've found us . . . and we both know how.

Men surrounded them. Others searched the neighboring rooms. Then the one who had threatened Naomi called to the door, switching to French. "*Tout est clair!*"

Upon this acknowledgment, two figures entered, a man and a woman, both dressed in suits and bundled in woolen overcoats. They were followed by a third who showed a clerical collar with a prominent crucifix hanging at his chest. Tag remembered the Rolls with Vatican plates outside their flat. All of this dashed any hope that these assailants were a local police force.

Still, Tag imagined this group must have gained some cooperation from the Italian authorities. He remembered Laurent's description of the enemy's convoluted ties to intelligence services across the EU and beyond. In addition, the bastards must have waited for the cover of the blizzard to time this assault, to further mask their actions.

Still, the end result was the same.

The *Confrérie* had found them.

The man in the suit crossed briskly toward them, carrying no weapon, only a briefcase. He stopped between Naomi and Tag.

"Where are the others?" he asked with no preamble, no gloating.

Naomi propped up on an elbow to answer. "They . . . they went off to a pub. I don't know where."

Tag tried to support this lie and nodded to the spread of drug paraphernalia. "We stayed to party on our own."

As the man frowned down at him, Tag squinted back, suddenly struck by how familiar this guy looked. Still, terror stifled his recall. He fought against it.

How could I possibly know this bastard?

Then knowledge struck him, maybe aided by the weed's tempering effects on his anxiety. Tag's eyes widened. He fought to hide his shock. After he graduated with a biochemistry degree, he had been headhunted by various companies, running the gamut from dreamy-eyed environmentalists to serious petrochemical reps. But by far, it had been pharmaceutical companies who had pursued him, especially due to his degree's emphasis on medical research. He had been aggressively hunted by one outfit in particular, the leading drug company in the EU—NeuVentis Pharma.

And here stood its CEO.

Keir Marchand.

Tag turned his face, trying to hide this knowledge. The woman—someone of Indian descent per her burnished complexion—came up alongside him.

"Surely they're lying," she scoffed. "No one else has been spotted in the area. If it wasn't for the patrol who sent out an alert, we might not have found these two."

"No doubt you're right, Burman."

Tag bit down a curse, remembering Naomi's tale of her drug buy and the fright she had experienced. The Carabinieri officers must have been on the lookout for them and had been warned to report any sightings, but not to apprehend them. And for good reason. The *Confrérie* wanted them in their clutches, not in a holding cell. Still, if the Brotherhood had reached San Vito this quickly, it meant the bastards must know about what was hidden at Monte Antelao.

The enemy's hack must have worked—but how well?

Tag tried to judge this. From the fact that the *Confrérie* had gone through such efforts to hunt down their group in town, it suggested the Brotherhood was still missing some critical data.

Like the exact location on the mountain.

This became clear with Keir's next words to Burman: "We'll have to coerce the information out of these two. Find out where the others went and what they know about this blasted mountain."

The woman glanced to the shattered door. "Perhaps we should move this pair to a more secure location. We may have this chalet locked down, but any loud screaming might unnerve other guests. Enough for someone to reach out and make contact beyond the sphere of my intelligence operations. Which could expose us."

Keir waved this away. "The wind and snow will cover any noise. And the blizzard has already knocked down most communication. But you are correct that we should be expeditious." Keir turned to the armored man who had called the all-clear. "Captain Ferhat, you have your dagger, yes?"

"*Oui.*" He unsheathed a long steel blade, serrated on one side, razor sharp on the other.

"We must pry one of their tongues loose." Keir looked between his captives, then pointed at Naomi. "Take off this one's ear if the gentleman refuses to answer our questions."

Naomi fought to squirm away, but another soldier grabbed a fistful of her hair and yanked her head back. Captain Ferhat closed on her with his blade.

Tag stared at Naomi. Her face had flushed with a mix of fury and terror.

"Don't tell them anything," she gasped out.

"He will," Keir warned.

Tag knew the man was right. He could not watch Naomi be tortured. He had to trust that cooperation would earn them a few hours of grace, especially as the bastards would want to corroborate anything told to them. And considering the blizzard outside, that might take until morning.

Still, in the end, Tag knew they would be killed. He was under no delusions otherwise. And anything he told them, if truthful, would only jeopardize his other friends, too.

He met Naomi's frightened eyes.

I'm sorry. It was my fault. I got you into this, exposed us.

He flicked his gaze to the side, then to the French doors, before returning his attention to Naomi.

And I'm going to get you out.

He stared hard at her, hoping she understood. He then snatched his toppled cane and tossed it under the coffee table and onto Naomi's lap. She grabbed it, spun it, and jabbed its end into her captor's throat.

The man coughed and let go of her hair.

Freed, she burst toward the French doors, still left unlocked. She yanked it open as gunshots shattered the glass over her head. She ducked through to the second-story balcony, rolled over its rail, and vanished into the snow.

Men shoved outside and searched below, but visibility had dropped to nearly zero.

"Go after her!" Keir shouted.

Two men leaped over the rail. Others fled out the door behind him.

Tag stayed on his knees, allowing a hard grin to show. Ferhat pointed his pistol at the back of Tag's head.

"What about him?" Burman asked.

Tag stiffened his back. "You won't get me to talk, Mister Marchand." He paused to enjoy the shock on the CEO's face at being recognized. "I declined your employment offer in the past. And I'll do so again."

Keir turned and eyed the dagger in Ferhat's other hand.

Tag shrugged, trying to sound brave. "Do your best. I've dealt with pain all my life."

"That may be true." Keir collected himself, turned, and placed his briefcase down, then snapped it open. "While this method will unfortunately take longer, it will get the job done."

Tag shifted higher and spotted an array of syringes and vials nestled inside the case.

"What about afterward?" Burman asked.

Keir sighed. "I suppose we must keep him alive. For now. At least until we recapture the girl."

As NeuVentis's CEO began prepping the syringes, Tag turned to the balcony. The door had been left open, allowing gusts of snow to sweep in along with the cold. A lone gunman stood outside, searching below.

Tag remembered his earlier statement about Naomi being his *lifesaver.*

He willed her to keep running, to buy him more time.

To be my lifesaver again.

45

7:04 p.m.

Naomi gasped as she fled through the blinding snow. Pain and terror drove her onward. Her twisted ankle stabbed fire up her leg with every step. Still, she dared not slow. Behind her, she had heard the heavy thud as men crashed with a clatter of armor behind her, taking the same hard exit as she had.

Her parka, still unzipped, flapped around her like the broken wings of a bird. Winds buffeted her, finding every way through her clothing to reach skin. By now, snow had started to crust over her. Still, adrenaline and terror kept her warm.

But for how much longer?

She fought to go faster, especially knowing she was leaving a trail through the snow. The storm sought to help her—by blowing powder and filling her prints—but she did not have enough of a lead for this to make a difference.

She searched for help, some straggler battling home, but she knew running into such a person would only get them both killed. The gloam of lights through heavy snowfall drew her onward. She prayed to find an open restaurant or shop, somewhere with enough people to ward off an attack, but everything had been shuttered tight.

She glanced back, rubbing the back of her wrist across her frozen eyelids, but she could see nothing except a blanket of white.

Still, she heard her pursuers steadily closing on her. The crunch of boots on ice, the rattle of body armor, the grunt of coordinated commands.

As she faced around, her foot slipped on a patch of ice. She lost her balance and slid headlong into the snow.

No . . .

Panicked, she struggled for half a breath before regaining her legs. She shoved off—but not before noting a darker shadow blooming in the snowfall behind her.

They're almost on me.

As she sped across the next intersection, a loud grumbling rose to her right. A glance over showed a growing well of brightness. She skidded into a turn and ran toward it, not with any plan, simply drawn by the instinct to flee the darkness for the light.

Or maybe it was something else, something her body reacted to before comprehension reached her mind.

Then she heard it.

A deep-throated scraping behind the engine's grumbling.

Please . . .

Ahead, the glow sharpened into spears of light, driving through the snow, sweeping past the next intersection. The brightness illuminated a huge snowplow. It shoved heavily past and continued onward until it vanished out of view.

As she ran, the noise of the machinery's passage obscured any audible sign of pursuit. Still, she refrained from looking back and only raced harder. She reached the intersection, and rather than striking off in the wake of the plow, she turned in the other direction. The street remained scraped enough to hide her footprints. She fled along the plow's path, pushed by the wind from behind. She prayed the hunters would think she had chased after the plow.

After she crossed another block, faint calls, muffled by the snow and wind, carried to her from behind. She recognized the sounds of momentary confusion and took advantage of it. While the hunters might split up, she trusted she had gained enough of a lead. She fled another three blocks, then ducked off the plowed road. By the time her pursuers hunted down this spot, the storm should have erased her path.

Or so she hoped.

She continued through town, lost, freezing, and hobbling worse as the adrenaline wore off. Her heart pounded in her throat, while terror strangled her. She fought to hold back tears that would only turn to ice. For the moment, she seemed to have shaken off her pursuers. Such a reprieve left her time to think about *who* she had left behind, *who* had helped her escape.

Tag . . .

She stumbled to a wall, leaning a shoulder against it. Would they torture him in her stead? Would he tell them where the others had gone? She stared in the direction of Monte Antelao, but there was no sign of the peak through the snow.

Fearing for the others, fearing for herself, she shoved off the wall and headed into the blizzard.

But where can I go?

46

7:55 p.m.

Sharyn continued deeper into the bunker. Behind her, the howling winds set her teeth on edge. Outside, the blizzard raged at full force, an icy beast at their door. It didn't help matters that the Castello proved to be a dank, frigid labyrinth covering three levels, each deeper than the next, connected by narrow stairwells.

She stayed next to Duncan, both carrying flashlights. The group had already searched the upper floor and its connected outer tower. The latter proved to be a hollow shaft, showing the stubs of old timbers that had supported floors long ago.

After that, they had descended to this second level, but it looked no more hopeful. It had become quickly evident that the old Axis bunker had been cleared of any sign of its former builders, leaving rooms scarred by graffiti and filled with garbage: broken bottles, crushed cans, a moldy mattress.

"Clearly, no one called in any housekeepers before locking this place up," Duncan commented.

She nodded and stepped around a charred spot on the floor, marking another old campsite. Throughout their search, they had found piles of dry branches, stacked or scattered across the levels. Trespassers in the past must have hauled in this supply to fuel their fires.

And we're now the beneficiary of their largesse.

Russo and her cat remained on the top floor, prepping a bonfire. The woman wanted it positioned near the open doorway to draw off smoke. No one wanted to be choked out during the night by smoldering fumes.

As Sharyn continued, Duncan ran his fingertips along a door-frame, where rusted hinges were nailed into raw stone. The whole place was like this—constructed from a mix of manmade and natural materials. Some of the rooms had walls composed of crumbling bricks. Others were chiseled straight out of dolomitic rock.

A low murmuring of voices echoed out of the darkness, rising from where Archie and Laurent searched a warren of rooms off to the left. It did not sound like they were having any better luck.

Duncan paused in the next chamber and tugged some wires sticking out of a wall. "I wonder if this was once an old radio shack. For communicating and coordinating Axis forces."

"Could be." She cast her gaze wider. "Though, as remote as this bunker is, I think its purpose was less about fighting and more about hiding. Meant as a shelter to retreat to in case of danger."

"You may be right. This place is certainly off the beaten track."

They continued on, searching room by room. After another ten minutes, the scuff of boots drew her attention. A glow of lights revealed the return of Laurent and Archie.

"Anything?" Duncan asked.

"*Non,*" Laurent reported. "And it's getting late. We'll do a sweep of the third level below. If we don't find anything, we should get some food in us, then bed down. As tired as we all are, we could easily be missing something."

"That's if there's anything here at all," Archie added sourly.

Laurent ignored him. "We can start fresh in the morning."

Sharyn longed for her bedroll and followed the others to the stairs that led down to the third level.

As they reached the steps, Russo called from above. "I've got the fire going. And some pans heating up. I also need to feed Katch. I've learned never to leave a cat hungry before going to bed."

The lynx had followed his mistress to the stairwell, but still, the cat hung back, his eyes aglow, sheltering behind the woman's legs. His gaze was fixed not on them, but on the twist of stairs heading deeper. His hackles remained up, shivering with tension. It had taken some convincing to get the beast to come even this far into the bunker.

"We'll join you shortly," Laurent said.

"Don't be long. Don't want to burn the sausages I brought."

Archie looked like he wanted to follow the woman, drawn by the promise of food, but Laurent grabbed his elbow and drew him away. They descended to the next level and spread out again. This floor was much like the others, ruined by age, neglect, and mischief. Only here, chamber after chamber held the oxidized skeletons of old bunk beds, now just metal frames, bent and beaten, and shoved haphazardly against walls or toppled over.

Sharyn and Duncan worked their way through this deadfall of rusted metal, risking tetanus with every step.

"This whole floor must have once served as the bunker's dormitory," Duncan said. "One large enough to house several hundred people. Which supports your theory of this being an evacuation shelter."

"Maybe . . ."

Duncan stared over at her, likely noting her hesitation.

She waved away any further inquiry, not sure what was nagging her.

After working through another dozen rooms, they rejoined Laurent. The tall man stood before a chiseled wall. He inspected the handiwork closely.

"What's got your attention?" Duncan asked.

Laurent turned to them, fingering a few marks. "This chiseling.

Both here and elsewhere. It's all far cruder than I'd expect. Like it was done with tools predating World War II."

Sharyn squinted closer, trusting his archaeological expertise. "Are you thinking these rooms had already been dug out *before* the arrival of the Axis forces?"

"I do. And if I'm right, then the locals would have surely known about this place. It reminds me of what Gabriel told us—how those limestone quarries under his family's château had once been used as a refuge for people fleeing the Napoleonic Wars. This may have served the same end."

"Until it was co-opted by the Italian army during the war," Duncan added.

Sharyn frowned. "If that's true, if this place is older, it would support that this could very well be the place we came to find."

Archie shrugged heavily. "Then *where's* the entrance to this bloody treasure trove." He swept his flashlight's beam across the spread of dark chambers. "Nothing's here."

"Maybe it got destroyed when the army remodeled the bunker," Duncan whispered, as if fearful of voicing this worrisome possibility too loudly.

Laurent rubbed his temples. "I don't know. But we'll think more clearly once we've gotten some sleep."

Sharyn offered no argument against this. Her head ached from the strain, from hunger, from exhaustion. As they all slogged back to the steps, something continued to nag at her, but she shoved it aside and focused on the mystery at hand.

Once on the stairs, Sharyn confronted Laurent. "Maybe it would help our search if we had a fuller understanding of what happened in the past. Of how the *Gardiens* discovered the gold cache in Libya."

"You're right." Laurent pointed to the flickering glow above. "But that's a story best told around a campfire."

47

8:19 p.m.

Duncan kept close to the flames, with his feet resting near the fire. He had tugged off his boots and let the heat dry his socks. He luxuriated in the warmth.

Russo had built the campsite inside the hollowed-out tower. Above, snow and wind whipped across a pair of high windows, fierce enough to draft the smoke outward like a chimney.

Though they were exposed to the blizzard beyond the bunker's main door, the enclosed walls of the tower helped trap in the heat. It had grown so warm that the group had shed their parkas. All their faces shone ruddy from the fire.

Dinner had also been shared. Sausages, hard cheese, and bread. In addition, Russo had brought forth a bottle of wine. Even Sharyn took a splash in the tin cup from Laurent's camping gear.

Russo finally stood up. "I need to feed Katch, if he'll eat." She grabbed a plastic container from her pack. "Raw meat. Best to do it from a distance as it whets his bloodlust. I'll take him down a level just in case."

Once the woman left with the cat, Sharyn broached the subject she had raised earlier, keeping her voice low and turning to Laurent. "What exactly happened in Libya? What lessons did the *Gardiens* learn during the recovery of the cache of gold coins?"

Laurent drained his cup. "Foremost, we learned *not* to discount the cunning of the *Confrérie*."

"Who stole the treasure from under you," Duncan said.

"Yes. While we were transporting the gold out of Africa. The Brotherhood somehow gleaned word of what was aboard our cargo ship. It was raided in the Mediterranean, and the ship hauled to Italy, where Axis forces eventually commandeered the bulk of the ancient coins."

Duncan frowned. "And you don't know what happened to it afterward."

"Throughout the war, the Nazis stole priceless art and treasures, then as the Reich fell, they shipped everything off by truck, boat, and train." Laurent shrugged. "We believe the gold ended up in Poland, where it later vanished. Either buried somewhere out there or maybe stolen in turn by the Russian army as it swept through the country."

Duncan remembered similar stories told to him by his grandfather. Of jewelry, art, currency, gold—all confiscated by the Germans. Most of it stolen from the Jewish people. Additionally, countless cultural artifacts had been removed from occupied countries. It all got whisked away. Gold was melted into bullion. Relics and artwork cloaked behind forged documentation. The treasures ended up being hidden in mines, castles, and bank vaults.

"But going back to your story," Sharyn pressed Laurent, "how were the coins found? You said the *Gardiens* deciphered the location from the First Adage, like we did the Second."

"Indeed."

Duncan pictured his grandmother's smiling face. "Using tools devised by the cryptographers at Bletchley Park."

Laurent nodded. "The site was located in central Libya. About eight hundred kilometers from the coast. Within the spread of a massive dormant volcanic field called the Haruj, which covers forty thousand square kilometers. Large enough to be visible from space."

Archie winced. "That's a lot of territory to search."

"The decryption of the First Adage pointed to a corner of this prehistoric flow, where it had shattered into deep chasms and eroded canyons, an area the Bedouins and other desert peoples eventually used as a mining site. My grandfather joined the expedition to search this region in 1940, during the height of the Western Desert campaign, when British, Italian, Egyptian, and German forces battled fiercely in the area."

"My grandfather fought in that same desert," Duncan noted, again feeling the twining of fate. "At the same time, too."

"And now here we are," Laurent said. "Continuing in their footsteps."

Duncan shivered despite the campfire's heat.

Sharyn shifted this narrative forward. "Back to the lava field. What did your grandfather say about the discovery of the treasure? Did he give any details? Any clues that could help us here."

"Less clues than warnings."

Archie shifted straighter. "What do you mean?"

"It took the team a month to uncover a hidden vault deep in a series of lava tubes. Especially as the group had to be careful of boobytraps left to protect the site from errant trespassers."

Sharyn glanced into the depths of the dark bunker. "What sort of traps?"

"Rockfalls, spiked pits. Even the treasure vault itself had an insidious pressure-triggered setup. When removing the gold, the entire cavern nearly caved in. Only the timely repositioning of a heavy ore cart stopped this from happening."

Duncan shared a worried look with the others. "If the same's true here, the Axis forces who refurbished this place might've inadvertently triggered one of those traps. It could've destroyed the entrance."

"I can't discount that. Or that we're even looking in the right spot."

"When this vault was eventually found in Libya," Sharyn asked, "what did the entrance look like? You told us before that Saint-Germain's book had been needed to open it."

"That's true. In deciphering the First Adage, Saint-Germain warned that his book was the doorway's key. But he offered no further elaboration. It took weeks before the team stumbled upon a small alcove, carved by hand, in a remote cavern. My grandfather had walked past it countless times. He had thought it was a niche for a mining lamp. But when the team tried to use it as such, they discovered their lamp clung stubbornly to the stone. Further inspection revealed the rock to be rich in magnetite."

"A magnetic ore," Sharyn whispered.

Laurent nodded. "The niche also matched the dimensions of the book. Once my grandfather set the tome inside and opened it there, the doorway unlocked, employing some alchemy of magnetism. A section of wall dropped away, revealing a tunnel that led to the hidden vault."

Duncan frowned. "I don't remember seeing any such niche down here."

"But many of the walls are bricked over," Sharyn reminded him.

Archie groaned. "Many? It's like half this place. If that alcove is hidden behind one of those walls, it'll take months to break through them all."

"And that's assuming it's even here," Duncan sighed.

"And not accidentally destroyed," Sharyn added.

"Or we could be wrong about this spot entirely," Laurent finished.

A low growl drew their attention from the fire. Past the tower's threshold, Russo reappeared with her flashlight, leading Katch, who looked anxious to return to the warmth—or maybe the cat simply wanted to get out of the shadowy depths of the bunker.

Russo confirmed this as she rejoined them, lifting her plastic container. "Could only get him to eat a few pieces. Between the wailing storm and his edginess in this confinement, he's not in the mood for dinner. I shouldn't have tried to take him down a level."

Archie shifted farther away as Katch shoved inside. The cat kept to the wall, his eyes on the doorway out of the tower.

"What's got him so nervous?" Sharyn asked.

Russo shrugged. "Ask him. He's always been a bit temperamental. I wouldn't read too much into his behavior."

"Or maybe, like I said before, he senses one of those witches you told us about." Archie tried to make it sound like a joke, but he was not convincing.

Russo didn't help matters. "It could be. The *anguana* are said to guard many caves up in these mountains." She then cast their group a hard look. "Especially if such a cavern should hold a great treasure."

Duncan winced. "You overheard us?"

"Acoustics underground are tricky."

Laurent eyed her. "Is this going to be a problem?"

Russo opened her container, pulled out a cube of meat dripping with blood, and tossed it on a hot pan still sitting at the edge of the fire. She then spun a finger next to one of her ears. "I think you're all *molto pazzo*. But if not, the species repopulation effort in these mountains could use a large boost in funding."

"I'm sure we can work something out," Laurent acknowledged. "If we find anything, that is."

Sharyn sighed softly, still staring off into the darkness beyond the firelit tower. "Those stories of witches . . ." she mumbled.

"What about them?" Duncan asked.

He was surprised Sharyn was giving any credence to such tales. She had never struck him as superstitious, especially for someone enrolled in a postgrad program on witchcraft.

She faced the fire and shook her head. "It's nothing."

Duncan frowned, noting the pinch to her eyes as she gazed into the flames. Something was clearly troubling her.

Before he could press her about it, Laurent stirred to his feet. “We should all try to get some sleep. We’ll rotate shifts. To keep the fire stoked.”

Duncan knew this wasn’t the only reason. He turned toward the outer bunker door, where the blizzard continued to blow outside. He remembered the helicopters descending into San Vito and accepted a hard truth.

Witches aren’t the only dangers in these mountains.

48

8:22 p.m.

Who holds a carnival during a blizzard?

From Naomi's perspective, that's what this boisterous and brightly lit corner of San Vito appeared to be. All this strangeness—the booming music, the glowing brilliance, the cheering voices—had drawn her out of the dark, snow-swept streets.

With her limp, she struggled down the pedestrian alleyway. Bars packed both sides. Sheltered by the press of tall buildings, snow fell heavily, but the winds were somewhat tamed.

But not the people.

Drunken revelers crowded the narrow street. All around, off-key choruses were shouted more than sung. Bottles clinked. Bodies bumped. A group of men caroused past in nothing but boxers, braving the snow, maybe celebrating the coming ski season. Or more likely simply using the storm as an excuse to let loose.

As she fought onward, someone grabbed her shoulder, nearly drawing a scream from her. She expected to feel a gun at her back or a knife in her ribs. Instead, she turned and found a familiar face leering down, cherry-cheeked and bleary-eyed.

The man—still in the same Moncler parka and Bogner cap—pinched his fingers at his lips, pantomiming smoking. "*Bene, sì?* You need more? I can get you."

Naomi searched around for this guy's drug-dealing partner—

the older woman—but there was no sign of her. Still, considering this raucous crowd, it was likely a good place to do business this night.

But that's not what I came here for.

She turned to the man, remembering his name. "Antonio, I need a phone."

It was her turn to play the mime, pretending to hold a cell to her ear. It was one of the reasons she had risked leaving the dark streets. That and she needed a port in this storm, to warm away the threat of frostbite, to gain the insulation of others around her.

"Phone no good," Antonio said. "No service. Towers snowed over."

She had feared as much, but she had a back-up plan. During her flight across town, she had made one stop. She had ducked into the lighted—and thankfully—warm vestibule of an Italian bank. For the first time since being thrust into all of this, she had used her debit card and withdrawn her maximum daily allowance.

Three hundred euros.

She saw no reason not to risk this. The Brotherhood already knew she was in town. After grabbing the cash, she had fled—though, with this storm, she doubted the notification of the withdrawal would reach her pursuers any time soon. Plus, her effort at the bank had not been solely to secure cash, but also to verify what she had hoped to be true.

The drug dealer had begun to turn away, but she grabbed him. "What about an internet café? Is there anything like that near here?"

From the success of her withdrawal, she hoped this meant the regional internet services remained operational.

Antonio scrunched up his face, then slowly nodded with a shrug. "But might be closed."

She knew most such cafés were open 24/7, so she was willing to take this chance. "Can you show me?"

He thrust out a palm. "Twenty euros."

She sighed, gave him a scathing look, and fingered out a single bill without revealing how much cash she had on hand. "Take me there."

He headed off, shoving through the drunken crowd, forging a path for her. He noted her limp. "You hurt."

"Don't worry about it."

"I get you oxy. *Molto bene*. You feel better."

She considered it, but she feared the current blizzard-pricing would drain her meager funds. "No. I'm fine."

The level of gouging became clearer when her guide turned the next corner. Steps away, a green sign glowed through the snow, emblazoned with a stylized cup of steaming coffee and the word *internet* stenciled beneath it.

Antonio waved with a great flourish. "Here it is."

She rolled her eyes, pushed past him, while offering a sarcastic, "*Grazie*."

"*Prego*," he responded and retreated into the riotous crowd.

As she entered the establishment, she found the place packed, which, for its small size, meant about seven patrons. Plainly, she was not the only one seeking a means of outside communication.

She headed to the café's barista, a sullen-looking teenager who was reading a curled-up paperback of Stephen King's *The Shining*. She found his choice of material especially appropriate considering the blizzard.

His gaze flicked to her without raising his face from the book.

"I . . . I need to buy twenty minutes," she said.

He simply pointed to a credit card reader.

"I'd rather pay in euros."

He shook his head and tapped the reader, making it clear this was a cash-free establishment.

She frowned and grabbed her wallet. She had already used her debit card, so what did one more hit on her account matter?

In for a penny, in for a pound.

She tapped her card, got assigned a computer, and set to work. She had to hurry knowing she had just given away her location. Still, she had no idea how long it would be before the enemy responded.

On the computer, she did a swift search for the email address of the British embassy in Rome. She then opened her Google account and dispatched a note with a header asking it to be forwarded to *Sir Avery Bailey.*

Archie's father.

While the man no longer worked at the embassy, someone over there surely still had his contact information. She was lucky to have learned his full name, knowledge she had gained from Archie bragging about his father being knighted. It also helped that Naomi had a nearly eidetic memory.

She quickly typed her note, trying to ignore the clock ticking in her head. She kept the gist of her message concise: *We're innocent. We're in trouble. Send help to San Vito di Cadore.*

She hit send. She felt relieved but far from hopeful. Especially knowing the snail's pace of British bureaucracy. There was no telling *when* her email would reach Archie's father—or anyone, for that matter.

Fears plagued her.

Will they even believe me? Will it do any good?

She moved on to another resource, one certain to garner more immediate attention. She shifted the corded eyeball of the computer's camera closer—and logged in to her TikTok account.

She recorded and posted a short personal plea to her followers, repeating the same message from her email. She prayed for it to light a firestorm.

But even then, would it be enough with time running so short?

Especially for one of us.

Once done, she hurried out of the café and into the street. After the warmth inside, the icy cold forced the air from her lungs. She gasped as she turned the corner—and ran straight into the Moncler-clad entrepreneur again.

Antonio steadied her. “Where are you going?”

She shoved past him and headed away. “To help a friend.”

49

11:51 p.m.

Aggravated, Sharyn kicked inside her bedroll and heaved onto her side. Though exhausted, sleep still escaped her. It wasn't due to the screaming winds, or the snap of a dry branch tossed into the fire by Russo, who had this watch. Or even Archie's snoring.

Instead, her mind kept working on a puzzle, one she could not solve, and she knew why.

I'm missing a piece, something right in front of me that I'm not seeing.

She turned over again and found a pair of eyes shining at her with concern.

Duncan shifted in his rumpled bag. "What's wrong?" he whispered.

"I don't know. Nothing. I'm just too much in my head."

He moved back and flipped up the edge of his bedroll. "Come here."

"I don't—"

"Just do it."

She gave in, too tired to argue, too lonely in her thoughts. She slipped out of her bedroll, crawled over to his, and tucked herself inside. Both were fully clothed, but she could still feel the furnace of his body as she settled against him. His arms pulled her deeper into that heat.

She remembered the last time they had shared a bed.

No doubt he did, too.

It kept them silent for several breaths.

She closed her eyes and rested her cheek in the crook of his shoulder. He leaned his chin near the nape of her neck, his stubble rough but reassuring.

"Do you want to talk about it?" he asked, his voice just an exhalation.

"No . . . not yet."

She feared if she spoke her concerns aloud, gave them too much weight, it would slip away from her. She simply needed the problem to steep inside her, to brew into something more substantial. By now, she knew she could not force it. It would have to come on its own.

Still, the pressure of time weighed on her. Anxiety kept her taut. Perhaps sensing this, Duncan spooned closer, cocooning her with his body. She let herself fall into his embrace, relaxing into it. He hardened in turn, but she felt no demand in his bodily response, only support, a silent promise that his steel was hers if she needed it.

Recognizing this, the tension sighed out her.

She began to drift off—when another sharp crackle of wood drew her attention. Through lids barely open, she watched Russo toss another branch into the flames, retrieving it from the pile she had gathered earlier, the refuse left over from prior trespassers.

Sharyn stared at the stack next to the fire.

All that wood . . .

Her breath caught in her throat, as something suddenly struck her.

Could that be it . . . the missing piece?

Duncan must have felt the shift inside her. "Sharyn . . ."

"Not yet," she whispered, repeating herself.

She still wanted to sleep on it, too exhausted to fully trust herself with this idea.

"In the morning . . ." she promised.

She knew she didn't have the complete answer, just a possibility. Still, it was enough for now, enough for her to relax more fully. The strong arms around her and the warm musk of Duncan's scent helped, too. As she snuggled deeper into his embrace, she felt his heartbeat as if it were her own.

"What about the morning?" Duncan mumbled back at her.

As her lids drowsed closed, she noted another set of eyes glowing out of the shadows and answered Duncan.

"Not sure . . . but I may need to borrow Russo's cat."

SIXTH

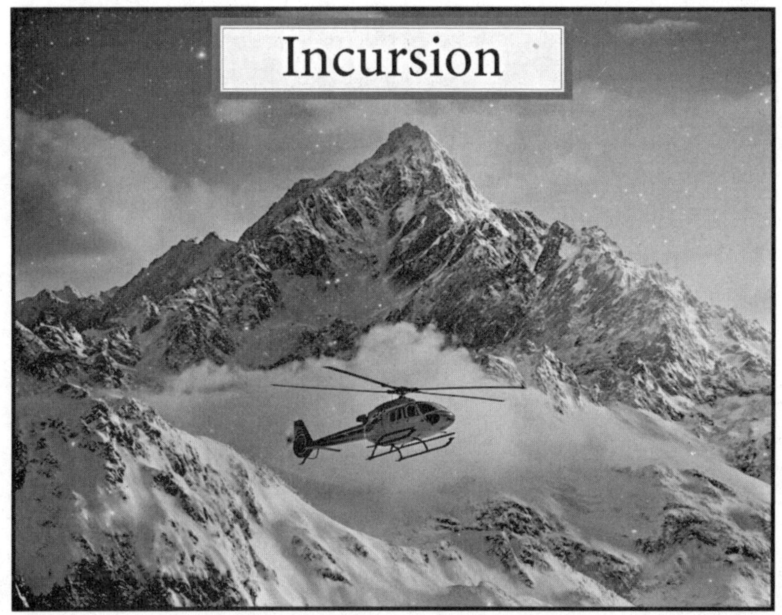

50

November 4, 7:03 a.m. CET

Monte Antelao, Italy

Sharyn stood at the bunker's door, staring out as a new day dawned. She cradled a tin cup of coffee in her hands, so hot it threatened to burn her palms. Russo had prepared the blend by balancing a dented, well-used percolator on hot ashes at the edge of the campfire.

She sipped at the steaming brew and surveyed the mountains outside. The blizzard had finally blown itself out sometime during the night, leaving behind skies that ached an impossible blue after such a fierce storm. A few straggling clouds marred the expanse, and pillows of ice-mist hugged the slopes and sifted through the lower forest.

Otherwise, the world outside had been sculpted of snow. Rolls of wind-swept powder formed ridges along the slopes. The narrow cliffside trail lay buried in white. Above, huge cornices hung in sharp-edged waves, frozen in place. Closer at hand, a waist-high mound filled the apron outside. The bunker might have been totally buried, except the fire in the tower had heated its stones, enough to hold the storm at bay.

Outside, snowmelt dripped and ran down the bricks. Huge icicles had formed a row of fangs across the top of the doorway. Higher up, streams of smoke trailed into the sky.

Duncan drew alongside her. "Everyone is finished with breakfast. Laurent wants us to begin a renewed search of the levels below."

She nodded and turned to him. "How are you feeling?"

"Tired and sore. You?"

"Same. But the coffee is helping." She squinted at him. Her inquiry to him had not been a casual one. "Yesterday, when we were down below, did you feel sick?"

"What do you mean?"

"I had a horrible headache. I thought it was from exertion and stress. But I saw Laurent rubbing his temples as if he were suffering the same."

Duncan's gaze turned into a long contemplative stare, then he slowly nodded. "I had felt a migraine coming on. I get them sometimes." He frowned at her. "What are you thinking?"

She headed back inside. "Let's check with the others first."

They crossed through the bunker's main chamber to the archway that led into the tower. The fire inside had turned the air stiflingly hot, especially after they had faced the frigid landscape outside.

Duncan challenged Archie with the same question.

His friend shrugged. "My sinuses always bother me. So, I can't say if it was any worse than usual."

Sharyn frowned, finding this far from conclusive.

Laurent drew closer. "I had a stabbing pain behind my eyes. But what are you getting at, Ms. Karr?"

She waved to the large stack of dry branches by the fire. "I don't think we were the first visitors to suffer this way. Past campers went to a lot of effort to haul up so much fuel for their fires. Yet, they never got through it all. Over the decades, more and more wood ended up accumulating here, abandoned as those who trespassed became sick and, either consciously or not—or maybe believing they were hungover—they got driven out."

Duncan's eyes widened. "You're thinking the air down below is bad. Stale, maybe poisoned by carbon dioxide. Like you find sometimes in deep caves."

"Not *gone* bad. I think it's *always* been bad." She turned to Russo, who had stopped stacking the tin breakfast plates to listen. "Your story of witches, those who cast spells that knocked out trespassers, then killed them—"

"The *anguana*."

Sharyn nodded. "It's almost as if that folk tale could have a natural basis, a way of explaining toxic caves like this one."

"Reminds me of the Salem witch trials," Duncan said. "Where the hallucinations and seizures that triggered the accusations are believed to have been caused by ergot poisoning, from a toxic fungus on moldy rye bread."

Archie added his support. "Or how the magic found in potions and herbal remedies often had a pharmacological basis. Like Tag always keeps harping about."

Sharyn pointed to the stairwell. "If this cavern system existed long before the bunker, I could see such a myth rising out of these depths. People could have been sheltering down here for centuries, especially if the spaces were made more habitable by chiseling them out."

"Like with the Barbiers' limestone quarry," Laurent noted.

She faced the group and broached a fear that was more speculative. "But I don't think it's carbon dioxide that's the source of the poisoning here. The bunker's lowest level isn't all that *deep*. I wouldn't expect the air to be all that bad."

"Then what is it?" Laurent pressed her.

She stared hard at him. "I think it's a boobytrap."

51

7:55 a.m.

Duncan kept well back from the frenzied lynx. Russo had attached a leash to the cat's collar and sought to draw Katch toward the stairwell. The lynx hissed and snarled. Claws dug at the stone, looking for traction. His entire coat bristled out, as if the beast had been shocked by a cattle prod.

Duncan frowned.

Even if we had such a weapon, I doubt it would move the cat down those steps.

Russo must have realized this, too, and glared at Sharyn. "*Signorina,* if you wish me to force Katch, I will need more of a reason to torture him like this."

Sharyn stood with her arms crossed, looking ill at the treatment of the cat. She swallowed and nodded. "I'm sorry. Truthfully, I don't know if this will accomplish anything. I was hoping that if we could get him into the lower levels, we could have him sniff out the wellspring of this toxin. It likely protects the doorway we're looking for."

"I don't smell anything," Archie said.

"It's clearly odorless. Same as carbon dioxide. But Katch is plainly responding to something. And a feline's nose is far stronger than ours."

Russo nodded. "Fourteen times as strong. Still, their sense of smell is not as acute as their sight and hearing. Lynxes are mainly nocturnal. Their night-vision is exceptional, as is their hearing, making them formidable hunters in the dark."

As if ready to demonstrate this talent, Katch bunched his haunches and growled.

"If we could borrow his keen nose," Sharyn explained, "it could help narrow down our search. To discover which, if any, of the brick walls might be hiding a secret door."

Laurent turned to Russo. "Is there any hope of gaining his co-operation?"

"I can try again."

Russo dropped to a knee and offered an open palm. She spoke firmly but softly in Italian. The cat's growl ebbed. His ears, which had flattened menacingly against his skull, lifted up, drawn by her voice.

Archie whispered, "I think it's—"

Katch snapped out a paw, lightning fast, and ripped claws across Russo's palm. The cat hissed and backed away.

Russo barely reacted, only showing a slight pinching of her eyes. Blood welled thickly and dripped to the floor. Though her hand had been gouged to the bone, the woman kept her arm out and continued talking calmly.

Clearly this wasn't her first mauling. Last night, while they were preparing dinner, Russo had stripped off her coat and rolled up her sleeves. Her leathery arms had been crisscrossed with ropes of scars.

Katch sank his belly to the floor. His eyes glowed on the blood, on the wound. His hissing quieted into a soft mewling, as if recognizing the damage he had wrought, grieving over it.

"*Va bene, Katch. Sto bene . . .*"

Finally, the lynx crawled forward, bowing his head. Russo reached her other hand and reassured him, still murmuring, rubbing the spots she must know well, earning the whisper of a purr.

Duncan held his breath, especially when Russo detached the lead from the cat's collar.

After another minute, Katch grew more relaxed. Russo leaned closer, nearly nose to nose. The cat bumped the tip of his muzzle into her, then rubbed his cheek across her chin.

Afterward, Russo stood slowly. She shook out a bandana from a pocket and bound her wounded hand, using her teeth to knot the bandage. "I should not have attached the lead. It's my fault. I've not leashed him in more than a year. I've been training him to be self-sufficient, readying him to be free. So, he's right to lash out. It's a good sign of the independence he will need in the wild."

Duncan took her at her word.

Sharyn stared toward the steps. "Do you think you can get him to follow you down?"

"Right now, he's feeling guilty, so he'll likely cooperate. But I can't say for how long."

"Then we should get going," Laurent warned.

52

8:48 a.m.

Sharyn waited with the others. The group gave Russo and Katch space to challenge the steps, then slowly followed behind.

As they descended, she remembered a moment yesterday on these same stairs, when Russo had told them the campfire was ready. The lynx had hidden behind the woman's legs and stared down—not at them, but at the steps heading deeper.

Knowing the cat's cooperation had a time limit, Sharyn offered a suggestion. "We should go straight to the third level. I think that floor spooks him the most."

Russo agreed. "When I fed him last night, I could only get him down one floor. He balked at going any farther."

"Makes sense," Archie said. "If I was hiding a door, I'd put it as deep as possible."

Russo kept her charge moving along the steps, skipping past the second level. Momentum and guilt got Katch all the way down. But as they exited onto the third floor, the group only managed to cross a handful of yards before Katch hissed and retreated to the left, banging into some of the rusted bunkbeds in his haste to escape.

Duncan pointed to the right. "He clearly doesn't like that direction."

"Then that's where we must go," Sharyn said.

Through trial and error and an angry spray of urine from Katch, they slowly narrowed the search to a corner of the floor. Already, Sharyn's headache had returned.

Others suffered, too.

"I feel a migraine coming on," Duncan noted with a wince.

"If we stay down here too long," Sharyn warned, "this boobytrap may prove deadly."

Laurent frowned. "Back in Libya, the traps were cruder, easier to avoid if one paid attention. This is far more insidious. Invisible and slow."

"It could be a reflection of the book," Duncan noted. "The encryptions got harder to solve between the First and Second Adages. Maybe these traps mirror the same escalating difficulty."

Finally, they reached a room that Katch refused to enter. His panic grew severe, far worse than when he had been leashed. He hissed and spat and finally fled off into the darkness, likely aiming for the steps to head up on his own.

Sharyn faced the room, which had its share of skeletal beds shoved to one side. All three walls were chiseled rock. The far side had been bricked over.

"Could that be it?" she whispered.

Duncan stepped over the threshold. "Only one way to find out."

They all followed him into the room, even Russo, who must have decided to give Katch some privacy and space to calm down.

Once at the wall, they spread out to inspect its length. It stretched five yards across and half that in height. Like many areas of the bunker, it had been heavily tagged with graffiti, marred by neon swaths of spray paint. Its surface was pitted and pocked by broken bricks. Sections showed crumbling mortar, forming deep crevices.

Sharyn pointed her flashlight into an empty pocket created by a pair of missing bricks. At the back, raw rock reflected her light's shine. The wall there showed the same chiseling as the others. As she reached in, she felt a slight gap between the masonry work and the imperfections of natural stone.

Archie called from a few steps away. "Look at this!"

She shifted over, drawing the others.

"Or I should say, *feel* this." Like her, Archie had stuck his hand into a hole formed by an *L*-shaped pattern of lost bricks. "There's a crack in the rock back here."

They each took turns to confirm it.

Sharyn probed the fissure, but her fingers were not long enough to discern how far it went. But she had a guess. "I wonder if this is the source of the gas, something seeping in from down deeper."

Laurent grabbed the ax he had slung over his shoulder. "If it is deadly, we should not waste any time."

No one argued.

Sharyn's head already pounded hard.

Working together, they used their collapsible shovels and Laurent's ax to begin pulling down the wall. The areas with missing bricks offered vantage points to pry and break their way through. Russo, with her injured hand, helped by hauling and tossing broken debris out of the way. As more and more of the bulwark fell to their efforts, the work quickened—especially as what slowly revealed itself became apparent.

In less than twenty minutes, most of the wall had been cleared.

They all stepped back and inspected their handiwork.

"Christ almighty," Archie mumbled.

"No wonder the army bricked this wall," Duncan said.

Sharyn stared at the cracks and fissures that radiated across the dolomitic rock. It looked like a dark spiderweb. She pictured gasses flowing out of that expanse, filling these levels more heavily with poison.

Duncan frowned. "Even if the Axis forces didn't know about the danger of seeping gas, they must have wanted to shore up this wall as a precaution."

Sharyn felt sick and was sure she looked it. "If the army hadn't bricked all this over, we might not have survived the night."

Laurent nodded. "For the unwary, death would have come quickly. Which might have birthed the legend of a witch who killed trespassers."

Sharyn swallowed. "To survive coming down here, to reach the hidden door, you'd need to move swiftly. To do that, you'd have to know in advance *what* you were looking for. Knowledge that would only be gained if you knew about the site in Libya and learned its lessons."

Laurent pointed to the wall. "You had to know to look for *that*."

Sharyn stared at the center of the poisonous spiderweb—where an alcove had been carved into the rock.

The perfect size to hold a book.

"We found it," she said. "The entrance to the Second Adage's vault."

As they all gaped at the wonder before them, a new noise intruded, echoing from above. A heavy thumping. Faint, muffled by rock, but swiftly growing.

Duncan stared toward the roof. "A helicopter."

The noise steadily rose—not only in volume but numbers.

"Not a copter," Archie said. "Copters."

Despite the poisonous air, Sharyn breathed harder. She knew what approached. It was not a group of heli-skiers looking for fresh powder. She pictured the aircraft descending upon San Vito.

She stated what they all knew. "The *Confrérie* found us."

"But how?" Duncan asked.

She knew that answer, too.

53

10:36 a.m.

Naomi spied upon the chalet from the backseat of a heated SUV. The vehicle was parked a block down from the hotel. Her knee jagged up and down, spurred by her anxiety.

"What's taking so long?" she whined to the woman next to her.

"*Pazienza.* Antonio is on his way."

Naomi stared out the SUV and scowled at the helmeted gunman posted at the hotel door. She had no idea how many more soldiers were inside. But if the chalet was still under guard, it offered some hope that Tag was still alive.

But for how much longer?

Half an hour ago, Naomi had watched a small army exit the hotel. They had swarmed around the man who had threatened her in the room, along with his companion in a clerical collar. They had left in a row of Land Rovers. Shortly thereafter, a trio of helicopters had lifted off from a site outside of town. The three aircraft had swung high in formation, then aimed for the neighboring mountain.

Naomi knew this was bad.

The bastards must have broken Tag, tortured him into giving up the others.

The only bit of fortune was that the enemy had been forced to wait out the storm before attempting a mountain assault. The delay had allowed Naomi to make her own plans, to build her own army.

She turned to the woman seated next to her, who fingered a salt-filled charm. Despite her pounding heart, Naomi had to trust this woman, whose name she had learned was Chiara.

Last night, after exiting the internet café into the blizzard, Naomi had initially brushed off Antonio, then realized she needed his help if she had any hope of rescuing Tag. She confronted the man and asked him to take her to his boss.

They met in a coffeehouse at the edge of town. Naomi sought to lean on the good graces of the woman, sharing a tale of kidnapping and torture. She also showed Chiara her TikTok plea, the one she had posted to her WitchTok site, hoping the commonality of their shared interest in magic might sway the woman.

It did not—at least, not entirely.

What did convince Chiara was a trip this morning to an Italian bank. With the storm ended, the establishment was open. Inside, Naomi had drained her checking and savings account, drawing out fifteen thousand euros. She had handed it all to Chiara—along with a promise of more if they were successful in freeing Tag.

"Antonio comes now." Chiara craned around and stared behind their SUV. "As I said."

Naomi turned to look and grabbed the door handle, but the woman reached to Naomi's knee and forced it to stop bobbing. Rather than urging patience again, Chiara passed her the necklace with its charm.

"Be safe," the woman urged.

Naomi accepted this amulet of protection, touched by the gesture and generosity. Then again, fifteen thousand euros was a steep price to pay for a salt-filled trinket.

As she donned the charm, a group of ten young men appeared from around a corner—dressed in nothing but boxers, boots, and scarves. Chiara and Antonio must have been inspired by the antics from last night. The group sang and hung on one another, clutching beer bottles. They passed the SUV and continued down the block toward the hotel.

Behind them, Antonio appeared, still in his Moncler parka and Bogner cap. Only now he wore a pair of Oakley sunglasses, which mirrored the bright morning.

Naomi donned a matching pair and exited the SUV. She had also been lent a Moncler parka, currently zippered over her old clothes.

As she joined Antonio, he slipped her arm under his.

"*Buongiorno,*" he said, leaning close.

At the moment, she found nothing *good* about this morning.

"Let us go visit your friend," Antonio encouraged her.

Ahead of them, the rowdy bunch reached the hotel and swarmed boisterously around the lone guard, who struggled to make sense of this group of half-naked men. They bumped and cajoled him, offering a bottle. He rested his hand on his holstered pistol, but before he could do more, a knife appeared out of nowhere. The tip was pressed against the man's carotid. Hands grabbed him roughly. The crowd, still smiling with good cheer, forced him from his post.

As he was dragged away, Naomi and Antonio ducked through the hotel doors and into the lobby. It was empty of patrons, with only a frightened-looking concierge at the front desk. It looked as if the marauders had cleared out most of the hotel.

Antonio laughed loudly at nothing, drawing the eye of another soldier standing at the base of the stairs. Arm in arm, they approached the gunman. Antonio shouted something in Italian to the man, whose face was unreadable behind the reflection of his helmet's face shield.

The guard blocked them with a raised arm, but Antonio pretended to stumble and jabbed the Taser he had palmed at his side. He struck the man under his armpit, where there was no armor.

The jolt was strong enough to lift the man off his feet, sending him crashing to the stairs. Antonio hit him again with the Taser, leaving him limp, then grabbed his side-arm. He passed his Taser over to Naomi.

Together, they raced up the stairs, fearing the noise might have alerted others. Once at the top, they found the hallway empty. Clearly, the leader of this mercenary force had pulled away most of his men for the mountain assault, leaving only a skeleton crew behind to guard their prisoner, a captive with cerebral palsy who offered little threat.

Ahead, the battered door to their hotel room hung crooked on its hinges and had been left partially ajar. Voices carried to them. A man and a woman. It sounded like they were arguing, angry or frustrated.

"Try again!" the woman shouted.

Naomi could guess who that was. The Indian woman—the one called Burman. Naomi had never seen her leave the hotel.

Antonio stepped forward, taking the lead. "Let me."

He peeked through a gap in the door jamb, took a breath, then shouldered into the room, his weapon leveled. A moment later, a blast made Naomi jump—only it hadn't come from Antonio's gun.

Antonio came crashing back into the hall, knocked into a hard spin by a bullet to the shoulder. His weapon went flying. Naomi fell back, landing on her backside. She managed to grab the skittering pistol as an armored figure shoved into the hall.

She struggled to get the weapon pointed.

The soldier had no such problem and aimed his pistol at Antonio's face.

Another thunderous blast deafened Naomi.

Only this time, the noise had come from behind her. She twisted to see Chiara standing there, a pistol smoking in her cradled grip. Ahead, the soldier gasped and choked, shot through the neck.

Antonio kicked the legs out from under the man.

Chiara pulled Naomi up. "Hurry."

As they reached Antonio, blood seeped through his parka.

Still, he relieved Naomi of her pistol. From inside the room, a door slammed.

Fearing for Tag, Naomi rushed with the others into the room. No other assailants were in view. The Indian woman—Burman—had retreated out the French doors to the balcony. She held a pistol in one hand and a thick-antennaed satellite phone in the other.

Chiara swept her aim around the room, wary of any other hidden gunmen. Antonio focused his fury on the lone target in sight. He fired at Burman. His round shattered the window. Outside, the woman lifted her pistol and tossed it aside, plainly knowing any resistance would only get her killed.

Still, she kept her phone at her ear.

Fearing a call for reinforcements, Naomi ran toward the French doors. As she passed the sofa, she spotted Tag sprawled there, limp and unmoving, his face blue, his eyes staring glassily at the ceiling. His shirt had been torn open, showing burn marks on his chest from a defibrillator sitting on the floor.

No . . .

Naomi screamed, a wordless cry of rage, and burst out to the balcony.

Burman backed to the rail, still clutching the phone. She must have gone outside to get a bead on a satellite, as cell service remained down. She finally gave up and held the device to the side.

"I . . . It's not my fault," the woman begged. "His body couldn't handle the recovery. Had a seizure. We tried to revive him. I swear."

Naomi didn't care. She led with the only weapon at hand. She jammed the Taser into the woman's belly. Burman screamed, her body stiffening into a trembling rod. Unable to stop the momentum of her charge, Naomi shouldered into the woman, catching a jolting trace of the Taser before it automatically cut off.

The impact threw Burman over the balcony's edge.

Naomi's belly struck the rail.

Below, limp from the attack, Burman fell headlong. Her skull cracked into the plowed pavement and snapped her neck sideways. As her body sprawled, it went into convulsion. She still lived, but not for long.

Naomi turned away and stumbled back into the room.

Chiara knelt next to Tag.

In the distance, sirens blared, no doubt racing here.

"*Aiutatemi!*" Chiara snapped to Antonio.

Naomi didn't understand.

Chiara twisted to her. "He still has a heartbeat."

54

10:45 a.m.

"What do we do now?" Sharyn asked, fighting down panic.

The sweep of the helicopters had grown deafening, even down this deep. It was loud enough to rattle the skeletal bedframes in the room. Then a huge gust of wind blew from the stairwell, carrying with it a trace of snowy powder.

Duncan craned up. "One of the helicopters must have buzzed the tower."

"It's not like they have to guess where we are," Archie said. "This bunker is a hot coal sitting in the snow."

"They'll be on us before long," Laurent agreed.

"Maybe not," Russo said.

They had already explained the danger to her.

Laurent frowned. "What do you mean—"

"I know these mountains. I can buy you some time." Russo pointed to Duncan. "With me, young man. And be quick about it."

Before anyone could object or question her, the woman set off, cradling her injured hand. Duncan looked back at the group, plainly as mystified as any of them, then took off.

Sharyn turned to the alcove in the wall and pulled off her cross-body bag. "Maybe we should burn the book."

Laurent looked aghast at this suggestion.

"It's the only key to the door," she explained. "If nothing else, we can keep the treasure from the Brotherhood's grasp."

"Destroying the book will only delay them. Once they eliminate us, they'll eventually bring in excavation equipment and dig the gold out."

"Even so, without Saint-Germain's diary, they'll lose the final treasure, whatever remains encrypted by the Third Adage."

Laurent slowly shook his head, his eyes pained. "Not only will the *Confrérie* suffer this loss, so will the world. I'd rather the Brotherhood win here and offer humanity some hope for a better outcome in the future."

"If the enemy is holding the key," Sharyn argued, "what hope is there? With the Brotherhood wielding the power behind the Third Adage, those murderous bastards could make things far worse for humanity."

"I'd still rather take that chance. The *Confrérie* are not of one mind. Various factions within their organization war with one another. We can only hope their better angels will eventually prevail."

Sharyn frowned at such an optimistic viewpoint. She remembered how she had prayed night after night for her father's *better angel* to show up.

It never did.

And the *Confrérie* were far worse.

Instead, she placed her trust in a proverb that had proven true throughout history: *Power corrupts, and absolute power corrupts absolutely.*

"Then what do we do?" Archie asked, repeating Sharyn's earlier question.

Laurent faced the alcove and sighed. "We open this door. Before I die, I would like to set eyes on the treasure beyond it."

Archie frowned. "I'd like to avoid the *die* part, if possible. Maybe there's a back door somewhere in there. A way to slip out."

Sharyn knew this was not likely. They had escaped out back

doors before. At the King's House, at the Barbiers' château. But that would not be possible here, of that she was certain.

Still, she unzipped her bag and pulled out the copper-clad volume, coming to a decision, agreeing with Laurent on one point:

I want to see this treasure, too.

She stepped over and placed the book into the alcove.

As she did, the roar of the helicopters died to a distant rumble. She glanced back. The trio of aircraft must have landed. Likely on the football field–size plateau nearby.

"We'd better be quick," Sharyn warned.

Laurent stepped forward and withdrew the small leather box from a pocket in his parka. He flipped it open and shook out two magnets into his palm.

Sharyn backed to give him room.

As before, Laurent set the poles of the magnetic rods to the top and bottom of the crystal orb, then slowly rotated the eye one full turn. Once this was done, the book's copper bands snapped open.

They all retreated.

Nothing happened.

Archie grimaced. "Maybe we should try—"

A gong-like chime sounded from the fissured wall. A rectangular crack appeared in the rock, framing the alcove—then the whole outlined section slowly sank away.

Sharyn recalled Laurent's words last night, explaining the source of this supposed magic: *an alchemy of magnetism* cast between the machinations inside Saint-Germain's diary and the magnetite impregnated in the surrounding rock.

"The book," Archie warned.

Sharyn flinched, then reacted quickly, alerted by his warning. She rushed forward and retrieved the volume from its niche before the slab dropped away. She hugged the book to her chest and stumbled back.

We dare not lose this.

As the slab receded into the floor, a stairway appeared beyond the threshold, descending deeper into the mountain.

Trembling, unsure how much time they had left, Sharyn moved closer. She stabbed the beam of her flashlight down its length. A wash of stale air exhaled out, no doubt ripe with poison.

Ignoring this danger, she took the first step toward the mystery below.

Let's go see what our deaths have bought us.

55

11:04 a.m.

Duncan huddled with Russo by the bunker's outer door. Off to the right, a localized blizzard obscured the large plateau that extended from the mountain's shoulder. Through the swirling snow, he watched a third helicopter descend and land, joining the two others. Its rotor wash swept the rock of powder, snow, and ice.

All three aircraft popped their hatches. Men in black armor and helmets piled into the snow, bearing weapons. Duncan tried to count their number, but the snowy squall made this difficult.

Still, if I can't see them, hopefully they can't see me.

He turned to Russo, who crouched over her open pack and got ready. He had already strapped a pair of snowshoes over his boots, as had she.

"We must move swiftly," Russo instructed. "Not only going out, but coming back."

He remained silent. He had no intention of staying out there any longer than necessary. As she sat back, she withdrew a yellow tube from her bag. It was as thick around as his forearm and as long. A fuse draped from one end.

She passed it to him. "This is packed with a kilo of TNT. So do not hesitate."

He nodded, spotting another charge inside her pack.

In case, I fail the first time.

He rubbed his shoulder, readying himself.

Russo pointed at the exit. “I can’t survey the landscape from this vantage. We’ll go out together. I’ll pick the best spot. Then you’d better prove your rugby skills.”

While she had prepped for this excursion, he had brought up his athletic prowess. It was less bragging as it was an attempt to reassure himself.

I can do this.

Russo squinted toward the open plateau, which remained clouded by mist and blown powder. “Let’s go.”

They exited the bunker, staying low, and ducked under the thick drape of icicles. Outside, their snowshoes aided the climb over the icy mound atop the apron. Russo led him to its far side and crossed over to the cliff’s edge, which dropped away into a precipitous plunge.

She turned her back on the danger and surveyed the challenge. Her gaze went high, to the top of the bluffs overlooking the bunker, where frozen cornices hung in huge swells and massive windblown curls.

As Russo surveyed them, harsh voices and shouted commands echoed from the neighboring plateau. Still, she remained calm. She rubbed her lips with her gloved fingers, squinting up, reading the ice and snow. She finally pointed her bandaged hand to a section of cornice that draped between the bunker and the cliff.

“There,” she said. “Can you throw the charge that far?”

“I had better.”

“*È vero,*” she agreed. “Then we run.”

Duncan held the yellow tube toward her. She flicked the lighter in her good hand and set the flame to the fuse. The cord flashed and burned a fiery eye that slowly worked down the line.

“Hurry,” Russo urged.

Duncan backed a step, careful of the drop behind him, and hauled his arm back.

Russo had already explained her expertise in such matters. Her occupation as a wildlife biologist had not been limited to fair weather. When it came to overseeing her project, she had spent many winter months in the mountains, where snowfall was unpredictable and avalanches a threat. For her own safety, she had learned to read such danger, anticipate them, and deal accordingly—by using explosive charges to trigger flows and release the pressure along a slope.

Duncan prayed her skills had not gone rusty over the summer.

Grimacing, he aimed for the spot she had pointed to, then whipped his arm forward with all the strength of his shoulder and back. Having held the position of a fly half on the rugby pitch, he had thrown plenty of balls far downfield, attempting a Hail Mary pass to change the outcome of a game.

None of them mattered more than this throw.

As the burning tube left his fingers, a spatter of gunfire erupted, sparking rounds off the bricks and stone. They'd been spotted.

Startled, Duncan's thumb nudged the red-capped end of the charge as it flew from his fingertips. The tube went cartwheeling wildly. He ducked low as the gunfire continued. Luckily, the distance and swirling snow made them hard targets.

At least for now.

Duncan winced and glanced high, judging his throw. The charge had struck a cornice overhead, impaling into the snow. It hung there precariously, ready to drop back. Unfortunately, he had also failed to hit the proper target.

With the bunker under fire, there would be no second chance.

Russo shouldered him away. "Move!"

Frogging in their snowshoes, they scaled back over the mound and dropped behind its ridge. Rounds tore into the snow and ricocheted off the bunker's façade.

Duncan craned up and saw his charge still hung in place, the fiery fuse flickering against the snow. But there was no time to appreciate his handiwork.

Russo grabbed his arm and hauled him toward the bunker door. Together, they dove headlong across the threshold. A fierce blast shook the world and deafened him for a breath. He skidded across the floor, then rolled around as a wall of snow crashed with a thunderous boom across the opening. A back wash of powder and ice buried his lower legs.

Gasping, he crab-crawled free and dragged Russo with him.

By now, the chamber had gone dark, lit only by the flickering glow of the neighboring fire in the tower. Ice crystals hung in the air, reflecting the flames, looking like burning ash.

He stared at the snowy wall blocking the exit. Faint light suffused through it, setting it aglow. It indicated that the barricade was not as thick as it could've been if his aim had been true.

Russo patted his leg. "You'll do better next time, *sì*?"

"There had better not be a next time," he muttered.

He stood up. Even with his bad toss, the enemy would have difficulty digging their way inside here. He turned to Russo and helped her to her feet.

"You bought us time," he said. "Like you promised."

"But not forever."

He understood and pointed toward the stairwell. "I'm going to head down and let the others know. They must be wondering about the blast."

"Do that. I'll keep watch." Russo searched around. "And be wary of Katch. He's somewhere in here and likely in a bad mood."

Him and me both.

Duncan glanced to the blockage of snow.

And maybe others.

56

11:19 a.m.

Red-faced and angry, Keir stomped from under the slowly spinning rotors. The pilots continued to keep the engines warm, not wanting them to seize up in the cold. He ducked out and crossed to Captain Ferhat.

"What do we do now?" Keir shouted, both out of fury and to be heard past the trio of idling aircraft.

Ferhat studied the snow-blasted face of the bunker with a pair of binoculars. "A moment," the man intoned.

Keir tried to read the captain's assessment, but his features were obscured by his helmet's polycarbonate face shield and a black balaclava—as was true for the thirteen men who made up his team.

Keir hunched into his parka, which came with a matching helmet, specially ordered for this sojourn. As an extra precaution, he wore a Kevlar vest under his coat. Still, it did little to hold back the cold, which burned his cheeks. Fine powder continued to swirl from the turning rotors. Each breath was like sucking ice into his lungs.

At least the bastard Tissot suffered the same. The cardinal and a younger cohort huddled together, whispering, so close it looked as if they were about to kiss. Keir had not bothered to supply them with helmets or body armor. Such neglect was punishment for their insistence on joining this expedition.

Ferhat finally lowered his binoculars.

"Well?" Keir pressed him.

"They were clever. I'll give them that." The captain swept an arm toward the precipitous path that ran from the plateau to the bunker. "We can clear the trail easily enough with shovels. It's too narrow to hold much snow. Take maybe an hour."

Keir nodded, satisfied with this timetable, but Ferhat was not done.

He shifted and pointed at the massive slide of snow covering the face of the bunker, sealing its entrance. "But that's a problem. It could take half a day or more to dig that out."

"We don't have that leeway. We must secure this site before too many eyes look this direction."

"Understood." Ferhat turned. "I anticipated that. And may have a solution to expedite matters. But it's not without risk."

"What?"

The captain turned and nodded toward two of his men. From the back of one of the helicopters, the pair carried forth a long gray tube with a metal bipod mounted under it.

Keir recognized the weapon, struggling to decide if Ferhat was clever or mad.

The two soldiers joined them and began setting up the rocket launcher.

57

11:21 a.m.

Sharyn crouched with Laurent and Archie on the dark stairs. They all carried flashlights, but the stygian blackness still hid what lay below. The steps ran in a straight course, angled steeply, heading toward the heart of the mountain.

A moment ago, a sharp blast had stopped their descent, echoing down from above. It was followed by a rush of noise that sounded like a freight train rolling overhead.

"Avalanche," Archie gasped out. "I've heard the same during snow control measures when I skied Zermatt a couple winters ago."

"Russo's delaying tactic," Laurent realized.

Sharyn pictured the bunker being buried. "How much time will that buy us?"

"No telling," Laurent said.

Archie glanced back up. "What about Duncan and Russo?"

Laurent shook his head. "We can't wait for them. Not with poison in the air. We keep going."

While fearful for the others, Sharyn did not argue. Her head hammered, and her vision had begun to pinch.

What manner of poison is this?

They continued down the steps, with Laurent leading. He set a swifter pace, likely equally afflicted. Sharyn still clutched Saint-Germain's book against her chest with one arm, while holding aloft her flashlight. The walls down here appeared less chiseled, nearly smooth, as if worn down by rushing water or melted through by some arcane means.

"The stairs end ahead," Laurent finally announced.

Thank god . . .

She closed upon the tall man, trying to see past his bulk. But as they neared the bottom, Laurent's flashlight revealed a tunnel continuing onward, heading even deeper into the core of the mountain.

How far does this go?

Laurent rubbed the heel of a hand between his eyes, clearly in pain, but it did not slow him—only distracted him. As he reached the bottom, the last step sank under his weight. Thrown off balance, he tripped forward into the tunnel and crashed to a knee.

No one spoke.

All held their breath.

Behind them, a familiar grating of stone echoed down the steps. Sharyn swung her flashlight's beam back up. Very faintly, she could spot movement. Still, it was enough to recognize their predicament.

"We're being sealed in," she said.

Archie glared at the offending step. "Another boobytrap."

Sharyn remembered Laurent's story of the pitfalls in Libya, both inside and outside the vault. He had even mentioned a pressure-sensitive trigger that had nearly collapsed the treasure cave.

"I've been foolish," Laurent admitted, standing up.

Sharyn took a deep breath, struggling to hold back nausea. She hoped it was born of stress and not toxicity.

"Stuck in here," she warned, "we won't last long."

Laurent turned and faced the tunnel. "Then pray there is not only treasure back there—but also a way to release the trap that holds us."

"If so," Archie said, "we'd better find it quick."

58

11:24 a.m.

Duncan pressed his palms to either side of the alcove in the wall. He then ran his fingers around the edges where a door should be. Even this close, he could not discern any outline. It had vanished amid all the chisel marks.

When he had rushed down here with his flashlight a moment ago, he had caught sight of a stone slab rising, accompanied by a low grinding of rock. By the time he reached it, the opening had sealed tight, as if it were never there.

He suppressed a moan and leaned back to shout. "Sharyn! Archie! Laurent!"

He doubted his voice would reach through the thick slab of dolomitic rock. Still, he leaned his ear to the array of cracks surrounding the alcove, hoping his call had carried through somehow. He strained for any response.

Nothing . . .

He backed a step, noting the book was gone, too, likely taken by the others. Without it, there would be no way to reopen the door. He swallowed hard, his head pounding, fiercer than the heartbeat in his throat. He felt ill and knew it wasn't just due to his panic. The toxin in the air was slowly poisoning him.

Now, with the outer bunker door blocked by snow, it would only grow more dangerous inside here. Even worse, the trio who had vanished below were sealed in even tighter and heading toward the source of the poison.

Duncan wrung his hands, something he hadn't done since he was a boy. He almost lost his grip on the flashlight.

What can I do?

He took a step back, then another, knowing the answer. To help the others, he could do only one thing: *Buy them time.* Enough of a window so they could figure a way out.

Recognizing this, he twisted around and rushed away from the fissured wall. He hit the stairs and headed up. As he did, he felt the spirit of his grandfather looking down upon him, helping Duncan accept his duty from here.

To defend this castle with my life.

59

11:27 a.m.

With the door sealed behind them, only one path remained open. Sharyn continued down the tunnel. Laurent limped a step ahead, having struck his knee hard when he fell. But his injury was the least of their problems.

Sharyn's stomach churned queasily. Her head pounded with every thud of her heart. Pain stabbed the back of her eyes, reaching all the way to the angle of her jaw. Still, she and the two men continued deeper down the poisonous passageway.

As they rounded a sharp curve, Laurent stumbled—but not because of his compromised leg. "We found it."

Sharyn and Archie crowded behind him.

Laurent edged forward slowly, pointing his flashlight.

Ahead, the passageway dumped into a cavernous space. The shine of their lights reflected back a golden sheen, as if setting fire to whatever lay inside. No one spoke as they crossed to the tunnel's end. They all held their breath as they stepped inside and gaped all around.

The cavern had been sculpted into a domed vault, held up by carved Doric pillars of dark dolomitic stone. The columns framed tiny chapels dug deeper. A few appeared to lead to other chambers farther back, likely forming a labyrinth of riches beyond measure.

In this chamber alone, gold shone everywhere. Yard-long trumpets hung on the walls, along with rows of gilded shields, which had turned into fiery mirrors. Overhead, dozens of massive lanterns and censers hung from the roof. On the floor, chests lay open, glittering with plates, cups, bowls, and crowns.

"The temple treasures," Archie murmured in awe.

Sharyn nodded.

Still, the chamber's most striking features were the massive seven-stemmed candelabras—ancient menorahs—sitting on pedestals carved out of the stone floor. While the modern Hanukkah menorah had nine branches, the oldest of them—still used as a symbol in synagogues and on the Israeli coat of arms—had only seven. Three of the towering relics rose on each side, standing as tall as Laurent's shoulders with stems as thick around as the man's wrist, all sculpted of pure gold.

Their group slowly worked deeper into the space.

"Look there," Laurent whispered, shining his light forward.

At the rear of the chamber, a seventh menorah beckoned. It stood in an arched alcove, set apart by itself. It was unlike the others in many ways. Not only was it larger by a third, but its branches were also thicker, more crudely sculpted. From the roughened surfaces, it looked as if it had grown in place versus being crafted by an artisan's hand. This illusion was amplified by its dark gray metal, nearly the same hue as the surrounding dolomitic rock.

But even that wasn't the strangest aspect to it.

"What's beneath it?" Archie asked.

They drew nearer, drawn forward by the mystery. Around the menorah's stone pedestal, a silvery moat shimmered, brimming with a dense liquid, as if a mirror had been melted and filled in around it. Once close enough, the vast breadth of this strange reservoir grew clearer. It wasn't just the foot-wide moat in front of the relic, but behind it, the alcove's archway opened into another chamber, even larger than this one. Back there, a sea of the same metallic-looking liquid filled the space, reflecting the beams of their flashlights.

"What the bloody hell is it?" Archie asked.

Sharyn knew and stepped away. "The source of the poison."

Archie turned to her. "What do you mean?"

"It's a lake of mercury," Sharyn said. "What used to be called quicksilver. While the metallic element remains a liquid at room temperature, it still gives off toxic vapors over time."

"A neurotoxin," Laurent clarified. "Such pools, far smaller, have been discovered in other archaeological sites. Back in 2014, mercury was found stored at the Temple of the Feathered Serpent in Mexico. The tomb of China's first emperor is rumored to flow with rivers of the stuff."

"We shouldn't be down here," Sharyn warned. "Not without ventilators and masks. We can only hope that the mercury here is less toxic. Maybe a safer amalgam of some sort."

Archie covered his mouth, as if that would help. "But why did Saint-Germain, or whoever built this place, fill it with something so dangerous? Just to make it a trap?"

Laurent answered. "Maybe not only that. Mercury was always revered by alchemists. They viewed it as the First Matter, the metal from which all other metals arose. It's why they believed mercury was so critical to their experiments with transmutation."

"Turning lead into gold," Sharyn said.

She retreated from the lone menorah, backdropped by its poisonous lake. To the left, a massive golden slab—three feet long and half as wide—stood like an altar, stacked with items of worship. Bowls, jars, dishes, lamps.

Laurent noted her attention. "It's another holy relic from the Second Temple. The Table of Showbread. During the Sabbath, twelve loaves of bread would be laid out, representing the twelve tribes of Israel, in honor of the manna given to the Jews fleeing through the desert."

Sharyn recognized the historical importance of such a discovery. Still, the bright gold only seemed to mock the dull candelabra in the alcove.

But was this done purposefully?

Archie pointed. "Do you think this is the same menorah stolen by the Romans? The holiest of holy Jewish relics?"

"It's not gold," Sharyn reminded him.

He nodded, accepting this.

"It's lead," she explained.

"What?"

She turned to Laurent. "I think I know how to get out of here."

60

11:40 a.m.

Sharyn waited as Laurent fished through his pack. He had dropped it from his shoulder and searched for what she had asked of him.

Archie stood to the side. "Why do we need a lighter?"

She pointed to the leaden menorah, as if this were obvious. "To prove we understand." She lifted the book still in her other hand and tapped her flashlight on its embossed cover. "Saint-Germain made this symbol his signature. Representing the four alchemical elements. Earth, fire, water, and air."

Archie shrugged, clearly baffled.

Sharyn gritted her teeth, fighting through her pounding headache to explain. "Someone crafted a lead copy of the holiest menorah. Maybe the true one lies hidden elsewhere down here. Or it could be lost to history. I don't know. But whoever fashioned this place—Saint-Germain or his network of savants—wanted us to understand the founding principles of alchemy."

She waved across the space. "Lead, mercury, gold. They all tie together. The only thing we're missing is what brings them all together."

Laurent answered, pulling out a stick lighter. "Alchemical fire."

She nodded, which only made her head pound worse.

We must get out of here.

Laurent crossed to the menorah and stood on his toes to peer at the tiny bowls that tipped each branch. "The cups are full of a black metallic slurry. Maybe another form of mercury. But there are no wicks."

Sharyn glanced down to the book, remembering what impregnated its pages. "Maybe the contents are flammable."

Laurent nodded, flicked his lighter, and sparked a flame. He reached out, while leaning his face away, and dabbed the fire into the bowl. The fuel ignited with a flash, flaring brightly.

"You were right," Archie gasped.

From the branch, the flame spun into a fiery torrent, rising a foot high. As it did, the very air seemed to glow around it.

Archie glanced back to the exit. "Keep going."

As Laurent moved to the second branch, Sharyn talked through her tension. "Back in Africa. In those volcanic fields. All the booby-traps had been about rock. Even the pressure-sensitive trigger that threatened a cave-in had been stopped by pushing a heavy ore cart onto it."

"What are you getting at?" Archie asked.

"I think the Libyan site represented the alchemical element of *earth*," she explained. "A veritable Temple of Earth."

Archie watched Laurent light the third branch, which further excited the air around it. "Then you think we're standing in the Temple of Fire."

"Maybe. We'll see."

They waited for Laurent to finish igniting all seven branches. As he continued down the line, the air scintillated and grew brighter, creating a nimbus around the menorah.

Sharyn peered closer, catching a whiff of hot metal. "I . . . I think whatever fuels this fire is burning the vapors out of the air. Demonstrating some strange trick of alchemy."

She glanced at the silvery lake, wondering if it was combustible, too. Though, if that were true, considering the reservoir's sheer size, any fire cast forth by that giant pool would quickly become an inferno.

Laurent lit the last stem, then retreated. "Whatever *strange trick of alchemy* this demonstrates," he said, using her description, "it's affecting more than just the air."

She pulled her attention back to the menorah. As the surrounding air became fiery in its own right, the surface of the candelabra began to soften, reacting to whatever alchemy had been ignited.

The lead—maybe an amalgam of the true element—had begun to drip in sludgy rivulets down its surface. As they all watched, the streaming slowly increased from a softening slurry to a rippling torrent. The lead flowed and wept down to the menorah's pedestal, spilling over into the silvery moat.

"My god," Archie moaned.

As the dull metal sloughed away, something new appeared beneath it.

Gold.

Like ice melting off a statue, the true relic revealed itself, shining in all its glory.

Sharyn knew what she was looking at. "I was wrong. It's not hidden elsewhere. Or lost to history. It's right *here*."

Laurent nodded. "The holiest of holy."

"What just happened?" Archie asked. "Did we turn lead to gold?"

Sharyn shook her head. "No. It's just a trick. A transformational representation of the long sought after goal of alchemy. To turn lead into gold. Maybe demonstrations like this gave birth to legends of alchemists succeeding in this task."

Laurent rubbed his chin. "Some indeed claimed Saint-Germain could perform this miracle."

From a few steps back, they kept vigil as the last of the lead—more than an inch thick across the menorah's surfaces—flowed away and vanished into the mercury pool. With all that weight melted off, one last miracle awaited them.

A sharp click sounded from the pedestal under the menorah.

"It's another pressure-sensitive switch," Sharyn whispered.

A faint grinding echoed behind them.

She turned, her eyes wide, knowing what this meant. "The door's opening. We've released the trap. We're free."

But some miracles come with a curse.

As the secret door opened wider, sharp blasts of gunfire echoed down to them.

Sharyn stared at the others, knowing what this meant.

I was wrong again. We're still trapped.

61

11:55 a.m.

Duncan continued his defense of the castle, though he wished it was from a less precarious perch. Under him, he balanced his feet on a pair of stubbed timbers sticking out of the tower's inner wall. His left hand clutched a rope hooked to a climbing piton, which was crammed into a crevice between two bricks. The elbow of his other arm rested in the open window, pointing Russo's pistol out into the cold.

Earlier, he had free-climbed up the wall, carrying the rope and pitons. He had found plenty of purchases for his toes and fingers due to the number of broken or missing bricks in the crumbling surface. Once up here, he had secured this high roost.

From the window's vantage, he could snipe down at the soldiers below as they struggled to clear the narrow cliffside trail. As they worked, he harried them as best he could. Still, he failed to do more than make them wary. Despite the danger, they continued to dig the snow off the path, keeping sheltered behind the icy mounds. At the same time, other men strafed the tower in short bursts, driving him back.

While Duncan had succeeded in slowing them down, the enemy continued to make steady progress.

And I'm down to my last magazine.

Russo called from below. "How far off are they?"

"Thirty yards."

Much too close.

He weighed an alternative plan, but he was saving it as a last resort.

Then rounds suddenly hammered the bricks outside in a fierce barrage. A few tore through the window and ricocheted off the far wall behind him. One rebound struck him in the lower back, like a mule's kick to his kidney. He lost his grip on the rope and slid down a couple feet before his fingers could clamp tight. Still, he kept his toes on the timbers and pushed himself back up.

As the onslaught continued, he kept below the window frame. Once the shooting stopped, he edged up and peered out again. He immediately recognized why the strafing had been so savage just now. On the cliffside path, the soldiers had abandoned their efforts and fled from their worksite, retreating back toward the plateau.

Duncan fired after the men. A lucky round nailed one in the leg, sending him crashing sideways, arms pinwheeling. The wounded man grabbed a neighbor, only to take them both tumbling over the cliff's edge.

Two birds, one stone.

Still, Duncan struggled to understand this sudden retreat.

He squinted toward the enemy's landing site. He noted a commotion, clustered around a pile of sandbags that had been stacked. Focused on the trail, he had failed to pay much attention to the activity atop the plateau, especially when being shot at from below.

Now he did.

The enemy must have been holding off until a good portion of the cliffside trail had been cleared before pulling out their big guns.

Really big guns.

Duncan recognized the tube of a rocket launcher.

Across the way, a soldier pressed his cheek to the weapon's scope and adjusted its aim.

Duncan swore and tucked his pistol into his waistband. The barrel remained hot enough to burn his hip. He ignored the pain, grabbed the line, and slid down its length to the floor. In his haste, he landed hard, jarring his teeth.

Russo looked on with concern. "What is—"

He lunged at her, scooped her waist, and hauled her with him. He fled out the tower and took two steps into the main chamber—then a loud boom, accompanied by a sharp whistle, chased him another step.

Before he could take a breath, the world exploded behind him.

The blast threw them both far, pummeling their bodies with rocks and debris. Duncan cradled Russo to him and rolled with the shockwave. Smoke and dust blinded him. The blast deafened the world to a steady high-pitched hum. As he slid to a stop, he coughed to clear his head, to force his crushed lungs to inflate again.

He got to his hands and knees and crawled farther away, pulling Russo by the arm. A glance back showed the woman's shin snapped at a sharp angle. Bone stuck from her pants. Blood poured.

"Leave me," she croaked. He barely heard her through his ringing ears. "Get to the others."

She somehow kept hold of her shotgun.

Duncan knew Russo could offer no meaningful defense. He stared past her. The sight outside stole what little breath he had left. As he watched, the whole tower slowly tipped outward, its foundation shattered from under it. Like a felled redwood, it continued to topple, tearing away bricks and stone. Then gravity took full hold and ripped it off the mountainside. The tower rolled and vanished over the cliff's edge.

Past the dust and smoke, blue skies and snowy distances opened up, the view far too panoramic due to the huge, gaping hole in the bunker's face.

Duncan helped Russo up, who grunted in agony. He carried her away. He wasn't about to leave her behind, knowing there was no stopping the enemy.

Any further defense was futile.

The castle had fallen.

62

12:32 p.m.

Keir strode behind the men pouring down the trail. A sniper had dropped two of their numbers, but the remaining dozen forged a path toward the wound in the side of the mountain. Rocks and bricks still trickled down. Smoke hung from the blast. But a wide swath of the snow and ice had been shattered away, along with a good portion of the bunker's façade.

He regretted doubting Ferhat's skill.

Still, triumph so buoyed him that he had little room in his heart for remorse or guilt. Not even for the deaths to come. One of the core tenets of longtermism was that present-day brutality and callousness held no sway when balanced against the future.

And when it came to the promise locked in Saint-Germain's book—of extending life to better the human condition—what else mattered? Birth rates were dropping in nations across the globe, threatening growth, productivity, and future prosperity. It was a danger greater than climate change.

And Saint-Germain's promise held the hope of stemming that tide.

And filling my own coffers.

Anxious for this next step forward—for him, for the world—Keir kept close to Ferhat's back. The captain whispered into his radio, commanding the men at the lead. After a brief pause, the front line entered the dark confines of the blasted bunker. The soldiers carried assault rifles equipped with bayonets. One hauled in an RPG launcher. Additionally, Ferhat had a bandolier over a shoulder, weighted down with grenades and other charges.

Maybe this was overkill, but Kier was done underestimating their adversaries. This close to victory, he felt generous enough to acknowledge the others' fierce struggle, to grant them a measure of earned respect.

But now it ends.

Behind him, Cardinal Tissot followed with his aide. Keir had tried to order the pair to stay with the helicopters, but they had refused. While he would have liked to have pushed both of them off the cliff, he knew Tissot still held great sway within the organization. And when it came to divining whatever key might be hidden within the treasure below or deciphering Saint-Germain's book, Keir recognized having an ally within the *Gardiens* could still prove useful.

So, he let the pair dog behind him.

He felt that gracious.

Ferhat turned to him. "Upper floor is clear. We're moving down."

Keir pointed ahead. "Then let's go collect our prize."

63

12:47 p.m.

Sharyn rushed forward as Archie and Duncan burst out of the tunnel and into the golden chamber. The pair dragged Russo between them. Minutes ago, they had all heard a mountain-quaking blast, followed by a thunderous crash of stones. She had feared the two defending the bunker had been killed. Then, Duncan had hollered for help, calling down from the entrance into the vault.

Tears welled at the sight of him.

Alive . . .

But she knew that might not last long. Some of her tears were for them all, for what would be lost here, handed to others who would abuse the wonders hidden at the heart of this mountain.

Laurent remained stoic. He eyed the incoming group and immediately recognized the damage. "I've a med-kit in my bag. We need to stop the bleeding. Get her leg splinted."

Clearly his training with the French armed forces had honed him for immediate action. He helped settle Russo to the floor, relieving Duncan, who weaved unsteadily on his legs. Blood covered half his face, flowing from a scalp cut. He was likely concussed, too.

She crossed and helped him sit on the closed lid of a chest.

He gaped around, blearily. "You found it."

She nodded, wishing she hadn't. She kept hold of his hand,

feeling the tremoring, the clammy chill to his skin, signs of pending shock.

"I . . . I couldn't stop them," he mumbled.

She wanted to tell him they had been doomed from the start, fighting a faceless enemy with near-unlimited resources. Instead, she offered him hope, knowing he needed it, even if it was a lie.

"It's not over yet," she whispered.

Voices, full of sharp command, carried down to them, echoing from above. Earlier, she had already tried stomping on the lowest step, to seal them back inside, to protect what was here. Still, it had failed, which was likely for the best. As Laurent had said, the enemy would've eventually found a way to dig down here.

And I would've never had a chance for this reunion, brief though it may be.

Duncan looked toward the stairs. "I thought maybe destiny brought us all together. That there was some guiding hand beyond blind chance and cruel coincidence." He shrugged heavily and turned back to her. "But it's only us."

"Maybe that's enough." She stared around the room, while clutching the book in her other hand. "Look at the miracle we uncovered."

She told him about the Temple of Fire, of lead turning to gold, and the transformation they had witnessed. As she did, he smiled at her through the blood and strain. He had never looked more handsome.

Then from the tunnel, a small metallic egg bounced and rattled into the chamber.

Archie backed away, naming the threat. "Grenade."

Before anyone could move, it exploded.

64

12:55 p.m.

Crouched on the dark steps, Keir clamped his palms over his ears. It wasn't enough. A shockwave pounded up the stairwell and crushed his chest. Even with his head turned, the fiery flash stung his eyes.

Still, he ignored the pain, too exulted to feel anything but triumph.

Earlier, a trail of blood had led them to a door at the bunker's lowest level, which opened onto this steep stair. Captain Ferhat had sent a man ahead, equipped with a night-vision scope. The soldier dropped down into a lower tunnel and reported a large chamber, fiery with gold. Their stubborn targets were holed up inside. To soften the enemy, Ferhat had his man toss in a flashbang charge.

Keir rubbed his eyes.

The blast certainly lived up to its name.

As it ended, Ferhat stabbed an arm ahead. "Go!"

A dozen men pounded down the last steps and into the tunnel. Ferhat reserved one man to keep at their side, then turned to Keir. "Do you wish to wait until we've fully secured the site?"

"Fuck that. Just get us down there." He glanced behind to Tissot and his aide. "We'll stay at the rear. But I want to ensure your men don't damage anything that might prove critical."

Especially Saint-Germain's book.

That was more important than a chamber full of gold.

For this reason, Keir had made sure only a flashbang had been deployed below and not one of the grenades hanging on the captain's bandolier. The site had to be preserved and protected. To that end, before entering the bunker, while he still had satellite contact, he had tried to reach Burman, to have her ready all their reserved forces. If anything important was found here, they needed to lock down this mountain.

Unfortunately, she never answered, which angered him at the time, but it hadn't deterred him from following Ferhat and his men into the bunker.

And it won't stop me now.

Keir waved to Ferhat. "Let's go."

The captain nodded crisply and set off with his man. Keir followed, keeping Tissot behind him—but not for the cardinal's safety. Keir wanted to be the first to enter, to make sure he secured Saint-Germain's volume for himself.

As they reached the tunnel, soldiers shouted ahead, barking orders, demanding a surrender of weapons. Bright lights shone around the curve of the passageway. Ferhat kept them moving cautiously. Keir had to refrain from pushing the captain to go faster.

Still, their small group finally rounded the curve. Ahead, a cavernous chamber opened, swirling with beams from flashlights mounted on the soldiers' rifles.

Someone inside called an all-clear.

Ferhat nodded back to Keir, then led their group the rest of the way.

As Keir stepped inside, the view inside strangled his breath. Gold shone everywhere, reflecting the lights into a fiery gleam. On the far side, flames danced atop a massive golden candelabra.

"*Mein Gott im Himmel,*" Tissot intoned, dropping to his native Swiss German before collecting himself. He gawked at the treasure, clearly with some recognition. "These relics . . . the menorahs . . . they must be from Jerusalem's Second Temple. All stolen by the Romans."

Keir pushed through his own shock—and not a small measure of avarice—to focus on the cluster of figures across the chamber. The group had retreated to the flaming candelabra. He watched the last of them, a young man, crawl on his hands and knees, wobbling from the effects of the flashbang. Blood flowed from his nostrils, coated his face.

The fleeing group had left behind a trail of weapons.

As a precaution, Ferhat's men swept in a wide arc and kept their rifles pointed at the captives. A few of the soldiers took furtive glances at the wealth amassed here. But the captain ran a tight crew. They all knew they would be well rewarded in the end.

Truthfully, Keir didn't care if they took *all* the gold, as long as the key hidden here by Saint-Germain was secured first. The *Confrérie* had lost the first one, when the African gold got divided, destroying its secret, which confounded both the Brotherhood and the *Gardiens.*

With no threat in sight, Keir pushed next to Ferhat and surveyed the situation. His gaze swept the room. He ignored the treasure around him and focused on the greater prize. He glared at the five clustered on the far side, all still dazed. Still, the captured group had accepted the inevitable. A few palms were raised in surrender. A large black man squatted next to an older woman with a broken shin, her pant leg soaked in blood. They all knew they were defeated.

Then he spotted it.

A young woman—Sharyn Karr, from all the reports—knelt before the hulking menorah and clutched a leathery book to her chest. From the little that Keir could see, copper straps bound the volume. His breath caught in his throat at the sight of it.

Just like it was described over the centuries.

Saint-Germain's text.

He stepped past Ferhat, ready to claim it for himself, for the Brotherhood, for the hope of humanity. As he continued across the chamber, he lifted an arm, drawn by the promise of immortality. It was almost within his grasp.

Then a loud blast deafened the space.

Keir got kicked in the spine, knocking him forward. Agony flared as he lost his footing and crashed to his knees, then down to one arm. He glanced back to see one of Ferhat's men, the soldier who had stayed behind with the captain, holding a smoking pistol.

Bastard shot me. In the back.

Keir only lived because of the Kevlar vest under his parka. Still, he had felt a rib shatter. Pain kept him immobilized, down on the ground. Bloody spittle dripped from his lips. He stared ahead at the treasure clutched to the young woman's chest.

So close . . .

He glanced back for some explanation.

It came in the form of Cardinal Tissot. The man stepped forward and settled his palm on the shooter's shoulder. It wasn't an act of friendship, but ownership.

This became even clearer when Ferhat stepped to the shooter's other side.

Tissot smiled sadly down at Kier. "*Vielen Dank, mein Freund.* But we'll take it from here."

65

1:09 p.m.

Sharyn struggled to understand the abrupt change in circumstance. It didn't help matters that her vision remained pinched, rimmed by an angry crimson. To her ears, the world had turned hollow, with audibility wavering in and out.

The explosive blast had left them all addled and damaged.

But alive.

For now.

A moment ago, she had watched one of the enemy stalk forward, his gaze fixed on the book hugged to her chest. Then a sudden gunshot made her jump, as it did with the others. The only one not to respond was Russo. She had lost so much blood that she hung limp in Laurent's arms. Already in shock and pain, the earlier blast had knocked her into a slack-necked daze.

"What's going on?" Duncan whispered, or at least it sounded that way to her dampened ears.

She shook her head, but she remembered Laurent mentioning the friction between various factions within the *Confrérie.*

Is that what we're witnessing?

She struggled to think of a way to turn this to her advantage, but she could come up with nothing. Especially with a dozen soldiers crowded in here. All with rifles leveled at their group. Their own weapons—a meager mix of pistols and one shotgun—lay out of reach on the floor.

She was not the only one frustrated.

The man who had been shot shoved around and turned his fury upon the figure at the shooter's side. This one wore a silver crucifix around his neck, resting over his coat, as if boasting of his rank for all to see.

"Cardinal Tissot," the injured man spat, clearly knowing who to blame. "What the hell are you doing? Are you mad?"

"Not mad, *Herr* Marchand, simply practical." A hand waved to the splendor in the room. "This is my birthright."

The man on the ground looked baffled.

The cardinal explained, "It was my father who was instrumental in securing the Solomon coins out of Libya."

"Which your father lost to the Nazis."

Tissot cocked his head. "Did he? Or did my father make it seem so? I understand it was very confusing at the end of the war."

These words clearly stunned Marchand.

Even Laurent cursed at the implication. "The bastard's father must've stolen the treasure from his own group, kept it for himself."

"The coins were melted down," the cardinal continued. "Then spread across Swiss banks, under various aliases and shells, all with the cooperation of my father's allies."

Marchand turned to the other man flanking the shooter. "Captain Ferhat, you went along with this betrayal? Why? You've been my man for over a decade."

Ferhat simply shrugged.

Tissot nodded to the captain. "He was never your *man*—only your *mercenary*. A soldier of *fortune*. For such men, it is gold that buys loyalty. And the more gold, the more loyalty."

Marchand looked agog at all of this. It took him a long sputtering moment before he could speak. "So, you orchestrated this betrayal . . . all to steal more gold?"

"*Nein.* Do you truly think so little of me? Gold is always useful." He lifted an arm to the wonders here. "I intend to melt it all down to aid our cause."

Sharyn quailed at this plan, knowing what would be lost. The archaeological, historical, and religious importance of this treasure far surpassed its weight in gold.

Marchand scowled at the cardinal. "What fucking cause?"

"The same as yours, *mein Freund.* I've not wavered in my commitment to securing and deciphering Saint-Germain's text. In fact, I went through great efforts to make sure it happens. I spent years cultivating contacts, buying access, until I was able to do something the Brotherhood had failed to do since its founding."

"Which is what?"

"To recognize the value of cooperation. To pool together the knowledge of the *Gardiens* with the resources of the *Confrérie.*" Cardinal Tissot motioned to the shooter. "I only had to find a like-minded soul."

The shooter stepped forward, separating from the two men. He holstered his pistol, reached up, and removed his helmet. Then with a little tugging, he pulled away the concealing balaclava.

Marchand gasped, falling back.

The shooter ignored him. His gaze continued past the injured man and focused across the room.

On Sharyn.

"Thank you, Ms. Karr, for protecting the book." Professor Julian Wright held out his hand. "But I'll take it back now."

SEVENTH

66

November 4, 1:25 p.m.
Cortina d'Ampezzo, Italy

Naomi rode in the back of the ambulance. It raced with sirens blaring down the winding mountain road. She clutched Tag's hand as he lay on the gurney beside her. His face remained tinged blue, but the hue had faded slightly.

Keep hanging in there.

The closest hospital lay eight miles away from San Vito, in the larger town of Cortina d'Ampezzo. They had just arrived at the city's outskirts after a jarring twenty-minute drive along roads with steep drops along one side.

An EMT crouched by Tag's head and adjusted a nasal canula inserted into his patient's nostrils, delivering a heavy flow of oxygen. The same man and another medic had stabilized Tag back at the hotel, bagging him fiercely until the last of the sedatives had worn off, enough for him to begin breathing on his own.

Prior to their arrival, Antonio had given Tag mouth-to-mouth while Chiara monitored his pulse. Once the authorities closed on the hotel, Naomi had sent the pair off. They didn't deserve to be dragged further into all of this. She was ready to assume all responsibility herself.

Which she had done.

A member of the Italian national police and an armed Carabinieri officer shared the cramped back of the ambulance. Naomi's right wrist had been handcuffed to a steel bar secured to one wall. She had pleaded to be allowed to come along with Tag. The EMT supported her, insisting Tag would have died if not for her efforts to keep him breathing. Still, this leniency was more likely born from the simple reason that the closest jail cell was also in Cortina.

Fingers tightened on her hand.

She stared down as Tag tilted his head, his eyes focusing more fully on her. He had faded in and out since stirring out of the sedation.

"Hi . . ." he said hoarsely, his gaze swinging around, looking confused. "Th . . . Think you may need to fill in some blanks."

A short laugh—full of relief—burst from her.

Thank god . . .

She squeezed his hand in turn. "It looked like you were dead back there for a minute."

He coughed softly. "On . . . on my bad days, people often think that. Even when I'm standing up. And this has been a bloody bad day."

"You weren't breathing. Your eyes were all glassy and unblinking."

"They drugged me. And not with the good stuff," he reminded her. "The palsy . . . it compromises my rib muscles, constricts my chest. I was probably breathing, but so weakly it looked like I wasn't. Those bastards probably thought I was dead, too."

"Maybe because you were so blue."

"Cyanosis." He waved his other hand dismissively. "I turn that color at the drop of a hat. You've seen it. Just climbing up to our flat. Plus, living like this, my body's acclimatized to low O2 by now."

"Tag." She lowered her voice with concern. "You had a seizure. At least, that's what the bitch told me."

She pictured Burman's body being hauled into another ambulance. Shockingly, the woman lived, too. Her neck had been secured in a red cushioned brace as she was whisked away. If she lived, she would surely be paralyzed, a quadriplegic for the rest of her days.

For Naomi, that wasn't punishment enough.

"I get seizures sometimes," Tag admitted. "It's just my body being irritable. Probably trying to shake off the drugs, in this case."

Despite attempting to downplay everything, Tag's face shone with fear—and not for himself. He swallowed, then spoke even more softly. "Naomi . . . I think I told them where the others went. Not sure."

She stayed silent, not wishing to burden him any further.

"Everything was foggy." He lifted his arm and rested his hand on his chest, wincing at the burn marks. "I did feel this. The pain . . . I think they stopped my heart with the first zap, then started it again with the second."

"But you're alive now. We're on the way to the hospital."

His gaze turned to the two armed escorts. "But is that the *only* place we're headed?"

"We'll worry about that later." She let go of his hand, reached to her neck, and pulled off Chiara's amulet. She placed it into Tag's hand and squeezed his fingers tightly. "You'd better keep this. For extra protection."

Tag lifted the salt-filled vial. "Where did you—"

"From a friend."

The ambulance made a sharp turn, throwing her to the side. The EMT leaned over Tag to hold him steady. The vehicle braked with a squeal that silenced the sirens.

They had reached the hospital. The two armed escorts stirred and spoke to each other in Italian, readying for the transfer of patient and prisoner. The rear doors popped open—only to reveal a chaos of flashing lights and clusters of figures, some in uniforms, others in suits.

Naomi retreated from the chaos.

A balding older gentleman dressed in business attire charged toward the ambulance, waving others aside.

The policeman lifted an arm to block him from getting too close. The Carabinieri officer rested a hand on his holstered weapon. The stranger ignored them both, his gaze fixed inside, taking in everything with a sweep of his eyes, before settling on her.

He pointed. "You're Naomi Wren."

She remained silent, not sure who this was, fearing it was a member of the *Confrérie.*

"I got your email. After my daughter alerted me to a post on TikTok." He stared hard at her. Only now did Naomi see the resemblance. "I'm Avery Bailey."

Archie's father.

The man's frantic gaze swept the interior of the ambulance again. "Where is my son? Is he safe?"

Past the man's shoulders, the snowy rise of Monte Antelao loomed beyond the city's edge. Naomi searched for any sign of the helicopters she had spotted earlier—some three hours ago.

She shook her head, knowing this for certain.

"He's far from safe."

67

1:37 p.m.
San Vito di Cadore, Italy

Sharyn fought through the shock at seeing a dead man resurrected before her. She struggled to understand how Julian Wright could be standing here. She searched his face, looking for those answers.

It was clearly the professor. Same silver hair, same trimmed goatee. The only differences to his features were the purpled bruising and a swelling under one eye. She remembered the CCTV footage of him being dragged into the Old Library by hooded figures. It clearly must have been a ruse, but one that required him to suffer a beating for it to be convincing.

She clutched Saint-Germain's book to her chest, as if it were a life preserver and she was lost in rocky seas—both of which were true at the moment.

"You proved a great adversary, Ms. Karr, better than I would've ever suspected." Julian stepped closer, clearly savoring her shock. "I picked poorly, it seems."

With her mind whirling, her world turned upside down, she grasped to one word. "*Picked?*" She shook her head. "To take the book. Why? Why didn't you take it yourself?"

"Ah, yes. Matters became very fluid and tight that night. I had not anticipated the bequeathment from the Twelfth Keeper would be so large. Or that it would take so long to search for one book among so many. Especially on my own."

She pictured the dozen large crates stacked in the library's strongroom. It was a daunting task for any one man. Plus, Wright had dared not involve any others. He hadn't even told Ms. Peele he was in the vault.

Julian continued. "I had gone to great lengths—aided by Cardinal Tissot's financial help—to convince the *Gardiens* to choose me as the book's Thirteenth Keeper. I set up the perfect library to hide it in. Petitioned for the role. Bribed where I needed to. And in the end, it worked."

"You were selected," Sharyn noted, appreciating that she was not the only one fooled by this man.

"It was only after I was tapped for this esteemed role that I learned the name of my predecessor, the Twelfth Keeper. By then, the book was already on its way to me. During a flurry of encrypted communications, an ally of Cardinal Tissot made a mistake that allowed the Keeper's name to reach Marchand and his *Confrérie* cohorts. There was nothing to be done about it. All I could do was hope Jakob Haugen would not tell them where the book was shipped to. But that got dashed due to a cocktail of drugs. And worse, the *Gardiens* also learned of the book's possible exposure after the death of Haugen."

Sharyn drew back to that day in the library, trying to imagine the dark forces closing upon her that night.

"With both the *Gardiens* and the *Confrérie* racing for the book, the timetable to execute our plans became exceptionally tight. Then came a call that made things worse."

She grimaced, remembering him arguing on the phone—in German or some other Nordic language.

"It was from Cardinal Tissot. He warned me that members of Marchand's faction had already been dispatched and would reach the library at any moment. Which required me to act with haste. I had to flee, but I couldn't take the book with me or leave it behind. I had to move it temporarily, to somewhere out of the way, to a place of safety."

"And I happened to be there . . ." she groaned.

Julian's brows raised. "Not *happened.* No, my dear, it was preplanned. You were always my back-up. It was not a coincidence you were at the Old Library on Halloween. As the former director of libraries, I made sure you did not have access to the Saxton Atlas—the book you requested—until I knew the shipment from the Twelfth Keeper had arrived safely."

She swallowed hard, remembering the long delay in gaining permission to photograph the book. It hadn't been due to bureaucracy, but from machinations far darker.

"I needed you there as a failsafe. Even if Ms. Peele hadn't brought you to the library's vault, I would've sought you out in the reading room if it proved necessary."

"But why . . . why me?"

"I read your application, Ms. Karr. Ran a background check. You were someone with a troubled past, abused, beaten down. Someone easily cowed and highly persuadable. Plus, you were a fish out of water in Exeter, with no resources and few friends locally. You seemed perfect. A mule I could use if needed to temporarily hide the book out of the way."

Sharyn stared at the others, her face burning, ashamed and guilty.

I got them all into this.

"Unfortunately, I failed to discern your other talents. With everything moving so swiftly, errors were made. Unnecessary delays. But with the book safely diverted, held by an easily secured target, we moved too slowly, too cautiously. Then again, we had much to do that night. Like staging my death. We needed to make it look like one of my students killed me in a ritual. Then, after setting up this tableau and torching the library, Cardinal Tissot and his men were supposed to grab the book, kill you, and leave behind a burned facsimile of Saint-Germain's text."

Sharyn found it harder to breathe. She remembered the Rolls parked in front of their flat, pictured the men rushing up the steps.

Before she could find her voice, Laurent challenged him. "But why do all this?"

"Why? To end a long impasse between our two organizations. We were only getting in each other's way. You must recognize this, Monsieur Laurent. I needed to make it look like this long trail of the book had finally come to an end. No one—not the *Gardiens*, not the *Confrérie*—would come looking for it if they believed it was destroyed."

Laurent looked aghast, his eyes flashing with fury. "Yet, you left my calling card with Sharyn. You sent her to me. Why?"

"Extra insurance. If we lost Ms. Karr, I had to ensure that she went somewhere I could still find her. And not just anywhere. Not with the treasure in her possession. The book still needed to be protected, especially from other members of the *Confrérie*." He motioned to Marchand. "And at the same time, I had to keep her within my own grasp. The *Gardiens* served both of these roles well. With the unwitting help of others in our group, and using various intermediaries and Cardinal Tissot's assets, I knew you'd be easy to track. That you'd keep in contact. Leave a trail back to Ms. Karr if she went missing."

Sharyn pictured the attack at the Tower of London, the ambush at the Barbiers' estate. The bastard had been using his own organization—a group who thought he was dead—to keep tabs on Laurent's movements.

"But again, you all proved very resourceful. Then went silent on us. If not for those intermediaries within the *Gardiens*, I might have lost you. As the cardinal and I were already gathering talented cryptographers for our cause, we tasked them to hack into the *Gardiens'* mainframe after it had become evident someone was engaging it from afar."

Laurent's jaw muscles tightened, hardening the edges of his face. "To do that, you must have still had your former access codes. No one thought to delete them after your death."

"Why would they?"

Archie stirred, kneeling next to Duncan. "But you *were* dead. A medical exam confirmed it was you."

Julian turned to him. "An easy deception, young man. Tissot found someone of my age and build. Then drugged and hauled him into the library when we all entered, hiding his presence under a robe. As to the rest of the deception, the flames did most of the work, burning away bodily details. We also made sure a beam fell and crushed the skull and jaw to erase any dental comparisons."

Duncan stirred. "Then how did the coroners mistakenly identify you?"

"Ah, another calling card I left behind." He rubbed a hand on his chest. "I suffer from arrythmias. Requiring a pacemaker."

Sharyn remembered Ms. Peele mentioning the professor had a heart condition. The librarian had even offered to stay behind and help him.

"Medical devices have identifying serial numbers. Using a private surgeon paid by Cardinal Tissot, it was only a matter of switching out mine for a new one and placing the old device inside our decoy. Once it was discovered by the coroner, especially with camera footage showing me being dragged into the library, the serial number would have left little doubt as to the identity of the burned body."

"You thought of everything," Sharyn admitted.

With layers upon layers of contingencies.

"This has been long in the planning," Julian admitted. "If frantic in its execution. For that, I must apologize. All of this need not have been so hard on you and your friends. It could've ended on Halloween night."

"What will you do now?" Duncan asked.

Julian glanced back. "As the cardinal attested, we will work together. I can bring to the table all the *Gardiens'* prior knowledge, its research, its deciphering tools. Much of which I amassed in secret."

Cardinal Tissot stepped forward. "And I will share the resources and assets of the *Confrérie*—who will never learn of today's treachery. Along with the vast wealth at my disposal. Both what was stolen in the past and what we will take from here now."

Julian nodded. "With such combined strength, we will achieve what the endless fighting between the *Gardiens* and the *Confrérie* only thwarted. We will fully decrypt Saint-Germain's book. Secure its mysteries and treasures, not just for ourselves, but for the world."

Sharyn lowered her gaze, wondering if these two, despite the carnage in their wake, were not entirely wrong.

Maybe this is the only way to discover Saint-German's last secrets.

Julian held out his hand. "So, as you see, Ms. Karr, it seems your duty as the Thirteenth Keeper has finally come to an end."

68

2:04 p.m.

Sharyn backed away from Julian Wright. A rising fury—stoked by his smug, self-satisfied look—pushed through her shock and dread. She had been used, deceived, and terrorized by this bastard. She had been chosen because she had survived childhood abuse and judged weak.

Julian remained standing in place, still holding out his hand. "Bring me the book."

Even now, he wanted to humiliate her, to make her deliver the volume to him. He could have easily come forward and taken it, but instead he continued this passive-aggressive torment.

Sick of such men in her life, she clutched the book harder.

Julian sighed and pulled out his pistol. He waved it negligently, like a teacher with a pointer. Only this lesson would be a grim one.

"I can make your deaths slow and painful," he warned. "Or mercifully quick."

He settled his aim and fired. The blast deafened. Russo's head snapped back, shot through the forehead. She slumped in Laurent's arms, his face spattered with blood.

"Like this," Julian said calmly, standing in place. "She was going to die anyway. Blood loss, sepsis. It's a kindness. One I can offer you all if you cooperate. Otherwise, I will let Captain Ferhat's men find some entertainment before we leave. Losing two of their men to a sniper has them looking for satisfaction."

Sharyn stumbled another step back, her legs shaking. "No . . ."

"A shame." Julian turned to the soldier next to the cardinal. "Captain Ferhat, maybe a demonstration is necessary after all."

The soldier unsheathed a long steel dagger.

"Wait," Sharyn gasped out. She steadied her stance and forced her legs to move her body forward.

Julian holstered his weapon. "Very wise, Ms. Karr."

She took the three steps to him and held out the book. "Take it. It's caused nothing but misery."

He smiled and reached for it.

She whipped forth her other arm and stabbed her karambit knife through his palm. As he screamed, she twisted on one leg, lowered her hip, and snapped out a kick with the other. Her boot heel struck him high in the midriff, under his ribs, hard enough to knock the wind out of him and lift him off his feet. He went flying backward.

She did not slow. She continued her turn, back to facing her friends, and lunged for the only path open to her. Toward the flaming menorah. She had already come to a decision, knowing what needed to be done. Saint-Germain had made it clear in this transformational Temple of Fire.

She remembered the horrors depicted in the Third Adage. Skinned and dissected bodies, cruel experimentations. It was a depravity of science. Even the skull that graced its title page was like a warning to those who dared delve deeper into the book.

She would not make that mistake.

She lifted the book—still loose and open after unlocking the secret door—and thrust it into the menorah's flames.

Cries rose behind her.

From Tissot, from Julian, even from Laurent.

The book's pages burst into fiery glory, as if waiting for this moment over centuries. She turned and held the book aloft, like a torch for all to see. Rifles leveled at her, but no one knew quite what to do at this moment.

The searing heat burned to her fingertips. The flames splayed the book wider, a fiery bible now. She cast it away, sending it spinning across the floor and behind the neighboring gold table.

"You fool!" Julian bellowed and yanked the impaled knife out of his hand.

The man thrust to his feet, gasping both from her kick and from the horror of her fiery act. In a stumbling run, he tried to reach the table and the flaming book, clearly in the desperate hope of snuffing out the flames and salvaging what he could.

Sharyn simply fell to her knees and stared behind the gold table, toward the burning pyre, recognizing she had made the right choice.

The book needed to be destroyed.

Julian continued his run. Others stirred behind him, unsure what to do.

But another had also come to a decision.

69

2:18 p.m.

Using this confusion, Duncan shoved to his feet. He turned his back to the soldiers, who continued to rustle and look for instructions. He stared up at the flaming menorah, as if casting a prayer, trying his best not to look like a threat.

Instead, he planned to follow Sharyn's example.

He had already silently shown her his intent, getting a nod from her and a whispered, "Wait for my signal."

Surely burning the book was that, a distraction if ever there was one.

From inside his half-zipped parka, torn and ripped by the rocket blast, he tugged up the yellow tube of the avalanche charge. The last of Russo's supply. He silently thanked the biologist for this hope, for this chance.

Earlier, he had tucked the tube into his parka when he had climbed up the tower to his sniper's roost. It was his *last resort*, his final means of defending the castle. He had intended to light its fuse and drop the kilo of TNT on top of the soldiers clearing the cliffside trail—if they ever got too close.

And they're bloody well too close now.

Keeping as hidden as possible, but moving quickly, he pulled the charge higher and wiggled its fuse up to the menorah's lowest branch. The incendiary cord burst into a fiery eye that quickly began eating down the line to its explosive core.

He spun back, knowing this threat would quickly be recognized.

In that fleeting moment, with adrenaline sharpening his focus, he took in the room.

—Archie gaped wide-eyed at him.

—Laurent still held Russo's body, as if disbelieving she was dead. Still, he stared to where Sharyn knelt, her gaze fixed to the flaming book behind the table.

—Julian ran toward her, close to reaching her, but Laurent thrust out a leg as the man passed and sent him sprawling.

Duncan yanked his arm back. With all the strength left to him, he threw the charge. A gunshot—coming from Captain Ferhat's pistol—struck his wrist, shattering bone. The charge flew wildly, making it only halfway across the chamber, landing some distance from the spread of soldiers.

Once again, his Hail Mary pass had failed.

The yellow tube struck the floor and skittered to the only man sitting there, still bent over after being shot in the back.

Kier Marchand picked up the tube and stared back at Duncan.

Their eyes met.

70

2:21 p.m.

Kier clutched the tube in his hand, noting the burning fuse. He had time to snuff it out, to stop this effort by the young man. Or he could toss it back to where it came from and eliminate the targets who had so plagued him.

But he knew who was ultimately at fault.

He turned back to Ferhat and Tissot and the flanking soldiers.

He remembered the cardinal's words a moment ago: *I will share the resources and assets of the Confrérie—who will never learn of today's treachery.* To cover up his betrayal of the Brotherhood, Tissot would never let Keir leave this cavern alive.

He had already accepted this fate.

But providence had granted him a gift. While it wasn't a reprieve from death, it was a means of revenge.

He flung his arm toward his former allies, letting the charge fly. Rounds pelted his body in an attempt to stop him, but the barrage came too late. His Kevlar vest and helmet protected him long enough to see the horror writ across the cardinal's face and the rare panic in the captain's eyes.

Then his world exploded.

71

2:22 p.m.

Duncan huddled over Sharyn. Both of them were sheltered behind the gold table as the blast pounded the room. Archie had followed, too, after noting Marchand's assist. Likewise, Laurent had abandoned Russo's body, snatched a pistol from the floor, then shoulder-rolled across the tabletop to join them.

The explosion crushed them all, deafened everyone.

A kilo of TNT has the power to destroy a small vehicle and kill anything within a few meters of its blast. The confines of the chamber amplified this danger. Even sheltered thirty yards away, the detonation felt like being stomped on by a giant. Rubble, most of it golden, shattered around them, accompanied by a hail of rocks. Other softer debris splattered, limbs and body parts, some pieces still bearing armor.

Finally, the barrage ended.

Duncan checked to make sure everyone was okay, then risked rising up. The view beyond their shelter showed the carnage left behind. A small smoking crater marked the epicenter of the blast. Golden artifacts—shields and trumpets—had been hammered from the walls, some crushed, others looking miraculously untouched. Elsewhere, lanterns had been blown off their gilded chains. Menorahs lay crooked in their alcoves.

Still, the cavern remained intact.

Duncan had feared the charge might cause a cave-in, but he had trusted the mountain could withstand such a blast. He was relieved to be proven right.

The soldiers in the room had not fared as well. Bodies lay everywhere. Broken, torn, smoking. Blood pooled and continued to spread. A few figures moved. One man crawled toward the exit, dragging a bloody stump. Another took a potshot toward them, but a sharp retort next to his ear made Duncan flinch to the side.

Laurent held out his pistol, ready to shoot again, but the gunman collapsed.

Momentarily distracted, they failed to note another.

Julian shoved to his knees, his face bloody, rising to the side of the table, only a couple yards away. He lay tangled in Russo's body, as if the dead woman had sought to exact her revenge. Unfortunately, Julian had vengeance on his mind, too. With pistol in hand, he fired nearly point blank, driving them all down.

A round clipped Laurent's cheek, breaking bone.

They dropped low and waited for Julian to stop shooting. Once he had emptied his magazine, Duncan and Laurent popped up. By now, using the cover of his barrage, Julian had retreated halfway across the chamber. He tossed aside his emptied pistol, snatched a bent gold shield in his bloody hand, and grabbed an abandoned rifle in the other.

Laurent returned fire, his aim shaky, clearly concussed from the shatter of his cheekbone. Still, his rounds pinged off gold or struck his target's body armor.

Julian shielded his head, while strafing blindly toward them. It was enough to force them back down, especially as the slide on Laurent's pistol had popped. He was out of bullets.

They had no way of stopping Julian's escape.

Worse, Duncan realized Ferhat and Cardinal Tissot had vanished, too. His last sight of them was when the pair had fled from the tossed charge. Ferhat had been pushing Tissot in front of him.

Had they made it out?

Across the chamber, Julian reached the exit, tossed the cumbersome shield aside, and dove into the tunnel.

Duncan cursed, ready to go after him. Blood dripped thickly from Duncan's wrist and pain stabbed up his limb. The bullet had broken his ulna, but not his radius, and seemed to have missed major arteries.

I can do this.

As he moved to follow, Julian came flying back into the room. The bastard crashed onto his back and slid. Atop his body rode a snarling, hissing monster. Julian raised a defensive arm, only to meet fangs that tore deep. A toss of the lynx's head ripped long lacerations across the man's forearm.

He screamed in pain, and surely some terror.

But Julian was not Katch's true focus. The lynx leaped away and stalked into the chamber, fur bristling, lips rippling from bloody fangs. Julian used this moment to roll to his feet and flee again.

Duncan was about to pursue him, but Laurent grabbed his arm. "Stay still."

Duncan obeyed, recognizing the threat closer at hand.

Katch edged toward them, moving low, haunches quivering. Still, for now, the cat ignored the group clustered behind the gold altar. He crossed to Russo's body, moving ever slower. Once he reached her, he nudged her with his muzzle, shifting a limp arm, then letting it rest. The cat sniffed at the blood, then shifted to her face, which lay turned on its side. He nosed her, as if trying to wake her. But he knew the truth. His hissing quieted to a low pained mewl. He rubbed his muzzle along her chin, no longer trying to stir her.

Only to say goodbye.

But like his mistress, Katch was not overly sentimental. He had done his duty, paid his respects. He backed a step, turned his head toward the exit, and chuffed at the air. A growl returned, flowing from deep inside, then rose to a ferocious yowl.

Duncan knew not all the blood soaking Julian's clothes had been his own. Russo's body had been blown against him, marking him as her killer.

Maybe Katch understood this, too.

Or maybe his fury simply called for blood.

The massive cat leaped away and raced for the exit.

Duncan remembered Russo telling him lynxes were ambush hunters, perfectly evolved to stalk in the dark. Intending to follow his example, Duncan slid on his hip across the table and set off after Katch—and the man he hunted.

But Julian wasn't the only danger. Ferhat and Tissot had possibly fled, too. None of them could get away, not with the knowledge they possessed.

As Duncan set off, Archie followed at his heels, ever his friend, ever his sidekick.

They both grabbed rifles.

"Stay with Sharyn!" Duncan called back to Laurent, knowing the big man wobbled on his legs. "In case anyone circles back."

72

2:33 p.m.

Even if Laurent were not compromised, Sharyn knew the man needed little convincing to stay behind. It wasn't only her that needed protecting. Even though much of the chamber was damaged, the archaeological and religious importance of this site had to be preserved.

It couldn't be lost to the enemy.

The *Confrérie* had already come too close to achieving that goal. And they might yet still.

Laurent swept out into the chamber, collected a rifle, then returned. By now, all the wounded had expired, leaving the room silent, turning it into a golden morgue. Laurent rejoined her, focusing his attention on what else had been lost this day, what lay in a ruin on the floor.

"Why?" he finally mumbled, unable to hold in the question any longer.

"It had to be done," she said, struggling how to justify her actions so they made sense.

She came up with nothing and simply stared at the wreckage. The fire had burned through the pages, scorched off the leather binding. All that was left were two copper plates that had been at the core of the covers and a melted tangle of copper sitting between them.

She reached down and retrieved one last artifact of the book's former glory—the crystal orb. She held it toward the menorah. The ancient relic had withstood the blast. Flames still danced from its branches, as if echoing the miracle that had made it a symbol of God's pact with the Jewish people.

"Look here." Sharyn showed the orb to Laurent. "It's been transformed, too. Like the menorah."

Prior to this, the crystal had been a perfect sphere. Now its surface was cut with a hundred tiny facets. In addition, its shape had somehow been sculpted into a pear, coming to a sharp point at the bottom.

"Looks like a diamond," Laurent murmured.

It certainly reflected the light as such, shining with a fiery brilliance, a last gift of Saint-Germain to the world.

"I doubt it's truly a diamond," Sharyn noted. "Another trick of alchemical fire. Like with the menorah. If you look closer, past the reflections, even the small astrological symbols are gone."

"Flaws," Laurent murmured with a nod. "Many claimed Saint-Germain possessed the ability to melt diamonds and remove their imperfections. Even King Louis XVI believed this."

Sharyn lowered the crystal. "Maybe even the wildest stories of Saint-Germain had some truth to them."

"By now, I would not doubt that." Laurent turned to the chamber, to the gold.

Sharyn searched the other way, toward the lake of mercury. It reminded her that the air remained poisonous. Though, at the moment, her head pounded less. Maybe this was due to the flush of adrenaline, or maybe the flames of the menorah had created a protective nimbus, burning away the closest toxins.

Laurent sighed heavily, accepting reality but not defeat. "We can only hope there remains some clue out there in all that gold. While the book is lost to us, some key might still be discovered, something for us to build on."

"Possibly," Sharyn said, but with little confidence.

She had already placed her trust elsewhere. She squeezed the crystal in her hand, as if trying to pressure it into a true diamond.

Before they could contemplate these mysteries further, a yowl of fury echoed down to them, muffled by distance and rock, but still ripe with anger.

It served as a reminder.

We're not safe yet.

73

2:39 p.m.

Drawn by the cat's scream, Duncan raced up the stairs toward the bunker's main floor, taking the steps two at a time. His shadow danced ahead of him, his body lit from behind by Archie's bobbling flashlight. With a broken wrist, Duncan could only manage the rifle. He carried it one-handed while resting its barrel on his bloody forearm.

As they neared the top floor, his shadow dissolved into the shine of daylight flowing through the bunker's blasted façade. He slowed, wary of an ambush, and paused at the last step. A quick peek showed the true extent of the rocket's damage. Boulders, bricks, and shattered sections of walls formed a treacherous labyrinth. Winds from outside stirred sand and dust into a haze.

He headed out, dashing for the closest cover.

Through all the debris, he could not see any sign of Julian.

Archie skidded next to Duncan. He had already tossed aside his flashlight, so it didn't give away their position. "Anything?" he whispered.

Duncan shook his head. "We keep going."

As he stepped out of cover, a burst of movement drew his eye. Julian fled toward the gaping exit. Once he crossed the threshold, he spun around and fired on full auto, backpedaling as he did so, propelled by both the rifle's recoil and terror.

Duncan retreated, bumping into Archie.

But none of the rounds came near them. Julian hadn't even been shooting in their direction. His angle of fire was too low, aimed toward the neighboring barricade of broken rocks. From that shelter, a tawny shape burst forth with a speed that seemed impossible, transforming flesh into shadow. None of the rounds seemed to strike the furious lynx.

Katch leaped and struck Julian in the chest, transforming from shadow back to savage muscle. The impact carried the cat's prey to the lip of the cliff—then over it.

Both man and beast plummeted away.

Julian continued to scream. Duncan pictured Katch ripping into the man as they fell. Then a long moment later, the agonized cries cut off with a distant thud of flesh on rock.

Archie stepped next to him, stunned into silence.

In respect for the dead.

But not for Julian, of course.

In that quiet, a new noise arose. The harsh rumble of a helicopter's engine. The reverberations quickly grew into a roar.

Duncan cringed at the implication, reminded that Julian wasn't the only concern here.

"Tissot and Ferhat!"

He and Archie ran for the exit. Each step shot pain up his arm, but he did not slow. Duncan burst outside. Above, a blue sky defied this dark day. Blinded by the brightness, he squinted toward the plateau.

One of the helicopter's blades spun into a blur. The other two followed to match.

"Over there!" Archie yelled and pointed to the far end of the trail.

Two figures rushed toward the plateau. Ferhat hauled Tissot by the arm. The captain must have radioed ahead, ordering an immediate evacuation.

Archie cursed loudly.

Duncan understood his fury.

No way we can reach them in time.

Then from around the mountain's shoulder, a trio of massive military choppers, badged with roundels of the Italian air force, swung into view. They swept down upon the plateau. From side hatches, soldiers fired at the helicopters, shattering canopies and rotors. One engine coughed up a spat of flames, then a gout of black smoke.

Ferhat shoved Tissot away, sending the cardinal into a faceplant on the rock. The captain tried to make a run for the slope that led to a neighboring bowl. But rounds sparked across the rock, caught him, and tore him apart.

Duncan retreated, pushing Archie toward the bunker's opening. He didn't want them to be mistaken for enemy combatants. To ensure that, he tossed his rifle down and waved for Archie to do the same.

One of the helicopters swept past the opening in a squall of hard wind. The open hatch faced them. Both Duncan and Archie lifted their arms high. A helmeted soldier manned a mounted gun, pointing its barrel at them.

Behind him, a smaller figure pushed forward and shouted—not at them, but at the gunman. Though buried in a vest and helmet, this one was easy enough to identify.

"Naomi . . ." Duncan gasped out.

Another figure, equally weighed down by armor, joined her.

Archie frowned. "Is that my dad?"

74

3:42 p.m.

Sharyn rode in the rear cabin of the medivac. As the helicopter made a wide sweep over the face of Monte Antelao, she was relieved to leave the chaos behind her. Only an hour had passed since the *Confrérie*'s stranglehold on the mountain had been broken, but already an ever-growing presence of military personnel and police forces descended on the peak to secure the treasure at its heart.

She had done her best to warn those incoming of the toxins that protected the gold, but her words fell on deaf ears. Orders were barked. Commands made. Mostly in Italian. Archie had tried to act as a translator, but even his efforts had little impact. Still, his father helped expedite their transfer to a local hospital, where Tag awaited them—and where undoubtedly weeks of questioning would follow.

For now, she simply pushed deeper under Duncan's arm, which draped over her shoulders. His other wrist bore a thick cotton wrap, a temporary splint until something more could be done.

Across from them, Archie bowed his head next to his dad, likely relating events in greater detail. But the roaring engine drowned them out. Still, she smiled as Archie's father pulled his son into a warm embrace, kissing the top of his head.

A twinge of envy at such clear affection rang through her. She tried not to think about what Julian Wright had said regarding *why* she had been selected to bear this burden, a detail that only reinforced how the shadow of her father's abuse still hung over her and continued to have repercussions.

Still, she also recognized that she lived only because of her father's training and lessons, and, yes, a love that still carried through all the hardship.

She knew it would take time to balance all of this.

For now, she pushed such thoughts away.

Naomi sat on Archie's other side. She looked exhausted with dark circles under her eyes. She had offered a thumbnail version of all that had transpired in San Vito. A fuller recounting would come later.

Past her friend, Laurent sat up front. His face bore a heavy wrap over his broken cheek, a temporary patch, like Duncan's soft splint. All of their injuries would need far more attention and time to heal, as would the wounds not visible. Sharyn even suspected Laurent had taken the seat next to the pilot because he did not fully trust the man not to betray them.

Don't blame him.

Not after all that had happened.

Still, Sharyn knew one person who had earned her full trust. She turned her head to stare into Duncan's eyes. He breathed heavily, both from pain and from the soporifics given to him.

Still, he smiled at her. "What is it?"

She lifted up, bringing her face close to his. He leaned down, expecting a kiss. That would come in a moment, but first she shared a secret.

One meant for him, for her friends, and no others.

She whispered it to his waiting lips.

"I know where the third treasure is hidden."

75

April 5, 10:08 a.m. CEST
Mellieħa, Republic of Malta

Duncan climbed out of the taxi van and into a sunny Maltese morning. He luxuriated in the warmth. It was nothing like the rainy skies and low clouds of springtime in Exeter. Still, the breeze reaching this hilltop from the Mediterranean's blue waters below required wearing a light jacket. He wished he could've donned shorts, but not knowing the terrain ahead, he had settled for khaki pants and stout boots.

He cleared out of the way for the other four. They were all similarly attired. Only, Naomi had added a wide-brimmed sunhat. And Sharyn had her usual ballcap with her ponytail tucked out the back.

Tag climbed out last, using his cane to help propel him. "Ready?"

"We'd better be," Archie said. "We've traveled a proper long distance to get here."

Duncan rubbed his wrist, which had long healed, but he still found himself massaging it when nervous.

For Easter Break, the five of them had flown to the Republic of Malta, a trio of islands about sixty miles south of Sicily. While other university students headed to parties in Spain or Greece, they had detoured here. Not for drunken festivities, but to hunt for confirmation of what they had worked on over these past five months. What

Naomi called their *private study club* and what Tag described as *our little* Gardiens *party*.

While they had reached some conclusions months ago—using charts, maps, and reading histories—they had waited for this school break. For a couple reasons. First, they wanted the heat to die down. After the events in the Dolomites, the spotlight had shone too strongly on them—both at school and far wider. The discovery of the lost treasures of the Second Temple had garnered much press, especially with the murderous conspiracy surrounding it.

The aftermath and repercussions still reverberated across intelligence agencies, financial institutions, and nations. Cardinal Tissot had been captured and imprisoned, but the ongoing efforts to root out other members of the *Confrérie* continued. This was aided by Saanvi Burman, who was confined to a prison hospital, paralyzed from the neck down, requiring help even breathing. Archie's father also worked diplomatic channels to further this effort. Though, knowing such organizations, the enemy would surely rise again in one form or another.

As Sir Kelly had once told them, *power does not tolerate a vacuum*.

Additionally, Duncan's dad—with his international ties to the banking world—worked alongside Archie's father to ferret out and confiscate all the gold hidden by Tissot's family. Any success in this regard would likely wound Tissot more than the decades of incarceration ahead of him.

Off in the Dolomites, Laurent continued working with a team of archaeologists, religious scholars, and other academics who painstakingly sought to extract the vast treasure. Duncan imagined he was also looking for Saint-Germain's key amid all that gold. This thought caused him some guilt, knowing what Sharyn had kept secret.

He stared up the curve of the narrow street. It led to a church with a tall belltower. The Sanctuary of Our Lady of Mellieħa. It was the oldest church in Malta, first consecrated in 1436. From their studies, this seemed like the best place to begin their search.

Naomi joined him, craning up at the stone structure. "And you think the Temple of Water is somewhere inside there?"

Duncan knew that that was exactly what they were looking for, a vault dedicated to *water.* Here on an island surrounded by the sea.

"Hopefully we'll find its door hidden in the church," Sharyn said. "But I'm certain the vault itself is buried somewhere in the limestone hill beneath it."

For now, they had to take her word on it. None of them had witnessed the miracle she had seen. He could still picture her kneeling at the foot of the flaming menorah, staring at the burning book.

"Let's go." Tag led the way up the hill with his cane. "If it's in there, I'm not missing out."

"Me neither," Naomi said. "Not this time."

Duncan rolled his eyes and followed, hooking his arm around Sharyn. Their relationship had grown over these past months. He had even spent February's half-semester break with her back in the States.

Naomi waved to the picturesque village that surrounded the church. "The name of this place. *Mellieħa.* Do you know what that translates to?"

Tag frowned at her. "What?"

She reached and tapped the amulet hanging around his neck. "Salt."

He gripped the tiny crystal vial. "Really?"

"Said to be named after the bay's ancient Roman salt pans." Naomi eyed him. "Hopefully it's a sign of good luck for us."

"I'll take it."

Duncan knew the story behind the charm. Naomi had sent a sizable wire payment to the two who had helped her in San Vito. Most of those funds had been contributed by Archie's dad, who had been equally appreciative.

Duncan took Sharyn's hand.

I am, too.

As the group continued upward, he surveyed the spread of neighboring valleys, all framed by white cliffs pocked by caves, once neolithic homes. Even the church ahead was the island's only surviving *troglodytic* sanctuary, meaning it had been built into caves, rising out of them from below.

Not unlike the bunker in the Dolomites.

For that reason alone, it was worth investigating.

But the more important reason strode alongside him. He glanced over to Sharyn and squeezed her fingers, expressing his trust.

Only she had witnessed the miracle that led them here.

76

10:49 a.m.

Sharyn passed through the gates of a monumental Baroque arch and entered the church's stone courtyard. High walls surrounded all sides. A towering statue of the Virgin Mary stood at the center, surrounded by a rod-iron fence. The church's façade rose to one side, the stones glowing a pinkish white under the midmorning sun.

She could sense the history of this place, like a physical weight.

Or maybe it's just worry.

She had drawn everyone here based on a brief glimpse of a miracle born of alchemical fire. As she stood here now, preparing for this search, she fell back to that moment at the heart of Monte Antelao, surrounded by a golden treasure tied not just to the Jewish faith, but to the history of humanity.

Her ultimate decision in that vault—to burn the book—had come to fruition much like Julian Wright's description of his own plot:

Long in planning, and frantic in execution.

After viewing the pages of the Third Adage back at the Barbiers' château, she had remained troubled, disturbed by the sights of skinned bodies, tortured skeletal shapes, and exposed organs. Such horrifying records of human experimentation had left her cold. None of it seemed to match the Saint-Germain described by history. According to those stories, the man had come off humble, wise, patient with his critics, always searching for enlightened paths to help better humanity.

Whoever penned the Third Adage seemed nothing like this man.

Even the skull on the title page appeared to her more like a warning than a decoration. It had reminded her of a skull-and-crossbones on a bottle of poison. Even the promise of immortality seemed too hard won if it required such ghastly procedures to achieve such an end.

Later, at the bunker, she had been reminded of the moral quandary faced by the medical community following World War II: whether or not to use Nazi research from their sadistic experimentation on prisoners. Such thoughts only whetted her misgivings. It was part of the reason she had suggested burning the book as they stood at the hidden door. It was not only to keep the *Confrérie* from the treasures beyond, but to perhaps end any further exploration into the dark section at the back of Saint-Germain's text.

Because of *all* of this, when she had faced Julian Wright, she knew she could never give him the book. By then, she had also come to suspect the nature of the *key* that was tied to this golden vault.

I had it in my hand.

The answer had been all around her.

In the room of transmutation, they had been forced to learn how to turn dull lead into bright gold. This act had been both a test and a lesson. Only by letting go of the promise of immortality—of recognizing that the Third Adage was an atrocity in written form—could one move forward. You had to be willing to burn it away, to purify the darkness to reveal the brighter treasure beyond.

She pictured the coarse menorah shedding its dross to shine in all its glory.

That was what Saint-Germain wanted us to take away from this demonstration.

To burn away dark ambition to gain the ultimate reward.

She also knew its trigger. Such a miracle would require more than ordinary fire. It would take the menorah's flames, a wonder fueled by alchemy.

So, in that frantic moment, she trusted herself, she trusted Saint-Germain, and she lit the book on fire.

And even if she was wrong, she knew she was right.

The book had cost too many lives. No one should have this power. It was time to end it either way. And more than anything, she refused to grant such miracles to the likes of Julian Wright.

Still, as the text burned in her hand, she did not know what to expect. She had tossed it behind the gold table to keep it out of sight, then dropped to her knees and watched closely, even as a firefight broke out.

As she did, she witnessed the *blooming* of the book.

There was no other way to describe it. She watched the flames burn away paper and leather, exposing its hard skeleton—a possible hint foretold by the Third Adage's macabre drawings of stripped bodies. Plates of copper took the place of leather covers, which fell open, freeing the metallic filaments that Laurent had described within, those fibrils veined through paper and woven in its bindings.

As the flames faded, the copper threads, strands, and fibers swirled into a mesh above the plates, fueled by whatever alchemy had melted lead off gold earlier. As she watched, the woven net formed a three-dimensional topographic map, showing a cluster of three islands.

Two small, one larger.

She let the shining image burn into her retina, knowing what was being shown to her. A map to the Temple of Water. As if confirming this, from the twining mass, a new sun rose. The crystal orb reappeared, transformed into a bright diamond, pear-shaped and pinched on the bottom.

The miracle rose and spun in place, its sharp tip pointing at the northern end of the largest island, near a tiny bay. She barely had time to fix the image in her mind's eye before the miracle collapsed, dissolving away, like a fading rose in winter.

Then it was gone, and the world crashed down upon her again.

Afterward, during the chaos, she had kept this secret to herself, not even trusting Laurent with the truth. She had learned another lesson from all of this: to give out her trust sparingly. Plus, she did not know how connected the *Confrérie* and the *Gardiens* might be after all of this.

So, instead, she had kept this revelation to her small group.

Working together, it had taken a month to try to figure out *where* the cluster of islands might be. It didn't help that her sketches, drawn from memory, had been crude, possibly full of errors. Finally, though, one location had seemed the most plausible.

The Republic of Malta.

Even still, Sharyn had begun to doubt herself, her memory.

Then additional support came from Duncan, who had unflaggingly believed in her, sometimes to the point of irritation. While seated in a booth at the Ram, Duncan had held down a map of the Mediterranean with pint glasses. He then took a ruler and drew a line from the volcanic fields in central Libya to the peak of Monte Antelao in northern Italy.

"See," he had said. "The line ends up running straight across the islands of Malta. And not only that, the country lies equidistant between those two locations. That can't be a coincidence."

Tag reached over and tapped the inked line. "The Temple of Earth lies at one end. The Temple of Fire at the other."

Naomi pointed to the middle. "With the Temple of Water between them. Malta must be right."

She had nodded. "A location surrounded by the seas."

And now here we are.

The village of Mellieħa sat at the edge of the bay pointed out by the spinning diamond-shaped orb. Months of further study had refined their search, pointing to this parish's ancient church.

She studied the stone façade, rising into a tall belltower. Several clues suggested this might be the best location to begin their search. The Sanctuary of Our Lady of Mellieħa had been a stable presence on the island going back to the fifteenth century, built into a massive cave. Geological studies also showed the whole region was burrowed with additional caverns. And only steps away from this courtyard, a revered grotto held a freshwater spring that was said to have healing properties.

It seemed the perfect location to hide the Temple of Water.

But am I right?

77

11:08 a.m.

Sharyn pushed through the main doors of the church and entered a hall lined by petitions, prayers, and votives. As her group passed through in respectful silence, she noted the walls were a mix of masonry and natural limestone. She ran a fingertip along the chipped stone, noting its similarity to the handiwork found inside the Dolomite bunker.

It was a reminder that the Sanctuary of Our Lady of Mellieħa had started out as a natural cave. According to legend, the grotto had been a place of worship for Calypso, the nymph from Homer's *Odyssey*. Then in AD 60, St. Paul and St. Luke were shipwrecked here and consecrated it as a Christian site, with Luke painting the image of the Madonna and Christ child on the cavern wall.

No one had proof of such stories, but the site had remained a place of Christian worship for centuries, with the church itself going through many renovations, while still rooted in the original sacred cave.

"We're already late," Archie warned, leading the way.

They were scheduled to meet the parish priest in the church's main sanctuary. Archie's father had arranged a special dispensation to allow them to explore the deeper reaches beneath the church. The Vatican—already humbled and seeking to atone for a certain cardinal—had facilitated matters.

Archie waved them brusquely through the door into the main nave. Wooden pews lined both sides. Overhead, high windows in the barrel-domed roof shone with sunlight, which reflected brightly off the marble walls.

Ahead, a figure dressed all in black with a clerical collar stood by the altar. He lifted an arm in greeting.

"That must be our guy." Archie set off to meet him, drawing their group with him. Once close enough, he called to the priest. "*Monsinjur Vella, grazzi talli akkomodajtna.*"

Sharyn looked to Duncan. "He speaks Maltese, too?"

Duncan shrugged. "Only because he knew we were coming here. He's a quick study."

Archie made their introductions, then conversed quietly with the monsignor, finalizing their arrangements.

Sharyn used this moment to study the sanctuary. With Easter approaching, the altar had been decorated with lilies and palm fronds. Candles burned everywhere. The scent of frankincense and myrrh lingered in the air. She had always found the smoking censers used in formal Masses to be cloying, but now it stirred memories.

During her winter break, she had returned home to Tulsa and attended a midnight service on Christmas Eve with her mother. It was a ceremony full of pomp and singing and moments of quieter contemplation. Following everything that had happened, Sharyn found solace and comfort in such rituals, something she had never felt before.

Afterward, as a light snow began to fall, she and her mother had visited her father's grave in the neighboring cemetery. Her mother had gripped Sharyn's hand, both to hold her there and to thank her. Sharyn had never visited this spot, not since the funeral. But it was time. She was ready. She asked her mother for a moment of privacy. Once alone, she placed a single red rose on his gravestone, the crimson petals stark against the white snow.

The gesture was not an act of forgiveness, or even an offering of thanks for giving her the tools necessary to survive. Instead, the gesture was simply a start, the first step toward peace—for herself.

"We're ready," Archie said, drawing her attention.

She focused back on the altar, noting the curve of raw rock framed behind it. It was part of the church's original cave. A Byzantine-style fresco adorned its wall, depicting the Virgin Mary holding the Christ child. But it was not the one painted by St. Luke. This one dated to the twelfth or thirteenth century. Still, many miracles had been attributed with it.

Let's hope it can spare one more.

78

11:22 a.m.

Duncan followed Monsignor Vella, a middle-aged man with sparkling eyes and salt-and-pepper hair. He led the group out a side door, through a sacristy, and into a maze of small chambers cut into the limestone.

Vella waved as they passed through, switching to English. "Back in the eighteenth century, Manuel Pinto da Fonseca, the sixty-eighth Grand Master of Malta, had this excavated to accommodate his visits to our parish. Many other pilgrims also sought such quiet spaces for contemplation."

Duncan searched ahead. "How deep do these excavations go?"

"Come see."

Vella led them down another narrow passageway. It ended at a black metal door, heavily riveted. A large padlock hung on it.

"Past here, the caves and diggings are considered treacherous. Down there, you'll find some of the oldest places of worship, going back to the Roman era." He glanced to them. "I understand that you're particularly interested in exploring that area."

"As part of an archaeological study," Naomi confirmed.

That was their cover story.

The monsignor gave them a long look, as if sensing the subterfuge, then took out a large black key and freed the lock. He opened the door with a complaint of hinges. "Do take care."

Duncan intended to follow that instruction.

Past the door, a short flight of carved steps cut through the natural limestone. They broke out flashlights and continued in silence, hushed by expectation and worry. Only their strained breathing and Tag's cane tapping on stone broke the quiet.

Once they reached the bottom, a small antechamber opened. From it, a warren of narrow, low-roofed tunnels headed off in multiple directions. Many looked barely wide enough to pass through sideways. It could take days to search this place.

But they had come prepared, knowing what they needed to find.

"We should get started," Sharyn said.

Naomi dropped her pack and withdrew a wide case. She snapped it open, revealing a boxy handheld unit nestled inside. She pulled it out and snapped the cord of a tubular wand to its side.

"Let's hope we don't run out of battery juice," Archie commented. "It looks like we've got a lot of ground to cover."

Naomi powered the unit up. "I have an extra battery pack. Just in case. But I'm certain this will shorten our search."

"My legs thank you for that," Tag said.

She shrugged. "As an archaeologist, it's not my first rodeo. We use magnetometers like this in the field. Helps pinpoint magnetic anomalies underground that can reveal buried items that don't belong there."

"And you truly think this can help us find the hidden door?" Duncan asked.

"I do. This is a *vector* magnetometer, made to measure the strength and direction of magnetic fields." She waved the wand like a steampunk witch. "If there's even a whiff of any magnetite down here, it'll sniff it out."

"Like Katch did with the poison back at the bunker." Archie then winced, looking guilty for reminding them.

A silence settled over the group. Dr. Bianca Russo had been buried in the Dolomites, near a spring that had been her favorite camping site, according to a colleague. Laurent had also kept his word and set up a large endowment, named after the biologist and funded by a Jewish organization, to finance the ongoing repopulation efforts in her beloved mountains.

But their group was not the only ones mourning the biologist.

Duncan pictured his last sight of Julian Wright, tumbling over the cliff's edge, being mauled by Katch. Days later, the professor's broken body had been discovered at the bottom, along with the shattered remains of a wildlife tracking device. There had been no sign of Katch. It seemed even lynxes landed on their feet—or maybe the impact of the long fall had been cushioned by Wright's bulk.

Either way, over the following months, the locals reported hearing yowls of a lone cat at night, often near the burial site by the spring. Duncan hoped somehow Russo heard her friend, knowing she had prepared him for this moment.

To be free.

Just as she wished for him.

"I'm getting a strong signal in this direction." Naomi pointed her wand toward one of the many tunnels.

They continued onward, following her lead, seeking their goal.

A hidden door rich in magnetite.

79

12:02 p.m.

Forty minutes later, Sharyn stood in what appeared to be a small chapel buried at the heart of the limestone hill. The air was dank, smelling of salt. They had passed many such rooms. Some larger, others smaller, a few mere cubbies.

This cavern appeared to be a microcosm of the church's main sanctuary. Raw stone framed one half. On the other, rock that had been chiseled and sculpted. Seven shallow alcoves had been carved into the wall, lined up in a row, like a bank of windows. Below them, low kneeling benches invited one to prayer.

Sharyn imagined holy relics or votive candles resting in those spaces. Only, they were empty now.

Except for one.

Naomi lowered her wand. "Getting crazy strong readings from there."

They edged closer, falling silent. The only sound was the water trickling down the back of the niche. It ran along the rock face and filled a basin cut into the bottom of the alcove. The water's surface shimmered like a black mirror. The overflow spilled down a channel cut in the front, then drained into a crack in the floor.

"Looks like a baptismal font," Duncan said.

"Or a drinking fountain for Calypso," Tag said. "The nymph's springs were said to be healing."

Naomi repacked her magnetometer, clearly believing they had reached the end of their search. "With all this wetness, this *must* be the door to a Temple of Water."

The three turned to Sharyn, knowing the next task was hers alone. They had already debated how to open this door. It posed a challenge as they no longer had Saint-Germain's book as its key.

Sharyn stepped forward and searched the alcove for a clue. Months ago, she had already guessed what she might need if she ever reached this spot.

Praying she was not wrong, she reached her hand into the basin and ran her palm along the curve of stone below the water's black mirror. The rock was smooth, nearly polished. Then her fingers found a hole at the center, like a drain. The opening was small, no larger than the tip of her pinkie.

"I think this is it." She turned to the others. "Help me splash the water out."

Duncan and Archie flanked her. Together, they scooped out handfuls, quickly emptying the basin, while soaking the front of their clothes.

"It's like we're being christened," Duncan mumbled. "Blessed before entering."

Archie frowned at him. "If this is holy water, I'm going straight to confession after this."

Once the basin had been mostly cleared, Sharyn pulled a scarf from her pack and dried the rest. She then pointed to the hole at the basin's center. "Looks about the right size. What do you think?"

"Try it," Duncan urged her.

She bit her lip and unzipped a pants pocket. She reached inside and removed a pear-shaped chunk of crystal, what had once been the orb gracing the cover of Saint-Germain's book.

She had stolen it from the gold chamber, sensing its importance even back then. Laurent had inquired about it later, after realizing it had vanished. She had lied and told him she had left it in the chamber. She suggested maybe it got bumped into the mercury pool.

Still, she could live with this deception. The crystal was too important to leave behind. Back at the bunker, it had gleamed like a beacon amidst the coppery ruins of the book, as if begging to be taken. And for good reason. The original orb had been the key to unlocking Saint-Germain's text *and* these secret doors.

She hoped it still remained a key.

Only one way to find out.

She lowered the crystal to the bottom of the basin. She inserted its pointy end into the hole, like planting a diamond into a precious setting.

Once done, she stepped back to the others. She tightened her fists, hoping there was some bit of alchemy left in the crystal, enough to stir the magnetic field of the surrounding rock.

After a full minute, Archie turned to her. "Nothing's happening."

"Maybe we need those magnetic rods," Duncan offered. "To zap it somehow."

Sharyn worried he might be right, but somewhere deep inside she sensed this wasn't necessary.

We're beyond that now.

Then a wet trickle seeped down the wall, ran across the basin, and touched the crystal. Upon contact with the water, the stone shimmered—at first softly, then brightening quickly.

"Something's happening," Tag said, his voice awed.

Sharyn remembered Duncan's words from a moment ago. "It's like the water christened it."

The crystal flared brilliantly—then lifted from its stone cradle. It slowly spun in place. Its radiant facets cast an iridescent shine across the inside of the alcove.

Duncan named the science behind this magic. "Magnetic levitation. Like what lifts some bullet trains off their tracks."

Sharyn slowly nodded, remembering Moira Kelly's scoffing at

the more fanciful claims about Saint-Germain, one of which included the man's supposed ability to levitate.

Maybe something like this was the basis for such tales.

Before she could consider it further, a familiar ringing chime sounded, followed by a heavy grinding. They all backed up another step. As lines formed in the stone around the watery alcove, the entire slab sank into the floor.

This time, Sharyn didn't need Archie to warn her. She hurried forward and grabbed the floating crystal from the niche. Its glow faded, but it remained warm in her palm, like a cooling coal from a fire.

She watched the door fully sink away.

They all drew closer.

Tag blew out his breath. "At least there aren't any stairs."

Past the door, a straight tunnel cut deeper into the hill.

Sharyn got them moving along it. She also passed on a warning, remembering the mistake Laurent had made. "Watch your step."

They dared not trip any boobytraps. She hoped—like with the magnetic rods—that they were finished with all that, too.

But when it came to Saint-Germain, one thing was certain:

More than his secrets, he loves his surprises.

80

12:18 p.m.

Beyond the doorway, the tunnel widened enough for them to walk side by side. Sharyn reached back and took Duncan's hand. Naomi and Tag trailed them, while Archie held up the rear. As a precaution, they all carried flashlights. Wary of each step, they proceeded slowly.

As they delved deeper, the air grew both drier and colder. The smell of salt faded into something less stringent, nearly smoky, but pleasantly so.

Something familiar about—

"What treasures do you think are hidden here?" Archie called up to them, breaking the silence, maybe in an attempt to break the tension, too.

Sharyn had pondered this same question and could only come up with one answer.

No clue.

But after several yards, it was clear they were about to find out. Ahead, the tunnel emptied into a cavernous space, perfectly circular, easily forty yards across. The roof, while high, was unadorned and flat. No gold reflected their lights as they searched.

"Nothing's here," Archie said, his voice heavy with disappointment.

Sharyn frowned, not with regret, but curiosity.

What is this place?

Tag headed deeper inside, leading with his flashlight. "It's not totally empty. There's a fence or something out there."

Sharyn followed with the others. Within a few steps, she saw her friend was correct. A waist-high iron barricade blocked the way. It was easy to miss, blending into the dark rock. As they got nearer, the run of the fence proved to be as circular as the surrounding walls. Like the arena of an equestrian training center.

"Careful," Duncan warned, spotting the danger first.

They slowed as they neared the barricade. Beyond it, there was no floor. The fence protected an open well that dropped straight into the earth. Once at the barrier, they spread out along it and cast their lights down.

Gasps followed—in recognition, in shock.

Below them, tier after tier of levels fell away, disappearing into the darkness, stretching beyond the reach of their lights. The floors were connected by a pair of staircases, which spiraled down in tandem, forming a pattern reminiscent of a DNA's double helix. Maybe this was purposeful, maybe happenstance. But it was a minor mystery compared to the grander one below.

Shelves, sculpted from stone, crowded each level and were packed with books. Other partitions had holes drilled into them, housing hundreds of curled scrolls. Elsewhere and everywhere, artifacts filled niches and cubbies: the yellowed skulls of long-dead animals, tall standing stones carved with writing, arcane tools of brass, rows of bottles holding unknown reagents. The sheer breadth of it all—the wealth, the history, the arc of humanity on display—strained the eyes to take it all in.

And what they viewed was only the barest edges of these uppermost levels.

Archie finally broke out a glow stick, snapped it brighter, and tossed it down the shaft. Its emerald shine tumbled down the well, falling and falling—then winking out.

"It's like there's no bottom," Naomi murmured.

"What are we looking at?" Tag asked. "Is this Saint-Germain's lost library?"

"No." She remembered Laurent's description of the man's journeys around the world. "It's not just *his* library. But the archive of *all* his savants. The sum total of their knowledge, stored and preserved for humanity."

She turned to the others and pointed down. "Here is true immortality. The permanence of ink on paper. The magic that can carry your thoughts, your lessons, your tales, your hopes, your dreams . . . far into the future. To share with others, so they can carry it on."

"You may be right," Duncan said.

Naomi offered a counterpoint. "It's not just that."

Sharyn turned to her.

"This is the Temple of *Water*," Naomi reminded her.

Sharyn immediately understood. Her eyes grew huge, while her vision narrowed with shock. She turned and pointed her light down into this cryptic well of lost knowledge.

She's right. It's not only that . . .

Sharyn breathed harder, trying to force the words out, to name what this place truly was. "It . . . It's the Fourth Adage."

Naomi nodded, looking both scared and exulted. "To lead us eventually to the Temple of *Air*."

"Aristotle's fourth element," Duncan mumbled.

Archie pointed his flashlight up, toward the heavens, as if searching for that temple now. Instead, he discovered the *gold* hidden in this cave.

Across the roof, engraved deep into the stone, gilded letters curved around the open space.

Tag squinted. "What does it say?"

To answer that, the group circled outward and danced their beams across this message from the library's builders.

Tag read aloud the passage closest to him. "*Studium Discere Crescere.*"

Naomi shouted on her side. "*Cum Paratus Es.*"

Duncan finished with the last word, yelling it like a call to arms. "*Veniemus!*"

Sharyn knew some Latin, but another in their group was far more fluent.

Archie pointed to each orator, starting with Tag, and translated, "*Study, Learn, Grow.*" Then he swung to Naomi. "*When you are ready.*" Finally, he shoved an arm toward his best friend. "*We will come!*"

As the others returned to her side, stumbling and stunned, Sharyn swept her gaze around the ring of writing, repeating the message in her head.

Study, learn, grow. When you are ready, we will come.

It was a promise to the future set in gold.

Now, if only the world could make this come true.

Duncan rejoined her, smiling, breathless. "What do you think?"

Her friends closed around them. Sharyn had stopped where one of the spiral staircases climbed to this level, welcoming them to venture deeper. She knew they would eventually have to share this with the greater world, but for now . . .

This is all ours.

Duncan flicked his gaze up, then to her again. "What about it? Are *you* ready?"

She stared into his shining eyes, recognizing what he was truly asking. It wasn't just about journeying into the unknown below—but about their future together.

She grasped his hand, holding tight, and answered both.

"Damn right, I am."

81

April 6, 5:33 p.m. CEST
London, England

Moira crossed the Tower Green, gripping a Starbucks cup. Only, it wasn't full of an over-sugared latte. Instead, it sloshed with pig's blood. She also carried loose biscuits in a pouch snapped around her waist. One wafer—a reward for Hugh—was already soaking in the cup.

The raven sat perched on a wall on the lawn's far side, dancing angrily back and forth on his claws.

My boyo is in an especially foul mood.

Hugh never liked his rehab sessions, but neither did Moira's father. The old man had healed from his surgery, but a post-op lung infection had complicated his recovery, which put him in bed for a long stretch. At the moment, he was working with a physical therapist over at King's House, trying to increase both his lung capacity and upper body strength.

Moira had used this time to exercise Hugh. The raven had mended from his heroic rescue of her, but his broken wing had healed crookedly, making it hard for him to manage more than short, uncoordinated flights. It had turned him sullen, irritable, and reluctant to take these short excursions with her. The Ravenmaster—the Yeoman Warder who oversaw the Tower's winged mascots—had said such hesitation wasn't due to embarrassment or pride, but more likely due to an innate desire not to show weakness, a trait that could make him an easy target for predation.

Regardless, Hugh had to keep moving.

Just like her father.

She reached the wall, fished out the soaked biscuit, and held it up. "C'mon, Hugh. A couple more laps around the green, and we'll call it a day."

He tilted his head and cast her a loathsome look. Then reinforced it with a string of expletives.

Moira glanced around. The Tower had closed only minutes ago. A few tourists straggled about, but luckily no one seemed to be in earshot.

She sighed and debated whether or not to grab a dustbin and use it as a ladder to reach him.

Hugh danced some more, turning his back on her. He was definitely in a mood. Then he whistled brightly, letting loose with an operatic riff—which he only did when he was happy. She hadn't heard it in months. Something must have caught his attention on the wall's far side, which overlooked a pedestrian walkway.

Then he dove off his perch and disappeared from view.

She grimaced, knowing she'd have to chase him down. But at least he was on the ground where she could nab him. She quickly circled around the wall to reach the walkway beyond it.

When she did, she spotted a strange sight. One of the tourists, a gentleman in an ankle-length great coat and matching cap, had grabbed Hugh and cradled him close, as if about to tuck the bird away and abscond with him.

Such manhandling was dangerous to both bird and man.

"Oi!" she hollered, drawing the attention of a few stragglers and one Beefeater. "Put the raven down! You know you're not supposed to harass them."

Though, to be honest, Hugh seemed perfectly content.

The stranger leaned closer, as if whispering a secret to the bird.

She couldn't make out the words, but the accent sounded French, almost aristocratic. Finally, he obeyed. Gripping the raven with both hands, he cast Hugh high into the air.

Moira gasped, panicked, knowing how compromised Hugh was. She twisted around as the raven struggled, bobbling back and forth—then his wings snapped straighter. He caught the air, then a breeze off the Thames. He sailed high, floating back and forth. Then with a cry of triumph, he dove and spun and whirled. His path scribed a sigil of joy across the bright blue sky.

She stared in amazement, struggling to understand.

She turned to the man who had cradled Hugh.

But he had vanished.

As if he was never there.

Author's Note to Readers: Truth or Fiction

All novels are constructed of fabrications, illusions, hopes, and lies, but their foundation is often built on a solid footing of the truth. So, I thought I'd spend these last few pages sharing the origins of this story and the facts upon which this novel was fashioned.

Let's start in the past and work our way forward.

* * *

Saint-Germain and the Countess

At the beginning of this book and throughout this story, I shared many details concerning Saint-Germain's life, his works, and the tales that surrounded him—some factual, others fanciful. I tried to adhere to Sir Kelly's philosophy of sticking to anecdotes and particulars that were based on written accounts by contemporaries of his time.

For example, in the prologue, I dramatized the story of Saint-Germain meeting Countess Gabrielle Pauline d'Adhémar, the former lady-in-waiting to Marie-Antoinette. I related the Countess's past ties to him, including his attempt to gain her assistance in warning King Louis XVI of the coming French Revolution. A fuller account of this effort can be found in great detail in the woman's memoir, *Souvenirs sur Marie-Antoinette,* which was published after her death. The italicized passages in my prologue relating to these events were paraphrased from her memoir. Even the promise made to the Countess—that Saint-Germain would visit her five more times, but never a sixth—is what she wrote herself.

If you'd care to explore this part of Saint-Germain's history—and so much more—I highly recommend reading the two books below, which offered great insight and inspiration for this novel:

The Comte de St. Germain, by Isabel Cooper-Oakley
Saint Germain on Alchemy: Formulas for Self-Transformation, by Mark L. Prophet and Elizabeth Clare Prophet

After learning of this connection between Count and Countess, I wanted to explore what might have happened during those five later meetings between the two, especially the last one, before he vanished from her side. It was this mystery that started me on this journey, one that I hope you enjoyed.

Yet, over the centuries, the story of Saint-Germain has only grown larger. Many still believe he was immortal, living for millennia on end. Supposed sightings of the Count were reported throughout history, even into modern times. In 1972, a French public figure, Richard Chanfray, appeared on television and claimed he was indeed this immortal count.

Still, despite such wild claims, Count Saint-Germain was a true historical figure, a man of astounding skill, talent, and wisdom. So much so that he became known as the "Wonderman" of his era. Of course, such acclaim led others, like Louis XVI's advisor, the Marquise de Maurepas, to vilify the man, declaring him a dangerous charlatan.

So, in the end, who was Saint-Germain? Wonderman or charlatan? For me, I place my faith in the wisdom that Duncan shared with Sharyn at the Old Library:

The truth probably lies somewhere in the cracks.

The City of Exeter and Its University

As mentioned in the foreword to this novel, the University of Exeter had begun offering a postgraduate degree in magic and occult science in 2024. As a thriller writer, especially one attracted to strange science and historical mysteries, how could I not build a story around its students?

I also wanted to bring my readers into the program and immerse them in the city, the university, and its surroundings. While I did burn down the Old Library on campus, it still stands. Other details of campus life—the Forum, the Ram, the Lemon Grove nightclub—are real locations. Even the placard memorializing the "Devon Witches" can be found in the shadow of Rougemont Castle. And yes, the women were hung nearby, and their bones are believed to be buried in unconsecrated ground on the University of Exeter campus—under a car park, as Naomi mentions. All of which seems fitting as Exeter has indeed been deemed "the most haunted city in all of England." So, maybe do visit there on Halloween; just don't accept any books from strangers.

One minor admission: The location for the best coffee in Exeter, the Toad on a Stool, is fictitious. Still, for a haunted city featuring a university program about witchcraft, a coffeehouse with the nickname "Toadstool" seemed appropriate. Someone should open it—if so, I want a highly caffeinated drink named after me.

The Tower of London

I've been to this site many times, and I always wanted to build an action set piece on its grounds. If I ever did, I swore to make it as accurate as possible, which I've hopefully done in this novel—while taking some very minor liberties.

First of all, the histories related to the Tower are factual. Or at least, as much as any history tells the full truth. But let's talk about some particulars.

Yes, in the summer, the Tower moat does get converted into a giant wonderland of flowers, winding paths, and sculptures. It's called the Superbloom, and I highly recommend you experience it yourself. Just be careful of all the bees (something I learned the hard way).

And as a veterinarian, how could I not feature the Tower's legendary ravens in this book? The Tower did have a breeding pair of ravens named Huginn and Muninn. Sadly, both have since died but are still well-regarded. As to "Hugh," since he's fictitious, I decided to make this pair of ravens, who were named after Odin's companions, *brothers*. For no other reason than Odin's ravens were supposedly males according to epic poems, like *Grímnismál*, which is best read in the original Old Norse. Okay, no, I don't read Old Norse. It's not even on my bucket list.

As to the diets of ravens, they are fed mostly raw meat, and yes, they are offered treats of blood-soaked biscuits. How could I not feature that detail in a book? And yes, the birds are excellent mimics and can speak as well as parrots. If you'd like to see this demonstrated, I suggest you do an internet search for "Fable the Raven" and watch the videos.

For an entertaining and informative read about ravens at the Tower, please do check this book out:

The Ravenmaster: My Life with the Ravens at the Tower of London, by Christopher Skaife

Speaking of those who make their home at the Tower, I was fascinated to learn that people *do* live within its grounds. I highly recommend watching TikTok videos of a stand-up comedian in the UK, named Tom Houghton, who lived with his father, the Constable of the Tower at the time, and recorded his experience living there. Like trying to order pizza. To check him and his videos out, go to @honourabletom on TikTok. See, not all research has to be arduous.

Since I love charts and maps (you know that, right?), I thought I'd include one here of the Tower of London. It shows my characters' arrival and their flight through the illustrious grounds. I did this in case you ever wanted to follow in their footsteps—and maybe record a TikTok video of your experience. Who knows? If you're lucky, someone might invite you to the private Beefeater's pub, The Keys. If so, save a seat for me.

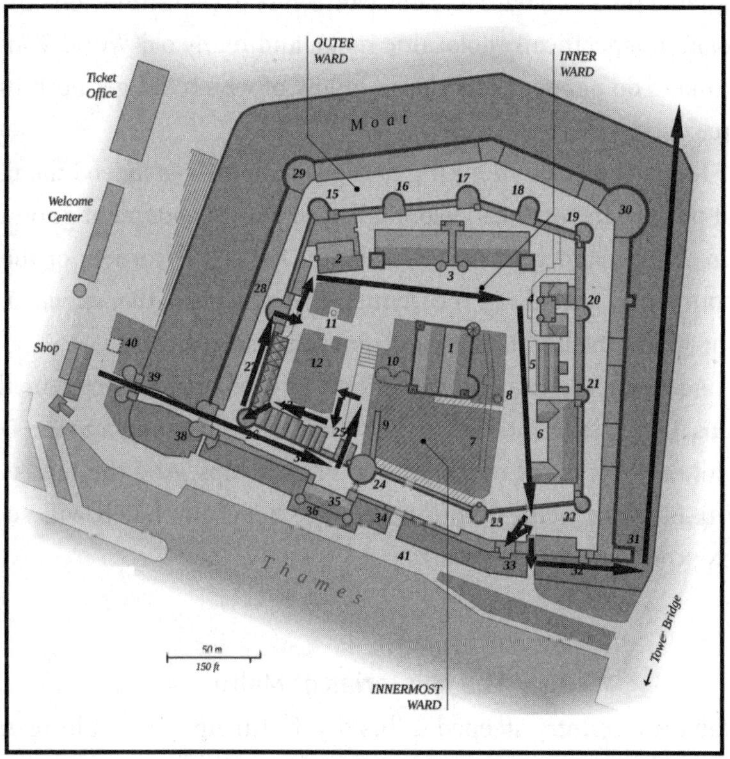

The Châteaus of Meaux

While the commune of Meaux near Paris is a real place, the Château de Barbier is not. The Dogue de Bordeaux are not only real, but also a wonderful breed—both great hunters and clowns. The detail regarding those old limestone mines being used as shelters for people during the Napoleonic Wars is factual. And yes, many of them have now been converted into large mushroom farms.

The Dolomites and Its Legends

I've only visited the Dolomites once, but the landscape and legends of these Italian Alps have stayed with me. I always wanted to highlight them in a novel, especially as an avid caver myself. The regional peaks do have lots of caverns due to their limestone composition (specifically dolomitic rock), and many old World War II bunkers do pepper their slopes, many of which did get built into preexisting caves.

Monte Antelao—the King of the Dolomites—is indeed the tallest peak in the eastern Dolomites. And stories abound of gnomes, sorceresses, and wild men who haunt the secret corners of these mountains, including the nymph-like witches—the *anguana*—who guard the highland caves from trespassers.

As to Dr. Bianca Russo's efforts to repopulate species in the Alps, this is indeed ongoing. Bears are making a return to the Dolomites. Wolf packs now hunt the French Alps. And the Eurasian lynx is slowly being reintroduced. So, hopefully Katch will soon have companions out there.

The Mysteries of Malta

Malta is a country steeped in history, featuring a rich culture and a stunning landscape. And yes, its islands do lie nearly exactly at the midpoint between the volcanic fields of Haruj in Libya and the peak of Monte Antelao in the Dolomites. All the details regarding the Sanctuary of Our Lady of Mellieħa—the history, the caves, the springs—are also all true.

A Final Few Miscellaneous Items

I bring up the philosophy of *longtermism* in this novel. At its purest form, it posits that it's the highest moral responsibility of the present to increase the odds of humanity's long-term survival—which is a grand ethical principle. It's also a growing movement and finds support among luminaries like Elon Musk, Peter Thiel, and Skype founder Jaan Tallinn, along with many others in Silicon Valley. If you'd like to learn more about this philosophy, I recommend reading this book:

What We Owe the Future, by William MacAskill

So why did I make the villain of this book such an advocate for longtermism? I wanted Keir Marchand to represent the darker side of this philosophy, where any cruelties, depravations, and brutalities in the present could be justified in the name of some future good. Keir serves as my cautionary warning about applying such extremes to this principle.

As to the efficacy of using marijuana to help treat cerebral palsy, studies continue to show great promise. Just ask Tag.

Regarding Naomi's participation and influence on a subsection of TikTok called *WitchTok*, it is indeed a vibrant and engaged group with some wonderful content and billions of views worldwide. I encourage you to explore—once you've finished watching all those cat videos, of course. See, again, research can be fun!

* * *

Of course, many other details, anecdotes, and claims populate this story. Hopefully this afterword offers some insight into the book's *foundations of truth*. As to the rest, please accept it all as factual. You trust me, right? Or maybe you'd best stick to the philosophy I used in naming this novel:

Trust no one.

Acknowledgments

No author is an island when it comes to crafting a novel. Many contribute to its production, polish, and eventual publication. To start, let me thank those who read the first rough pages and offered wise counsel and discerning eyes, but who also shared their generous friendship and firm support: Chris Crowe, Lee Garrett, Matt Orr, Judy Prey, Steve Prey, Caroline Williams, Sadie Davenport, Lisa Goldkuhl, Dave Meeks, Laura Rinaldi, James Auld, Vanessa Bedford, and a longstanding member of our group who passed away this year, Denny Grayson, whose wisdom and generosity touched this book in so many ways. I must also single out David Sylvian for his hard work and dedication in the digital sphere, all to make me shine brighter. Of course, none of this would happen without an astounding team of industry professionals whom I defy anyone to surpass. To everyone at William Morrow, thank you for always having my back, especially Liate Stehlik, Kaitlin Harri, Josh Marwell, Richard Aquan, Lindsey Kennedy, Beatrice Jason, and Caitlin Garing. Last, of course, a special acknowledgment to the people instrumental to all levels of production: my distinguished editor, Jennifer Brehl, and her industrious colleague Nate Lanman; and for all their hard work, my agents, Russ Galen and Danny Baror (along with his daughter Heather Baror). And as always, I must stress that any and all errors of fact or detail in this book fall squarely on my shoulders.

Acknowledgments

Rights and Attributions for the Artwork in This Novel

p. XI—Engraving of Saint-Germain
Public Domain

p. XVIII—Saint-Germain Book Symbol
Graphic created by author with Midjourney and edited by author

p. 1—Statue of Richard Hooker
Secured with an Enhanced License
ID 2232198091 © PhotoFires | Shutterstock.com
(image edited by author)

p. 6—Witch Plaque
Public Domain (Photographer: Totnesmartin)

p. 51—Big Ben and Trees
Secured with an Enhanced License
ID 133105034 © Petar Paunchev | Shutterstock.com
(image edited by author)

p. 62—License Plate Number
Created by author

p. 75—Sagittarius Constellation
Secured with an Enhanced License
ID 506941522 © iiga | Shutterstock.com
(image edited by author)

p. 103—Raven at Tower of London
Secured with an Enhanced License
ID 1321866731 © Michael Cordone | Shutterstock.com
(image edited by author)

p. 121—Alchemical Symbol Comparison
Gottfried Wilhelm Leibniz, Public Domain, via Wikimedia Commons
In conjunction with:
Graphic created by author with Midjourney and edited by author

p. 147—Open Book
Graphic created by author with Midjourney and edited by author

p. 191—Second Adage
Graphic created by author with Midjourney and edited by author

p. 198—Mountain
Graphic created by author with Midjourney and edited by author

p. 199—Mountain
Graphic created by author with Midjourney and edited by author

p. 200—Third Adage
Graphic created by author with Midjourney and edited by author

p. 201—Skeleton (Top)
Graphic created by author with Midjourney and edited by author

p. 201—Skeleton (Bottom)

Graphic created by author with Midjourney and edited by author

p. 206—Arch of Titus

Jebulon, CC0, via Wikimedia Commons, Public Domain

p. 208—Pixelated Mountain

Graphic created by author with Midjourney and edited by author

p. 210—Bluebell

Combination of graphic created by author with Midjourney and edited by author

and

Bluebell photo secured with an Enhanced License
ID 94113289 © Daniel Prudek | Shutterstock.com
(image edited by author)

p. 219—Mountain Bunker

Graphic created by author with Midjourney and edited by author

p. 283—Monte Antelao

Graphic created by author with Midjourney and edited by author

p. 339—Revelation

Graphic created by author with Midjourney and edited by author

p. 399—Tower of London

Thomas Römer, CC BY-SA 3.0 <https://creativecommons.org/licenses/by-sa/3.0>, via Wikimedia Commons; edited by author

About the Author

James Rollins is the #1 *New York Times* bestselling author of international thrillers that have been translated into more than forty languages. His Sigma Force series has been lauded as one of the "top crowd-pleasers" (*The New York Times*) and one of the "hottest summer reads" (*People*). In each novel, acclaimed for its originality, Rollins unveils unseen worlds, scientific breakthroughs, and historical secrets—and he does it all at breakneck speed and with stunning insight. He lives in the Sierra Nevada mountains.